Nora Roberts is the *New*
ore than one hundred
toryteller, she creates a blend of warmth, humour and
poignancy that speaks directly to her readers and has
arned her almost every award for excellence in her field.
The youngest of five children, Nora lives in western
Maryland. She has two sons.

isit her website at www.noraroberts.com

Nora Roberts

Long Summer Days

MILLS & BOON

This edition published in Great Britain 2017
By Mills & Boon, an imprint of HarperCollins*Publishers*
1 London Bridge Street, London, SE1 9GF

Treasures Lost, Treasures Found © 1986 Nora Roberts

Temptation © 1987 Nora Roberts

ISBN: 978-0-263-92747-4

29-0617

Our policy is to use papers that are natural, renewable and recyclable products and made from wood grown in sustainable forests. The logging and manufacturing processes conform to the legal environmental regulations of the country of origin.

Printed and bound
by CPI Group (UK) Ltd, Croydon, CRO 4YY

Treasures Lost, Treasures Found

To Dixie Browning, the true lady of the island.

Chapter 1

He had believed in it. Edwin J. Hardesty hadn't been the kind of man who had fantasies or followed dreams, but sometime during his quiet, literary life he had looked for a pot of gold. From the information in the reams of notes, the careful charts and the dog-eared research books, he thought he'd found it.

In the panelled study, a single light shot a beam across a durable oak desk. The light fell over a hand—narrow, slender, without the affectation of rings or polish. Yet even bare, it remained an essentially feminine hand, the kind that could be pictured holding a porcelain cup or waving a feather fan. It was a surprisingly elegant hand for a woman who didn't consider herself elegant, delicate or particularly feminine. Kathleen Hardesty was, as her father had been, and as he'd directed her to be, a dedicated educator.

Minds were her concern—the expanding and the fulfilling of them. This included her own as well as every one of her students'. For as long as she could remember, her father had impressed upon her the importance of education. He'd stressed the priority of it over every other aspect of life. Education was the cohesiveness that held civilization together. She grew up surrounded by the dusty smell of books and the quiet, placid tone of patient instruction.

She'd been expected to excel in school, and she had. She'd been expected to follow her father's path into education. At twenty-eight, Kate was just finishing her first year at Yale as an assistant professor of English literature.

In the dim light of the quiet study, she looked the part. Her light brown hair was tidily secured at the nape of her neck with all the pins neatly tucked in. Her practical tortoiseshell reading glasses seemed dark against her milk-pale complexion. Her high cheekbones gave her face an almost haughty look that was often dispelled by her warm, doe-brown eyes.

Though her jacket was draped over the back of her chair, the white blouse she wore was still crisp. Her cuffs were turned back to reveal delicate wrists and a slim Swiss watch on her left arm. Her earrings were tasteful gold studs given to Kate by her father on her twenty-first birthday, the only truly personal gift she could ever remember receiving from him.

Seven long years later, one short week after her father's funeral, Kate sat at his desk. The room still carried the scent of his cologne and a hint of the pipe tobacco he'd only smoked in that room.

She'd finally found the courage to go through his papers.

She hadn't known he was ill. In his early sixties, Hardesty had looked robust and strong. He hadn't told his daughter about his visits to the doctor, his check-ups, ECG results or the little pills he carried with him everywhere. She'd found his pills in his inside pocket after his fatal heart attack. Kate hadn't known his heart was weak because Hardesty never shared his shortcomings with anyone. She hadn't known about the charts and research papers in his desk; he'd never shared his dreams either.

Now that she was aware of both, Kate wasn't certain she ever really knew the man who'd raised her. The memory of her mother was dim; that was to be expected after more than twenty years. Her father had been alive just a week before.

Leaning back for a moment, she pushed her glasses up and rubbed the bridge of her nose between her thumb and forefinger. She tried, with only the desk lamp between herself and the dark, to think of her father in precise terms.

Physically, he'd been a tall, big man with a full head of steel-gray hair and a patient face. He had favored dark suits and white shirts. The only vanity she could remember had been his weekly manicures. But it wasn't a physical picture Kate struggled with now. As a father...

He was never unkind. In all her memories, Kate couldn't remember her father ever raising his voice to her, ever striking her. He never had to, she thought with a sigh. All he had to do was express disappointment, disapproval, and that was enough.

He had been brilliant, tireless, dedicated. But all of that had been directed toward his vocation. As a father, Kate reflected... He'd never been unkind. That was all that would come to her, and because of it she felt a fresh wave of guilt and grief.

She hadn't disappointed him, that much she could cling to. He had told her so himself, in just those words, when she was accepted by the English Department at Yale. Nor had he expected her ever to disappoint him. Kate knew, though it had never been discussed, that her father wanted her to become head of the English Department within ten years. That had been the extent of his dream for her.

Had he ever realized just how much she'd loved him? She wondered as she shut her eyes, tired now from the hours of reading her father's handwriting. Had he ever known just how desperately she'd wanted to please him? If he'd just once said he was proud...

In the end, she hadn't had those few intense last moments with her father one reads about in books or sees in the movies. When she'd arrived at the hospital, he was already gone. There'd been no time for words. No time for tears.

Now she was on her own in the tidy Cape Cod house she'd shared with him for so long. The housekeeper would still come on Wednesday mornings, and the gardener would come on Saturdays to cut the grass. She alone would have to deal with the paperwork, the sorting, the shifting, the clearing out.

That could be done. Kate leaned back farther in her father's worn leather chair. It could be done because all of those things were practical matters. She dealt easily with the practical. But what about these papers she'd found? What would she do about the carefully drawn charts, the notebooks filled with information, directions, history, theory? In part, because she was raised to be logical, she considered filing them neatly away.

But there was another part, the part that enabled one to lose oneself in fantasies, in dreams, in the "perhapses" of life. This was the part that allowed Kate to lose herself totally in the possibilities of the written word, in the wonders of a book. The papers on her father's desk beckoned her.

He'd believed in it. She bent over the papers again. He'd believed in it or he never would have wasted his time documenting, searching, theorizing. She would never be able to discuss it with him. Yet, in a way, wasn't he telling her about it through his words?

Treasure. Sunken treasure. The stuff of fiction and Hollywood movies. Judging by the stack of papers and notebooks on his desk, Hardesty must have spent months, perhaps years, compiling information on the location of an English merchant ship lost off the coast of North Carolina two centuries before.

It brought Kate an immediate picture of Edward Teach—Blackbeard, the bloodthirsty pirate with the crazed superstitions and reign of terror. The stuff of romances, she thought. Of romance…

Ocracoke Island. The memory was sharp, sweet and painful. Kate had blocked out everything that had happened that summer four years before. Everything and everyone. Now, if she was to make a rational decision about what was to be done, she had to think of those long, lazy months on the remote Outer Banks of North Carolina.

She'd begun work on her doctorate. It had been a surprise when her father had announced that he planned to spend the summer on Ocracoke and invited her to accompany him. Of course, she'd gone, taking her portable typewriter, boxes of books, reams of paper. She hadn't expected to be seduced by white sand beaches and the call of gulls. She hadn't expected to fall desperately and insensibly in love.

Insensibly, Kate repeated to herself, as if in defense. She'd have to remember that was the most apt adjective. There'd been nothing sensible about her feelings for Ky Silver.

Even the name, she mused, was unique, unconventional, flashy. They'd been as suitable for each other as a peacock and a wren. Yet that hadn't stopped her from losing her head, her heart and her innocence during that balmy, magic summer.

She could still see him at the helm of the boat her father had rented, steering into the wind, laughing, dark hair flowing wildly. She could still remember that heady, weightless feeling when they'd gone scuba diving in the warm coastal waters. Kate had been too caught up in what was happening to herself to think about her father's sudden interest in boating and diving.

She'd been too swept away by her own feelings of astonishment that a man like Ky Silver should be attracted to someone like her to notice her father's pre-occupation with currents and tides. There'd been too much excitement for her to realize that her father never bothered with fishing rods like the other vacationers.

But now her youthful fancies were behind her, Kate told herself. Now, she could clearly remember how many hours her father had closeted himself in his hotel room, reading book after book that he brought with him from the mainland library. He'd been researching even then. She was sure he'd continued that research in the following summers when she had refused to go back. Refused to go back, Kate remembered, because of Ky Silver.

Ky had asked her to believe in fairy tales. He asked her to give him the impossible. When she refused, frightened, he shrugged and walked away without a second look. She had never gone back to the white sand and gulls since then.

Kate looked down again at her father's papers. She had to go back now—go back and finish what her father had started. Perhaps, more than the house, the trust fund, the antique jewelry that had been her mother's, this was her father's legacy to her. If she filed those papers neatly away, they'd haunt her for the rest of her life.

She had to go back, Kate reaffirmed as she took off her glasses and folded them neatly on the blotter. And it was Ky Silver she'd have to go to. Her father's aspirations had drawn her away from Ky once; now, four years later, they were drawing her back.

But Dr. Kathleen Hardesty knew the difference between fairy tales and reality. Reaching in her father's desk drawer, she drew out a sheet of thick creamy stationery and began to write.

Ky let the wind buffet him as he opened the throttle. He liked speed in much the same way he liked a lazy afternoon in the hammock. They were two of the things that made life worthwhile. He was used to the smell of salt spray, but he still inhaled deeply. He was well accustomed to the vibration of the deck under his feet, but he still felt it. He wasn't a man to let anything go unnoticed or unappreciated.

He grew up in this quiet, remote little coastal town, and though he'd traveled and intended to travel more, he didn't plan to live anywhere else. It suited him—the freedom of the sea, and the coziness of a small community.

He didn't resent the tourists because he knew they helped keep the village alive, but he preferred the island in winter. Then the storms blew wild and cold, and only the hearty would brave the ferry across Hatteras Inlet.

He fished, but unlike the majority of his neighbors, he rarely sold what he caught. What he pulled out of the sea, he ate. He dove, occasionally collecting shells, but again, this was for his own pleasure. Often he took tourists out on his boat to fish or to scuba dive, because there were times he enjoyed the company. But there were afternoons, like this sparkling one, when he simply wanted the sea to himself.

He had always been restless. His mother had said that he came into the world two weeks early because he grew impatient waiting. Ky turned thirty-two that spring, but was far from settled. He knew what he wanted—to live as he chose. The trouble was that he wasn't certain just what he wanted to choose.

At the moment, he chose the open sky and the endless sea. There were other moments when he knew that that wouldn't be enough.

But the sun was hot, the breeze cool and the shoreline was drawing near. The boat's motor was purring smoothly and in the small cooler was a tidy catch of fish he'd cook up for his supper that night. On a crystal, sparkling afternoon, perhaps it was enough.

From the shore he looked like a pirate might if there were pirates in the twentieth century. His hair was long enough to curl over his ears and well over the collar of a shirt had he worn one. It was black, a rich, true black that might have come from his Arapaho or Sicilian blood. His eyes were the deep, dark green of the sea on a cloudy day. His skin was bronzed from years in the sun, taut from the years of swimming and pulling in nets. His bone structure was also part of his heritage, sculpted, hard, defined.

When he smiled as he did now, racing the wind to shore, his face took on that reckless freedom women found irresistible. When he didn't smile, his eyes could turn as cold as a lion's before a leap. He discovered long ago that women found that equally irresistible.

Ky drew back on the throttle so that the boat slowed, rocked, then glided into its slip in Silver Lake Harbor. With the quick, efficient movements of one born to the sea, he leaped onto the dock to secure the lines.

"Catch anything?"

Ky straightened and turned. He smiled, but absently, as one does at a brother seen almost every day of one's life. "Enough. Things slow at the Roost?"

Marsh smiled, and there was a brief flicker of family resemblance, but his eyes were a calm light brown and his hair was carefully styled. "Worried about your investment?"

Ky gave a half-shrug. "With you running things?"

Marsh didn't comment. They knew each other as intimately as men ever know each other. One was restless, the other calm. The opposition never seemed to matter. "Linda wants you to come up for dinner. She worries about you."

She would, Ky thought, amused. His sister-in-law loved to mother and fuss, even though she was five years younger than Ky. That was one of the reasons the restaurant she ran with Marsh was such a success—that, plus Marsh's business sense and the hefty investment and shrewd renovations Ky had made. Ky left the managing up to his brother and his sister-in-law. He didn't mind owning a restaurant, even keeping half an eye on the profit and loss, but he certainly had no interest in running one.

After the lines were secure, he wiped his palms down the hips of his cut-offs. "What's the special tonight?"

Marsh dipped his hands into his front pockets and rocked back on his heels. "Bluefish."

Grinning, Ky tossed back the lid of his cooler revealing his catch. "Tell Linda not to worry. I'll eat."

"That's not going to satisfy her." Marsh glanced at

his brother as Ky looked out to sea. "She thinks you're alone too much."

"You're only alone too much if you don't like being alone." Ky glanced back over his shoulder. He didn't want to debate now, when the exhilaration of the speed and the sea were still upon him. But he'd never been a man to placate. "Maybe you two should think about having another baby, then Linda would be too busy to worry about big brothers."

"Give me a break. Hope's only eighteen months old."

"You've got to add nine to that," Ky reminded him carelessly. He was fond of his niece, despite—no, because she was a demon. "Anyway, it looks like the family lineage is in your hands."

"Yeah." Marsh shifted his feet, cleared his throat and fell silent. It was a habit he'd carried since childhood, one that could annoy or amuse Ky depending on his mood. At the moment, it was only mildly distracting.

Something was in the air. He could smell it, but he couldn't quite identify it. A storm brewing, he wondered? One of those hot, patient storms that seemed capable of brewing for weeks. He was certain he could smell it.

"Why don't you tell me what else is on your mind?" Ky suggested. "I want to get back to the house and clean these."

"You had a letter. It was put in our box by mistake."

It was a common enough occurrence, but by his brother's expression Ky knew there was more. His sense of an impending storm grew sharper. Saying nothing, he held out his hand.

"Ky..." Marsh began. There was nothing he could say, just as there'd been nothing to say four years before. Reaching in his back pocket, he drew out the letter.

The envelope was made from heavy cream-colored paper. Ky didn't have to look at the return address. The handwriting and the memories it brought leaped out at him. For a moment, he felt his breath catch in his lungs as it might if someone had caught him with a blow to the solar plexus. Deliberately, he expelled it. "Thanks," he said, as if it meant nothing. He stuck the letter in his pocket before he picked up his cooler and gear.

"Ky—" Again Marsh broke off. His brother had turned his head, and the cool, half-impatient stare said very clearly—back off. "If you change your mind about dinner," Marsh said.

"I'll let you know." Ky went down the length of the dock without looking back.

He was grateful he hadn't bothered to bring his car down to the harbor. He needed to walk. He needed the fresh air and the exercise to keep his mind clear while he remembered what he didn't want to remember. What he never really forgot.

Kate. Four years ago she'd walked out of his life with the same sort of cool precision with which she'd walked into it. She had reminded him of a Victorian doll—a little prim, a little aloof. He'd never had much patience with neatly folded hands or haughty manners, yet almost from the first instant he'd wanted her.

At first, he thought it was the fact that she was so different. A challenge—something for Ky Silver to conquer. He enjoyed teaching her to dive, and watch-

ing the precise step-by-step way she learned. It hadn't
been any hardship to look at her in a snug scuba suit,
although she didn't have voluptuous curves. She had a
trim, neat, almost boylike figure and what seemed like
yards of thick, soft hair.

He could still remember the first time she took it
down from its pristine knot. It left him breathless, hurting, fascinated. Ky would have touched it—touched her
then and there if her father hadn't been standing beside
her. But if a man was clever, if a man was determined,
he could find a way to be alone with a woman.

Ky had found ways. Kate had taken to diving as
though she'd been born to it. While her father had buried himself in his books, Ky had taken Kate out on
the water—under the water, to the silent, dreamlike
world that had attracted her just as it had always attracted him.

He could remember the first time he kissed her. They
had been wet and cool from a dive, standing on the
deck of his boat. He was able to see the lighthouse behind her and the vague line of the coast. Her hair had
flowed down her back, sleek from the water, dripping
with it. He'd reached out and gathered it in his hand.

"What are you doing?"

Four years later, he could hear that low, cultured,
eastern voice, the curiosity in it. It took no effort for
him to see the curiosity that had been in her eyes.

"I'm going to kiss you."

The curiosity had remained in her eyes, fascinating
him. "Why?"

"Because I want to."

It was as simple as that for him. He wanted to. Her body had stiffened as he'd drawn her against him. When her lips parted in protest, he closed his over them. In the time it takes a heart to beat, the rigidity had melted from her body. She'd kissed him with all the young, stored-up passion that had been in her—passion mixed with innocence. He was experienced enough to recognize her innocence, and that too had fascinated him. Ky had, foolishly, youthfully and completely, fallen in love.

Kate had remained an enigma to him, though they shared impassioned hours of laughter and long, lazy talks. He admired her thirst for learning and she had a predilection for putting knowledge into neat slots that baffled him. She was enthusiastic about diving, but it hadn't been enough for her simply to be able to swim freely underwater, taking her air from tanks. She had to know how the tanks worked, why they were fashioned a certain way. Ky watched her absorb what he told her, and knew she'd retain it.

They had taken walks along the shoreline at night and she had recited poetry from memory. Beautiful words, Byron, Shelley, Keats. And he, who'd never been overly impressed by such things, had eaten it up because her voice had made the words somehow personal. Then she'd begin to talk about syntax, iambic pentameters, and Ky would find new ways to divert her.

For three months, he did little but think of her. For the first time, Ky had considered changing his lifestyle. His little cottage near the beach needed work. It needed furniture. Kate would need more than milk crates and the hammock that had been his style. Because he'd been young and had never been in love before, Ky had taken his own plans for granted.

She'd walked out on him. She'd had her own plans, and he hadn't been part of them.

Her father came back to the island the following summer, and every summer thereafter. Kate never came back. Ky knew she had completed her doctorate and was teaching in a prestigious ivy league school where her father was all but a cornerstone. She had what she wanted. So, he told himself as he swung open the screen door of his cottage, did he. He went where he wanted, when he wanted. He called his own shots. His responsibilities extended only as far as he chose to extend them. To his way of thinking, that itself was a mark of success.

Setting the cooler on the kitchen floor, Ky opened the refrigerator. He twisted the top off a beer and drank half of it in one icy cold swallow. It washed some of the bitterness out of his mouth.

Calm now, and curious, he pulled the letter out of his pocket. Ripping it open, he drew out the single neatly written sheet.

Dear Ky,
You may or may not be aware that my father suffered a fatal heart attack two weeks ago. It was very sudden, and I'm currently trying to tie up the many details this involves.

In going through my father's papers, I find that he had again made arrangements to come to the island this summer, and engage your services. I now find it necessary to take his place. For reasons which I'd rather explain in person, I need your help. You have my father's deposit. When I arrive in Ocracoke on the fifteenth, we can discuss terms.

If possible, contact me at the hotel, or leave a message. I hope we'll be able to come to a mutually agreeable arrangement. Please give my best to Marsh. Perhaps I'll see him during my stay.

Best,
Kathleen Hardesty

So the old man was dead. Ky set down the letter and lifted his beer again. He couldn't say he'd had any liking for Edwin Hardesty. Kate's father had been a stringent, humorless man. Still, he hadn't disliked him. Ky had, in an odd way, gotten used to his company over the last few summers. But this summer, it would be Kate.

Ky glanced at the letter again, then jogged his memory until he remembered the date. Two days, he mused. She'd be there in two days...to discuss terms. A smile played around the corners of his mouth but it didn't have anything to do with humor. They'd discuss terms, he agreed silently as he scanned Kate's letter again.

She wanted to take her father's place. Ky wondered if she'd realized, when she wrote that, just how ironic it was. Kathleen Hardesty had been obediently dogging her father's footsteps all her life. Why should that change after his death?

Had she changed? Ky wondered briefly. Would that fascinating aura of innocence and aloofness still cling to her? Or perhaps that had faded with the years. Would that rather sweet primness have developed into a rigidity? He'd see for himself in a couple of days, he realized, but tossed the letter onto the counter rather than into the trash.

So, she wanted to engage his services, he mused. Leaning both hands on either side of the sink, he looked out the window in the direction of the water he could smell, but not quite see. She wanted a business arrangement—the rental of his boat, his gear and his time. He felt the bitterness well up and swallowed it as cleanly as he had the beer. She'd have her business arrangement. And she'd pay. He'd see to that.

Ky left the kitchen with his catch still in the cooler. The appetite he'd worked up with salt spray and speed had vanished.

Kate pulled her car onto the ferry to Ocracoke and set the brake. The morning was cool and very clear. Even so, she was tempted to simply lean her head back and close her eyes. She wasn't certain what impulse had pushed her to drive from Connecticut rather than fly, but now that she'd all but reached her destination, she was too weary to analyze.

In the bucket seat beside her was her briefcase, and inside, all the papers she'd collected from her father's desk. Perhaps once she was in the hotel on the island, she could go through them again, understand them better. Perhaps the feeling that she was doing the right thing would come back. Over the last few days she'd lost that sense.

The closer she came to the island, the more she began

to think she was making a mistake. Not to the island, Kate corrected ruthlessly—the closer she came to Ky. It was a fact, and Kate knew it was imperative to face facts so that they could be dealt with logically.

She had a little time left, a little time to calm the feelings that had somehow gotten stirred up during the drive south. It was foolish, and somehow it helped Kate to remind herself of that. She wasn't a woman returning to a lover, but a woman hoping to engage a diver in a very specific venture. Past personal feelings wouldn't enter into it because they were just that. Past.

The Kate Hardesty who'd arrived on Ocracoke four years ago had little to do with the Dr. Kathleen Hardesty who was going there now. She wasn't young, inexperienced or impressionable. Those reckless, wild traits of Ky's wouldn't appeal to her now. They wouldn't frighten her. They would be, if Ky agreed to her terms, business partners.

Kate felt the ferry move beneath her as she stared through the windshield. Yes, she thought, unless Ky had changed a great deal, the prospect of diving for treasure would appeal to his sense of adventure.

She knew enough about diving in the technical sense to be sure she'd find no one better equipped for the job. It was always advisable to have the best. More relaxed and less weary, Kate stepped out of her car to stand at the rail. From there she could watch the gulls swoop and the tiny uninhabited islands pass by. She felt a sense of homecoming, but pushed it away. Connecticut was home. Once Kate did what she came for, she'd go back.

The water swirled behind the boat. She couldn't hear it over the motor, but looking down she could watch the wake. One island was nearly imperceptible under a flock of big, brown pelicans. It made her smile, pleased to see the odd, awkward-looking birds again. They passed the long spit of land, where fishermen parked trucks and tried their luck, near the point where bay met sea. She could watch the waves crash and foam where there was no shore, just a turbulent marriage of waters. That was something she hadn't forgotten, though she hadn't seen it since she left the island. Nor had she forgotten just how treacherous the current was along that verge.

Excitement. She breathed deeply before she turned back to her car. The treacherous was always exciting.

When the ferry docked, she had only a short wait before she could drive her car onto the narrow blacktop. The trip to town wouldn't take long, and it wasn't possible to lose your way if you stayed on the one long road. The sea battered on one side, the sound flowed smoothly on the other—both were deep blue in the late morning light.

Her nerves were gone, at least that's what she told herself. It had just been a case of last minute jitters—very normal. She was prepared to see Ky again, speak to him, work with him if they could agree on the terms.

With the windows down, the soft moist air blew around her. It was soothing. She'd almost forgotten just how soothing air could be, or the sound of water lapping constantly against sand. It was right to come. When she saw the first faded buildings of the village, she felt a wave of relief. She was here. There was no turning back now.

The hotel where she had stayed that summer with her father was on the sound side of the island. It was small and quiet. If the service was a bit slow by northern standards, the view made up for it.

Kate pulled up in front and turned off the ignition. Self-satisfaction made her sigh. She'd taken the first step and was completely prepared for the next.

Then as she stepped out of the car, she saw him. For an instant, the confident professor of English literature vanished. She was only a woman, vulnerable to her own emotions.

Oh God, he hasn't changed. Not at all. As Ky came closer, she could remember every kiss, every murmur, every crazed storm of their loving. The breeze blew his hair back from his face so that every familiar angle and plane was clear to her. With the sun warm on her skin, bright in her eyes, she felt the years spin back, then forward again. He hadn't changed.

He hadn't expected to see her yet. Somehow he thought she'd arrive that afternoon. Yet he found it necessary to go by the Roost that morning knowing the restaurant was directly across from the hotel where she'd be staying.

She was here, looking neat and a bit too thin in her tailored slacks and blouse. Her hair was pinned up so that the soft femininity of her neck and throat were revealed. Her eyes seemed too dark against her pale skin—skin Ky knew would turn golden slowly under the summer sun.

She looked the same. Soft, prim, calm. Lovely. He ignored the thud in the pit of his stomach as he stepped in front of her. He looked her up and down with the arrogance that was so much a part of him. Then he grinned because he had an overwhelming urge to strangle her.

"Kate. Looks like my timing's good."

She was almost certain she couldn't speak and was therefore determined to speak calmly. "Ky, it's nice to see you again."

"Is it?"

Ignoring the sarcasm, Kate walked around to her trunk and released it. "I'd like to get together with you as soon as possible. There are some things I want to show you, and some business I'd like to discuss."

"Sure, always open for business."

He watched her pull two cases from her trunk, but didn't offer to help. He saw there was no ring on her hand—but it wouldn't have mattered.

"Perhaps we can meet this afternoon then, after I've settled in." The sooner the better, she told herself. They would establish the purpose, the ground rules and the payment. "We could have lunch in the hotel."

"No, thanks," he said easily, leaning against the side of her car while she set her cases down. "You want me, you know where to find me. It's a small island."

With his hands in the pockets of his jeans, he walked away from her. Though she didn't want to, Kate remembered that the last time he'd walked away, they'd stood in almost the same spot.

Picking up her cases, she headed for the hotel, perhaps a bit too quickly.

Chapter 2

She knew where to find him. If the island had been double in size, she'd still have known where to find him. Kate acknowledged that Ky hadn't changed. That meant if he wasn't out on his boat, he would be at home, in the small, slightly dilapidated cottage he owned near the beach. Because she felt it would be a strategic error to go after him too soon, she dawdled over her unpacking.

But there were memories even here, where she'd spent one giddy, whirlwind night of love with Ky. It had been the only time they were able to sleep together through the night, embracing each other in the crisp hotel sheets until the first light of dawn crept around the edges of the window shades. She remembered how reckless she'd felt during those few stolen hours, and how dull the morning had seemed because it brought them to an end.

Now she could look out the same window she had

stood by then, staring out in the same direction she'd stared out then when she watched Ky walk away. She remembered the sky had been streaked with a rose color before it had brightened to a pure, pale blue.

Then, with her skin still warm from her lover's touch and her mind glazed with lack of sleep and passion, Kate had believed such things could go on forever. But of course they couldn't. She had seen that only weeks later. Passion and reckless nights of loving had to give way to responsibilities, obligations.

Staring out the same window, in the same direction, Kate could feel the sense of loss she'd felt that long ago dawn without the underlying hope that they'd be together again. And again.

They wouldn't be together again, and there'd been no one else since that one heady summer. She had her career, her vocation, her books. She had had her taste of passion.

Turning away, she busied herself by rearranging everything she'd just arranged in her drawers and closet. When she decided she'd stalled in her hotel room long enough, Kate started out. She didn't take her car. She walked, just as she always walked to Ky's home.

She told herself she was over the shock of seeing him again. It was only natural that there be some strain, some discomfort. She was honest enough to admit that it would have been easier if there'd been only strain and discomfort, and not that one sharp quiver of pleasure. Kate acknowledged it, now that it had passed.

No, Ky Silver hadn't changed, she reminded herself. He was still arrogant, self-absorbed and cocky. Those traits might have appealed to her once, but she'd been very young. If she were wise, she could use those same traits to persuade Ky to help her. Yes, those traits, she thought, and the tempting offer of a treasure hunt. Even at her most pessimistic, she couldn't believe Ky would refuse. It was his nature to take chances.

This time she'd be in charge. Kate drew in a deep breath of warm air that tasted of sea. Somehow she felt it would steady her. Ky was going to find she was no longer naive, or susceptible to a few careless words of affection.

With her briefcase in hand, Kate walked through the village. This too was the same, she thought. She was glad of it. The simplicity and solitude still appealed to her. She enjoyed the dozens of little shops, the restaurants and small inns tucked here and there, all somehow using the harbor as a central point, the lighthouse as a landmark. The villagers still made the most of their notorious one-time resident and permanent ghost, Blackbeard. His name or face was lavishly displayed on store signs.

She passed the harbor, unconsciously scanning for Ky's boat. It was there, in the same slip he'd always used—clean lines, scrubbed deck, shining hardware. The flying bridge gleamed in the afternoon light and looked the same as she remembered. Reckless, challenging. The paint was fresh and there was no film of salt spray on the bridge windows. However careless Ky had been about his own appearance or his home, he'd always pampered his boat.

The *Vortex*. Kate studied the flamboyant lettering

on the stern. He could pamper, she thought again, but he also expected a lot in return. She knew the speed he could urge out of the second-hand cabin cruiser he'd lovingly reconstructed himself. Nothing could block the image of the days she'd stood beside him at the helm. The wind had whipped her hair as he'd laughed and pushed for speed, and more speed. Her heart thudded, her pulse raced until she was certain nothing and no one could catch them. She'd been afraid, of him, of the rush of wind—but she'd stayed with both. In the end, she'd left both.

He enjoyed the demanding, the thrilling, the frightening. Kate gripped the handle of her briefcase tighter. Isn't that why she came to him? There were dozens of other experienced divers, many, many other experts on the coastal waters of the Outer Banks. There was only one Ky Silver.

"Kate? Kate Hardesty?"

At the sound of her name, Kate turned and felt the years tumble back again. "Linda!" This time there was no restraint. With an openness she showed to very few, Kate embraced the woman who dashed up to her, "It's wonderful to see you." With a laugh, she drew Linda away to study her. The same chestnut hair cut short and pert, the same frank, brown eyes. It seemed very little had changed on the island. "You look wonderful."

"When I looked out the window and saw you, I could hardly believe it. Kate, you've barely changed at all." With her usual candor and lack of pretension, Linda took a quick, thorough survey. It was quick only because she did things quickly, but it wasn't subtle. "You're too thin," she decided. "But that might be jealousy."

"You still look like a college freshman," Kate returned. "That is jealousy."

As swiftly as the laugh had come, Linda sobered. "I'm sorry about your father, Kate. These past weeks must've been difficult for you."

Kate heard the sincerity, but she'd already tied up her grief and stored it away. "Ky told you?"

"Ky never tells me anything," Linda said with a sniff. In an unconscious move, she glanced in the direction of his boat. It was in its slip and Kate had been walking north—in the direction of Ky's cottage. There could be only one place she could have been going. "Marsh did. How long are you going to stay?"

"I'm not sure yet." She felt the weight of her briefcase. Dreams held the same weight as responsibilities. "There are some things I have to do."

"One of the things you have to do is have dinner at the Roost tonight. It's the restaurant right across from your hotel."

Kate looked back at the rough wooden sign. "Yes, I noticed it. Is it new?"

Linda glanced over her shoulder with a self-satisfied nod. "By Ocracoke standards. We run it."

"We?"

"Marsh and I." With a beaming smile, Linda held out her left hand. "We've been married for three years." Then she rolled her eyes in a habit Kate remembered.

"It only took me fifteen years to convince him he couldn't live without me."

"I'm happy for you." She was, and if she felt a pang, she ignored it. "Married and running a restaurant. My father never filled me in on island gossip."

"We have a daughter too. Hope. She's a year and a half old and a terror. For some reason, she takes after Ky." Linda sobered again, laying a hand lightly on Kate's arm. "You're going to see him now." It wasn't a question; she didn't bother to disguise it as one.

"Yes." Keep it casual, Kate ordered herself. Don't let the questions and concern in Linda's eyes weaken you. There were ties between Linda and Ky, not only newly formed family ones, but the older tie of the island. "My father was working on something. I need Ky's help with it."

Linda studied Kate's calm face. "You know what you're doing?"

"Yes." She didn't show a flicker of unease. Her stomach slowly wrapped itself in knots. "I know what I'm doing."

"Okay." Accepting Kate's answer, but not satisfied, Linda dropped her hand. "Please come by—the restaurant or the house. We live just down the road from Ky. Marsh'll want to see you, and I'd like to show off Hope—and our menu," she added with a grin. "Both are outstanding."

"Of course I'll come by." On impulse, she took both of Linda's hands. "It's really good to see you again. I know I didn't keep in touch, but—"

"I understand." Linda gave her hands a quick squeeze.

"That was yesterday. I've got to get back, the lunch crowd's pretty heavy during the season." She let out a little sigh, wondering if Kate was as calm as she seemed. And if Ky were as big a fool as ever. "Good luck," she murmured, then dashed across the street again.

"Thanks," Kate said under her breath. She was going to need it.

The walk was as beautiful as she remembered. She passed the little shops with their display windows showing handmade crafts or antiques. She passed the blue and white clapboard houses and the neat little streets on the outskirts of town with their bleached green lawns and leafy trees.

A dog raced back and forth on the length of his chain as she wandered by, barking at her as if he knew he was supposed to but didn't have much interest in it. She could see the tower of the white lighthouse. There'd been a keeper there once, but those days were over. Then she was on the narrow path that led to Ky's cottage.

Her palms were damp. She cursed herself. If she had to remember, she'd remember later, when she was alone. When she was safe.

The path was as it had been, just wide enough for a car, sparsely graveled, lined with bushes that always grew out a bit too far. The bushes and trees had always had a wild, overgrown look that suited the spot. That suited him.

Ky had told her he didn't care much for visitors. If he wanted company, all he had to do was go into town where he knew everyone. That was typical of Ky Silver, Kate mused. If I want you, I'll let you know. Otherwise, back off.

He'd wanted her once.... Nervous, Kate shifted the briefcase to her other hand. Whatever he wanted now, he'd have to hear her out. She needed him for what he was best at—diving and taking chances.

When the house came into view, she stopped, staring. It was still small, still primitive. But it no longer looked as though it would keel over on its side in a brisk wind.

The roof had been redone. Obviously Ky wouldn't need to set out pots and pans during a rain any longer. The porch he'd once talked vaguely about building now ran the length of the front, sturdy and wide. The screen door that had once been patched in a half a dozen places had been replaced by a new one. Yet nothing looked new, she observed. It just looked right. The cedar had weathered to silver, the windows were untrimmed but gleaming. There was, much to her surprise, a spill of impatiens in a long wooden planter.

She'd been wrong, Kate decided as she walked closer. Ky Silver had changed. Precisely how, and precisely how much, she had yet to find out.

She was nearly to the first step when she heard sounds coming from the rear of the house. There was a shed back there, she remembered, full of boards and tools and salvage. Grateful that she didn't have to meet him in the house, Kate walked around the side to the tiny backyard. She could hear the sea and knew it was less than a two-minute walk through high grass and sand dunes.

Did he still go down there in the evenings? she won-

dered. Just to look, he'd said. Just to smell. Sometimes
he'd pick up driftwood or shells or whatever small treasures the sea gave up to the sand. Once he'd given her a
small smooth shell that fit into the palm of her hand—
very white with a delicate pink center. A woman with
her first gift of diamonds could not have been more
thrilled.

Shaking the memories away, she went into the shed.
It was as tall as the cottage and half as wide. The last
time she'd been there, it'd been crowded with planks
and boards and boxes of hardware. Now she saw the
hull of a boat. At a worktable with his back to her, Ky
sanded the mast.

"You've built it." The words came out before she
could stop them, full of astonished pleasure. How many
times had he told her about the boat he'd build one day?
It had seemed to Kate it had been his only concrete ambition. Mahogany on oak, he'd said. A seventeen-foot
sloop that would cut through the water like a dream.
He'd have bronze fastenings and teak on the deck. One
day he'd sail the inner coastal waters from Ocracoke
to New England. He'd described the boat so minutely
that she'd seen it then just as clearly as she saw it now.

"I told you I would." Ky turned away from the mast
and faced her. She, in the doorway, had the sun at her
back. He was half in shadow.

"Yes." Feeling foolish, Kate tightened her grip on
the briefcase. "You did."

"But you didn't believe me." Ky tossed aside the
sandpaper. Did she have to look so neat and cool, and
impossibly lovely? A trickle of sweat ran down his

back. "You always had a problem seeing beyond the moment."

Reckless, impatient, compelling. Would he always bring those words to her mind? "You always had a problem dealing with the moment," she said.

His brow lifted, whether in surprise or derision she couldn't be sure. "Then it might be said *we* always had a problem." He walked to her, so that the sun slanting through the small windows fell over him, then behind him. "But it didn't always seem to matter." To satisfy himself that he still could, Ky reached out and touched her face. She didn't move, and her skin was as soft and cool as he remembered. "You look tired Kate."

The muscles in her stomach quivered, but not her voice. "It was a long trip."

His thumb brushed along her cheekbone. "You need some sun."

This time she backed away. "I intend to get some."

"So I gathered from your letter." Pleased that she'd retreated first, Ky leaned against the open door. "You wrote that you wanted to talk to me in person. You're here. Why don't you tell me what you want?"

The cocky grin might have made her melt once. Now it stiffened her spine. "My father was researching a project. I intend to finish it."

"So?"

"I need your help."

Ky laughed and stepped past her into the sunlight. He needed the air, the distance. He needed to touch her again. "From your tone, there's nothing you hate more than asking me for it."

"No." She stood firm, feeling suddenly strong and bitter. "Nothing."

There was no humor in his eyes as he faced her again. The expression in them was cold and flat. She'd seen it before. "Then let's understand each other before we start. You left the island and me, and took what I wanted."

He couldn't make her cringe now as he once had with only that look. "What happened four years ago has nothing to do with today."

"The hell it doesn't." He came toward her again so that she took an involuntary step backward. "Still afraid of me?" he asked softly.

As it had a moment ago, the question turned the fear to anger. "No," she told him, and meant it. "I'm not afraid of you, Ky. I've no intention of discussing the past, but I will agree that I left the island and you. I'm here now on business. I'd like you to hear me out. If you're interested, we'll discuss terms, nothing else."

"I'm not one of your students, professor." The drawl crept into his voice, as it did when he let it. "Don't instruct."

She curled her fingers tighter around the handle of her briefcase. "In business, there are always ground rules."

"Nobody agreed to let you make them."

"I made a mistake," Kate said quietly as she fought for control. "I'll find someone else."

She'd taken only two steps away when Ky grabbed her arm. "No, you won't." The stormy look in his eyes made her throat dry. She knew what he meant. She'd never find anyone else that could make her feel as he made her feel, or want as he made her want. Deliberately, Kate removed his hand from her arm.

"I came here on business. I've no intention of fighting with you over something that doesn't exist any longer."

"We'll see about that." How long could he hold on? Ky wondered. It hurt just to look at her and to feel her withdrawing with every second that went by. "But for now, why don't you tell me what you have in that businesslike briefcase, professor."

Kate took a deep breath. She should have known it wouldn't be easy. Nothing was ever easy with Ky. "Charts," she said precisely. "Notebooks full of research, maps, carefully documented facts and precise theories. In my opinion, my father was very close to pinpointing the exact location of the *Liberty*, an English merchant vessel that sank, stores intact, off the North Carolina coast two hundred and fifty years ago."

He listened without a comment or a change of expression from beginning to end. When she finished, Ky studied her face for one long moment. "Come inside," he said and turned toward the house. "Show me what you've got."

His arrogance made her want to turn away and go back to town exactly as she'd come. There were other divers, others who knew the coast and the waters as well as Ky did. Kate forced herself to calm down, forced herself to think. There were others, but if it was a choice between the devil she knew and the unknown, she had no choice. Kate followed him into the house.

This, too, had changed. The kitchen she remembered had had a paint splattered floor, with the only usable counter space being a tottering picnic table. The floor had been stripped and varnished, the cabinets redone, and scrubbed butcher block counters lined the sink. He had put in a skylight so that the sun spilled down over the picnic table, now re-worked and re-painted, with benches along either side.

"Did you do all of this yourself?"

"Yeah. Surprised?"

So he didn't want to make polite conversation. Kate set her briefcase on the table. "Yes. You always seemed content that the walls were about to cave in on you."

"I was content with a lot of things, once. Want a beer?"

"No." Kate sat down and drew the first of her father's notebooks out of her briefcase. "You'll want to read these. It would be unnecessary and time-consuming for you to read every page, but if you'd look over the ones I've marked, I think you'll have enough to go by."

"All right." Ky turned from the refrigerator, beer in hand. He sat, watching her over the rim as he took the first swallow, then he opened the notebook.

Edwin Hardesty's handwriting was very clear and precise. He wrote down his facts in didactic, unromantic terms. What could have been exciting was as dry as a thesis, but it was accurate. Ky had no doubt of that.

The *Liberty* had been lost, with its stores of sugar, tea, silks, wine and other imports for the colonies. Hardesty had listed the manifest down to the last piece of hardtack. When it had left England, the ship had also been carrying gold. Twenty-five thousand in coins of the realm. Ky glanced up from the notebook to see Kate watching him.

"Interesting," he said simply, and turned to the next page she marked.

There'd been only three survivors who'd washed up on the island. One of the crew had described the storm that had sunk the *Liberty*, giving details on the height of the waves, the splintering wood, the water gushing into the hole. It was a grim, grisly story which Hardesty had recounted in his pragmatic style, complete with footnotes. The crewman had also given the last known location of the ship before it had gone down. Ky didn't require Hardesty's calculations to figure the ship had sunk two-and-a-half miles off the coast of Ocracoke.

Going from one notebook to another, Ky read through Hardesty's well-drafted theories, his clear to-the-point documentations, corroborated and recorroborated. He scanned the charts, then studied them with more care. He remembered the man's avid interest in diving, which had always seemed inconsistent with his precise lifestyle.

So he'd been looking for gold, Ky mused. All these years the man had been digging in books and looking for gold. If it had been anyone else, Ky might have dismissed it as another fable. Little towns along the coast were full of stories about buried treasure. Edward Teach had used the shallow waters of the inlets to frustrate and outwit the crown until his last battle off the shores of Ocracoke. That alone kept the dreams of finding sunken treasures alive.

But it was Dr. Edwin J. Hardesty, Yale professor, an unimaginative, humorless man who didn't believe there was time to be wasted on the frivolous, who'd written these notebooks.

Ky might still have dismissed it, but Kate was sitting across from him. He had enough adventurous blood in him to believe in destinies.

Setting the last notebook aside, he picked up his beer again. "So, you want to treasure hunt."

She ignored the humor in his voice. With her hands folded on the table, she leaned forward. "I intend to follow through with what my father was working on."

"Do you believe it?"

Did she? Kate opened her mouth and closed it again. She had no idea. "I don't believe that all of my father's time and research should go for nothing. I want to try. As it happens, I need you to help me do it. You'll be compensated."

"Will I?" He studied the liquid left in the beer bottle with a half smile. "Will I indeed?"

"I need you, your boat and your equipment for a month, maybe two. I can't dive alone because I just don't know the waters well enough to risk it, and I don't have the time to waste. I have to be back in Connecticut by the end of August."

"To get more chalk dust under your fingernails."

She sat back slowly. "You have no right to criticize my profession."

"I'm sure the chalk's very exclusive at Yale," Ky commented. "So you're giving yourself six weeks or so to find a pot of gold."

"If my father's calculations are viable, it won't take that long."

"If," Ky repeated. Setting down his bottle, he leaned forward. "I've got no timetable. You want six weeks of my time, you can have it. For a price."

"Which is?"

"A hundred dollars a day and fifty percent of whatever we find."

Kate gave him a cool look as she slipped the notebooks back into her briefcase. "Whatever I was four years ago, Ky, I'm not a fool now. A hundred dollars a day is outrageous when we're dealing with monthly rates. And fifty percent is out of the question." It gave her a certain satisfaction to bargain with him. This made it business, pure and simple. "I'll give you fifty dollars a day and ten percent."

With the maddening half grin on his face he swirled the beer in the bottle. "I don't turn my boat on for fifty a day."

She tilted her head a bit to study him. Something tore inside him. She'd often done that whenever he said something she wanted to think over. "You're more mercenary than you once were."

"We've all got to make a living, professor." Didn't she feel anything? he thought furiously. Wasn't she suffering just a little, being in the house where they'd made love their first and last time? "You want a service," he said quietly, "you pay for it. Nothing's free. Seventy-five a day and twenty-five percent. We'll say it's for old-times' sake."

"No, we'll say it's for business' sake." She made herself extend her hand, but when his closed over it, she regretted the gesture. It was callused, hard, strong. Kate knew how his hand felt skimming over her skin, driving her to desperation, soothing, teasing, seducing.

"We have a deal." Ky thought he could see a flash of remembrance in her eyes. He kept her hand in his knowing she didn't welcome his touch. Because she didn't. "There's no guarantee you'll find your treasure."

"That's understood."

"Fine. I'll deduct your father's deposit from the total."

"All right." With her free hand, she clutched at her briefcase. "When do we start?"

"Meet me at the harbor at eight tomorrow." Deliberately, he placed his other free hand over hers on the leather case. "Leave this with me. I want to look over the papers some more."

"There's no need for you to have them," Kate began, but his hands tightened on hers.

"If you don't trust me with them, you take them along." His voice was very smooth and very quiet. At its most dangerous. "And find yourself another diver."

Their gazes locked. Her hands were trapped and so was she. Kate knew there would be sacrifices she'd have to make. "I'll meet you at eight."

"Fine." He released her hands and sat back. "Nice doing business with you, Kate."

Dismissed, she rose. Just how much had she sacrificed already? she wondered. "Goodbye."

He lifted and drained his half-finished beer when the screen shut behind her. Then he made himself sit there until he was certain that when he rose and walked to the window she'd be out of sight. He made himself sit there until the air flowing through the screens had carried her scent away.

Sunken ships and deep-sea treasure. It would have excited him, captured his imagination, enthusiasm and interest if he hadn't had an overwhelming urge to just get in his boat and head toward the horizon. He hadn't believed she could still affect him that way, that much, that completely. He'd forgotten that just being within touching distance of her tied his stomach in knots.

He'd never gotten over her. No matter what he filled his life with over the past four years, he'd never gotten over the slim, intellectual woman with the haughty face and doe's eyes.

Ky sat, staring at the briefcase with her initials stamped discreetly near the handle. He'd never expected her to come back, but he'd just discovered he'd never accepted the fact that she'd left him. Somehow, he'd managed to deceive himself through the years. Now, seeing her again, he knew it had just been a matter of pure survival and nothing to do with truth. He'd had to go on, to pretend that that part of his life was behind him, or he would have gone mad.

She was back now, but she hadn't come back to him. A business arrangement. Ky ran his hand over the smooth leather of the case. She simply wanted the best diver she knew and was willing to pay for him. Fee for services, nothing more, nothing less. The past meant little or nothing to her.

Fury grew until his knuckles whitened around the

bottle. He'd give her what she paid for, he promised himself. And maybe a bit extra.

This time when she went away, he wouldn't be left feeling like an inadequate fool. She'd be the one who would have to go on pretending for the rest of her life. This time when she went away, he'd be done with her. God, he'd have to be.

Rising quickly, he went out to the shed. If he stayed inside, he'd give in to the need to get very, very drunk.

Chapter 3

Kate had the water in the tub so hot that the mirror over the white pedestal sink was fogged. Oil floated on the surface, subtly fragrant and soothing. She'd lost track of how long she lay there—soaking, recharging. The next irrevocable step had been taken. She'd survived. Somehow during her discussion with Ky in his kitchen she had fought back the memories of laughter and passion. She couldn't count how many meals they'd shared there, cooking their catch, sipping wine.

Somehow during the walk back to her hotel, she'd overcome the need to weep. Tomorrow would be just a little easier. Tomorrow, and every day that followed. She had to believe it.

His animosity would help. His derision toward her kept Kate from romanticizing what she had to tell herself had never been more than a youthful summer fling.

Perspective. She'd always been able to stand back and
align everything in its proper perspective.

Perhaps her feelings for Ky weren't as dead as she
had hoped or pretended they were. But her emotions
were tinged with bitterness. Only a fool asked for more
sorrow. Only a romantic believed that bitterness could
ever be sweet. It had been a long time since Kate had
been a romantic fool. Even so, they would work together because both had an interest in what might be
lying on the sea floor.

Think of it. Two hundred and fifty years. Kate closed
her eyes and let her mind drift. The silks and sugar
would be gone, but would they find brass fittings deep
in corrosion after two-and-a-half centuries? The hull
would be covered with fungus and barnacles, but how
much of the oak would still be intact? Might the log
have been secured in a waterproof hold and still be leg-
ible? It could be donated to a museum in her father's
name. It would be something—the last something she
could do for him. Perhaps then she'd be able to lay all
her ambiguous feelings to rest.

The gold, Kate thought as she rose from the tub, the
gold would survive. She wasn't immune to the lure of
it. Yet she knew it would be the hunt that would be exciting, and somehow fulfilling. If she found it...

What would she do? Kate wondered. She dropped the
hotel towel over the rod before she wrapped herself in
her robe. Behind her, the mirror was still fogged with
steam from the water that drained slowly from the tub.
Would she put her share tidily in some conservative investments? Would she take a leisurely trip to the Greek

islands to see what Byron had seen and fallen in love with there? With a laugh, Kate walked through to the other room to pick up her brush. Strange, she hadn't thought beyond the search yet. Perhaps that was for the best, it wasn't wise to plan too far ahead.

You always had a problem seeing beyond the moment.

Damn him! With a sudden fury, Kate slammed the brush onto the dresser. She'd seen beyond the moment. She'd seen that he'd offered her no more than a tentative affair in a run-down beach shack. No guarantees, no commitment, no future. She only thanked God she'd had enough of her senses left to understand it and to walk away from what was essentially nothing at all. She'd never let Ky know just how horribly it had hurt to walk away from nothing at all.

Her father had been right to quietly point out the weaknesses in Ky, and her obligation to herself and her chosen profession. Ky's lack of ambition, his careless attitude toward the future weren't qualities, but flaws. She'd had a responsibility, and by accepting it had given herself independence and satisfaction.

Calmer, she picked up her brush again. She was dwelling on the past too much. It was time to stop. With the deft movements of habit, she secured her hair into a sleek twist. From this time on, she'd think only of what was to come, not what had, or might have been.

She needed to get out.

With panic just under the surface, Kate pulled a dress out of her closet. It no longer mattered that she was tired, that all she really wanted to do was to crawl into bed and let her mind and body rest. Nerves wouldn't permit it. She'd go across the street, have a drink with Linda and Marsh. She'd see their baby, have a long, extravagant dinner. When she came back to the hotel, alone, she'd make certain she'd be too tired for dreams.

Tomorrow, she had work to do.

Because she dressed quickly, Kate arrived at the Roost just past six. What she saw, she immediately approved of. It wasn't elegant, but it was comfortable. It didn't have the dimly lit, cathedral feel of so many of the restaurants she'd dined in with her father, with colleagues, back in Connecticut. It was relaxed, welcoming, cozy.

There were paintings of ships and boats along the stuccoed walls, of armadas and cutters. Throughout the dining room was other sailing paraphernalia—a ship's compass with its brass gleaming, a colorful spinnaker draped behind the bar with the stools in front of it shaped like wooden kegs. There was a crow's nest spearing toward the ceiling with ferns spilling out and down the mast.

The room was already half full of couples and families, the bulk of whom Kate identified as tourists. She could hear the comforting sound of cutlery scraping lightly over plates. There was the smell of good food and the hum of mixed conversations.

Comfortable, she thought again, but definitely well organized. Waiters and waitresses in sailor's denims moved smoothly, making every second count without looking rushed. The window opened out to a full evening view of Silver Lake Harbor. Kate turned her back on it because she knew her gaze would fall on the *Vortex* or its empty slip.

Tomorrow was soon enough for that. She wanted one night without memories.

"Kate."

She felt the hands on her shoulders and recognized the voice. There was a smile on her face when she turned around. "Marsh, I'm so glad to see you."

In his quiet way, he studied her, measured her and saw both the strain and the relief. In the same way, he'd had a crush on her that had faded into admiration and respect before the end of that one summer. "Beautiful as ever. Linda said you were, but it's nice to see for myself."

She laughed, because he'd always been able to make her feel as though life could be honed down to the most simple of terms. She'd never questioned why that trait had made her relax with Marsh and tingle with Ky.

"Several congratulations are in order, I hear. On your marriage, your daughter and your business."

"I'll take them all. How about the best table in the house?"

"No less than I expected." She linked her arm through his. "Your life agrees with you," she decided as he led her to a table by the window. "You look happy."

"Look and am." He lifted a hand to brush hers. "We were sorry to hear about your father, Kate."

"I know. Thank you."

Marsh sat across from her and fixed her with eyes so much calmer, so much softer than his brother's. She'd always wondered why the man with the dreamer's eyes had been so practical while Ky had been the real dreamer. "It's tragic, but I can't say I'm sorry it brought you back to the island. We've missed you." He paused, just long enough for effect. "All of us."

Kate picked up the square carmine-colored napkin and ran it through her hands. "Things change," she said deliberately. "You and Linda are certainly proof of that. When I left, you thought she was a bit of a nuisance."

"That hasn't changed," he claimed and grinned. He glanced up at the young, pony-tailed waitress. "This is Cindy, she'll take good care of you, Miss Hardesty—" He looked back at Kate with a grin. "I guess I should say Dr. Hardesty."

"Miss'll do," Kate told him. "I've taken the summer off."

"Miss Hardesty's a guest, a special one," he added, giving the waitress a smile. "How about a drink before you order? Or a bottle of wine?"

"Piesporter," the reply came from a deep, masculine voice.

Kate's fingers tightened on the linen, but she forced herself to look up calmly to meet Ky's amused eyes.

"The professor has a fondness for it."

"Yes, Mr. Silver."

Before Kate could agree or disagree, the waitress had dashed off.

"Well, Ky," Marsh commented easily. "You have a way of making the help come to attention."

With a shrug, Ky leaned against his brother's chair. If the three of them felt the air was suddenly tighter, each concealed it in their own way. "I had an urge for scampi."

"I can recommend it," Marsh told Kate. "Linda and the chef debated the recipe, then babied it until they reached perfection."

Kate smiled at Marsh as though there were no dark, brooding man looking down at her. "I'll try it. Are you going to join me?"

"I wish I could. Linda had to run home and deal with some crisis—Hope has a way of creating them and browbeating the babysitter—but I'll try to get back for coffee. Enjoy your dinner." Rising, he sent his brother a cool, knowing look, then walked away.

"Marsh never completely got over that first case of adulation," Ky commented, then took his brother's seat without invitation.

"Marsh has always been a good friend." Kate draped the napkin over her lap with great care. "Though I realize this is your brother's restaurant, Ky, I'm sure you don't want my company for dinner any more than I want yours."

"That's where you're wrong." He sent a quick, dashing smile at the waitress as she brought the wine. He didn't bother to correct Kate's assumption on the Roost's ownership. Kate sat stone-faced, her manners too good to allow her to argue, while Cindy opened the bottle and poured the first sip for Ky to taste.

"It's fine," he told her. "I'll pour." Taking the bottle, he filled Kate's glass to within half an inch of the rim. "Since we've both chosen the Roost tonight, why don't we have a little test?"

Kate lifted her glass and sipped. The wine was cool and dry. She remembered the first bottle they'd shared—sitting on the floor of his cottage the night she gave him her innocence. Deliberately, she took another swallow. "What kind of test?"

"We can see if the two of us can share a civilized meal in public. That was something we never got around to before."

Kate frowned as he lifted his glass. She'd never seen Ky drink from a wineglass. The few times they had indulged in wine, it had been drunk out of one of the half a dozen water glasses he'd owned. The stemware seemed too delicate for his hand, the wine too mellow for the look in his eye.

No, they'd never eaten dinner in public before. Her father would have exuded disapproval for socializing with someone he'd considered an employee. Kate had known it, and hadn't risked it.

Things were different now, she told herself as she lifted her own glass. In a sense, Ky was now her employee. She could make her own judgments. Recklessly, she toasted him. "To a profitable arrangement then."

"I couldn't have said it better myself." He touched the rim of his glass to hers, but his gaze was direct and uncomfortable. "Blue suits you," he said, referring to her dress, but not taking his eyes off hers. "The deep midnight blue that makes your skin look like something that should be tasted very, very carefully."

She stared at him, stunned at how easily his voice could take on that low, intimate tone that had always made the blood rush out of her brain. He'd always been able to make words seem something dark and secret. That had been one of his greatest skills, one she had never been prepared for. She was no more prepared for it now.

"Would you care to order now?" The waitress stopped beside the table, cheerful, eager to please.

Ky smiled when Kate remained silent. "We're having scampi. The house dressing on the salads will be fine." He leaned back, glass in hand, still smiling. But the smile on his lips didn't connect with his eyes. "You're not drinking your wine. Maybe I should've asked if your taste has changed over the years."

"It's fine." Deliberately she sipped, then kept the glass in her hand as though it would anchor her. "Marsh looks well," she commented. "I was happy to hear about him and Linda. I always pictured them together."

"Did you?" Ky lifted his glass toward the lowering evening light slanting through the window. He watched the colors spear through the wine and glass and onto Kate's hand. "He didn't. But then…" Shifting his gaze, he met her eyes again. "Marsh always took more time to make up his mind than me."

"Recklessness," she continued as she struggled just to breathe evenly, "was always more your style than your brother's."

"But you didn't come to my brother with your charts and notes, did you?"

"No." With an effort she kept her voice and her eyes level. "I didn't. Perhaps I decided a certain amount of recklessness had its uses."

"Find me useful, do you, Kate?"

The waitress served the salads but didn't speak this time. She saw the look in Ky's eyes.

So had Kate. "When I'm having a job done, I've found that it saves a considerable amount of time and trouble to find the most suitable person." With forced calm, she set down her wine and picked up her fork. "I wouldn't have come back to Ocracoke for any other reason." She tilted her head, surprised by the quick surge of challenge that rushed through her. "Things will be simpler for both of us if that's clear up front."

Anger moved through him, but he controlled it. If they were playing word games, he had to keep his wits. She'd always been clever, but now it appeared the cleverness was glossed over with sophistication. He remembered the innocent, curious Kate with a pang. "As I recall, you were always one for complicating rather than simplifying. I had to explain the purpose, history and mechanics of every piece of equipment before you'd take the first dive."

"That's called caution, not complication."

"You'd know more about caution than I would. Some people spend half their lives testing the wind." He drank deeply of the wine. "I'd rather ride with it."

"Yes." This time it was she who smiled with her lips only. "I remember very well. No plans, no ties, tomorrow the wind might change."

"If you're anchored in one spot too long, you can become like those trees out there." He gestured out the window where a line of sparse junipers bent away from the sea. "Stunted."

"Yet you're still here, where you were born, where you grew up."

Slowly Ky poured her more wine. "The island's too isolated, the life a bit too basic for some. I prefer it to those structured little communities with their parties and country clubs."

Kate looked like she belonged in such a place, Ky thought as he fought against the frustrated desire that ebbed and flowed inside him. She belonged in an elegant silk suit, holding a Dresden cup and discussing an obscure eighteenth-century English poet. Was that why she could still make him feel rough and awkward and too full of longings?

If they could be swept back in time, he'd have stolen her, taken her out to open sea and kept her there. They would have traveled from port to exotic port. If having her meant he could never go home again, then he'd have sailed until his time was up. But he would have had her. Ky's fingers tightened around his glass. By God, he would have had her.

The main course was slipped in front of him discreetly. Ky brought himself back to the moment. It wasn't the eighteenth century, but today. Still, she had brought him the past with the papers and maps. Perhaps they'd both find more than they'd bargained for.

"I looked over the things you left with me."

"Oh?" She felt a quick tingle of excitement but speared the first delicate shrimp as though it were all that concerned her.

"Your father's research is very thorough."

"Of course."

Ky let out a quick laugh. "Of course," he repeated, toasting her. "In any case, I think he might have been on the right track. You do realize that the section he narrowed it down to goes into a dangerous area."

Her brows drew together, but she continued to eat. "Sharks?"

"Sharks are a little difficult to confine to an area," he said easily. "A lot of people forget that the war came this close in the forties. There are still mines all along the coast of the Outer Banks. If we're going down to the bottom, it'd be smart to keep that in mind."

"I've no intention of being careless."

"No, but sometimes people look so far ahead they don't see what's under their feet."

Though he'd eaten barely half of his meal, Ky picked up his wine again. How could he eat when his whole system was aware of her? He couldn't stop himself from wondering what it would be like to pull those confining pins out of her hair as he'd done so often in the past. He couldn't prevent the memory from springing up about what it had been like to bundle her into his arms and just hold her there with her body fitting so neatly against his. He could picture those long, serious looks she'd give him just before passion would start to take over, then the freedom he could feel racing through her in those last heady moments of love-making.

How could it have been so right once and so wrong now? Wouldn't her body still fit against his? Wouldn't her hair flow through his hands as it fell—that quiet brown that took on such fascinating lights in the sun. She'd always murmur his name after passion was spent, as if the sound alone sustained her. He wanted to hear her say it, just once more, soft and breathless while they were tangled together, bodies still warm and pulsing. He wasn't sure he could resist it.

Absently Ky signaled for coffee. Perhaps he didn't want to resist it. He needed her. He'd forgotten just how sharp and sure a need could be. Perhaps he'd take her. He didn't believe she was indifferent to him—certain things never fade completely. In his own time, in his own way, he'd take what he once had from her. And pray it would be enough this time.

When he looked back at her, Kate felt the warning signals shiver through her. Ky was a difficult man to understand. She knew only that he'd come to some decision and that it involved her. Grateful for the warming effects of the coffee, she drank. She was in charge this time, she reminded herself, every step of the way and she'd make him aware of it. There was no time like the present to begin.

"I'll be at the harbor at eight," she said briskly. "I'll require tanks of course, but I brought my own wet suit. I'd appreciate it if you'd have my briefcase and its contents on board. I believe we'd be wise to spend between six and eight hours out a day."

"Have you kept up with your diving?"

"I know what to do."

"I'd be the last to argue that you had the best teacher." He tilted his cup back in a quick, impatient gesture Kate found typical of him. "But if you're rusty, we'll take it slow for a day or two."

"I'm a perfectly competent diver."

"I want more than competence in a partner."

He saw the flare in her eyes and his need sharpened. It was a rare and arousing thing to watch her controlled and reasonable temperament heat up. "We're not partners. You're working for me."

"A matter of viewpoint," Ky said easily. He rose, deliberately blocking her in. "We'll be putting in a full day tomorrow, so you'd better go catch up on all the sleep you've been missing lately."

"I don't need you to worry about my health, Ky."

"I worry about my own," he said curtly. "You don't go under with me unless you're rested and alert. You come to the harbor in the morning with shadows under your eyes, you won't make the first dive." Furiously she squashed the urge to argue with the reasonable. "If you're sluggish, you make mistakes," Ky said briefly. "A mistake you make can cost me. That logical enough for you, professor?"

"It's perfectly clear." Bracing herself for the brush of bodies, Kate rose. But bracing herself didn't stop the jolt, not for either of them.

"I'll walk you back."

"It's not necessary."

His hand curled over her wrist, strong and stubborn. "It's civilized," he said lazily. "You were always big on being civilized."

Until you'd touch me, she thought. No, she wouldn't remember that, not if she wanted to sleep tonight. Kate merely inclined her head in cool agreement. "I want to thank Marsh."

"You can thank him tomorrow." Ky dropped the waitress's tip on the table. "He's busy."

She started to protest, then saw Marsh disappear into what must have been the kitchen. "All right." Kate moved by him and out into the balmy evening air.

The sun was low, though it wouldn't set for nearly an hour. The clouds to the west were just touched with mauve and rose. When she stepped outside, Kate decided there were more people in the restaurant than there were on the streets.

A charter fishing boat glided into the harbor. Some of the tourists would be staying on the island, others would be riding back across Hatteras Inlet on one of the last ferries of the day.

She'd like to go out on the water now, while the light was softening and the breeze was quiet. Now, she thought, while others were coming in and the sea would stretch for mile after endless empty mile.

Shaking off the mood, she headed for the hotel. What she needed wasn't a sunset sail but a good solid night's sleep. Daydreaming was foolish, and tomorrow too important.

The same hotel. Ky glanced up at her window. He already knew she had the same room. He'd walked her there before, but then she'd have had her arm through his in that sweet way she had of joining them together. She'd have looked up and laughed at him over something that had happened that day. And she'd have kissed him, warm, long and lingeringly before the door would close behind her.

Because her thoughts had run the same gamut, Kate

turned to him while they were still outside the hotel. "Thank you, Ky." She made a business out of shifting her purse strap on her arm. "There's no need for you to go any further out of your way."

"No, there isn't." He'd have something to take home with him that night, he thought with sudden, fierce impatience. And he'd leave her something to take up to the room where they'd had one long, glorious night. "But then we've always looked at needs from different angles." He cupped his hand around the back of her neck, holding firm as he felt her stiffen.

"Don't." She didn't back away. Kate told herself she didn't back away because to do so would make her seem vulnerable. And she was, feeling those long hard fingers play against her skin again.

"I think this is something you owe me," he told her in a voice so quiet it shivered on the air. "Maybe something I owe myself."

He wasn't gentle. That was deliberate. Somewhere inside him was a need to punish for what hadn't been—or perhaps what had. The mouth he crushed on hers hungered, the arms he wrapped around her demanded. If she'd forgotten, he thought grimly, this would remind her. And remind her.

With her arms trapped between them, he could feel her hands ball into tight fists. Let her hate him, loathe him. He'd rather that than cool politeness.

But God she was sweet. Sweet and as delicate as one of the frothy waves that lapped and spread along the shoreline. Dimly, distantly, he knew he could drown in her without a murmur or complaint.

She wanted it to be different. Oh, how she wanted it to be different so that she'd feel nothing. But she felt everything.

The hard, impatient mouth that had always thrilled and bemused her—it was the same. The lean restless body that fit so unerringly against her—no different. The scent that clung to him, sea and salt—hadn't changed. Always when he kissed her, there'd been the sounds of water or wind or gulls. That, too, remained constant. Behind them boats rocked gently in their slips, water against wood. A gull resting on pilings let out a long, lonely call. The light dimmed as the sun dropped closer to the sea. The flood of past feelings rose up to merge and mingle with the moment.

She didn't resist him. Kate had told herself she wouldn't give him the satisfaction of a struggle. But the command to her brain not to respond was lost in the thin clouds of dusk. She gave because she had to. She took because she had no choice.

His tongue played over hers and her fists uncurled until Kate's palms rested against his chest. So warm, so hard, so familiar. He kissed as he always had, with complete concentration, no inhibitions and little patience.

Time tumbled back and she was young and in love and foolish. Why, she wondered while her head swam, should that make her want to weep?

He had to let her go or he'd beg. Ky could feel it rising in him. He wasn't fool enough to plead for what was already gone. He wasn't strong enough to accept that he had to let go again. The tug-of-war going on inside him was fierce enough to make him moan. On the sound he pulled away from her, frustrated, infuriated, bewitched.

Taking a moment, he stared down at her. Her look was the same, he realized—that half surprised, half speculative look she'd given him after their first kiss. It disoriented him. Whatever he'd sought to prove, Ky knew now he'd only proven that he was still as much enchanted with her as he'd ever been. He bit back an oath, instead, giving her a half-salute as he walked away.

"Get eight hours of sleep," he ordered without turning around.

Chapter 4

Some mornings the sun seemed to rise more slowly than others, as if nature wanted to show off her particular majesty just a bit longer. When she'd gone to bed, Kate had left her shades up knowing that the morning light would awaken her before the travel alarm beside her bed rang.

She took the dawn as a gift to herself, something individual and personal. Standing at the window, she watched it bloom. The first quiet breeze of morning drifted through the screen to run over her hair and face, through the thin material of her nightshirt, cool and promising. While she stood, Kate absorbed the colors, the light and the silent thunder of day breaking over water.

The lazy contemplation was far different from her structured routine of the past months and years. Mornings had been a time to dress, a time to run over her

schedule and notes for the day's classes over two cups
of coffee and a quick breakfast. She never had time to
give herself the dawn, so she took it now.

She slept better than she'd expected, lulled by the
quiet, exhausted by the days of traveling and the strain
on her emotions. There'd been no dreams to haunt her
from the time she'd turned back the sheets until the first
light had fallen over her face. Then she rose quickly.
There'd be no dreams now.

Kate let the morning wash over her with all its new
promises, its beginnings. Today was the start. Everything, from the moment she'd taken out her father's
papers until she'd seen Ky again, had been a prelude.
Even the brief, torrid embrace of the night before had
been no more than a ghost of the past. Today was the
real beginning.

She dressed and went out into the morning.

Breakfast was impossible. The excitement she'd so
meticulously held off was beginning to strain for freedom. The feeling that what she was doing was right
was back with her. Whatever it took, whatever it cost
her, she'd look for the gold her father had dreamed of.
She'd follow his directions. If she found nothing, she'd
have looked anyway.

In looking, Kate had come to believe she'd lay all
her personal ghosts to rest.

Ky's kiss. It had been aching, disturbing as it had always been. She'd been absorbed, just as she'd always
been. Though she knew she had to face both Ky and
the past, she hadn't known it would be so frighten-

ingly easy to go back—back to that dark, dreamy world where only he had taken her.

Now that she knew, now that she'd faced even that, Kate had to prepare to fight the wind.

He'd never forgiven her, she realized, for saying no. For bruising his pride. She'd gone back to her world when he'd asked her to stay in his. Asked her to stay, Kate remembered, without offering anything, not even a promise. If he'd given her that, no matter how casual or airy the promise might have been, she wouldn't have gone. She wondered if he knew that.

Perhaps he thought if he could make her lose herself to him again, the scales would be even. She wouldn't lose. Kate stuck her hands into the pockets of her brief pleated shorts. No, she didn't intend to lose. If he had pressed her last night, if he'd known just how weakened she'd been by that one kiss...

But he wouldn't know, she told herself. She wouldn't weaken again. For the summer, she'd make the treasure her goal and her one ambition. She wouldn't leave the island empty-handed this time.

He was already on board the *Vortex*. Kate could see him stowing gear, his hair tousled by the breeze that flowed in from the sea. With only cut-offs and a sleeveless T-shirt between him and the sun she could see the muscles coil and relax, the skin gleam.

Magnificent. She felt the dull ache deep in her stomach and tried to rationalize it away. After all, a well-honed masculine build should make a woman respond. It was natural. One could even call it impersonal, Kate decided. As she started down the dock she wished she could believe it.

He didn't see her. A fishing boat already well out on the water had caught his attention. For a moment, she stopped, just watching him. Why was it she could always sense the restlessness in him? There was movement in him even when he was still, sound even when he was silent. What was it he saw when he looked out over the sea? Challenge? Romance?

He was a man who always seemed poised for action, for doing. Yet he could sit quietly and watch the waves as if there were nothing more important than that endless battle between earth and water.

Just now he stood on the deck of his boat, hands on hips, watching the tubby fishing vessel putt toward the horizon. It was something he'd seen countless times, yet he stopped to take it in again. Kate looked where Ky looked and wished she could see what he was seeing.

Quietly she went forward, her deck shoes making no sound, but he turned, eyes still intense. "You're early," he said, and with no more greeting reached out a hand to help her on board.

"I thought you might be as anxious to start as I am."

Palm met palm, rough against smooth. Both of them broke contact as soon as possible.

"It should be an easy ride." He looked back to sea, toward the boat, but this time he didn't focus on it. "The wind's coming in from the north, no more than ten knots."

"Good." Though it wouldn't have mattered to her

nor, she thought, to him, if the wind had been twice as fast. This was the morning to begin.

She could sense the impatience in him, the desire to be gone and doing. Wanting to make things as simple as possible Kate helped Ky cast off, then walked to the stern. That would keep the maximum distance between them. They didn't speak. The engine roared to life, shattering the calm. Smoothly, Ky maneuvered the small cruiser out of the harbor, setting up a small wake that caused the water to lap against pilings. He kept the same steady even speed while they sailed through the shallows of Ocracoke Inlet. Looking back, Kate watched the distance between the boat and the village grow.

The dreamy quality remained. The last thing she saw was a child walking down a pier with a rod cocked rakishly over his shoulder. Then she turned her face to the sea.

Warm wind, glaring sun. Excitement. Kate hadn't been sure the feelings would be the same. But when she closed her eyes, letting the dull red light glow behind her lids, the salty mist touch her face, she knew this was a love that had remained constant, one that had waited for her.

Sitting perfectly still, she could feel Ky increase the speed until the boat was eating its way through the water as sleekly as a cat moves through the jungle. With her eyes closed, she enjoyed the movement, the speed, the sun. This was a thrill that had never faded. Tasting it again, she understood that it never would.

She'd been right, Kate realized, the hunt would be

much more exciting than the final goal. The hunt, and no matter how cautious she was, the man at the helm.

He'd told himself he wouldn't look back at her. But he had to—just once. Eyes closed, a smile playing around her mouth, hair dancing around her face where the wind nudged it from the pins. It brought back a flash of memory—to the first time he'd seen her like that and realized he had to have her. She looked calm, totally at peace. He felt there was a war raging inside him that he had no control over.

Even when he turned back to sea again Ky could see her, leaning back against the stern, absorbing what wind and water offered. In defense, he tried to picture her in a classroom, patiently explaining the intricacies of *Don Juan* or *Henry IV*. It didn't help. He could only imagine her sitting behind him, soaking up sun and wind as if she'd been starved for it.

Perhaps she had been. Though she didn't know what direction Ky's thoughts had taken, Kate realized she'd never been further away from the classroom or the demands she placed on herself there than she was at this moment. She was part teacher, there was no question of that, but she was also, no matter how she'd tried to banish it, part dreamer.

With the sun and the wind on her skin, she was too exhilarated to be frightened by the knowledge, too content to worry. It was a wild, free sensation to experience again something known, loved, then lost.

Perhaps... Perhaps it was too much like the one frenzied kiss she'd shared with Ky the night before, but she needed it. It might be a foolish need, even a dangerous one. Just once, only this once, she told herself, she wouldn't question it.

Steady, strong, she opened her eyes again. Now she could watch the sun toss its diamonds on the surface of the water. They rippled, enticing, enchanting. The fishing boat Ky had watched move away from the island before them was anchored, casting its nets. A purse seiner, she remembered. Ky had explained the wide, weighted net to her once and how it was often used to haul in menhaden.

She wondered why he'd never chosen that life, where he could work and live on the water day after day. But not alone, she recalled with a ghost of a smile. Fishermen were their own community, on the sea and off it. It wasn't often Ky chose to share himself or his time with anyone. There were times, like this one, when she understood that perfectly.

Whether it was the freedom or the strength that was in her, Kate approached him without nerves. "It's as beautiful as I remember."

He dreaded having her stand beside him again. Now, however, he discovered the tension at the base of his neck had eased. "It doesn't change much." Together they watched the gulls swoop around the fishing boat, hoping for easy pickings. "Fishing's been good this year."

"Have you been doing much?"

"Off and on."

"Clamming?"

He had to smile when he remembered how she'd

looked, jeans rolled up to her knees, bare feet full of sand as he'd taught her how to dig. "Yeah."

She, too, remembered, but her only memories were of warm days, warm nights. "I've often wondered what it's like on the island in winter."

"Quiet."

She took the single careless answer with a nod. "I've often wondered why you preferred that."

He turned to her, measuring. "Have you?"

Perhaps that had been a mistake. Since it had already been made, Kate shrugged. "It would be foolish of me to say I hadn't thought of the island or you at all during the last four years. You've always made me curious."

He laughed. It was so typical of her to put things that way. "Because all your tidy questions weren't answered. You think too much like a teacher, Kate."

"Isn't life a multiple choice?" she countered. "Maybe two or three answers would fit, but only one's ultimately right."

"No, only one's ultimately wrong." He saw her eyes take on that thoughtful, considering expression. She was, he knew, weighing the pros and cons of his statement. Whether she agreed or not, she'd consider all the angles. "You haven't changed either," he murmured.

"I thought the same of you. We're both wrong. Neither of us have stayed the same. That's as it should be." Kate looked away from him, further east, then gave a quick cry of pleasure. "Oh, look!" Without thinking, she put her hand on his arm, slender fingers gripping taut muscle. "Dolphins."

She watched them, a dozen, perhaps more, leap and

dive in their musical pattern. Pleasure was touched with envy. To move like that, she thought, from water to air and back to water again. It was a freedom that might drive a man mad with the glory of it. But what a madness…

"Fantastic, isn't it?" she murmured. "To be part of the air and the sea. I'd nearly forgotten."

"How much?" Ky studied her profile until he could have etched the shape of it on the wind. "How much have you nearly forgotten?"

Kate turned her head, only then realizing just how close they stood. Unconsciously, she'd moved nearer to him when she'd seen the dolphins. Now she could see nothing but his face, inches from hers, feel nothing but the warm skin beneath her hand. His question, the depth of it, seemed to echo off the surface of the water to haunt her.

She stepped back. The drop before her was very deep and torn with rip tides. "All that was necessary," she said simply. "I'd like to look over my father's charts. Did you bring them on board?"

"Your briefcase is in the cabin." His hands gripped the wheel tightly, as though he were fighting against a storm. Perhaps he was. "You should be able to find your way below."

Without answering, Kate walked around him to the short steep steps that led belowdecks.

There were two narrow bunks with the spreads taut enough to bounce a coin if one was dropped. The galley just beyond would have all the essentials, she knew, in small, efficient scale. Everything would be in its place, as tidy as a monk's cell.

Kate could remember lying with Ky on one of the pristine bunks, flushed with passion while the boat swayed gently in the current and the music from his radio played jazz.

She gripped the leather of her case as if the pain in her fingers would help fight off the memories. To fight everything off entirely was too much to expect, but the intensity eased. Carefully she unfolded one of her father's charts and spread it on the bunk.

Like everything her father had done, the chart was precise and without frills. Though it had certainly not been his field, Hardesty had drawn a chart any sailor would have trusted.

It showed the coast of North Carolina, Pamlico Sound and the Outer Banks, from Manteo to Cape Lookout. As well as the lines of latitude and longitude, the chart also had the thin crisscrossing lines that marked depth.

Seventy-six degrees north by thirty-five degrees east. From the markings, that was the area her father had decided the *Liberty* had gone down. That was southeast of Ocracoke by no more than a few miles. And the depth... Yes, she decided as she frowned over the chart, the depth would still be considered shallow diving. She and Ky would have the relative freedom of wet suits and tanks rather than the leaded boots and helmets required for deep-sea explorations.

X marks the spot she thought, a bit giddy, but made herself fold the chart with the same care she'd used to open it. She felt the boat slow then heard the resounding silence when the engines shut off. A fresh tremor of anticipation went through her as she climbed the steps into the sunlight again.

Ky was already checking the tanks though she knew he would have gone over all the equipment thoroughly before setting out. "We'll go down here," he said as he rose from his crouched position. "We're about half a mile from the last place your father went in last summer."

In one easy motion he pulled off his shirt. Kate knew he was self-aware, but he'd never been self-conscious. Ky had already stripped down to brief bikini trunks before she turned away for her own gear.

If her heart was pounding, it was possible to tell herself it was in anticipation of the dive. If her throat was dry, she could almost believe it was nerves at the thought of giving herself to the sea again. His body was hard and brown and lean, but she was only concerned with his skill and his knowledge. And he, she told herself, was only concerned with his fee and his twenty-five percent of the find.

She wore a snug tank suit under her shorts that clung to subtle curves and revealed long, slender legs that Ky knew were soft as water, strong as a runner's. He began to pull on the thin rubber wet suit. They were here to look for gold, to find a treasure that had been lost. Some treasures, he knew, could never be recovered.

As he thought of it, Ky glanced up to see Kate draw the pins from her hair. It fell, soft and slow, over, then past her shoulders. If she'd shot a dart into his chest, she couldn't have pierced his heart more accurately. Swearing under his breath, Ky lifted the first set of tanks.

"We'll go down for an hour today."

"But—"

"An hour's more than enough," he interrupted without sparing her a glance. "You haven't worn tanks in four years."

Kate slipped into the set he offered her, securing the straps until they were snug, but not tight. "I didn't tell you that."

"No, but you'd sure as hell have told me if you had." The corner of his mouth lifted when she remained silent. After attaching his own tanks, Ky climbed over the side onto the ladder. She could either argue, he figured, or she could follow.

To clear his mask, he spat into it, rubbed, then reached down to rinse it in salt water. Pulling it over his eyes and nose, Ky dropped into the sea. It took less than ten seconds before Kate plunged into the water beside him. He paused a moment, to make certain she didn't flounder or forget to breathe, then he headed for greater depth.

No, she wouldn't forget to breathe, but the first breath was almost a sigh as her body submerged. It was as thrilling to her as it had been the first time, this incredible ability to stay beneath the ocean's surface and breathe air.

Kate looked up to see the sun spearing through the water, and held out a hand to watch the watery light play on her skin. She could have stayed there, she realized, just reveling in it. But with a curl of her body and a kick, she followed Ky into depth and dimness.

Ky saw a school of menhaden and wondered if they'd end up in the net of the fishing boat he'd watched that morning. When the fish swerved in a mass and rushed past him, he turned to Kate again. She'd been right when she'd told him she knew what to do. She swam as cleanly and as competently as ever.

He expected her to ask him how he intended to look for the *Liberty*, what plan he'd outlined. When she hadn't, Ky had figured it was for one of two reasons. Either she didn't want to have any in-depth conversation with him at the moment, or she'd already reasoned it out for herself. It seemed more likely to be the latter, as her mind was also as clean and competent as ever.

The most logical method of searching seemed to be a semi-circular route around Hardesty's previous dives. Slowly and methodically, they would widen the circle. If Hardesty had been right, they'd find the *Liberty* eventually. If he'd been wrong…they'd have spent the summer treasure hunting.

Though the tanks on her back reminded Kate not to take the weightless freedom for granted, she thought she could stay down forever. She wanted to touch—the water, the sea grass, the soft, sandy bottom. Reaching out toward a school of bluefish she watched them scatter defensively then regroup. She knew there were times when, as a diver moved through the dim, liquid world, he could forget the need for the sun. Perhaps Ky had been right in limiting the dive. She had to be careful not to take what she found again for granted.

The flattened disklike shape caught Ky's attention. Automatically, he reached for Kate's arm to stop her forward progress. The stingray that scuttled along the bottom looking for tasty crustaceans might be amusing to watch, but it was deadly. He gauged this one to be as long as he was tall with a tail as sharp and cruel as a razor. They'd give it a wide berth.

Seeing the ray reminded Kate that the sea wasn't all beauty and dreams. It was also pain and death. Even as she watched, the stingray struck out with its whiplike tail and caught a small, hapless bluefish. Once, then twice. It was nature, it was life. But she turned away. Through the protective masks, her eyes met Ky's.

She expected to see derision for an obvious weakness, or worse, amusement. She saw neither. His eyes were gentle, as they were very rarely. Lifting a hand, he ran his knuckles down her cheek, as he'd done years before when he'd chosen to offer comfort or affection. She felt the warmth, it reflected in her eyes. Then, as quickly as the moment had come, it was over. Turning, Ky swam away, gesturing for her to follow.

He couldn't afford to be distracted by those glimpses of vulnerability, those flashes of sweetness. They had already done him in once. Top priority was the job they'd set out to do. Whatever other plans he had, Ky intended to be in full control. When the time was right, he'd have his fill of Kate. That he promised himself. He'd take exactly what he felt she owed him. But she wouldn't touch his emotions again. When he took her to bed, it would be with cold calculation.

That was something else he promised himself.

Though they found no sign of the *Liberty*, Ky saw wreckage from other ships—pieces of metal, rusted, covered with barnacles. They might have been from a sub or a battleship from World War II. The sea absorbed what remained in her.

He was tempted to swim farther out, but knew it would take twenty minutes to return to the boat. Circling around, he headed back, overlapping, double-checking the area they'd just covered.

Not quite a needle in a haystack, Ky mused, but close. Two centuries of storms and currents and sea quakes. Even if they had the exact location where the *Liberty* had sunk, rather than the last known location, it took calculation and guesswork, then luck to narrow the field down to a radius of twenty miles.

Ky believed in luck much the same way he imagined Hardesty had believed in calculation. Perhaps with a mixture of the two, he and Kate would find what was left of the *Liberty*.

Glancing over, he watched Kate gliding beside him. She was looking everywhere at once, but Ky didn't think her mind was on treasure or sunken ships. She was, as she'd been that summer before, completely enchanted with the sea and the life it held. He wondered if she still remembered all the information she'd demanded of him before the first dive. What about the physiological adjustments to the body? How was the CO_2 absorbed? What about the change in external pressure?

Ky felt a flash of humor as they started to ascend. He was dead sure Kate remembered every answer he'd given her, right down to the decimal point in pounds of pressure per square inch.

The sun caught her as she rose toward the surface, slowly. It shone around and through her hair, giving her an ethereal appearance as she swam straight up, legs kicking gently, face tilted toward sun and surface. If there were mermaids, Ky knew they'd look as she did—slim, long, with pale loose hair free in the water. A man could only hold on to a mermaid if he accepted the world she lived in as his own. Reaching out, he caught the tip of her hair in his fingers just before they broke the surface together.

Kate came up laughing, letting her mouthpiece fall and pushing her mask up. "Oh, it's wonderful! Just as I remembered." Treading water, she laughed again and Ky realized it was a sound he hadn't heard in four years. But he remembered it exactly.

"You looked like you wanted to play more than you wanted to look for sunken ships." He grinned at her, enjoying her pleasure and the ease of a smile he'd never expected to see again.

"I did." Almost reluctant, she reached out for the ladder to climb on board. "I never expected to find anything the first time down, and it was so wonderful just to dive again." She stripped off her tanks then checked the valves herself before she set them down. "Whenever I go down I begin to believe I don't need the sun anymore. Then when I come up it's warmer and brighter than I remember."

With the adrenaline still flowing, she peeled off her

flippers, then her mask, to stand, face lifted toward the sun. "There's nothing else exactly like it."

"Skin diving." Ky tugged down the zipper of his wet suit. "I tried some in Tahiti last year. It's incredible being in that clear water with no equipment but a mask and flippers, and your own lungs."

"Tahiti?" Surprised and interested, Kate looked back as Ky stripped off the wet suit. "You went there?"

"Couple of weeks late last year." He dropped the wet suit in the big plastic can he used for storing equipment before rinsing.

"Because of your affection for islands?"

"And grass skirts."

The laughter bubbled out again. "I'm sure you'd look great in one."

He'd forgotten just how quick she could be when she relaxed. Because the gesture appealed, Ky reached over and gave her hair a quick tug. "I wish I'd taken snapshots." Turning, he jogged down the steps into the cabin.

"Too busy ogling the natives to put them on film for posterity?" Kate called out as she dropped down on the narrow bench on the starboard side.

"Something like that. And of course trying to pretend I didn't notice the natives ogling me."

She grinned. "People in grass skirts," she began then let out a muffled shout as he tossed a peach in her direction. Catching it cleanly, Kate smiled at him before she bit into the fruit.

"Still have good reflexes," Ky commented as he came up the last step.

"Especially when I'm hungry." She touched her tongue to her palm where juice dribbled. "I couldn't eat this morning, I was too keyed up."

He held out one of two bottles of cold soda he'd taken from the refrigerator. "About the dive?"

"That and..." Kate broke off, surprised that she was talking to him as if it had been four years before.

"And?" Ky prompted. Though his tone was casual, his gaze had sharpened.

Aware of it, Kate rose, turning away to look back over the stern. She saw nothing there but sky and water. "It was the morning," she murmured. "The way the sun came up over the water. All that color." She shook her head and water dripped from the ends of her hair onto the deck. "I haven't watched a sunrise in a very long time."

Making himself relax again, Ky leaned back, biting into his own peach as he watched her. "Why?"

"No time. No need."

"Do they both mean the same thing to you?"

Restless, she moved her shoulders. "When your life revolves around schedules and classes, I suppose one equals the other."

"That's what you want? A daily timetable?"

Kate looked back over her shoulder, meeting his eyes levelly. How could they ever understand each other? she wondered. Her world was as foreign to him as his to her. "It's what I've chosen."

"One of your multiple choices of life?" Ky countered, giving a short laugh before he tilted his bottle back again.

"Maybe, or maybe some parts of life only have one choice." She turned completely around, determined not to lose the euphoria that had come to her with the dive. "Tell me about Tahiti, Ky. What's it like?"

"Soft air, soft water. Blue, green, white. Those are the colors that come to mind, then outrageous splashes of red and orange and yellow."

"Like a Gauguin painting."

The length of the deck separated them. Perhaps that made it easier for him to smile. "I suppose, but I don't think he'd have appreciated all the hotels and resorts. It isn't an island that's been left to itself."

"Things rarely are."

"Whether they should be or not."

Something in the way he said it, in the way he looked at her, made Kate think he wasn't speaking of an island now, but of something more personal. She drank, cooling her throat, moistening her lips. "Did you scuba?"

"Some. Shells and coral so thick I could've filled a boat with them if I'd wanted. Fish that looked like they should've been in an aquarium. And sharks." He remembered one that had nearly caught him half a mile out. Remembering made him grin. "The waters off Tahiti are anything but boring."

Kate recognized the look, the recklessness that would always surface just under his skill. Perhaps he didn't look for trouble, but she thought he'd rarely sidestep it. No, she doubted they'd ever fully understand each other, if they had a lifetime.

"Did you bring back a shark's tooth necklace?"

"I gave it to Hope." He grinned again. "Linda won't let her have it yet."

"I should think not. Does it feel odd, being an uncle?"

"No. She looks like me."

"Ah, the male ego."

Ky shrugged, aware that he had a healthy share and was comfortable with it. "I get a kick out of watching her run Marsh and Linda in circles. There's not much entertainment on the island."

She tried to imagine Ky being entertained by something as tame as a baby girl. She failed. "It's strange," Kate said after a moment. "Coming back to find Marsh and Linda married and parents. When I left Marsh treated Linda like his little sister."

"Didn't your father keep you up on progress on the island?"

The smile left her eyes. "No."

Ky lifted a brow. "Did you ask?"

"No."

He tossed his empty bottle into a small barrel. "He hadn't told you anything about the ship either, about why he kept coming back to the island year after year."

She tossed her drying hair back from her face. It hadn't been put in the tone of a question. Still, she answered because it was simpler that way. "No, he never mentioned the *Liberty* to me."

"That doesn't bother you?"

The ache came, but she pushed it aside. "Why should it?" she countered. "He was entitled to his own life, his privacy."

"But you weren't."

She felt the chill come and go. Crossing the deck, Kate dropped her bottle beside Ky's before reaching for her shirt. "I don't know what you mean."

"You know exactly what I mean." He closed his hand over hers before she could pull the shirt on. Because it would've been cowardly to do otherwise, she lifted her head and faced him. "You know," he said again, quietly. "You just aren't ready to say it out loud yet."

"Leave it alone, Ky." Her voice trembled, and though it infuriated her, she couldn't prevent it. "Just leave it."

He wanted to shake her, to make her admit, so that he could hear, that she'd left him because her father had preferred it. He wanted her to say, perhaps sob, that she hadn't had the strength to stand up to the man who had shaped and molded her life to suit his values and wants.

With an effort, he relaxed his fingers. As he had before, Ky turned away with something like a shrug. "For now," he said easily as he went back to the helm. "Summer's just beginning." He started the engine before turning around for one last look. "We both know what can happen during a summer."

Chapter 5

"The first thing you have to understand about Hope," Linda began, steadying a vase the toddler had jostled, "is that she has a mind of her own."

Kate watched the chubby black-haired Hope climb onto a wing-backed chair to examine herself in an ornamental mirror. In the fifteen minutes Kate had been in Linda's home, Hope hadn't been still a moment. She was quick, surprisingly agile, with a look in her eyes that made Kate believe she knew exactly what she wanted and intended to get it, one way or the other. Ky had been right. His niece looked like him, in more ways than one.

"I can see that. Where do you find the energy to run a restaurant, keep a home and manage a fireball?"

"Vitamins," Linda sighed. "Lots and lots of vitamins. Hope, don't put your fingers on the glass."

"Hope!" the toddler cried out, making faces at herself in the mirror. "Pretty, pretty, pretty."

"The Silver ego," Linda commented. "It never tarnishes."

With a chuckle, Kate watched Hope crawl backwards out of the chair, land on her diaper-padded bottom and begin to systematically destroy the tower of blocks she'd built a short time before. "Well, she is pretty. It only shows she's smart enough to know it."

"It's hard for me to argue that point, except when she's spread toothpaste all over the bathroom floor." With a contented sigh, Linda sat back on the couch. She enjoyed having Monday afternoons off to play with Hope and catch up on the dozens of things that went by the wayside when the restaurant demanded her time. "You've been here over a week now, and this is the first time we've been able to talk."

Kate bent over to ruffle Hope's hair. "You're a busy woman."

"So are you."

Kate heard the question, not so subtly submerged in the statement, and smiled. "You know I didn't come back to the island to fish and wade, Linda."

"All right, all right, the heck with being tactful." With a mother's skill, she kept her antenna honed on her active toddler and leaned toward Kate. "What *are* you and Ky doing out on his boat every day?"

With Linda, evasions were neither necessary nor advisable. "Looking for treasure," Kate said simply.

"Oh." Expressing only mild surprise, Linda saved a budding African violet from her daughter's curious fingers. "Blackbeard's treasure." She handed Hope a rubber duck in lieu of the plant. "My grandfather still tells stories about it. Pieces of eight, a king's ransom and bottles of rum. I always figured that it was buried on land."

Amused at the way Linda could handle the toddler without breaking rhythm, Kate shook her head. "No, not Blackbeard's."

There were dozens of theories and myths about where the infamous pirate had hidden his booty, and fantastic speculation on just how rich the trove was. Kate had never considered them any more than stories. Yet she supposed, in her own way, she was following a similar fantasy.

"My father'd been researching the whereabouts of an English merchant ship that sank off the coast here in the eighteenth century."

"Your father?" Instantly Linda's attention sharpened. She couldn't conceive of the Edwin Hardesty she remembered from summers past as a treasure searcher. "That's why he kept coming to the island every summer? I could never figure out why…" She broke off, grimaced, then plunged ahead. "I'm sorry, Kate, but he never seemed the type to take up scuba diving as a hobby, and I never once saw him with a fish. He certainly managed to keep what he was doing a secret."

"Yes, even from me."

"You didn't know?" Linda glanced over idly as Hope began to beat on a plastic bucket with a wooden puzzle piece.

"Not until I went through his papers a few weeks ago. I decided to follow through on what he'd started."

"And you came to Ky."

"I came to Ky." Kate smoothed the material of her thin summer skirt over her knees. "I needed a boat, a diver, preferably an islander. He's the best."

Linda's attention shifted from her daughter to Kate. There was simple understanding there, but it didn't completely mask impatience. "Is that the only reason you came to Ky?"

Needs rose up to taunt her. Memories washed up in one warm wave. "Yes, that's the only reason."

Linda wondered why Kate should want her to believe what Kate didn't believe herself. "What if I told you he's never forgotten you?"

Kate shook her head quickly, almost frantically. "Don't."

"I love him." Linda rose to distract Hope who'd discovered tossing blocks was more interesting than stacking them. "Even though he's a frustrating, difficult man. He's Marsh's brother." She set Hope in front of a small army of stuffed animals before she turned and smiled. "He's my brother. And you were the first mainlander I was ever really close to. It's hard for me to be objective."

It was tempting to pour out her heart, her doubts. Too tempting. "I appreciate that, Linda. Believe me, what was between Ky and me was over a long time ago. Lives change."

Making a neutral sound, Linda sat again. There were some people you didn't press. Ky and Kate were both the same in that area, however diverse they were otherwise. "All right. You know what I've been doing the past four years." She sent a long-suffering look in Hope's direction. "Tell me what your life's been like."

"Quieter."

Linda laughed. "A small border war would be quieter than life in this house."

"Earning my doctorate as early as I did took a lot of concentrated effort." She'd needed that one goal to keep herself level, to keep herself...calm. "When you're teaching as well it doesn't leave much time for anything else." Shrugging, she rose. It sounded so staid, she realized. So dull. She'd wanted to learn, she'd wanted to teach, but in and of itself, it sounded hollow.

There were toys spread all over the living room, tiny pieces of childhood. A tie was tossed carelessly over the back of a chair next to a table where Linda had dropped her purse. Small pieces of a marriage. Family. She wondered, with a panic that came and went quickly, how she would ever survive the empty house back in Connecticut.

"This past year at Yale has been fascinating and difficult." Was she defending or explaining? Kate wondered impatiently. "Strange, even though my father taught, I didn't realize that being a teacher is just as hard and demanding as being a student."

"Harder," Linda declared after a moment. "You have to have the answers."

"Yes." Kate crouched down to look at Hope's collection of stuffed animals. "I suppose that's part of the appeal, though. The challenge of either knowing the answer or reasoning it out, then watching it sink in."

"Hoping it sinks in?" Linda ventured.

Kate laughed again. "Yes, I suppose that's it. When it does, that's the most rewarding aspect. Being a mother can't be that much different. You're teaching every day."

"Or trying to," Linda said dryly.

"The same thing."

"You're happy?"

Hope squeezed a bright pink dragon then held it out for Kate. Was she happy? Kate wondered as she obliged by cuddling the dragon in turn. She'd been aiming for achievement, she supposed, not happiness. Her father had never asked that very simple, very basic question. She'd never taken the time to ask herself. "I want to teach," she answered at length. "I'd be unhappy if I couldn't."

"That's a roundabout way of answering without answering at all."

"Sometimes there isn't any yes or no."

"Ky!" Hope shouted so that Kate jolted, whipping her head around to the front door.

"No." Linda noted the reaction, but said nothing. "She means the dragon. He gave it to her, so it's Ky."

"Oh." She wanted to swear but managed to smile as she handed the baby back her treasured dragon. It wasn't reasonable that just his name should make her hands unsteady, her pulse unsteady, her thoughts unsteady. "He wouldn't pick the usual, would he?" she asked carelessly as she rose.

"No." She gave Kate a very direct, very level look. "His tastes have always run to the unique."

Amusement helped to relax her. Kate's brow rose as she met the look. "You don't give up, do you?"

"Not on something I believe in." A trace of stubbornness came through. The stubbornness, Kate mused, that had kept her determinedly waiting for Marsh to fall in love with her. "I believe in you and Ky," Linda continued. "You two can make a mess of it for as long as you want, but I'll still believe in you."

"You haven't changed," Kate said on a sigh. "I came back to find you a wife, a mother, and the owner of a restaurant, but you haven't changed at all."

"Being a wife and mother only makes me more certain that what I believe is right." She had her share of arrogance, too, and used it. "We don't own the restaurant," she added as an afterthought.

"No?" Surprised, Kate looked up again. "But I thought you said the Roost was yours and Marsh's."

"We run it," Linda corrected. "And we do have a twenty percent interest." Sitting back, she gave Kate a pleased smile. There was nothing she liked better than to drop small bombs in calm water and watch the ripples. "Ky owns the Roost."

"Ky?" Kate couldn't have disguised the astonishment if she'd tried. The Ky Silver she thought she knew hadn't owned anything but a boat and a shaky beach cottage. He hadn't wanted to. Buying a restaurant, even a small one on a remote island took more than capital. It took ambition.

"Apparently he didn't bother to mention it."

"No." He'd had several opportunities, Kate recalled, the night they'd had dinner. "No, he didn't. It doesn't seem characteristic," she murmured. "I can picture him buying another boat, a bigger boat or a faster boat, but I can't imagine him buying a restaurant."

"I guess it surprised everyone except Marsh—but then Marsh knows Ky better than anyone. A couple of weeks before we were married, Ky told us he'd bought the place and intended to remodel. Marsh was ferrying over to Hatteras every day to work, I was helping out in my aunt's craft shop during the season. When Ky asked if we wanted to buy in for twenty percent and take over as managers, we jumped at it." She smiled, pleased, and perhaps relieved. "It wasn't a mistake for any of us."

Kate remembered the homey atmosphere, the excellent seafood, the fast service. No, it hadn't been a mistake, but Ky… "I just can't picture Ky in business, not on land anyway."

"Ky knows the island," Linda said simply. "And he knows what he wants. To my way of thinking, he just doesn't always know how to get it."

Kate was going to avoid that area of speculation. "I'm going to take a walk down to the beach," she decided. "Would you like to come?"

"I'd love to, but—" With a gesture of her hand Linda indicated why Hope had been quiet for the last few minutes. With her arm hooked around her dragon, she was sprawled over the rest of the animals, sound asleep.

"It's either stop or go with her, isn't it?" Kate observed with a laugh.

"The nice thing is that when she stops, so can I." Expertly Linda gathered up Hope, cradling her daughter on her shoulder. "Have a nice walk, and stop into the Roost tonight if you have the chance."

"I will." Kate touched Hope's head, the thick, dark, disordered hair that was so much like her uncle's. "She's beautiful, Linda. You're very lucky."

"I know. It's something I don't ever forget."

Kate let herself out of the house and walked along the quiet street. Clouds were low, making the light gloomy, but the rain held off. She could taste it in the breeze, the clean freshness of it, mixed with the faintest hint of the sea. It was in that direction she walked.

On an island, she'd discovered, you were much more drawn to the water than to the land. It was the one thing she'd understood completely about Ky, the one thing she'd never questioned.

It had been easier to avoid going to the beach in Connecticut, though she'd always loved the rocky, windy New England coast. She'd been able to resist it, knowing what memories it would bring back. Pain. Kate had learned there were ways of avoiding pain. But here, knowing you could reach the edge of land by walking in any direction, she couldn't resist. It might have been wiser to walk to the sound, or the inlet. She walked to the sea.

It was warm enough that she needed no more than the sheer skirt and blouse, breezy enough so that the material fluttered around her. She saw two men, caps low over foreheads, their rods secured in the sand, talking together while they sat on buckets and waited for a strike. Their voices didn't carry above the roar and thunder of surf, but she knew their conversation would deal with bait and lures and yesterday's catch. She wouldn't disturb them, nor they her. It was the way of the islander to be friendly enough, but not intrusive.

The water was as gray as the sky, but she didn't mind. Kate had learned not just to accept its moods but to appreciate the contrasts of each one. When the sea was like this, brooding, with threats of violence on the surface, that meant a storm. She found it appealed to a restlessness in herself she rarely acknowledged.

Whitecaps tossed with systematic fever. The spray rose high and wide. The cry of gulls didn't seem lonely or plaintive now, but challenging. No, a gray gloomy sky meeting a gray sea was anything but dull. It teamed with energy. It boiled with life.

The wind tugged at her hair, loosening pins. She didn't notice. Standing just away from the edge of the surf, Kate faced wind and sea with her eyes wide. She had to think about what she'd just discovered about Ky. Perhaps what she had been determined not to discover about herself.

Thinking there, alone in the gray threatening light before a storm, was what Kate felt she needed. The constant wind blowing in from the east would keep her head clear. Maybe the smells and sounds of the sea would remind her of what she'd had and rejected, and what she'd chosen to have.

Once she'd had a powerful force that had held her swirling, breathless. That force was Ky, a man who could pull on your emotions, your senses, by simply being. The recklessness had attracted her once, the tough arrogance combined with unexpected gentleness. What she saw as his irresponsibility had disturbed her. Kate sensed that he was a man who would drift through life when she'd been taught from birth to seek out a goal and work for it to the exclusion of all else. It was that very different outlook on life that set them poles apart.

Perhaps he had decided to take on some responsibility in his life with the restaurant, Kate decided. If he had she was glad of it. But it couldn't make any difference. They were still poles apart.

She chose the calm, the ordered. Success was satisfaction in itself when success came from something loved. Teaching was vital to her, not just a job, not even a profession. The giving of knowledge fed her. Perhaps for a moment in Linda's cozy, cluttered home it hadn't seemed like enough. Not quite enough. Still, Kate knew if you wished for too much, you often received nothing at all.

With the wind whipping at her face she watched the rain begin far out to sea in a dark curtain. If the past had been a treasure she'd lost, no chart could take her back. In her life, she'd been taught only one direction.

Ky never questioned his impulses to walk on the beach. He was a man who was comfortable with his own mood swings, so comfortable, he rarely noticed them. He hadn't deliberately decided to stop work on his boat at a certain time. He simply felt the temptation of sea and storm and surrendered to it.

Ky watched the seas as he made his way up and over the hill of sand. He could have found his way without faltering in the dark, with no moon. He'd stood on shore and watched the rain at sea before, but repetition didn't lessen the pleasure. The wind would bring it to the island, but there was still time to seek shelter if shelter were desired. More often than not, Ky would let the rain flow over him while the waves rose and fell wildly.

He'd seen his share of tropical storms and hurricanes. While he might find them exhilarating, he appreciated the relative peace of a summer rain. Today he was grateful for it. It had given him a day away from Kate.

They had somehow reached a shaky, tense coexistence that made it possible for them to be together day after day in a relatively small space. The tension was making him nervy; nervy enough to make a mistake when no diver could afford to make one.

Seeing her, being with her, knowing she'd withdrawn from him as a person was infinitely more difficult than being apart from her. To Kate, he was only a means to an end, a tool she used in the same way he imagined she used a textbook. If that was a bitter pill, he felt he had only himself to blame. He'd accepted her terms. Now all he had to do was live with them.

He hadn't heard her laugh again since the first dive. He missed that, Ky discovered, every bit as much as he missed the taste of her lips, the feel of her in his arms. She wouldn't give him any of it willingly, and he'd nearly convinced himself he didn't want her any other way.

But at night, alone, with the sound of the surf in his

head, he wasn't sure he'd survive another hour. Yet he had to. It was the fierce drive for survival that had gotten him through the last years. Her rejection had eaten away at him, then it had pushed him to prove something to himself. Kate had been the reason for his risking every penny he'd had to buy the Roost. He'd needed something tangible. The Roost had given him that, in much the same way the charter boat he'd recently bought gave him a sense of worth he once thought was unnecessary.

So he owned a restaurant that made a profit, and a boat that was beginning to justify his investment. It had given his innate love of risk an outlet. It wasn't money that mattered, but the dealing, the speculation, the possibilities. A search for sunken treasure wasn't much different.

What was she looking for really? Ky wondered. Was the gold her objective? Was she simply looking for an unusual way to spend her holiday? Was she still trying to give her father the blind devotion he'd expected all her life? Was it the hunt? Watching the wall of rain move slowly closer, Ky found of all the possibilities he wanted it to be the last.

With perhaps a hundred yards between them, both Kate and Ky looked out to the sea and the rain without being aware of each other. He thought of her and she of him, but the rain crept closer and time slipped by. The wind grew bolder. Both of them could admit to the restlessness that churned inside them, but neither could acknowledge simple loneliness.

Then they turned to walk back up the dunes and saw each other.

Kate wondered how long he'd been there, and how, when she could feel the waves of tension and need, she hadn't known the moment he'd stepped onto the beach. Her mind, her body—always so calm and co-operative—sprang to fevered life when she saw him. Kate knew she couldn't fight that, only the outcome. Still she wanted him. She told herself that just wanting was asking for disaster, but that didn't stop the need. If she ran from him now she'd admit defeat. Instead Kate took the first step across the sand toward him.

The thin white cotton of her skirt flapped around her, billowing, then clinging to the slender body he already knew. Her skin seemed very pale, her eyes very dark. Again Ky thought of mermaids, of illusions and of foolish dreams.

"You always liked the beach before a storm," Kate said when she reached him. She couldn't smile though she told herself she would. She wanted, though she told herself she wouldn't.

"It won't be much longer." He hooked his thumbs into the front pockets of his jeans. "If you didn't bring your car, you're going to get wet."

"I was visiting Linda." Kate turned her head to look back at the rain. No, it wouldn't be much longer. "It doesn't matter," she murmured. "Storms like this are over just as quickly as they begin." Storms like this, she thought, and like others. "I met Hope. You were right."

"About what?"

"She looks like you." This time she did manage to

smile, though the tension was balled at the base of her neck. "Did you know she named a doll after you?"

"A dragon's not a doll," Ky corrected. His lips curved. He could resist a great deal, be apathetic about a great deal more, but he found it virtually impossible to do either when it came to his niece. "She's a great kid. Hell of a sailor."

"You take her out on your boat?"

He heard the astonishment and shrugged it away. "Why not? She likes the water."

"I just can't picture you..." Breaking off, Kate turned back to the sea again. No, she couldn't picture him entertaining a child with toy dragons and boat rides, just as she couldn't picture him in the business world with ledgers and accountants. "You surprise me," she said a bit more casually. "About a lot of things."

He wanted to reach out and touch her hair, wrap those loose blowing ends around his finger. He kept his hands in his pockets. "Such as?"

"Linda told me you own the Roost."

He didn't have to see her face to know it would hold that thoughtful, considering expression. "That's right, or most of it anyway."

"You didn't mention it when we were having dinner there."

"Why should I?" She didn't have to see him to know he shrugged. "Most people don't care who owns a place as long as the food's good and the service is quick."

"I guess I'm not most people." She said it quietly, so quietly the words barely carried over the sound of the waves. Even so, Ky tensed.

"Why would it matter to you?"

Before she could think, she turned back, her eyes full of emotion. "Because it all matters. The whys, the hows. Because so much has changed and so much is the same. Because I want..." Breaking off, she took a step back. The look in her eyes turned to panic just before she started to dash away.

"What?" Ky demanded, grabbing her arm. "What do you want?"

"I don't know!" she shouted, unaware that it was the first time she'd done so in years. "I don't know what I want. I don't understand why I don't."

"Forget about understanding." He pulled her closer, holding her tighter when she resisted—or tried to. "Forget everything that's not here and now." The nights of restlessness and frustration already had his mercurial temperament on edge. Seeing her when he hadn't expected to made his emotions teeter. "You walked away from me once, but I won't crawl for you again. And you," he added with his eyes suddenly dark, his face suddenly close, "you damn well won't walk away as easily this time, Kate. Not this time."

With his arms wrapped around her he held her against him. His lips hovered above hers, threatening, promising. She couldn't tell. She didn't care. It was their taste she wanted, their pressure, no matter how harsh, how demanding. No matter what the consequence. Intellect and emotion might battle, and the battle might be eternal. Yet as she stood there crushed against him, feeling the wind whip at both of them, she already knew what the inevitable outcome would be.

"Tell me what you want, Kate." His voice was low, but as demanding as a shout. "Tell me what you want—now."

Now, she thought. If there could only be just now. She started to shake her head, but his breath feathered over her skin. That alone made future and past fade into insignificance.

"You," she heard herself murmur. "Just you." Reaching up she drew his face down to hers.

A wild passionate wind, a thunderous surf, the threat of rain just moments away. She felt his body—hard and confident against hers. She tasted his lips—soft, urgent. Over the thunder in her head and the thunder to the east, she heard her own moan. She wanted, as long as the moment lasted.

His tongue tempted; she surrendered to it. He dove deep and took all, then more. It might never be enough. With no hesitation, Kate met demand with demand, heat with heat. While mouth sought mouth, her hands roamed his face, teaching what she hadn't forgotten, reacquainting her with the familiar.

His skin was rough with a day's beard, the angle of cheek and jaw, hard and defined. As her fingers inched up she felt the soft brush of his hair blown by the wind. The contrast made her tremble before she dove her fingers deeper.

She could make him blind and deaf with needs. Knowing it, Ky couldn't stop it. The way she touched him, so sure, so sweet while her mouth was molten fire. Desire boiled in him, rising so quickly he was weak with it before his mind accepted what his body couldn't deny. He held her closer, hard against soft, rough against smooth, flame against flame.

Through the thin barrier of her blouse he felt her flesh warm to his touch. He knew the skin here would be delicate, as fragile as the underside of a rose. The scent would be as sweet, the taste as honeyed. Memories, the moment, the dream of more, all these combined to make him half mad. He knew what it would be like to have her, and knowing alone aroused. He felt her now, and feeling made him irrational.

He wanted to take her right there, next to the sea, while the sky opened up and poured over them.

"I want you." With his face buried against her neck he searched for all the places he remembered. "You know how much. You always knew."

"Yes." Her head was spinning. Every touch, every taste added speed to the whirl. Whatever doubts she'd had, Kate had never doubted the want. She hadn't always understood it, the intensity of it, but she'd never doubted it. It was pulling at her now—his, hers—the mutual, mindless passion they'd always been able to ignite in one another. She knew where it would lead—to dark, secret places full of sound and velocity. Not the eye of the hurricane, never the calm with him, but full fury from beginning to end. She knew where it would lead, and knew there'd be glory and freedom. But Ky had spoken no less than the truth when he'd said she wouldn't walk away so easily this time. It was that truth that made her reach for reason, when it would have been so simple to reach for madness.

"We can't." Breathless, she tried to turn in his arms.

"Ky, *I* can't." This time when she took his face in her hands it was to draw it away from hers. "This isn't right for me."

Fury mixed with passion. It showed in his eyes, in the press of his fingers on her arms. "It's right for you. It's never been anything but right for you."

"No." She had to deny it, she had to mean it, because he was so persuasive. "No, it's not. I've always been attracted to you. It'd be ridiculous for me to try to pretend otherwise, but this isn't what I want for myself."

His fingers tightened. If they brought her pain neither of them acknowledged it. "I told you to tell me what you wanted. You did."

As he spoke the sky opened, just as he'd imagined. Rain swept in from the sea, tasting of salt, the damp wind and mystery. Instantly drenched, they stood just as they were, close, distant, with his hands firm on her arms and hers light on his face. She felt the water wash over her body, watched it run over his. It stirred her. She couldn't say why, she wouldn't give in to it.

"At that moment I did want you, I can't deny it."

"And now?" he demanded.

"I'm going back to the village."

"Damn it, Kate, what else do you want?"

She stared at him through the rain. His eyes were dark, stormy as the sea that raged behind him. Somehow he was more difficult to resist when he was like this, volatile, on edge, not quite controlled. She felt desire knot in her stomach, and swim in her head. That was all, Kate told herself. That was all it had ever been.

Desire without understanding. Passion without future. Emotion without reason.

"Nothing you can give me," she whispered, knowing she'd have to dig for the strength to walk away, dig for it even to take the first step. "Nothing we can give to each other." Dropping her hands she stepped back. "I'm going back."

"You'll come back to me," Ky said as she took the first steps from him. "And if you don't," he added in a tone that made her hesitate, "it won't make any difference. We'll finish what's been started again."

She shivered, but continued to walk. Finish what's been started again. That was what she most feared.

Chapter 6

The storm passed. In the morning the sea was calm and blue, sprinkled with diamonds of sunlight from a sky where all clouds had been whisked away. It was true that rain freshened things—the air, grass, even the wood and stone of buildings.

The day was perfect, the wind calm. Kate's nerves rolled and jumped.

She'd committed herself to the project. It was her agreement with Ky that forced her to go to the harbor as she'd been doing every other morning. It made her climb on deck when she wanted nothing more than to pack and leave the island the way she'd come. If Ky could complete the agreement after what had passed between them on the beach, so could she.

Perhaps he sensed the fatigue she was feeling, but he made no comment on it. They spoke only when necessary as he headed out to open sea. Ky stood at the helm, Kate at the stern. Still, even the roar of the engine didn't disguise the strained silence. Ky checked the boat's compass, then cut the engines. Silence continued, thunderously.

With the deck separating them, each began to don their equipment—wet suits, the weight belts that would give them neutral buoyancy in the water, headlamps to light the sea's dimness, masks for sight. Ky checked his depth gauge and compass on his right wrist, then the luminous dial of the watch on his left while Kate attached the scabbard for her diver's knife onto her leg just below the knee.

Without speaking, they checked the valves and gaskets on the tanks, then strapped them on, securing buckles. As was his habit, Ky went into the water first, waiting until Kate joined him. Together they jackknifed below the surface.

The familiar euphoria reached out for her. Each time she dived, Kate expected the underwater world to become more commonplace. Each time it was still magic. She acknowledged what made it possible for her to join creatures of the sea—the regulator with its mouthpiece and hose that brought her air from the tanks on her back, the mask that gave her visibility. She knew the importance of every gauge. She acknowledged the technology, then put it in the practical side of her brain while she simply enjoyed.

They swam deeper, keeping in constant visual contact. Kate knew Ky often dived alone, and that doing so was always a risk. She also knew that no matter how much anger and resentment he felt toward her, she could trust him with her life.

She relied on Ky's instincts as much as his ability. It was his expertise that guided her now, perhaps more than her father's careful research and calculations. They were combing the very edge of the territory her father had mapped out, but Kate felt no discouragement. If she hadn't trusted Ky's skill and instincts, she would never have come back to Ocracoke.

They were going deeper now than they had on their other dives. Kate equalized by letting a tiny bit of air into her suit. Feeling the "squeeze" on her eardrums at the change in pressure, she relieved it carefully. A damaged eardrum could mean weeks without being able to dive.

When Ky signaled for her to switch on her headlamp she obeyed without question. Excitement began to rise.

The sunlight was fathoms above them. The world here never saw it. Sea grass swayed in the current. Now and then a fish, curious and brave enough, would swim along beside them only to vanish in the blink of an eye at a sudden movement.

Ky swam smoothly through the water, using his feet to propel him at a steady pace. Their lamps cut through the murk, surprising more fish, illuminating rock formations that had existed under the sea for centuries. Kate discovered shapes and faces in them.

No, she could never dive alone, Kate decided as Ky slowed his pace to keep rhythm with her more meandering one. It was so easy for her to lose her sense of time and direction. Air came into her lungs with a simple drawing of breath as long as the tanks held oxygen, but the gauges on her wrist only worked if she remembered to look at them.

Even mortality could be forgotten in enchantment. And enchantment could too easily lead to a mistake. It was a lesson she knew, but one that could slip away from her. The timelessness, the freedom was seductive. The feeling was somehow as sensual as the timeless freedom felt in a lover's arms. Kate knew this pleasure could be as dangerous as a lover, but found it as difficult to resist.

There was so much to see, to touch. Crustaceans of different shapes, sizes and hues. They were alive here in their own milieu, so different from when they washed up helplessly on the beach for children to collect in buckets. Fish swam in and out of waving grass that would be limp and lifeless on land. Unlike dolphins or man, some creatures would never know the thrill of both air and water.

Her beam passed over another formation, crusted with barnacles and sea life. She nearly passed it, but curiosity made her turn back so that the light skimmed over it a second time. Odd, she thought, how structured some of the shapes could be. It almost looked like...

Hesitating, using her arms to reverse her progress, Kate turned in the water to play her light over the shape from end to end. Excitement rose so quickly she grabbed Ky's arm in a grip strong enough to make him stop to search for a defect in her equipment. With a shake of her head Kate warded him off, then pointed.

When their twin lights illuminated the form on the

ocean floor, Kate nearly shouted with the discovery. It wasn't a shelf of rock. The closer they swam toward it the more apparent that became. Though it was heavily corroded and covered with crustaceans, the shape of the cannon remained recognizable.

Ky swam around the barrel. When he removed his knife and struck the cannon with the hilt the metallic sound rang out strangely. Kate was certain she'd never heard anything more musical. Her laughter came out in a string of bubbles that made Ky look in her direction and grin.

They'd found a corroded cannon, he thought, and she was as thrilled as if they'd found a chest full of doubloons. And he understood it. They'd found something perhaps no one had seen for two centuries. That in itself was a treasure.

With a movement of his hand he indicated for her to follow, then they began to swim slowly east. If they'd found a cannon, it was likely they'd find more.

Reluctant to leave her initial discovery, Kate swam with him, looking back as often as she looked ahead. She hadn't realized the excitement would be this intense. How could she explain what it felt like to discover something that had lain untouched on the sea floor for more than two centuries? Who would understand more clearly, she wondered, her colleagues at Yale or Ky? Somehow she felt her colleagues would understand intellectually, but they would never understand the exhilaration. Intellectual pleasure didn't make you giddy enough to want to turn somersaults.

How would her father have felt if he'd found it? She

wished she knew. She wished she could have given him that one instant of exultation, perhaps shared it with him as they'd so rarely shared anything. He'd only known the planning, the theorizing, the book-work. With one long look at that ancient weapon, she'd known so much more.

When Ky stopped and touched her shoulders, her emotions were as mixed as her thoughts. If she could have spoken she'd have told him to hold her, though she wouldn't have known why. She was thrilled, yet running through the joy was a thin shaft of sorrow— for what was lost, she thought. For what she'd never be able to find again.

Perhaps he knew something of what moved her. They couldn't communicate with words, but he touched her cheek—just a brush of his finger over her skin. It was more comforting to her than a dozen soft speeches.

She understood then that she'd never stopped lov-ing him. No matter how many years, how many miles had separated them, what life she had she'd left with him. The time in between had been little more than existence. It was possible to live with emptiness, even to be content with it until you had that heady taste of life again.

She might have panicked. She might have run if she hadn't been trapped there, fathoms deep in the midst of a discovery. Instead she accepted the knowledge, hoping that time would tell her what to do.

He wanted to ask her what was going through her mind. Her eyes were full of so many emotions. Words would have to wait. Their time in the sea was almost up. He touched her face again and waited for the smile. When she gave it to him, Ky pointed at something behind her that he had just noticed moments before.

An oaken plank, old, splintered and bumpy with parasites. For the second time Ky removed his knife and began to pry the board from its bed. Silt floated up thinly, cutting visibility before it settled again. Replacing his knife, Ky gave the thumbs-up signal that meant they'd surface. Kate shook her head indicating that they should continue to search, but Ky merely pointed to his watch, then again to the surface.

Frustrated with the technology that allowed her to dive, but also forced her to seek air again, Kate nodded.

They swam west, back toward the boat. When she passed the cannon again, Kate felt a quick thrill of pride. She'd found it. And the discoveries were only beginning.

The moment her head was above water, she started to laugh. "We found it!" She grabbed the ladder with one hand as Ky began to climb up, placing his find and his tanks on the deck first. "I can't believe it, after hardly more than a week. It's incredible, that cannon lying down there all these years." Water ran down her face but she didn't notice. "We have to find the hull, Ky." Impatient, she released her tanks and handed them up to him before she climbed aboard.

"The chances are good—eventually."

"Eventually?" Kate tossed her wet hair out of her eyes. "We found this in just over a week." She indicated the board on the deck. She crouched over it, just wanting to touch. "We found the *Liberty*."

"We found a wreck," he corrected. "It doesn't have to be the *Liberty*."

"It is," she said with a determination that caused his brow to lift. "We found the cannon and this just on the edge of the area my father had charted. It all fits too well."

"Regardless of what wreck it is, it's undocumented. You'll get your name in the books, professor."

Annoyed she rose. They stood facing each other on either side of the plank they'd lifted out of the sea. "I don't care about having my name in the books."

"Your father's name then." He unzipped his wet suit to let his skin dry.

She remembered her feelings after spotting the cannon, how Ky had seemed to understand them. Could they only be kind to each other, only be close to each other, fathoms under the surface? "Is there something wrong with that?"

"Only if it's an obsession. You always had a problem with your father."

"Because he didn't approve of you?" she shot back.

His eyes took on that eerily calm, almost flat expression that meant his anger was lethal. "Because it mattered too much to you what he approved of."

That stung. The truth often did. "I came here to finish my father's project," she said evenly. "I made that clear from the beginning. You're still getting your fee."

"You're still following directions. His directions." Before she could retort, he turned toward the cabin. "We'll eat and rest before we go back under."

With an effort, she held on to her temper. She wanted

to dive again, badly. She wanted to find more. Not for her father's approval, Kate thought fiercely. Certainly not for Ky's. She wanted this for herself. Pulling down the zipper of her wet suit, she went down the cabin steps.

She'd eat because strength and energy were vital to a diver. She'd rest for the same reason. Then, she determined, she'd go back to the wreck and find proof that it was the *Liberty*.

Calmer, she watched Ky go through a small cupboard. "Peanut butter?" she asked when she saw the jar he pulled out.

"Protein."

Her laugh helped her to relax again. "Do you still eat it with bananas?"

"It's still good for you."

Though she wrinkled her nose at the combination, she reminded herself that beggars couldn't be choosers. "When we find the treasure," she said recklessly, "I'll buy you a bottle of champagne."

Their fingers brushed as he handed her the first sandwich. "I'll hold you to it." He picked up his own sandwich and a quart of milk. "Let's eat on deck."

He wasn't certain if he wanted the sun or the space, but it wasn't any easier to be with her in that tiny cabin than it had been the first time, or the last. Taking her assent for granted, Ky went up the stairs again, without looking back. Kate followed.

"It might be good for you," Kate commented as she took the first bite, "but it still tastes like something you give five-year-olds when they scrape their knees."

"Five-year-olds require a lot of protein."

Giving up, Kate sat cross-legged on the deck. The sun was bright, the movement of the boat gentle. She wouldn't let his digs get to her, nor would she dig back. They were in this together, she reminded herself. Tension and sniping wouldn't help them find what they sought.

"It's the *Liberty*, Ky," she murmured, looking at the plank again. "I know it is."

"It's possible." He stretched out with his back against the port side. "But there are a lot of wrecks, unidentified and otherwise, all through these waters. Diamond Shoals is a graveyard."

"Diamond Shoals is fifty miles north."

"And the entire coastline along these barrier islands is full of littoral currents, rip currents and shifting sand ridges. Two hundred years ago they didn't have modern navigational devices. Hell, they didn't even have the lighthouses until the nineteenth century. I couldn't even give you an educated guess as to how many ships went down from the time Columbus set out until World War II."

Kate took another bite. "We're only concerned with one ship."

"Finding one's no big problem," he returned. "Finding a specific one's something else. Last year, after a couple of hurricanes breezed through, they found wrecks uncovered on the beach on Hatteras. There are plenty of houses on the island that were built from pieces of wreckage like that." He pointed to the plank with the remains of his sandwich.

Kate frowned at the board again. "It could be the *Liberty* just as easily as it couldn't."

"All right." Appreciating her stubbornness, Ky grinned. "But whatever it is, there might be treasure. Anything lost for more than two hundred years is pretty much finders keepers."

She didn't want to say that it wasn't any treasure she wanted. Just the *Liberty*'s. From what he said before, Kate was aware he already understood that. It was simply different for him. She took a long drink of cold milk. "What do you plan to do with your share?"

With his eyes half closed, he shrugged. He could do as he pleased now, a cache of gold wouldn't change that. "Buy another boat, I imagine."

"With what two-hundred-year-old gold would be worth today, you'd be able to buy a hell of a boat."

He grinned, but kept his eyes shaded. "I intend to. What about you?"

"I'm not sure." She wished she had some tangible goal for the money, something exciting, even fanciful. It just didn't seem possible to think beyond the hunt yet. "I thought I might travel a bit."

"Where?"

"Greece maybe. The islands."

"Alone?"

The food and the motion of the boat lulled her. She made a neutral sound as she shut her eyes.

"Isn't there some dedicated teacher you'd take with you? Someone you could discuss the Trojan War with?"

"Mmm, I don't want to go to Greece with a dedicated teacher."

"Someone else?"

"There's no one."

Sitting on the deck with her face lifted, her hair blowing, she looked like a finely crafted piece of porcelain. Something a man might look at, admire, but not touch. When her eyes were open, hot, her skin flushed with passion, he burned for her. When she was like this, calm, distant, he ached. He let the needs run through him because he knew there was no stopping them.

"Why?"

"Hmm?"

"Why isn't there anyone?"

Lazily she opened her eyes. "Anyone?"

"Why don't you have a lover?"

The sleepy haze cleared from her eyes instantly. He saw her fingers tense on the dark blue material that stretched snugly over her knees. "It's none of your business whether I do or not."

"You've just told me you don't."

"I told you there's no one I'd travel with," she corrected, but when she started to rise, he put a hand on her shoulder.

"It's the same thing."

"No, it's not, but it's still none of your business, Ky, any more than your personal life is mine."

"I've had women," he said easily. "But I haven't had a lover since you left the island."

She felt the pain and the pleasure sweep up through her. It was dangerous to dwell on the sensation. As dangerous as it was to lose yourself deep under the ocean.

"Don't." She lifted her hand to remove his from her shoulder. "This isn't good for either of us."

"Why?" His fingers linked with hers. "We want each other. We both know the rules this time around."

Rules. No commitment, no promises. Yes, she understood them this time, but like mortality during a dive, they could easily be forgotten. Even now, with his eyes on hers, her fingers caught in his, the structure of those rules became dimmer and dimmer. He would hurt her again. There was never any question of that. Somehow, in the last twenty-four hours, it had become a matter of *how* she would deal with the pain, not *if*.

"Ky, I'm not ready." Her voice was low, not pleading, but plainly vulnerable. Though she wasn't aware of it, there was no defense she could put to better use.

He drew her up so that they were both standing, touching only hand to hand. Though she was tall, her slimness made her appear utterly fragile. It was that and the way she looked at him, with her head tilted back so their eyes could meet, that prevented him from taking what he was determined to have, without questions, without her willingness. Ruthlessly, that was how he told himself he wanted to take her, even though he knew he couldn't.

"I'm not a patient man."

"No."

He nodded, then released her hand while he still could. "Remember it," he warned before he turned to go to the helm. "We'll take the boat east, over the wreck and dive again."

An hour later they found a piece of rigging, broken

and corroded, less than three yards from the cannon. By hand signals, Ky indicated that they'd start a stockpile of the salvage. Later they'd come back with the means of bringing it up. There were more planks, some too big for a man to carry up, some small enough for Kate to hold in one hand.

When she found a pottery bowl, miraculously unbroken, she realized just what an archaeologist must feel after hours of digging when he unearths a fragment of another era. Here it was, cupped in her hand, a simple bowl, covered with silt, covered with age. Someone had eaten from it once, a seaman, relaxing briefly below deck, perhaps on his first voyage across the Atlantic to the New World. His last journey in any event, Kate mused as she turned the bowl over in her hand.

The rigging, the cannon, the planks equaled ship. The bowl equaled man.

Though she put the bowl with the other pieces of their find, she intended to take it up with her on this dive. Whatever other artifacts they found could go to a museum, but the first, she'd keep.

They found pieces of glass that might have come from bottles that held whiskey, chunks of crockery that hadn't survived intact like the bowl. Bits of cups, bowls, plates littered the sea floor.

The galley, she decided. They must have found the galley. Over the years, the water pressure would have simply disintegrated the ship until it was all pieces spread on and under the floor of the ocean. It would, in essence, have become part of the sea, a home for the creatures and plant life that dwelt there.

But they'd found the galley. If they could find something, just one thing with the ship's name inscribed on it, they'd be certain.

Diligently, using her knife as a digging tool, Kate worked at the floor of the sea. It wasn't a practical way to search, but she saw no harm in trying her luck. They'd found crockery, glass, the unbroken bowl. Even as she glanced up she saw Ky examining what might have been half a dinner plate.

When she unearthed a long wooden ladle, Kate found that her excitement increased. They *had* found the galley, and in time, she'd prove to Ky that they'd found the *Liberty.*

Engrossed in her find, she turned to signal to Ky and moved directly into the path of a stingray.

He saw it. Ky was no more than a yard from Kate when the movement of the ray unearthing itself from its layer of sand and silt had caught his eye. His movement was pure reflex, done without thought or plan. He was quick. But even as he grabbed Kate's hand to swing her back behind him, out of range, the wicked, saw-toothed tail lashed out.

Her scream was muffled by the water, but the sound went through Ky just as surely as the stingray's poison went through Kate. Her body went stiff against his, rigid in pain and shock. The ladle she'd found floated down, out of her grip, until it landed silently on the bottom.

He knew what to do. No rational diver goes down unless he has a knowledge of how to handle an emergency. Still Ky felt a moment of panic. This wasn't just another diver, it was Kate. Before his mind could clear, her stiffened body went limp against him. Then he acted.

Cool, almost mechanically, he tilted her head back with the chin carry to keep her air passage open. He held her securely, pressing his chest into her tanks, keeping his hand against her ribcage. It ran through his mind that it was best she'd fainted. Unconscious she wouldn't struggle as she might had she been awake and in pain. It was best she'd fainted because he couldn't bear to think of her in pain. He kicked off for the surface.

On the rise he squeezed her, hard, forcing expanding air out of her lungs. There was always the risk of embolism. They were going up faster than safety allowed. Even while he ventilated his own lungs, Ky kept a lookout. She would bleed, and blood brought sharks.

The minute they surfaced, Ky released her weight belt. Supporting her with his arm wrapped around her, his hand grasping the ladder, Ky unhooked his tanks, slipped them over the side of the boat, then removed Kate's. Her face was waxy, but as he pulled the mask from her face she moaned. With that slight sound of life some of the blood came back to his own body. With her draped limply over his shoulder, he climbed the ladder onto the *Vortex*.

He laid her down on the deck, and with hands that didn't hesitate, began to pull the wet suit from her. She moaned again when he drew the snug material over the wound just above her ankle, but she didn't reach the surface of consciousness. Grimly, Ky examined the laceration the ray had caused. Even through the protection of her suit, the tail had penetrated deep into her skin. If Ky had only been quicker...

Cursing himself, Ky hurried to the cabin for the first aid kit.

As consciousness began to return, Kate felt the ache swimming up from her ankle to her head. Spears of pain shot through her, sharp enough to make her gasp and struggle, as if she could move away from it and find ease again.

"Try to lie still."

The voice was gentle and calm. Kate balled her hands into fists and obeyed it. Opening her eyes, she stared up at the pure blue sky. Her mind whirled with confusion, but she stared at the sky as though it were the only tangible thing in her life. If she concentrated, she could rise above the hurt. The ladle. Opening her hand she found it empty, she'd lost the ladle. For some reason it seemed vital that she have it.

"We found the galley." Her voice was hoarse with anguish, but her one hand remained open and limp. "I found a ladle. They'd have used it for spooning soup into that bowl. The bowl—it wasn't even broken. Ky..." Her voice weakened with a new flood of sensation as memory began to return. "It was a stingray. I wasn't watching for it, it just seemed to be there. Am I going to die?"

"No!" His answer was sharp, almost angry. Bending over her, he placed both hands on her shoulders so that she'd look directly into his face. He had to be sure she understood everything he said. "It was a stingray," he confirmed, not adding that it had been a good ten feet long. "Part of the spine's broken off, lodged just above your ankle."

He watched her eyes cloud further, part pain, part fear. His hands tightened on her shoulders. "It's not in deep. I can get it out, but it'll hurt like hell."

She knew what he was saying. She could stay as she was until he got her back to the doctor on the island, or she could trust him to treat her now. Though her lips trembled, she kept her eyes on his and spoke clearly.

"Do it now."

"Okay." He continued to stare at her, into the eyes that were glazed with shock. "Hang on. Don't try to be brave. Scream as much as you want but try not to move. I'll be quick." Bending farther, he kissed her hard. "I promise."

Kate nodded, then concentrating on the feeling of his lips against hers, shut her eyes. He was quick. Within seconds she felt the hurt rip through her, over the threshold she thought she could bear and beyond.... She pulled in air to scream, but went back under the surface into liquid dimness.

Ky let the blood flow freely onto the deck for a moment, knowing it would wash away some of the poison. His hands had been rock steady when he'd pulled the spine from her flesh. His mind had been cold. Now with her blood on his hands, they began to shake. Ignoring them, and the icy fear of seeing Kate's smooth skin ripped and raw, Ky washed the wound, cleansed it, bound it. Within the hour, he'd have her to a doctor.

With unsteady fingers, he checked the pulse at the

base of her neck. It wasn't strong, but it was steady. Lifting an eyelid with his thumb, he checked her pupils. He didn't believe she was in shock, she'd simply escaped from the pain. He thanked God for that.

On a long breath he let his forehead rest against hers, only for a moment. He prayed that she'd remain unconscious until she was safely under a doctor's care.

He didn't take the time to wash her blood from his hands before he took the helm. Ky whipped the boat around in a quick circle and headed full throttle back to Ocracoke.

Chapter 7

As she started to float toward consciousness, Kate focused, drifted, then focused again. She saw the whirl of a white ceiling rather than the pure blue arc of sky. Even when the mist returned she remembered the hurt and thrashed out against it. She couldn't face it a second time. Yet she found as she rose closer to the surface that she didn't have the will to fight against it. That brought fear. If she'd had the strength, she might have wept.

Then she felt a cool hand on her cheek. Ky's voice pierced the last layers of fog, low and gentle. "Take it easy, Kate. You're all right now. It's all over."

Though her breath hitched as she inhaled, Kate opened her eyes. The pain didn't come. All she felt was his hand on her cheek, all she saw was his face. "Ky." When she said his name, Kate reached for his hand, the one solid thing she was sure of. Her own voice frightened her. It was hardly more than a wisp of air.

"You're going to be fine. The doctor took care of you." As he spoke, Ky rubbed his thumb over her knuckles, establishing a point of concentration, and kept his other hand lightly on her cheek, knowing that contact was important. He'd nearly gone mad waiting for her to open her eyes again. "Dr. Bailey, you remember. You met him before."

It seemed vital that she should remember so she forced her mind to search back. She had a vague picture of a tough, weathered old man who looked more suited to the sea than the examining room. "Yes. He likes…likes ale and flounder."

He might have laughed at her memory if her voice had been stronger. "You're going to be fine, but he wants you to rest for a few more days."

"I feel…strange." She lifted a hand to her own head as if to assure herself it was still there.

"You're on medication, that's why you're groggy. Understand?"

"Yes." Slowly she turned her head and focused on her surroundings. The walls were a warm ivory, not the sterile white of a hospital. The dark oak trim gleamed dully. On the hardwood floor lay a single rug, its muted Indian design fading with age. It was the only thing Kate recognized. The last time she'd been in Ky's bedroom only half the drywall had been in place and one of the windows had had a long thin crack in the bottom pane. "Not the hospital," she managed.

"No." He stroked her head, needing to touch as much as to check for her fever that had finally broken near dawn. "It was easier to bring you here after Bailey took care of you. You didn't need a hospital, but neither of us liked the idea of your being in a hotel right now."

"Your house," she murmured, struggling to concentrate her strength. "This is your bedroom, I remember the rug."

They'd made love on it once. That's what Ky remembered. With an effort, he kept his hands light. "Are you hungry?"

"I don't know." Basically, she felt nothing. When she tried to sit up, the drug spun in her head, making both the room and reality reel away. That would have to stop, Kate decided while she waited for the dizziness to pass. She'd rather have some pain than that helpless, weighted sensation.

Without fuss, Ky moved the pillows and shifted her to a sitting position. "The doctor said you should eat when you woke up. Just some soup." Rising he looked down on her, in much the same way, Kate thought, as he'd looked at a cracked mast he was considering mending. "I'll fix it. Don't get up," he added as he walked to the door. "You're not strong enough yet."

As he went into the hall he began to swear in a low steady stream.

Of course she wasn't strong enough, he thought with a last vicious curse. She was pale enough to fade into the sheets she lay on. No resistance, that's what Bailey had said. Not enough food, not enough sleep, too much strain. If he could do nothing else, Ky determined as he pulled open a kitchen cupboard, he could do something about that. She was going to eat, and lie flat on her back until the doctor said otherwise.

He'd known she was weak, that was the worst of it. Ky dumped the contents of a can into a pot then hurled the empty container into the trash. He'd seen the strain on her face, the shadows under her eyes, he'd heard the traces of fatigue come and go in her voice, but he'd been too wrapped up in his own needs to do anything about it.

With a flick of the wrist, he turned on the burner under the soup, then the burner under the coffee. God, he needed coffee. For a moment he simply stood with his fingers pressed against his eyes waiting for his system to settle.

He couldn't remember ever spending a more frantic twenty-four hours. Even after the doctor had checked and treated her, even when Ky had brought her home and she'd been fathoms deep under the drug, his nerves hadn't eased. He'd been terrified to leave the room for more than five minutes at a time. The fever had raged through her, though she'd been unaware. Most of the night he'd sat beside her, bathing away the sweat and talking to her, though she couldn't hear.

Through the night he'd existed on coffee and nerves. With a half-laugh he reached for a cup. It looked like that wasn't going to change for a while yet.

He knew he still wanted her, knew he still felt something for her, under the bitterness and anger. But until he'd seen her lying unconscious on the deck of his boat, with her blood on his hands, he hadn't realized that he still loved her.

He'd known what to do about the want, even the bitterness, but now, faced with love, Ky hadn't a clue. It didn't seem possible for him to love someone so frail, so calm, so…different than he. Yet the emotion he'd once felt for her had grown and ripened into something so solid he couldn't see any way around it. For now, he'd concentrate on getting her on her feet again. He poured the soup into a bowl and carried it upstairs.

It would have been an easy matter to close her eyes and slide under again. Too easy. Willing herself to stay awake, Kate concentrated on Ky's room. There were a number of changes here as well, she mused. He'd trimmed the windows in oak, giving them a wide sill where he'd scattered the best of his shells. A piece of satiny driftwood stood, beautiful as a piece of sculpture. There was a paneled closet door with a faceted glass knob where there'd once been a rod, a round-backed rattan chair where there'd been packing crates.

Only the bed was the same, she mused. The wide four-poster had been his mother's. She knew he'd given the rest of his family's furniture to Marsh. Ky had told her once he'd felt no need or desire for it, but he kept the bed. He was born there, unexpectedly, during a night in which the island had been racked by a storm.

And they'd made love there, Kate remembered as she ran her fingers over the sheets. The first time, and the last.

Stopping the movement of her fingers, she looked over as Ky came back into the room. Memories had to be pushed aside. "You've done a lot of work in here."

"A bit." He set the tray over her lap as he sat on the edge of the bed.

As the scent of the soup reached her, Kate shut her

eyes. Just the aroma seemed to be enough. "It smells wonderful."

"The smell won't put any meat on you."

She smiled, and opened her eyes again. Then before she'd realized it, Ky had spoon-fed her the first bite. "It tastes wonderful too." Though she reached for the spoon, he dipped it into the bowl himself then held it to her lips. "I can do it," she began, then was forced to swallow more broth.

"Just eat." Fighting off waves of emotion he spoke briskly. "You look like hell."

"I'm sure I do," she said easily. "Most people don't look their best a couple of hours after being stung by a stingray."

"Twenty-four," Ky corrected as he fed her another spoon of soup.

"Twenty-four what?"

"Hours." Ky slipped in another spoonful when her eyes widened.

"I've been unconscious for twenty-four hours?" She looked to the window and the sunlight as if she could find some means of disproving it.

"You slipped in and out quite a bit before Bailey gave you the shot. He said you probably wouldn't remember." Thank God, Ky added silently. Whenever she'd fought her way back to consciousness, she'd been in agony. He could still hear her moans, feel the way she'd clutched him. He never knew a person could suffer physically for another's pain the way he'd suffered for hers. Even now it made his muscles clench.

"That must've been some shot he gave me."

"He gave you what you needed." His eyes met hers. For the first time Kate saw the fatigue in them, and the anger.

"You've been up all night," she murmured. "Haven't you had any rest at all?"

"You needed to be watched," he said briefly. "Bailey wanted you to stay under, so you'd sleep through the worst of the pain, and so you'd just sleep period." His voice changed as he lost control over the anger. He couldn't prevent the edge of accusation from showing, partly for her, partly for himself. "The wound wasn't that bad, do you understand? But you weren't in any shape to handle it. Bailey said you've been well on the way to working yourself into exhaustion."

"That's ridiculous. I don't—"

Ky swore at her, filling her mouth with more soup. "Don't tell me it's ridiculous. I had to listen to him. I had to look at you. You don't eat, you don't sleep, you're going to fall down on your face."

There was too much of the drug in her system to allow her temper to bite. Instead of annoyance, her words came out like a sigh. "I didn't fall on my face."

"Only a matter of time." Fury was coming too quickly. Though his fingers tightened on the spoon, Ky held it back. "I don't care how much you want to find the treasure, you can't enjoy it if you're flat on your back."

The soup was warming her. As much as her pride urged her to refuse, her system craved the food. "I won't be," she told him, not even aware that her words were beginning to slur. "We'll dive again tomorrow, and I'll prove it's the *Liberty*."

He started to swear at her, but one look at the heavy eyes and the pale cheeks had him swallowing the words. "Sure." He spooned in more soup knowing she'd be asleep again within moments.

"I'll give the ladle and the rigging and the rest to a museum." Her eyes closed. "For my father."

Ky set the tray on the floor. "Yes, I know."

"It was important to him. I need… I just need to give him something." Her eyes fluttered open briefly. "I didn't know he was ill. He never told me about his heart, about the pills. If I'd known…"

"You couldn't have done any more than you did." His voice was gentle again as he shifted the pillows down.

"I loved him."

"I know you did."

"I could never seem to make the people I love understand what I need. I don't know why."

"Rest now. When you're well, we'll find the treasure."

She felt herself sinking into warmth, softness, the dark. "Ky." Kate reached out and felt his fingers wrap around hers. With her eyes closed, it was all the reality she needed.

"I'll stay," he murmured, brushing the hair from her cheek. "Just rest."

"All those years…" He could feel her fingers relaxing in his as she slipped deeper. "I never forgot you. I never stopped wanting you. Not ever…"

He stared down at her as she slept. Her face was utterly peaceful, pale as marble, soft as silk. Unable to resist, he lifted her fingers to his own cheek, just to feel her flesh against his. He wouldn't think about what she'd said now. He couldn't. The strain of the last day had taken a toll on him as well. If he didn't get some rest, he wouldn't be able to care for her when she woke again.

Rising, Ky pulled down the shades, and took off his shirt. Then he lay down next to Kate in the big four-poster bed and slept for the first time in thirty-six hours.

The pain was a dull, consistent throb, not the silvery sharp flash she remembered, but a gnawing ache that wouldn't pass. When it woke her, Kate lay still, trying to orient herself. Her mind was clearer now. She was grateful for that, even though with the drug out of her system she was well aware of the wound. It was dark, but the moonlight slipped around the edges of the shades Ky had drawn. She was grateful for that too. It seemed she'd been a prisoner of the dark for too long.

It was night. She prayed it was only hours after she'd last awoken, not another full day later. She didn't want that quick panic at the thought of losing time again. Because she needed to be certain she was in control this time, she went over everything she remembered.

The pottery bowl, the ladle, then the stingray. She closed her eyes a moment, knowing it would be a very long time before she forgot what it had felt like to be struck with that whiplike tail. She remembered waking up on the deck of the *Vortex,* the pure blue sky overhead, and the strong, calm way Ky had spoken to her before he'd pulled out the spine. That pain, the horror of that one instant was very clear. Then, there was nothing else.

She remembered nothing of the journey back to the island, or of Dr. Bailey's ministrations or of being transported to Ky's home. Her next clear image was of waking in his bedroom, of dark oak trim on the windows, wide sills with shells set on them.

He'd fed her soup—yes, that was clear, but then things started to become hazy again. She knew he'd been angry, though she couldn't remember why. At the moment, it was more important to her that she could put events in some sort of sequence.

As she lay in the dark, fully awake and finally aware, she heard the sound of quiet, steady breathing beside her. Turning her head, Kate saw Ky beside her, hardly more than a silhouette with the moonlight just touching the skin of his chest so that she could see it rise and fall.

He'd said he would stay, she remembered. And he'd been tired. Abruptly Kate remembered there'd been fatigue in his eyes as well as temper. He'd been caring for her.

A mellow warmth moved through her, one she hadn't felt in a very long time. He had taken care of her, and though it had made him angry, he'd done it. And he'd stayed. Reaching out, she touched his cheek.

Though the gesture was whisper light, Ky awoke immediately. His sleep had been little more than a half doze so that he could recharge his system yet be aware of any sign that Kate needed attention. Sitting up, he shook his head to clear it.

He looked like a boy caught napping. For some reason the gesture moved Kate unbearably. "I didn't mean to wake you," she murmured.

He reached for the lamp beside the bed and turned it on low. Though his body revolted against the interruption, his mind was fully awake. "Pain?"

"No."

He studied her face carefully. The glazed look from the drug had left her eyes, but the color hadn't returned. "Kate."

"All right. Some."

"Bailey left some pills."

As he started to rise, Kate reached for him again. "No, I don't want anything. It makes me groggy."

"It takes away the pain."

"Not now, Ky, please. I promise I'll tell you if it gets bad."

Because her voice was close to desperate he made himself content with that. At the moment, she looked too fragile to argue with. "Are you hungry?"

She smiled, shaking her head. "No. It must be the middle of the night. I was only trying to orient myself." She touched him again, in gratitude, in comfort. "You should sleep."

"I've had enough. Anyway, you're the patient."

Automatically, he put his hand to her forehead to check for fever. Touched, Kate laid hers over it. She felt the quick reflexive tensing of his fingers.

"Thank you." When he would have removed his hand, she linked her fingers with his. "You've been taking good care of me."

"You needed it," he said simply and much too swiftly. He couldn't allow her to stir him now, not when they were in that big, soft bed surrounded by memories.

"You haven't left me since it happened."

"I had no place to go."

His answer made her smile. Kate reached up her free hand to touch his cheek. There had been changes, she thought, many changes. But so many things had stayed the same. "You were angry with me."

"You haven't been taking care of yourself." He told himself he should move away from the bed, from Kate, from everything that weakened him there.

He stayed, leaning over her, one hand caught in hers. Her eyes were dark, soft in the dim light, full of the sweetness and innocence he remembered. He wanted to hold her until there was no more pain for either of them, but he knew, if he pressed his body against hers now, he wouldn't stop. Again he started to move, pulling away the hand that held hers. Again Kate stopped him.

"I would've died if you hadn't gotten me up."

"That's why it's smarter to dive with a partner."

"I might still have died if you hadn't done everything you did."

He shrugged this off, too aware that the fingers on his face were stroking lightly, something she had done in the past. Sometimes before they'd made love, and often afterward, when they'd talked in quiet voices, she'd stroke his face, tracing the shape of it as though she'd needed to memorize it. Perhaps she, too, sometimes awoke in the middle of the night and remembered too much.

Unable to bear it, Ky put his hand around her wrist and drew it away. "The wound wasn't that bad," he said simply.

"I've never seen a stingray that large." She shivered and his hand tightened on her wrist.

"Don't think about it now. It's over."

Was it? she wondered as she lifted her head and looked into his eyes. Was anything ever really over? For four years she'd told herself there were joys and pains that could be forgotten, absorbed into the routine that was life as it had to be lived. Now, she was no longer sure. She needed to be. More than anything else, she needed to be sure.

"Hold me," she murmured.

Was she trying to make him crazy? Ky wondered. Did she want him to cross the border, that edge he was trying so desperately to avoid? It took most of the strength he had left just to keep his voice even. "Kate, you need to sleep now. In the morning—"

"I don't want to think about the morning," she murmured. "Only now. And now I need you to hold me." Before he could refuse, she slipped her arms around his waist and rested her head on his shoulder.

She felt his hesitation, but not his one vivid flash of longing before his arms came around her. On a long breath Kate closed her eyes. Too much time had passed since she'd had this, the gentleness, the sweetness she'd experienced only with Ky. No one else had ever held her with such kindness, such simple compassion. Somehow, she never found it odd that a man could be so reckless and arrogant, yet kind and compassionate at the same time.

Perhaps she'd been attracted to the recklessness, but it had been the kindness she had fallen in love with. Until now, in the quiet of the deep night, she hadn't understood. Until now, in the security of his arms, she hadn't accepted what she wanted.

Life as it had to be lived, she thought again. Was taking what she so desperately needed part of that?

She was so slender, so soft beneath the thin nightshirt. Her hair lay over his skin, loose and free, its color muted in the dim light. He could feel her palms against his back, those elegant hands that had always made him think more of an artist than a teacher. Her breathing was quiet, serene, as he knew it was when she slept. The light scent of woman clung to the material of the nightshirt.

Holding her didn't bring the pain he'd expected but a contentment he'd been aching for without realizing it. The tension in his muscles eased, the knot in his stomach vanished. With his eyes closed, he rested his cheek on her hair. It seemed like a lifetime since he'd known the pleasure of quiet satisfaction. She'd asked him to hold her, but had she known he needed to be held just as badly?

Kate felt him relax degree by degree and wondered if it had been she who'd caused the tension in him, and she who'd ultimately released it. Had she hurt him more than she'd realized? Had he cared more than she'd dared to believe? Or was it simply that the physical need never completely faded? It didn't matter, not tonight.

Ky was right. She knew the rules this time around. She wouldn't expect more than he offered. Whatever he offered was much, much more than she'd had in the long, dry years without him. In turn, she could give what she ached to give. Her love.

"It's the same for me as it always was," she murmured. Then, tilting her head back, she looked at him. Her hair streamed down her back, her eyes were wide and honest. He felt the need slam into him like a fist.

"Kate—"

"I never expected to feel the same way when I came back," she interrupted. "I don't think I'd have come. I wouldn't have had the courage."

"Kate, you're not well." He said it very slowly, as if he had to explain to them both. "You've lost blood, had a fever. It's taken a lot out of you. It'd be best, I think, if you tried to sleep now."

She felt no fever now. She felt cool and light and full of needs. "That day on the beach during the storm, you said I'd come to you." Kate brought her hands up his back until they reached his shoulders. "Even then I knew you were right. I'm coming to you now. Make love with me, Ky, here, in the bed where you loved me that first time."

And the last, he remembered, fighting back a torrent of desire. "You're not well," he managed a second time.

"Well enough to know what I want." She brushed her lips over his chin where his beard grew rough with neglect. So long…that was all that would come clearly to her. It had been so long. Too long. "Well enough to know what I need. It's always been you." Her fingers tightened on his shoulders, her lips inches from his. "It's only been you."

Perhaps moving away from her was the answer. But some answers were impossible. "Tomorrow you may be sorry."

She smiled in her calm, quiet way that always moved him. "Then we'll have tonight."

He couldn't resist her. The warmth. He didn't want to hurt her. The softness. The need building inside him threatened to send them both raging even though he knew she was still weak, still fragile. He remembered how it had been the first time, when she'd been innocent. He'd been so careful, though he had never felt the need to care before, and hadn't since. Remembering that, he laid her back.

"We'll have tonight," he repeated and touched his lips to hers.

Sweet, fresh, clean. Those words went through his head, those sensations went through his system as her lips parted for his. So he lingered over her kiss, enjoying with tenderness what he'd once promised himself to take ruthlessly. His mouth caressed, without haste, without pressure. Tasting, just tasting, while the hunger grew.

Her hands reached for his face, fingers stroking, the rough, the smooth. She could hear her own heart beat in her head, feel the slow, easy pleasure that came in liquid waves. He murmured to her, lovely, quiet words that made her thrill when she felt them formed against her mouth. With his tongue he teased hers in long, lazy sweeps until she felt her mind cloud as it had under the drug. Then when she felt the first twinge of desperation, he kissed her with an absorbed patience that left her weak.

He felt it—that initial change from equality to submission that had always excited him. The aggression would come later, knocking the breath from him, taking him to the edge. He knew that too. But for the moment, she was soft, yielding.

He slid his hands over the nightshirt, stroking, lingering. The material between his flesh and hers teased them both. She moved to his rhythm, glorying in the steady loss of control. He took her deeper with a touch, still deeper with a taste. She dove, knowing the full pleasure of ultimate trust. Wherever he took her, she wanted to go.

With a whispering movement he took his hand over the slender curve of her breast. She was soft, the material smooth, making her hardening nipple a sensuous contrast. He loitered there while her breathing grew unsteady, reveling in the changes of her body. Lingering over each separate button of her nightshirt, Ky unfastened them, then slowly parted the material, as if he were unveiling a priceless treasure.

He'd never forgotten how lovely she was, how exciting delicacy could be. Now that he had her again, he allowed himself the time to look, to touch carefully, all the while watching the contact of his lean tanned hand against her pale skin. With tenderness he felt seldom and demonstrated rarely, he lowered his mouth, letting his lips follow the progress his fingers had already begun.

She was coming to life under him. Kate felt her blood begin to boil as though it had lain dormant in her veins for years. She felt her heart begin to thump as though it had been frozen in ice until that moment. She heard her name as only he said it. As only he could.

Sensations? Could there be so many of them? Could she have known them all once, experienced them all once, then lived without them? A whisper, a sigh, the brush of a fingertip along her skin. The scent of a man touched by the sea, the taste of her lover lingering yet on her lips. The glow of soft lights against closed lids. Time faded. No yesterday. No tomorrow.

She could feel the slick material of the nightshirt slide away, then the warm, smooth sheets beneath her back. The skim of his tongue along her ribcage incited a thrill that began in her core and exploded inside her head.

She remembered the dawn breaking slowly over the sea. Now she knew the same magnificence inside her own body. Light and warmth spread through her, gradually, patiently, until she was glowing with a new beginning.

He hadn't known he could hold such raging desire in check and still feel such complete pleasure, such whirling excitement. He was aware of every heightening degree of passion that worked through her. He understood the changing, rippling thrill she felt if he used more pressure here, a longer taste there. It brought him a wild sense of power, made only more acute by the knowledge that he must harness it. She was fluid. She was silk. And then with a suddenness that sent him reeling, she was fire.

Her body arched on the first tumultuous crest. It ripped through her like a madness. Greedy, ravenous for more, she began to demand what he'd only hinted at. Her hands ran over him, nearly destroying his control in a matter of seconds. Her mouth was hot, hungry, and sought his with an urgency he couldn't resist. Then she rained kisses over his face, down his throat until he gripped the sheets with his hands for fear of crushing her too tightly and bruising her skin.

She touched him with those slender, elegant fingers so that the blood rushed fast and furious into his head. "You make me crazy," he murmured.

"Yes." She could do no more than whisper, but her eyes opened. "Yes."

"I want to watch you go up," he said softly as he slid into her. "I want to see what making love with me does to you."

She arched again, the moan inching out of her as she experienced a second wild peak. He saw her eyes darken, cloud as he took her slowly, steadily toward the verge between passion and madness. He watched the color come into her cheeks, saw her lips tremble as she spoke his name. Her hands gripped his shoulders, but neither of them knew her short tapered nails dug into his skin.

They moved together, neither able to lead, both able to follow. As pleasure built, he never took his eyes from her face.

All sensation focused into one. They were only one. With a freedom that reaches perfection only rarely, they gave perfection to each other.

Chapter 8

She was sleeping soundly when Ky woke. Ky observed a hint of color in her cheeks and was determined to see that it stayed there. The touch of his hand to her hair was gentle but proprietary. Her skin was cool and dry, her breathing quiet but steady.

What she'd given him the night before had been offered with complete freedom, without shadows of the past, with none of the bitter taste of regret. It was something else he intended to keep constant.

No, he wasn't going to allow her to withdraw from him again. Not an inch. He'd lost her four years ago, or perhaps he'd never really had her—not in the way he'd believed, not in the way he'd taken for granted. But this time, Ky determined, it would be different.

In his own way, he needed to take care of her. Her fragility drew that from him. In another way, he needed a partner on equal terms. Her strength offered him that.

For reasons he never completely understood, Kate was exactly what he'd always wanted.

Clumsiness, arrogance, inexperience, or perhaps a combination of all three made him lose her once. Now that he had a second chance, he was going to make sure it worked. With a little more time, he might figure out how.

Rising, he dressed in the shaded light of the bedroom, then left her to sleep.

When she woke slowly, Kate was reluctant to surface from the simple pleasure of a dream. The room was dim, her mind was hazy with sleep and fantasy. The throb in her leg came as a surprise. How could there be pain when everything was so perfect? With a sigh, she reached for Ky and found the bed empty.

The haze vanished immediately, as did all traces of sleep and the pretty edge of fantasy. Kate sat up, and though the movement jolted the pain in her leg, she stared at the empty space beside her.

Had that been a dream as well? she wondered. Tentatively, she reached out and found the sheets cool. All a fantasy brought on by medication and confusion? Unsure, unsteady, she pushed the hair away from her face. Was it possible that she'd imagined it all—the gentleness, the sweetness, the passion?

She'd needed Ky. That hadn't been a dream. Even now she could feel the dull ache in her stomach that came from need. Had the need caused her to fantasize all that strange, stirring beauty during the night? The bed beside her was empty, the sheets cool. She was alone.

The pleasure she awoke with drained, leaving her empty, leaving her grateful for the pain that was her only grip on reality. She wanted to weep, but found she hadn't the energy for tears.

"So you're up."

Ky's voice made her whip her head around. Her nerves were strung tight. He walked into the bedroom carrying a tray, wearing an easy smile.

"That saves me from having to wake you up to get some food into you." Before he approached the bed, he went to both windows and drew up the shades. Light poured into the room and the warm breeze that had been trapped behind the shades rushed in to ruffle the sheets. Feeling it, she had to control a shudder. "How'd you sleep?"

"Fine." The awkwardness was unexpected. Kate folded her hands and sat perfectly still. "I want to thank you for everything you've done."

"You've already thanked me once. It wasn't necessary then or now." Because her tone had put him on guard, Ky stopped next to the bed to take a good long look at her. "You're hurting."

"It's not bad."

"This time you take a pill." After setting the tray on her lap, he walked to the dresser and picked up a small bottle. "No arguments," he said, anticipating her refusal.

"Ky, it's really not bad." When had he offered her a pill before? The struggle to remember brought only more frustration. "There's barely any pain."

"Any pain's too much." He sat on the bed, and putting the pill into her palm curled her hand over it with his own. "When it's you."

With her fingers curled warmly under his, she knew. Elation came so quietly she was afraid to move and chase it away. "I didn't dream it, did I?" she whispered.

"Dream what?" He kissed the back of her hand before he handed her the glass of juice.

"Last night. When I woke up, I was afraid it had all been a dream."

He smiled and, bending, touched his lips to hers. "If it was, I had the same dream." He kissed her again, with humor in his eyes. "It was wonderful."

"Then it doesn't matter whether it was a dream or not."

"Oh no, I prefer reality."

With a laugh, she started to drop the pill on the tray, but he stopped her. "Ky—"

"You're hurting," he said again. "I can see it in your eyes. Your medication wore off hours ago, Kate."

"And kept me unconscious for an entire day."

"This is mild, just to take the edge off. Listen—" His hand tightened on hers. "I had to watch you in agony."

"Ky, don't."

"No, you'll do it for me if not for yourself. I had to watch you bleed and faint and drift in and out of consciousness." He ran his hand down her hair, then cupped her face so she'd look directly into his eyes. "I can't tell you what it did to me because I don't know how to describe it. I know I can't watch you in pain anymore."

In silence, she took the pill and drained the glass of

juice. For him, as he said, not for herself. When she swallowed the medication, Ky tugged at her hair. "It hardly has more punch than an aspirin, Kate. Bailey said he'd give you something stronger if you needed it, but he'd rather you go with this."

"It'll be fine. It's really more uncomfortable than painful." It wasn't quite the truth, nor did he believe her, but they both let it lie for the moment. Each of them moved cautiously, afraid to spoil what might have begun to bloom again. Kate glanced down at the empty juice glass. The cold, fresh flavor still lingered on her tongue. "Did Dr. Bailey say when I could dive again?"

"Dive?" Ky's brows rose as he uncovered the plate of bacon, eggs and toast. "Kate, you're not even getting up out of bed for the rest of the week."

"Out of bed?" she repeated. "A week?" She ignored the overloaded plate of food as she gaped at him. "Ky, I was stung by a stingray, not attacked by a shark."

"You were stung by a stingray," he agreed. "And your system was so depleted Bailey almost sent you to a hospital. I realize things might've been rough on you since your father died, but you haven't helped anything by not taking care of yourself."

It was the first time he'd mentioned her father's death, and Kate noted he still expressed no sympathy. "Doctors tend to fuss," she began.

"Bailey doesn't," he interrupted. The anger came back and ran along the edge of his words. "He's a tough, cynical old goat, but he knows his business. Hc told me that you'd apparently worked yourself right to the edge of exhaustion, that your resistance was nil, and that you were a good ten pounds underweight." He held out the fork. "We're going to do something about that, professor. Starting now."

Kate looked down at what had to be four large eggs, scrambled, six slices of bacon and four pieces of toast. "I can see you intend to," she murmured.

"I'm not having you sick." He took her hand again and his grip was firm. "I'm going to take care of you, Kate, whether you like it or not."

She looked back at him in her calm, considering way. "I don't know if I do like it," she decided. "But I suppose we'll both find out."

Ky dipped the fork into the eggs. "Eat."

A smile played at the corners of her mouth. She'd never been pampered in her life and thought it might be entirely too easy to get used to it. "All right, but this time I'll feed myself."

She already knew she'd never finish the entire meal, but for his sake, and the sake of peace, she was determined to deal with half of it. That had been precisely his strategy. If he'd have brought her a smaller portion, she'd have eaten half of that, and have eaten less. He knew her better than either one of them fully realized.

"You're still a wonderful cook," she commented, breaking a piece of bacon in half. "Much better than I."

"If you're good, I might broil up some flounder tonight."

She remembered just how exquisitely he prepared fish. "How good?"

"As good as it takes." He accepted the slice of toast she offered him but dumped on a generous slab of jam.

"Maybe I'll beg some of the hot fudge cake from the Roost."

"Looks like I'll have to be on my best behavior."

"That's the idea."

"Ky..." She was already beginning to poke at her eggs. Had eating always been quite such an effort? "About last night, what happened—"

"Should never have stopped," he finished.

Her lashes swept up, and her eyes were quiet and candid. "I'm not sure."

"I am," he countered. Taking her face in his hands, he kissed her, softly, with only a hint of passion. But the hint was a promise of much more. "Let it be enough for now, Kate. If it has to get complicated, let's wait until other things are a little more settled."

Complicated. Were commitments complicated, the future, promises? She looked down at her plate knowing she simply didn't have the strength to ask or to answer. Not now. "In a way I feel as though I'm slipping back—to that summer four years ago. And yet..."

"It's like a step forward."

Kate looked at him again, but this time reached out. He'd always understood. Though he said little, though his way was sometimes rough, he'd always understood. "Yes. Either way it's a little unnerving."

"I've never liked smooth water. You get a better ride with a few waves."

"Perhaps." She shook her head. Slipping back, stepping forward, it hardly mattered. Either way, she was moving toward him. "Ky, I can't eat any more."

"I figured." Easily, he picked up an extra fork from

the tray and began eating the cooling eggs himself. "It's still probably more than you eat for breakfast in a week."

"Probably," she agreed in a murmur, realizing just how well he'd maneuvered her. Kate lay back against the propped-up pillows, annoyed that she was growing sleepy again. No more medication, she decided silently as Ky polished off their joint breakfast. If she could just avoid that, and go out for a little while, she'd be fine. The trick would be to convince Ky.

Kate looked toward the window, and the sunshine. "I don't want to lose a week's time going over the wreck."

He didn't have to follow the direction of her gaze to follow the direction of her thoughts. "I'll be going down," he said easily. "Tomorrow, the next day anyway." Sooner, he thought to himself, depending on how Kate mended.

"Alone?"

He caught the tone as he bit into the last piece of bacon. "I've gone down alone before."

She would have protested, stating how dangerous it was, if she'd believed it would have done any good. Ky did a great deal alone because that was how he preferred it. Instead, Kate chose another route.

"We're looking for the *Liberty* together, Ky. It isn't a one-man operation."

He sent her a long, quiet look before he picked up the coffee she hadn't touched. "Afraid I'll take off with the treasure?"

"Of course not." She wouldn't allow her emotions to get in the way. "If I hadn't trusted your integrity," she said evenly, "I wouldn't have shown you the chart in the first place."

"Fair enough," he allowed with a nod. "So if I continue to dive while you're recuperating, we won't lose time."

"I don't want to lose you either." It was out before she could stop it. Swearing lightly, Kate looked toward the window again. The sky was the pale blue sometimes seen on summer mornings.

Ky merely sat for a moment while the pleasure of her words rippled through him. "You'd worry about me?"

Angry, Kate turned back. He looked so smug, so infuriatingly content. "No, I wouldn't worry. God usually makes a point of looking after fools."

Grinning, he set the tray on the floor beside the bed. "Maybe I'd like you to worry, a little."

"Sorry I can't oblige you."

"Your voice gets very prim when you're annoyed," he commented. "I like it."

"I'm not prim."

He ran a hand down her loosened hair. No, she looked anything but prim at the moment. Soft and feminine, but not prim. "Your voice is. Like one of those pretty, lacy ladies who used to sit in parlors eating finger sandwiches."

She pushed his hand aside. He wouldn't get around her with charm. "Perhaps I should shout instead."

"Like that too, but more..." He kissed one cheek, then the other. "I like to see you smile at me. The way you smile at nobody else."

Her skin was already beginning to warm. No, he

might not get around her with charm, but…he'd distract her from her point if she wasn't careful. "I'd be bored, that's all. If I have to sit here, hour after hour with nothing to do."

"I've got lots of books." He slipped her nightshirt down her shoulder then kissed her bare skin with the lightest of touches. "Probably lay my hands on some crossword puzzles, too."

"Thanks a lot."

"There's a copy of Byron downstairs."

Despite her determination not to, Kate looked toward him again. "Byron?"

"I bought it after you left. The words are wonderful." He had the three buttons undone with such quick expertise, she never noticed. "But I could always hear the way you'd say them. I remember one night on the beach, when the moon was full on the water. I don't remember the name of the poem, but I remember how it started, and how it sounded when you said it. 'It is the hour'," he began, then smiled at her.

"'It is the hour'," Kate continued, "'when from the boughs the nightingale is heard/It is the hour when lovers' vows seem sweet in every whisper'd word/And gentle winds, and waters near make music to the lonely ear'…" She trailed off, remembering even the scent of that night. "You were never very interested in Byron's technique."

"No matter how hard you tried to explain it to me."

Yes, he was distracting her. Kate was already finding it difficult to remember what point she'd been trying to make. "He was one of the leading poets of his day."

"Hmm." Ky caught the lobe of her ear between his teeth.

"He had a fascination for war and conflict, and yet he had more love affairs in his poems than Shelley or Keats."

"How about out of his poems?"

"There too." She closed her eyes as his tongue began to do outrageous things to her nervous system. "He used humor, satire as well as a pure lyrical style. If he'd ever completed *Don Juan*..." She trailed off with a sigh that edged toward a moan.

"Did I interrupt you?" Ky brushed his fingers down her thigh. "I really love to hear you lecture."

"Yes."

"Good." He traced her lips with his tongue. "I just thought maybe I could give you something to do for a while." He skimmed his hand over her hip then up to the side of her breast. "So you won't be bored by staying in bed. Want to tell me more about Byron?"

With a long quiet breath, she wound her arms around his neck. The point she'd been trying to make didn't seem important any longer. "No, but I might like staying in bed after all, even without the crossword puzzles."

"You'll relax." He said it softly, but the command was unmistakable. She might have argued, but the kiss was long and lingering, leaving her slow and helplessly yielding.

"I don't have a choice," she murmured. "Between the medication and you."

"That's the idea." He'd love her, Ky thought, but so

gently she'd have nothing to do but feel. Then she'd sleep. "There are things I want from you." He lifted his head until their eyes met. "Things I need from you."

"You never tell me what they are."

"Maybe not." He laid his forehead on hers. Maybe he just didn't know how to tell her. Or how to ask. "For now, what I want is to see you well." Again he lifted his head, and his eyes focused on hers. "I'm not an unselfish man, Kate. I want that just as much for myself as I want it for you. I fully intended to have you back in my bed, but I didn't want it for you. I fully intended to have you back in my bed, but I didn't care to have you unconscious here first."

"Whatever you intended, I make my own choices." Her hands slid up his shoulders to touch his face. "I chose to make love with you then. I choose to make love with you now."

He laughed and pressed her palm to his lips. "Professor, you think I'd have given you a choice? Maybe we don't know each other as well as we should at this point, but you should know that much."

Thoughtfully, she ran her thumb down his cheekbone. It was hard, elegantly defined. Somehow it suited him in the same way the unshaven face suited him. But did she? Kate wondered. Were they, despite all their differences, right for each other?

It seemed when they were like this, there was no question of suitability, no question of what was right or wrong. Each completed the other. Yet there had to be more. No matter how much each of them denied it on the surface, there had to be more. And ultimately, there had to be a choice.

"When you take what isn't offered freely, you have nothing." She felt the rough scrape of his unshaven face on her palm and the thrill went through her system. "If I give, you have whatever you need without asking."

"Do I?" he murmured before he touched his lips to hers again. "And you? What do you have?"

She closed her eyes as her body drifted on a calm, quiet plane of pleasure. "What I need."

For how long? The question ran through his mind, prodding against his contentment. But he didn't ask. There'd be a time, he knew, for more questions, for the hundreds of demands he wanted to make. For ultimatums. Now she was sleepy, relaxed in the way he wanted her to be.

With no more words he let her body drift, stroking gently, letting her system steep in the pleasure he could give. With no one else could he remember asking so little for himself and receiving so much. She was the hinge that could open or close the door on the better part of him.

He listened to her sigh as he touched her. The second was a kind of pure contentment that mirrored his own feelings. It seemed neither of them required any more.

Kate knew it shouldn't be so simple. It had never been simple with anyone else, so that in the end she'd never given herself to anyone else. Only with Ky had she ever known that full excitement that left her free. Only with Ky had she ever known the pure ease that felt so right.

They'd been apart four years, yet if it had been forty, she would have recognized his touch in an instant. That touch was all she needed to make her want him.

She remembered the demands and fire that had always been threaded through their lovemaking before. It had been the excitement she'd craved even while it had baffled her. Now there was patience touched with a consideration she didn't know he was capable of.

Perhaps if she hadn't loved him already, she would have fallen in love at that moment when the sun filtered through the windows and his hands were on her skin. She wanted to give him the fire, but his hands kept it banked. She wanted to meet any demands, but he made none. Instead, she floated on the clouds he brought to her.

Though the heat smoldered inside him, she kept him sane. Just by her pliancy. Though passion began to take over, she kept him calm. Just by her serenity. He'd never looked for serenity in his life. It had simply come to him, as Kate had. He'd never understood what it meant to be calm, but he had known the emptiness and the chaos of living without it.

Without urgency or force, he slipped inside her. Slowly, with a sweetness that made her weak, he gave her the ultimate gift. Passion, fulfillment, with the softer emotions covering a need that seemed insatiable.

Then she slept, and he left her to her dreams.

When she awoke again, Kate wasn't groggy, but weak. Even as sleep cleared, a sense of helpless annoyance went though her. It was midafternoon. She didn't need a clock, the angle of the sunlight that slanted through the window across from the bed told her what time it was. More hours had been lost without her knowledge. And where was Ky?

Kate groped for her nightshirt and slipped into it. If he followed his pattern, he'd be popping through the door with a loaded lunch tray and a pill. Not this time, Kate determined as she eased herself out of bed. Nothing else was going into her system that made her lose time.

But as she stood, the dregs of the medication swam in her head. Reflexively, she nearly sat again before she stopped herself. Infuriated, she gripped the bedpost, breathed deeply then put her weight on her injured foot. It took the pain to clear her head.

Pain had its uses, she thought grimly. After she'd given the hurt a moment to subside, it eased into a throb. That could be tolerated, she told herself and walked to the mirror over Ky's dresser.

She didn't like what she saw. Her hair was listless, her face washed-out and her eyes dull. Swearing, she put her hands to her cheeks and rubbed as though she could force color into them. What she needed, Kate decided, was a hot shower, a shampoo and some fresh air. Regardless of what Ky thought, she was going to have them.

Taking a deep breath, she headed for the door. Even as she reached for the knob, it opened.

"What're you doing up?"

Though they were precisely the words she'd expected, Kate had expected them from Ky, not Linda. "I was just—"

"Do you want Ky to skin me alive?" Linda demanded, backing Kate toward the bed with a tray of steaming soup in her hand. "Listen, you're supposed to rest and eat, then eat and rest. Orders."

Realizing abruptly that she was retreating, Kate held her ground. "Whose?"

"Ky's. And," she continued before Kate could retort, "Dr. Bailey's."

"I don't have to take orders from either of them."

"Maybe you don't," Linda agreed dryly. "But I don't argue with a man who's protecting his woman, or with the man who poked a needle into my bottom when I was three. Both of them can be nasty. Now lie down."

"Linda..." Though she knew the sigh sounded long suffering, Kate couldn't prevent it. "I've a cut on my leg. I've been in bed for something like forty-eight hours straight. If I don't have a shower and a breath of air soon, I'm going to go crazy."

A smile tugged at Linda's mouth that she partially concealed by nibbling on her lower lip. "A bit grumpy, are we?"

"I can be more than a bit." This time the sigh was simply bad tempered. "Look at me!" Kate demanded, tugging on her hair. "I feel as though I've just crawled out from under a rock."

"Okay. I know how I felt after I'd delivered Hope. After I'd had my cuddle with her I wanted a shower and shampoo so bad I was close to tears." She set the tray on the table beside the bed. "You can have ten minutes in the shower, then you can eat while I change your bandage. But Ky made me swear I'd make you eat every bite." She put her hands on her hips. "So that's the deal."

"He's overreacting," Kate began. "It's absurd. I don't need to be babied this way."

"Tell me that when you don't look like I could blow you over. Now come on, I'll give you a hand in the shower."

"No, damn it, I'm perfectly capable of taking a shower by myself." Ignoring the pain in her leg, she stormed out of the room, slamming the door at her back. Linda swallowed a laugh and sat down on the bed to wait.

Fifteen minutes later, refreshed and thoroughly ashamed of herself, Kate came back in. Wrapped in Ky's robe, she rubbed a towel over her hair. "Linda—"

"Don't apologize. If I'd been stuck in bed for two days, I'd snap at the first person who gave me trouble. Besides—" Linda knew how to play her cards "—if you're really sorry you'll eat all your soup, so Ky won't yell at me."

"All right." Resigned, Kate sat back in the bed and took the tray on her lap. She swallowed the first bite of soup and stifled her objection as Linda began to fiddle with her bandage. "It's wonderful."

"The seafood chowder's one of our specialties. Oh, honey." Linda's eyes darkened with concern after she removed the gauze. "This must've hurt like hell. No wonder Ky's been frantic."

Drumming up her courage, Kate leaned over enough to look at the wound. There was no inflammation as she'd feared, no puffiness. Though the slice was six inches in length, it was clean. Her stomach muscles unknotted. "It's not so bad," she murmured. "There's no infection."

"Look, I've been caught by a stingray, a small one. I probably had a cut half an inch across and I cried like a baby. Don't tell me it's not so bad."

"Well, I slept through most of it." She winced, then deliberately relaxed her muscles.

Linda narrowed her eyes as she studied Kate's face. "Ky said you should have a pill if there was any pain when you woke."

"If you want to do me a favor, you can dump them out." Calmly, Kate ate another spoonful of soup. "I really hate to argue with him, or with you, but I'm not taking any more pills and losing any more time. I appreciate the fact that he wants to pamper me. It's unexpectedly sweet, but I can only take it so far."

"He's worried about you. He feels responsible."

"For my carelessness?" With a shake of her head, Kate concentrated on finishing the soup. "It was an accident, and if there's blame, it's mine. I was so wrapped up in looking for salvage I didn't take basic precautions. I practically bumped into the ray." With an effort, she controlled a shudder. "Ky acted much more quickly than I. He'd already started to pull me out of range. If he hadn't, things would have been much more serious."

"He loves you."

Kate's fingers tightened on the spoon. With exaggerated care, she set it back on the tray. "Linda, there's a vast difference between concern, attraction, even affection and love."

Linda simply nodded in agreement. "Yes. I said Ky loves you."

She managed to smile and pick up the tea that had been cooling beside the soup. *"You* said," Kate returned simply. *"Ky* hasn't."

"Well neither did Marsh until I was ready to strangle him, but that didn't stop me."

"I'm not you." Kate lay back against the pillows, grateful that most of the weakness and the weariness had passed. "And Ky isn't Marsh."

Impatient, Linda rose and swirled around the room. "People who complicate simple things make me so mad!"

Smiling, Kate sipped her tea. "Others simplify the complicated."

With a sniff, Linda turned back. "I've known Ky Silver all my life. I watched him bounce around from one cute girl to the next, then one attractive woman to another until I lost count. Then you came along." Stopping, she leaned against the bedpost. "It was as if someone had hit him over the head with a blunt instrument. You dazed him, Kate, almost from the first minute. You fascinated him."

"Dazing, fascinating." Kate shrugged while she tried to ignore the ache in her heart. "Flattering, I suppose, but neither of those things equals love."

The stubborn line came and went between Linda's brows. "I don't believe love comes in an instant, it grows. If you could have seen the way Ky was after you left four years ago, you'd know—"

"Don't tell me about four years ago," Kate interrupted. "What happened four years ago is over. Ky and I are two different people today, with different expectations. This time…" She took a deep breath. "This time when it ends, I won't be hurt because I know the limits."

"You've just gotten back together and you're already talking about endings and limitations!" Dragging a hand through her hair, Linda came forward to sit on the edge of the bed. "What's wrong with you? Don't you know how to wish anymore? How to dream?"

"I was never very good at either. Linda…" She hesitated, wanting to choose her phrasing carefully. "I don't want to expect any more from Ky than what he can easily give. After August, I know we'll each go back to our separate worlds—there's no bridge between them. Maybe I was meant to come back so we could make up for whatever pain we caused each other before. This time I want to leave still being friends. He's…" She hesitated again because this phrasing was even more important. "He's always been a very important part of my life."

Linda waited a moment, then narrowed her eyes. "That's about the dumbest thing I've ever heard."

Despite herself, Kate laughed. "Linda—"

Holding up her hands, she shook her head and cut Kate off. "No, I can't talk about it anymore, I get too mad and I'm supposed to be taking care of you." She let out her breath on a huff as she removed Kate's tray. "I just can't understand how anyone so smart could be so stupid, but the more I think about it the more I can see that you and Ky deserve each other."

"That sounds more like an insult than a compliment."

"It was."

Kate pushed her tongue against her teeth to hold back a smile. "I see."

"Don't look so smug just because you've made me so angry I don't want to talk about it anymore." She drew her shoulders back. "I might just give Ky a piece of my mind when he gets home."

"That's his problem," Kate said cheerfully. "Where'd he go?"

"Diving."

Amusement faded. "Alone?"

"There's no use worrying about it." Linda spoke briskly as she cursed herself for not thinking of a simple lie. "He dives alone ninety percent of the time."

"I know." But Kate folded her hands, preparing to worry until he returned.

Chapter 9

"I'm going with you."

The sunlight was strong, the scent of the ocean pure. Through the screen the sound of gulls from a quarter of a mile away could be heard clearly. Ky turned from the stove where he poured the last cup of coffee and eyed Kate as she stood in the doorway.

She'd pinned her hair up and had dressed in thin cotton pants and a shirt, both of which were baggy and cool. It occured to him that she looked more like a student than a college professor.

He knew enough of women and their illusions to see that she'd added color to her cheeks. She hadn't needed blusher the evening before when he'd returned from the wreck. Then she had been angry, and passionate. He nearly smiled as he lifted his cup.

"You wasted your time getting dressed," he said easily. "You're going back to bed."

Kate disliked stubborn people, people who demanded their own way flatly and unreasonably. At that moment, she decided they were *both* stubborn. "No." On the surface she remained as calm as he was while she walked into the kitchen. "I'm going with you."

Unlike Kate, Ky never minded a good argument. Preparing for one, he leaned back against the stove. "I don't take down a diver against doctor's orders."

She'd expected that. With a shrug, she opened the refrigerator and took out a bottle of juice. She knew she was being bad tempered, and though it was completely out of character, she was enjoying the experience. The simple truth was that she had to do something or go mad.

As far as she could remember, she'd never spent two more listless days. She had to move, think, feel the sun. It might have been satisfying to stomp her feet and demand, but, she thought, fruitless. If she had to compromise to get her way, then compromise she would.

"I can rent a boat and equipment and go down on my own." With the glass in hand, she turned, challenging. "You can't stop me."

"Try me."

It was said simply, quietly, but she'd seen the flare of anger in his eyes. Better, she thought. Much better. "I've a right to do precisely as I choose. We both know it." Perhaps her leg was uncomfortable, but as to the rest of her body, it was charged up and ready to move. Nor was there anything wrong with her mind. Kate had plotted her strategy very well. After all, she thought grimly, there'd certainly been enough time to think it through.

"We both know you're not in any shape to dive." His first urge was to carry her back to bed, his second to shake her until she rattled. Ky did neither, only drank his coffee and watched her over the rim. A power struggle wasn't something he'd expected, but he wouldn't back away from it. "You're not stupid, Kate. You know you can't go down yet, and you know I won't let you."

"I've rested for two days. I feel fine." As she walked toward him she was pleased to see him frown. He understood she had a mind of her own, and that he had to deal with it. The truth was, she was stronger than either of them had expected her to be. "As far as diving goes, I'm willing to leave that to you for the next couple of days, but..." She paused, wanting to be certain he knew she was negotiating, not conceding. "I'm going out on the *Vortex* with you. And I'm going out this morning."

He lifted a brow. She'd never intended to dive, but she'd used it as a pressure point to get what she wanted. He couldn't blame her. Ky remembered recovering from a broken leg when he was fourteen. The pain was vague in his mind now, but the boredom was still perfectly clear. "You'll lie down in the cabin when you're told."

She smiled and shook her head. "I'll lie down in the cabin if I need to."

He took her chin in his hand and squeezed. "Damn right you will. Okay, let's go. I want an early start."

Once he was resigned, Ky moved quickly. She could either keep up, or be left behind. Within minutes he parked his car near his slip at Silver Lake Harbor and was boarding the *Vortex*. Content, Kate took a seat beside him at the helm and prepared to enjoy the sun and the wind. Already she felt the energy begin to churn.

"I've done a chart of the wreck as of yesterday's dive," he told her as he maneuvered out of the harbor.

"A chart?" Automatically she pushed at her hair as she turned toward him. "You didn't show me."

"Because you were asleep when I finished it."

"I've been asleep ninety percent of the time," she mumbled.

As he headed out to sea, Ky laid a hand on her shoulder. "You look better, Kate, no shadows. No strain. That's more important."

For a moment, just a moment, she pressed her cheek against his hand. Few women could resist such soft concern, and yet...she didn't want his concern to cloud their reason for being together. Concern could turn to pity. She needed him to see her as a partner, as equal. As long as she was his lover, it was vital that they meet on the same ground. Then when she left... When she left there'd be no regrets.

"I don't need to be pampered anymore, Ky."

His shoulders moved as he glanced at the compass. "I enjoyed it."

She was resisting being cared for. He understood it, appreciated it and regretted it. There had been something appealing about seeing to her needs, about having her depend on him. He didn't know how to tell her he wanted her to be well and strong just as much as he wanted her to turn to him in times of need.

Somehow, he felt their time together had been too short for him to speak. He didn't deal well with caution. As a diver, he knew its importance, but as a man... As a man he fretted to go with his instincts, with his impulses.

His fingers brushed her neck briefly before he turned to the wheel. He'd already decided he'd have to approach his relationship with Kate as he'd approach a very deep, very dangerous dive—with an eye on currents, pressure and the unexpected.

"That chart's in the cabin," he told her as he cut the engine. "You might want to look it over while I'm down."

She agreed with a nod, but the restlessness was already on her as Ky began to don his equipment. She didn't want to make an issue of his diving alone. He wouldn't listen to her in any case; if anything came of it, it would only be an argument. In silence she watched him check his tanks. He'd be down for an hour. Kate was already marking time.

"There are cold drinks in the galley." He adjusted the strap of his mask before climbing over the side. "Don't sit in the sun too long."

"Be careful," she blurted out before she could stop herself.

Ky grinned, then was gone with a quiet splash.

Though she ran over to the side, Kate was too late to watch him dive. For a long time after, she simply leaned over the boat, staring at the water's surface. She imagined Ky going deeper, deeper, adjusting his pressure, moving out with power until he'd reached the bottom and the wreck.

He'd brought back the bowl and ladle the evening before. They sat on the dresser in his bedroom while the broken rigging and pieces of crockery were stored downstairs. Thus far he'd done no more than gather what they'd already found together, but today, Kate thought with a twinge of impatience, he'd extend the search. Whatever he found, he'd find alone.

She turned away from the water, frustrated that she was excluded. It occurred to her that all her life she'd been an onlooker, someone who analyzed and explained the action rather than causing it. This search had been her first opportunity to change that, and now she was back to square one.

Stuffing her hands in her pockets, Kate looked up at the sky. There were clouds to the west, but they were thin and white. Harmless. She felt too much like that herself at the moment—something unsubstantial. Sighing, she went below deck. There was nothing to do now but wait.

Ky found two more cannons and sent up buoys to mark their position. It would be possible, if he didn't find something more concrete, to salvage the cannons and have them dated by an expert. Though he swam from end to end, searching carefully, he knew it was unlikely he'd find a date stamp through the layers of corrosion. But in time… Satisfied, he swam north.

If he accomplished nothing else on this dive, he wanted to establish the size of the site. With luck it would be fairly small, perhaps no bigger than a football field. However, there was always the chance that the wreckage could be scattered over several square miles. Before they brought in a salvage ship, he wanted to take a great deal of care with the preliminary work.

They would need tools. A metal detector would be invaluable. Thus far, they'd done no more than find a wreck, no matter how certain Kate was that it was the *Liberty*. For the moment he had no way to determine the origin of the ship, he had to find cargo. Once he'd found that, perhaps treasure would follow.

Once he'd found the treasure… Would she leave? Would she take her share of the gold and the artifacts and drive home?

Not if he could help it, Ky determined as he shone his headlamp over the sea floor. When the search was over and they'd salvaged what could be salvaged from the sea, it would be time to salvage what they'd once had—what had perhaps never truly been lost. If they could find what had been buried for centuries, they could find what had been buried for four years.

He couldn't find much without tools. Most of the ship—or what remained of it—was buried under silt. On another dive, he'd use the prop-wash, the excavation device he'd constructed in his shop. With that he could blow away inches of sediment at a time—a slow but safe way to uncover artifacts. But someone would have to stay on board to run it.

He thought of Kate and rejected the idea immediately. Though he had no doubt she could handle the technical aspect—it would only have to be explained to her once—she'd never go for it. Ky began to think it was time they enlisted Marsh.

He knew his air time was almost up and he'd have to surface for fresh tanks. Still, he lingered near the bottom, searching, prodding. He wanted to take something up for Kate, something tangible that would put the enthusiasm back in her eyes.

It took him more than half of his allotted time to find it, but when Ky held the unbroken bottle in his hand, he knew Kate's reaction would be worth the effort. It was a common bottle, not priceless crystal, but he could see no mold marks, which meant it had been hand blown. Crust was weathered over it in layers, but Ky took the time to carefully chip some away, from the bottom only. If the date wasn't on the bottom, he'd need the crust to have the bottle dated. Already he was thinking of the Corning Glass Museum and their rate of success.

Then he saw the date, and with a satisfied grin placed the find in the goodie bag on his belt. With his air supply running short, he started toward the surface.

His hour was up. Or so nearly up, Kate thought, that he should have surfaced already if he'd allowed himself any safety factor. She paced from port to starboard and back again. Would he always risk his own welfare to the limit?

She'd long since given up sitting quietly in the cabin, going over the makeshift chart Ky had begun. She'd found a book on shipwrecks that Ky had obviously purchased recently, and though it had also been among her father's research books, she'd skimmed through it again.

It gave a detailed guide to identifying and excavating a wreck, listed common mistakes and hazards. She found it difficult to read about hazards while Ky was alone beneath the surface. Still, even the simple language of the book couldn't disguise the adventure. For perhaps half the time Ky had been gone, she'd lost herself in it. Spanish galleons, Dutch merchant ships, English frigates.

She'd found the list of wrecks off North Carolina alone extensive. But these, she'd thought, had already been located, documented. The adventure there was over. One day, because of the chain her father had started and she'd continued, the *Liberty* would be among them.

Fretfully, Kate waited for Ky to surface. She thought of her father. He'd pored over this same book as well—planning, calculating. Yet his calculations hadn't taken him beyond the initial stage. If he'd shared his goal with her, would he have taken her on his summer quests? She'd never know, because she'd never been given the choice.

She was making her own choices now, Kate mused. Her first had been to return to Ocracoke, accepting the consequences. Her next had been to give herself to Ky without conditions. Her last, she thought as she stared down at the quiet water, would be to leave him again. Yet, in reality, perhaps she'd still been given no choice. It was all a matter of currents. She could only swim against them for so long.

Relief washed over her when she spotted the flow of

bubbles. Ky grabbed the bottom rung of the ladder as he pushed up his mask. "Waiting for me?"

Relief mixed with annoyance for the time she'd spent worrying about him. "You cut it close."

"Yeah, a little." He passed up his tanks. "I had to stop and get you a present."

"It's not a joke, Ky." Kate watched him come over the side, agile, lean and energetic. "You'd be furious with me if I'd cut my time that close."

"Leave it up to Linda to fuss," he advised as he pulled down the zipper of his wet suit. "She was born that way." Then he grabbed her, crushing her against him so that she felt the excitement he'd brought up with him. His mouth closed over hers, tasting of salt from the sea. Because he was wet, her clothes clung to him, binding them together for the brief instant he held her. But when he would have released her, she held fast, drawing the kiss out into something that warmed his cool skin.

"I worry about you, Ky." For one last moment, she held on fiercely. "Damn it, is that what you want to hear?"

"No." He took her face in his hands and shook his head. "No."

Kate broke away, afraid she'd say too much, afraid she'd say things neither of them were ready to hear. She knew the rules this time. She groped for something calm, something simple. "I suppose I got a bit frantic waiting up here. It's different when you're down."

"Yeah." What did she want from him? he wondered. Why was it that every time she started to show her concern for him, she clammed up? "I've got some more things to add to the chart."

"I saw the buoys you sent up." Kate moistened her lips and relaxed, muscle by muscle.

"Two more cannons. From the size of them, I'd say she was a fairly small ship. It's unlikely she was constructed for battle."

"She was a merchant ship."

"Maybe. I'm going to take the metal detector down and see what I come up with. From the stuff we've found, I don't think she's buried too deep."

Kate nodded. Delve into business, keep the personal aspect light. "I'd like to send off a piece of the planking and some of the glass to be analyzed. I think we'll have more luck with the glass, but it doesn't hurt to cover all the angles."

"No, it doesn't. Don't you want your present?"

At ease again, she smiled. "I thought you were joking. Did you bring me a shell?"

"I thought you'd like this better." Reaching into his bag, Ky brought out the bottle. "It's too bad it's not still corked. We could've had wine with peanut butter."

"Oh, Ky, it's not damaged!" Thrilled, she reached out for it, but he pulled it back out of reach and grinned.

"Bottoms up," he told her and turned the bottle upside down.

Kate stared at the smeared bottom of the bottle. "Oh, God," she whispered. "It's dated. 1749." Gingerly, she took the bottle in both hands. "The year before the *Liberty* sank."

"It's another ship, maybe," Ky reminded her. "But it does narrow down the time element."

"Over two hundred years," she murmured. "Glass, it's so breakable, so vulnerable, and yet it survived two centuries." Her eyes lit with enthusiasm as she looked back at him. "Ky, we should be able to find out where the bottle was made."

"Probably, but most glass bottles found on wrecks from the seventeenth and eighteenth century were manufactured in England anyway. It wouldn't prove the ship was English."

She let out a huff of breath, but her energy hadn't dimmed. "You've been doing your research."

"I don't go into any project until I know the angles." Ky knelt down to check the fresh tanks.

"You're going back down now?"

"I want to get as much mapped out as I can before we start dealing with too much equipment."

She'd done enough homework herself to know that the most common mistake of the modern day salvor was in failing to map out a site. Yet she couldn't stem her impatience. It seemed so time-consuming when they could be concentrating on getting under the layers of silt.

It seemed to her that she and Ky had changed positions somehow. She'd always been the cautious one, proceeding step by logical step, while he'd taken the risks. Struggling with the impotence of having to wait and watch, she stood back while he strapped on the fresh tanks. As she watched, Ky picked up a brass rod.

"What's that for?"

"It's the base for this." He held out a device that resembled a compass. "It's called an azimuth circle. It's a cheap, effective way to map out the site. I drive this into the approximate center of the wreck so that it becomes the datum point, align the circle with the magnetic north, then I use a length of chain to measure the distance to the cannons, or whatever I need to map. After I get it set, I'll be back up for the metal detector."

Frustration built again. He was doing all the work while she simply stood still. "Ky, I feel fine. I could help if—"

"No." He didn't bother to argue or list reasons. He simply went over the side and under.

It was midafternoon when they started back. Ky spent the last hour at sea adding to the chart, putting in the information he'd gathered that day. He'd brought more up in his goodie bag—a tankard, spoons and forks that might have been made of iron. It seemed they had indeed found the galley. Kate decided she'd begin a detailed list of their finds that evening. If it was all she could do at the moment, she'd do it with pleasure.

Her mood had lifted a bit since she'd caught three good-sized bluefish while Ky had been down at the wreck the second time. No matter how much Ky argued, she fully intended to cook them herself and eat them sitting at the table, not lying in bed.

"Pretty pleased with yourself, aren't you?"

She gave him a cool smile. They were cruising back toward Silver Lake Harbor and though she felt a weariness, it was a pleasant feeling, not the dragging fatigue of the past days. "Three bluefish in that amount of time's a very respectable haul."

"No argument there. Especially since I intend to eat half of them."

"I'm going to grill them."

"Are you?"

She met his lifted brow with a neutral look. "I caught, I cook."

Ky kept the boat at an even speed as he studied her. She looked a bit tired, but he thought he could convince her to take a nap if he claimed he wanted one himself. She was healing quickly. And she was right. He couldn't pamper her. "I could probably bring myself to start the charcoal for you."

"Fair enough. I'll even let you clean them."

He laughed at the bland tone and ruffled her hair until the pins fell out.

"Ky!" Automatically, Kate reached up to repair the damage.

"Wear it up in the school room," he advised, tossing some of the pins overboard. "I find it difficult to resist you when your hair's down and just a bit mussed."

"Is that so?" She debated being annoyed, then decided there were more productive ways to pass the time. Kate let the wind toss her hair as she moved closer to him so that their bodies touched. She smiled at the quick look of surprise in his eyes as she slipped both hands under his T-shirt. "Why don't you turn off the engine and show me what happens when you stop resisting?"

For all her generosity and freedom in lovemaking,

she'd never been the initiator. Ky found himself both baffled and aroused as she smiled up at him, her hands stroking slowly over his chest. "You know what happens when I stop resisting," he murmured.

She gave a low, quiet laugh. "Refresh my memory." Without waiting for an answer, she drew back on the throttle herself until the boat was simply idling. "You didn't make love with me last night." Her hands slid around and up his back.

"You were sleeping." She was seducing him in the middle of the afternoon, in the middle of the ocean. He found he wanted to savor the new experience as much as he wanted to bring it to fruition.

"I'm not sleeping now." Rising on her toes, she brushed her lips over his, lightly, temptingly. She felt his heartbeat race against her body and reveled in a sense of power she'd never explored. "Or perhaps you're in a hurry to get back, and uh, clean fish."

She was taunting him. Why had he never seen the witch in her before? Ky felt his stomach knot with need, but when he drew her closer, she resisted. Just slightly. Just enough to torment. "If I make love with you now, I won't be gentle."

She kept her lips inches from his. "Is that a warning?" she whispered. "Or a promise?"

He felt the first tremor move through him and was astonished. Not even for her had he ever trembled. Not even for her. The need grew, stretching restlessly, recklessly. "I'm not sure you know what you're doing, Kate."

Nor did she, but she smiled because it no longer mattered. Only the outcome mattered. "Come down to the cabin with me and we'll both find out." She slipped away from him and without a word disappeared below deck.

His hand wasn't steady when he reached for the key to turn off the engines. He needed a moment, perhaps a bit more, to regain the control he'd held so carefully since they'd become lovers again. Ever since he'd had her blood on his hands, he had a tremendous fear of hurting her. Since he'd had a taste of her again, he had an equal fear of driving her away. Caution was a strain, but he'd kept it in focus with sheer will. As Ky started down the steps, he told himself he'd continue to be cautious.

She'd unbuttoned her blouse but hadn't removed it. When he came into the narrow cabin with her, Kate smiled. She was afraid, though she hardly knew why. But over the fear was a heady sense of power and strength that fought for full release. She wanted to take him to the edge, to push him to the limits of passion. At that moment, she was certain she could.

When he came no closer to her, Kate stepped forward and pulled his shirt over his head. "Your skin's gold," she murmured. "It's always excited me." Taking her pleasure slowly, she ran her hands up his sides, feeling the quiver she caused. "You've always excited me."

Her hands were steady, her pulse throbbed as she unsnapped his cut-offs. With her eyes on his, she slowly, slowly, undressed him. "No one's ever made me want the way you make me want."

He had to stop her and take control again. She couldn't know the effect of those long, fragile fingers when they brushed easily over his skin, or how her calm eyes made him rage inside.

"Kate..." He took her hands in his and bent to kiss her. But she turned her head, meeting his neck with warm lips that sent a spear of fire up his spine.

Then her body was pressed against his, flesh meeting flesh where her blouse parted. Her mouth trailed over his chest, her hands down his back to his hips. He felt the fury of desire whip through him as though it had sharp, hungry teeth.

So he forgot control, gentleness, vulnerability. She drove him to forget. She intended to.

They were tangled on the narrow bunk, her blouse halfway down her back and parted so that her breasts pushed into his chest, driving him mad with their firm, subtle curves. She nipped at his lips, demanding, pushing for more, still more. Waves of passion overtook them.

His need was incendiary. She was like a flame, impossible to hold, searing here, singeing there until his body was burning with needs and fierce fantasies.

Her hands were swift, sending sharp gasping pleasure everywhere at once until he wasn't sure he could take it anymore. Yet he no longer thought of stopping her. Less of stopping himself.

His hands gripped her with an urgency that made her moan from the sheer strength in them. She wanted his strength now—mindless strength that would carry them both to a place they'd never gone before. And she was leading. The knowledge made her laugh aloud as she tasted his skin, his lips, his tongue.

She slid down his body, feeling each jolt of pleasure as it shot through him. There could be no slow, lingering loving now. They'd pushed each other beyond reason. The air here was dark and thin and whirling with sound. Kate drank it in.

When he found her moist, hot and ready she let him take her over peak after shuddering peak, knowing as he drove her, she drove him. Her body was filled with sensations that came and went like comets, slipped away and burst on her again, and again. Through the thunder in her head she heard herself say his name, clear and quick.

On the sound, she took him into her and welcomed the madness.

Chapter 10

She was wrong.

Kate had thought she'd be ready, even anxious to dive again. There hadn't been a day during her recuperation that she hadn't thought of going down. Every time Ky had brought back an artifact, she was thrilled with the discovery and frustrated with her own lack of participation. Like a schoolgirl approaching summer, she'd begun to count the days.

Now, a week after the accident, Kate stood on the deck of the *Vortex* with her mouth dry and her hands trembling as she pulled on her wet suit. She could only be grateful that Ky was already over the side, hooking up his home-rigged prop-wash to the boat's propeller. Drafted to the crew, Marsh stood at the stern watching his brother. With Linda's eager support, he'd agreed to give Ky a few hours a day of his precious free time while he was needed.

Kate took the moment she had alone to gather her thoughts and her nerve.

It was only natural to be anxious about diving after the experience she'd had. Kate told herself that was logical. But it didn't stop her hands from trembling as she zipped up her suit. She could equate it with falling off a horse and having to mount again. It was psychological. But it didn't ease the painful tension in her stomach.

Trembling hands and nerves. With or without them she told herself as she hooked on her weight belt, she was going down. Nothing, not even her own fears, was going to stop her from finishing what she'd begun.

"He's got it," Marsh called out when Ky signaled him.

"I'll be ready." Kate picked up the cloth bag she'd use to bring up small artifacts. With luck, and if the prop-wash did its job, she knew they'd soon need more sophisticated methods to bring up the salvage.

"Kate."

She didn't look up, but continued to hook on the goodie bag. "Yes?"

"You know it's only natural that you'd be nervous going down." Marsh touched a hand to her shoulder, but she busied herself by strapping on her diving knife. "If you want a little more time, I'll work with Ky and you can run the wash."

"No." She said it too quickly, then cursed herself. "It's all right, Marsh." With forced calm she hung the underwater camera she'd purchased only the day before around her neck. "I have to take the first dive sometime."

"It doesn't have to be now."

She smiled at him again thinking how calm, how steady he appeared when compared to Ky. This was the sort of man it would have made sense for her to be attracted to. Confused emotions made no sense. "Yes, it does. Please." She put her hand on his arm before he could speak again. "Don't say anything to Ky."

Did she think he'd have to? Marsh wondered as he inclined his head in agreement. Unless he was way off the mark, Marsh was certain Ky knew every expression, every gesture, every intonation of her voice.

"Let's run it a couple of minutes at full throttle." Ky climbed over the side, dripping and eager. "With the depth and the size of the prop, we're going to have to test the effect. There might not be enough power to do us any good."

In agreement, Marsh went to the helm. "Are you thinking about using an air lift?"

Ky's only answer was a noncommittal grunt. He had thought of it. The metal tube with its stream of compressed air was a quick, efficient way to excavate on silty bottoms. They might get away with the use of a small air lift, if it became necessary. But perhaps the prop-wash would do the job well enough. Either way, he was thinking more seriously about a bigger ship, with more sophisticated equipment and more power. As he saw it, it all depended on what they found today.

He picked up one last piece of equipment—a small powerful spear gun. He'd take no more chances with Kate.

"Okay, slow it down to the minimum," he ordered.

"And keep it there. Once Kate and I are down, we don't want the prop-wash shooting cannonballs around."

Kate stopped the deep breathing she was using to ease tension. Her voice was cool and steady. "Would it have that kind of power?"

"Not at this speed." Ky adjusted his mask then took her hand. "Ready?"

"Yes."

Then he kissed her, hard. "You've got guts, professor," he murmured. His eyes were dark, intense as they passed over her face. "It's one of the sexiest things about you." With this he was over the side.

He knew. Kate gave a quiet unsteady sigh as she started down the ladder. He knew she was afraid, and that had been his way of giving her support. She looked up once and saw Marsh. He lifted his hand in salute. Throat dry, nerves jumping, Kate let the sea take her.

She felt a moment's panic, a complete disorientation the moment she was submerged. It ran through her head that down here, she was helpless. The deeper she went, the more vulnerable she became. Choking for air, she kicked back toward the surface and the light.

Then Ky had her hands, holding her to him, holding her under. His grip was firm, stilling the first panic. Feeling the wild race of her pulse, he held on during her first resistance.

Then he touched her cheek, waiting until she'd calmed enough to look at him. In his eyes she saw strength and challenge. Pride alone forced her to fight her way beyond the fear and meet him, equal to equal.

When she'd regulated her breathing, accepting that

her air came through the tanks on her back, he kissed the back of her hand. Kate felt the tension give. She wouldn't be helpless, she reminded herself. She'd be careful.

With a nod, she pointed down, indicating she was ready to dive. Keeping hands linked, they started toward the bottom.

The whirlpool action created by the wash of the prop had already blasted away some of the sediment. At first glance Ky could see that if the wreck was buried under more than a few feet, they'd need something stronger than his home-made apparatus and single prop engine. But for now, it would do. Patience, which came to him only with deliberate effort, was more important at this stage than speed. With the wreck, he thought, and—he glanced over at the woman beside him—with a great deal more. He had to take care not to hurry.

It was still working, blowing away some of the overburden at a rate Ky figured would equal an inch per minute. He and Kate alone couldn't deal with any more speed. He watched the swirl of water and sediment while she swam a few feet away to catalog one of the cannons on film. When she came closer, he grinned as she placed the camera in front of her face again. She was relaxed, her initial fear forgotten. He could see it simply in the way she moved. Then she let the camera fall so they could begin the search again.

Kate saw something solid wash away from the hole being created by the whirl of water. Grabbing it up, she found herself holding a candlestick. In her excitement, she turned it over and over in her hand.

Silver? she wondered with a rush of adrenaline. Had they found their first real treasure? It was black with oxidation, so it was impossible to be certain what it was made of. Still, it thrilled her. After days and days of only waiting, she was again pursuing the dream.

When she looked up, Ky was already gathering the uncovered items and laying them in the mesh basket. There were more candleholders, more tableware, but not the plain unglazed pottery they'd found before. Kate's pulse began to drum with excitement while she meticulously snapped pictures. They'd be able to find a hallmark, she was certain of it. Then they'd know if they had indeed found a British ship. Ordinary seamen didn't use silver, or even pewter table service. They'd uncovered more than the galley now. And they were just beginning.

When Ky found the first piece of porcelain he signaled to her. True, the vase—if that's what it once had been—had suffered under the water pressure and the years. It was broken so that only half of the shell remained, but so did the manufacturer's mark.

When Kate read it, she gripped Ky's arm. *Whieldon.* English. The master potter who'd trained the likes of Wedgwood. Kate cupped the broken fragment in her hands as though it were alive. When she lifted her eyes to Ky's they were filled with triumph.

Fretting against her inability to speak, Kate pointed to the mark again. Ky merely nodded and indicated the basket. Though she was loath to part with it, Kate found herself even more eager to discover more. She settled the porcelain in the mesh. When she swam back, Ky's hands were filled with other pieces. Some were hardly more than shards, others were identifiable as pieces left from bowls or lids.

No, it didn't prove it was a merchant ship, Kate told herself as she gathered what she could herself. So far, it only proved that the officers and perhaps some passengers had eaten elegantly on their way to the New World. English officers, she reminded herself. In her mind they'd taken the identification that far.

The force of the wash sent an object shooting up. Ky reached out for it and found a crusted, filthy pot he guessed would have been used for tea or coffee. Perhaps it was cracked under the layers, but it held together in his hands. He tapped on his tank to get Kate's attention.

She knew it was priceless the moment she saw it. Stemming impatience, she signaled for Ky to hold it out as she lifted the camera again. Obliging, he crossed his legs like a genie and posed.

It made her giggle. They'd perhaps just found something worth thousands of dollars, but he could still act silly. Nothing was too serious for Ky. As she brought him into frame, Kate felt the same foolish pleasure. She'd known the hunt would be exciting, perhaps rewarding, but she'd never known it would be fun. She swam forward and reached for the pot herself.

Running her fingers over it, she could detect some kind of design under the crust. Not ordinary pottery, she was sure. Not utility-ware. She held something elegant, something well crafted.

He understood its worth as well as she. Taking it from her, Ky indicated they would bring it and the rest of the morning's salvage to the surface. Pointing to his watch he showed her that their tanks were running low.

She didn't argue. They'd come back. The *Liberty* would wait for them. Each took a handle of the mesh basket and swam leisurely toward the surface.

"Do you know how I feel?" Kate demanded the moment she could speak.

"Yes." Ky gripped the ladder with one hand and waited for her to unstrap her tanks and slip them over onto the deck. "I know just how you feel."

"The teapot." Breathing fast, she hauled herself up the ladder. "Ky, it's priceless. It's like finding a perfectly formed rose inside a mass of briars." Before he could answer, she was laughing and calling out to Marsh. "It's fabulous! Absolutely fabulous."

Marsh cut the engine then walked over to help them. "You two work fast." Bending he touched a tentative finger to the pot. "God, it's all in one piece."

"We'll be able to date it as soon as it's cleaned. But look." Kate drew out the broken vase. "This is the mark of an English potter. English," she repeated, turning to Ky. "He trained Wedgwood, and Wedgwood didn't begin manufacturing until the 1760s, so—"

"So this piece more than likely came from the era we're looking for," Ky finished. "*Liberty* or not," he continued, crouching down beside her. "It looks like you've found yourself an eighteenth-century wreck that's probably of English origin and certainly hasn't been recorded before." He took one of her hands between both of his. "Your father would've been proud of you."

Stunned, she stared at him. Emotions raced through her with such velocity she had no way of controlling or channeling them. The hand holding the broken vase began to tremble. Quickly, she set it down in the basket again and rose.

"I'm going below," she managed and fled.

Proud of her. Kate put a hand over her mouth as she stumbled into the cabin. His pride, his love. Wasn't it all she'd really ever wanted from her father? Was it possible she could only gain it after his death?

She drank in deep gulps of air and struggled to level her emotions. No, she wanted to find the *Liberty*, she wanted to bring her father's dream to reality, have his name on a plaque in a museum with the artifacts they'd found. She owed him that. But she'd promised herself she'd find the *Liberty* for herself as well. For herself.

It was her choice, her first real decision to come in from the sidelines and act on her own. For herself, Kate thought again as she brought the first surge of emotion under control.

"Kate?"

She turned, and though she thought she was perfectly calm, Ky could see the turmoil in her eyes. Unsure how to handle it, he spoke practically.

"You'd better get out of that suit."

"But we're going back down."

"Not today." To prove his point he began to strip out of his own suit just as Marsh started the engines.

Automatically, she balanced herself as the boat turned. "Ky, we've got two more sets of tanks. There's no reason for us to go back when we're just getting started."

"Your first dive took most of the strength you've built up. If you want to dive tomorrow, you've got to take it slow today."

Her anger erupted so quickly, it left them both astonished. "The hell with that!" she exploded. "I'm sick to death of being treated as if I don't know my own limitations or my own mind and body."

Ky walked into the galley and picked up a can of beer. With a flick of his wrist, air hissed out. "I don't know what you're talking about."

"I lay in bed for the better part of a week because of pressure from you and Linda and anyone else who came around me. I'm not tolerating this any longer."

With one hand, he pushed dripping hair from his forehead as he lifted the can. "You're tolerating exactly what's necessary until I say differently."

"You say?" she tossed back. Cheeks flaming, she strode over to him. "I don't have to do what you say, or what anyone says. Not anymore. It's about time you remember just who's in charge of this salvage operation."

His eyes narrowed. "In charge?"

"I hired you. Seventy-five a day and twenty-five percent. Those were the terms. There was nothing in there about you running my life."

He abruptly went still. For a moment, all that could be heard over the engines was her angry breathing. Dollars and percents, he thought with a deadly sort of calm. Just dollars and percents. "So that's what it comes down to?"

Too overwrought to see beyond her own anger, she continued to lash out. "We made an agreement. I fully intend to see that you get everything we arranged, but I won't have you telling me when I can go down. I won't have you judging when I'm well and when I'm not. I'm sick to death of being dictated to. And I won't be—not by you, not by anyone. Not any longer."

The metal of the can gave under his fingers. "Fine. You do exactly what you want, professor. But while you're about it, get yourself another diver. I'll send you a bill." Ky went up the cabin steps the way he came down. Quickly and without a sound.

With her hands gripped together, Kate sat down on the bunk and waited until she heard the engines stop again. She refused to think. Thinking hurt. She refused to feel. There was too much to feel. When she was certain she was in control, she stood and went up on deck.

Everything was exactly as she'd left it—the wire basket filled with bits of porcelain and tableware, her nearly depleted tanks. Ky was gone. Marsh walked over from the stern where he'd been waiting for her.

"You're going to need a hand with these."

Kate nodded and pulled a thigh length T-shirt over her tank suit. "Yes. I want to take everything back to my room at the hotel. I have to arrange for shipping."

"Okay." But instead of reaching down for the basket, he took her arm. "Kate, I don't like to give advice."

"Good." Then she swore at her own rudeness. "I'm sorry, Marsh. I'm feeling a little rough at the moment."

"I can see that, and I know things aren't always smooth for you and Ky. Look, he has a habit of closing himself up, of not saying everything that's on his mind. Or worse," Marsh added. "Of saying the first thing that comes to mind."

"He's perfectly free to do so. I came here for the specific purpose of finding and excavating the *Liberty*. If Ky and I can't deal together on a business level, I have to do without his help."

"Listen, he has a few blind spots."

"Marsh, you're his brother. Your allegiance is with him as it should be."

"I care about both of you."

She took a deep breath, refusing to let the emotion surface and carry her with it. "I appreciate that. The best thing you can do for me now, perhaps for both of us, is to tell me where I can rent a boat and some equipment. I'm going back out this afternoon."

"Kate."

"I'm going back out this afternoon," she repeated. "With or without your help."

Resigned, Marsh picked up the mesh basket. "All right, you can use mine."

It took the rest of the morning for Kate to arrange everything, including the resolution of a lengthy argument with Marsh. She refused to let him come with her, ending by saying she'd simply rent a boat and do without his assistance altogether. In the end, she stood at the helm of his boat alone and headed out to sea.

She craved the solitude. Almost in defiance, she pushed the throttle forward. If it was defiance, she didn't care, any more than she cared whom she was defying. It was vital to do this one act for herself.

She refused to think about Ky, about why she'd exploded at him. If her words had been harsh, they'd also been necessary. She comforted herself with that. For too long, for a lifetime, she'd been influenced by someone else's opinion, someone else's expectations.

Mechanically, she stopped the engines and put on her equipment, checking and rechecking as she went. She'd never gone down alone before. Even that seemed suddenly a vital thing to do.

With a last look at her compass, she took the mesh basket over the side.

As she went deep, a thrill went through her. She was alone. In acres and acres of sea, she was alone. The water parted for her like silk. She was in control, and her destiny was her own.

She didn't rush. Kate found she wanted that euphoric feeling of being isolated under the sea where only curious fish bothered to give her a passing glance. Ultimately, her only responsibility here was to herself. Briefly, she closed her eyes and floated. At last, only to herself.

When she reached the site, she felt a new surge of pride. This was something she'd done without her father. She wouldn't think of the whys or the hows now, but simply the triumph. For two centuries, it had waited. And now, *she'd* found it. She circled the hole the propwash had created and began to fan using her hand.

Her first find was a dinner plate with a flamboyant floral pattern around the rim. She found one, then half a dozen, two of which were intact. On the back was the mark of an English potter. There were cups as well, dainty, exquisite English china that might have graced the table of a wealthy colonist, might have become a beloved heirloom, if nature hadn't interfered. Now they looked like something out of a horror show—crusted, misshapen with sea life. They couldn't have been more beautiful to her.

As she continued to fan, Kate nearly missed what appeared to be a dark sea shell. On closer examination she saw it was a silver coin. She couldn't make out the currency, but knew it didn't matter. It could just as easily be Spanish, as she'd read that Spanish currency had been used by all European nations with settlements in the New World.

The point was, it was a coin. The first coin. Though it was silver, not gold, and unidentifiable at the moment, she'd found it by herself.

Kate started to slip it into her goodie bag when her arm was jerked back.

The thrill of fear went wildly from her toes to her throat. The spear gun was on board the *Vortex*. She had no weapon. Before she could do more than turn in defense, she was caught by the shoulders with Ky's furious hands.

Terror died, but the anger in his eyes only incited her own. Damn him for frightening her, for interfering. Shaking him away, Kate signaled for him to leave. With one arm, he encircled her waist and started for the surface.

Only once did she even come close to breaking away from him. Ky simply banded his arm around her again, more tightly, until she had a choice between submitting or cutting off her own air.

When they broke the surface, Kate drew in breath to shout, but even in this, she was out-maneuvered.

"Idiot!" he shouted at her, dragging her to the ladder. "One day off your back and you jump into forty feet of water by yourself. I don't know why in hell I ever thought you had any brains."

Breathless, she heaved her tanks over the side. When she was on solid ground again, she intended to have her say. For now, she'd let him have his.

"I take my eyes off you for a couple hours and you go off half-cocked. If I'd murdered Marsh, it would have been on your head."

To her further fury, Kate saw that she'd boarded the *Vortex*. Marsh's boat was nowhere in sight.

"Where's the *Gull*?" she demanded.

"Marsh had the sense to tell me what you were doing." The words came out like bullets as he stripped off his gear. "I didn't kill him because I needed him to come out with me and take the *Gull* back." He stood in front of her, dripping, and as furious as she'd ever seen him. "Don't you have any more sense than to dive out here alone?"

She tossed her head back. "Don't you?"

Infuriated, he grabbed her and started to peel the wet suit from her himself. "We're not talking about me, damn it. I've been diving since I was six. I know the currents."

"*I* know the currents."

"And I haven't been flat on my back for a week."

"I was flat on my back for a week because you were overreacting." She struggled away from him, and because the wet suit was already down to her waist, peeled it off. "You've no right to tell me when and where I can dive, Ky. Superior strength gives you no right to drag me up when I'm in the middle of salvaging."

"The hell with what I have a right to do." Grabbing her again, he shook her with more violence than he'd ever shown her. A dozen things might have happened to her in the thirty minutes she'd been down. A dozen things he knew too well. "I make my own rights. You're not going down alone if I have to chain you up to stop it."

"You told me to get another diver," she said between her teeth. "Until I do, I dive alone."

"You threw that damn business arrangement in my face. Percentages. Lousy percentages and a daily rate. Do you know how that made me feel?"

"No!" she shouted, pushing him away. "No, I don't know how that made you feel. I don't know how anything makes you feel. You don't tell me." Dragging both hands through her dripping hair she walked away. "We agreed to the terms. That's all I know."

"That was before."

"Before what?" she demanded. Tears brimmed for no reason she could name, but she blinked them back again. "Before I slept with you?"

"Damn it, Kate." He was across the deck, backing her into the rail before she could take a breath. "Are you trying to get at me for something I did or didn't do four years ago? I don't even know what it is. I don't know what you want from me or what you don't want and I'm sick of trying to outguess you."

"I don't want to be pushed into a corner," she told him fiercely. "That's what I don't want. I don't want to be expected to fall in passively with someone else's plans for me. That's what I don't want. I don't want it assumed that I simply don't have any personal goals or wishes of my own. Or any basic competence of my own. *That's* what I don't want!"

"Fine." They were both losing control, but he no longer gave a damn. Ky ripped off his wet suit and tossed it aside. "You just remember something, lady. I don't expect anything of you and I don't assume. Once maybe, but not anymore. There was only one person who ever pushed you into a corner and it wasn't me." He hurled his mask across the deck where it bounced and smacked into the side. "I'm the one who let you go."

She stiffened. Even with the distance between them he could see her eyes frost over. "I won't discuss my father with you."

"You caught on real quick though, didn't you?"

"You resented him. You—"

"I?" Ky interrupted. "Maybe you better look at yourself, Kate."

"I loved him," she said passionately. "All my life I tried to show him. You don't understand."

"How do you know that I don't understand?" he exploded. "Don't you know I can see what you're feeling every time we find something down there? Do you think I'm so blind I don't see that you're hurting because *you* found it, not him? Don't you think it tears me apart to see that you punish yourself for not being what you think he wanted you to be? And I'm tired," he continued as her breath started to hitch. "Damn tired of being compared to and measured by a man you loved without ever being close to him."

"I don't." She covered her face, hating the weakness but powerless against it. "I don't do that. I only want..."

"What?" he demanded. "What do you want?"

"I didn't cry when he died," she said into her hands. "I didn't cry, not even at the funeral. I owed him tears, Ky. I owed him something."

"You don't owe him anything you didn't already give him over and over again." Frustrated, he dragged a hand through his hair before he went to her. "Kate." Because words seemed useless, he simply gathered her close.

"I didn't cry."

"Cry now," he murmured. He pressed his lips to the top of her head. "Cry now."

So she did, desperately, for what she'd never been able to quite touch, for what she'd never been able to quite hold. She'd ached for love, for the simple companionship of understanding. She wept because it was too late for that now from her father. She wept because she wasn't certain she could ask for love again from anyone else.

Ky held her, lowering her onto the bench as he cradled her in his lap. He couldn't offer her words of comfort. They were the most difficult words for him to come by. He could only offer her a place to weep, and silence.

As the tears began to pass, she kept her face against

his shoulder. There was such simplicity there, though it came from a man of complications. Such gentleness, though it sprang from a restless nature. "I couldn't mourn for him before," she murmured. "I'm not sure why."

"You don't have to cry to mourn."

"Maybe not," she said wearily. "I don't know. But it's true, what you said. I've wanted to do all this for him because he'll never have the chance to finish what he started. I don't know if you can understand, but I feel if I do this I'll have done everything I could. For him, and for myself."

"Kate." Ky tipped back her head so he could see her face. Her eyes were puffy, rimmed with red. "I don't have to understand. I just have to love you."

He felt her stiffen in his arms and immediately cursed himself. Why was it he never said things to her the way they should be said? Sweetly, calmly, softly. She was a woman who needed soft words, and he was a man who always struggled with them.

She didn't move, and for a long, long moment, they stayed precisely as they were.

"Do you?" she managed after a moment.

"Do I what?"

Would he make her drag it from him? "Love me?"

"Kate." Frustrated, he drew away from her. "I don't know how else to show you. You want bouquets of flowers, bottles of French champagne, poems? Damn it, I'm not made that way."

"I want a straight answer."

He let out a short breath. Sometimes her very calmness drove him to distraction. "I've always loved you. I've never stopped."

That went through her, sharp, hot, with a mixture of pain and pleasure she wasn't quite sure how to deal with. Slowly, she rose out of his arms, and walking across the deck, looked out to sea. The buoys that marked the site bobbed gently. Why were there no buoys in life to show you the way?

"You never told me."

"Look, I can't even count the number of women I've said it to." When she turned back with her brow raised, he rose, uncomfortable. "It was easy to say it to them because it didn't mean anything. It's a hell of a lot harder to get the words out when you mean them, and when you're afraid someone's going to back away from you the minute you do."

"I wouldn't have done that."

"You backed away, you went away for four years, when I asked you to stay."

"You asked me to stay," she reminded him. "You asked me not to go back to Connecticut, but to move in with you. Just like that. No promises, no commitment, no sign that you had any intention of building a life with me. I had responsibilities."

"To do what your father wanted you to do."

She swallowed that. It was true in its way. "All right, yes. But you never said you loved me."

He came closer. "I'm telling you now."

She nodded, but her heart was in her throat. "And I'm not backing away. I'm just not sure I can take the next step. I'm not sure you can either."

"You want a promise."

She shook her head, not certain what she'd do if indeed he gave her one. "I want time, for both of us. It seems we both have a lot of thinking to do."

"Kate." Impatient, he came to her, taking her hands. They trembled. "Some things you don't have to think about. Some things you can think about too much."

"You've lived your life a certain way a long time, and I mine," she said quickly. "Ky, I've just begun to change—to feel the change. I don't want to make a mistake, not with you. It's too important. With time—"

"We've lost four years," he interrupted. He needed to resolve something, he discovered, and quickly. "I can't wait any longer to hear it if it's inside you."

Kate let out the breath she'd been holding. If he could ask, she could give. It would be enough. "I love you, Ky. I never stopped either. I never told you when I should have."

He felt the weight drain from his body as he cupped her face. "You're telling me now."

It was enough.

Chapter 11

Love. Kate had read hundreds of poems about that one phenomenon. She'd read, analyzed and taught from countless novels where love was the catalyst to all action, all emotion. With her students, she'd dissected innumerable lines from books, plays and verse that all led back to that one word.

Now, for perhaps the first time in her life, it was offered to her. She found it had more power than could possibly be taught. She found she didn't understand it.

Ky hadn't Byron's way with words, or Keat's romantic phrasing. What he'd said, he'd said simply. It meant everything. She still didn't understand it.

She could, in her own way, understand her feelings. She'd loved Ky for years, since that first revelation one summer when she'd come to know what it meant to want to fully share oneself with another.

But what, she wondered, did Ky find in her to love?

It wasn't modesty that caused her to ask herself this question, but the basic practicality she'd grown up with. Where there was an effect, there was a cause. Where there was reaction, there was action. The world ran on this principle. She'd won Ky's love—but how?

Kate had no insecurity about her own intelligence. Perhaps, if anything, she overrated her mind, and it was this that caused her to underrate her other attributes.

He was a man of action, of restless and mercurial nature. She, on the other hand, considered herself almost blandly level. While she thrived on routine, Ky thrived on the unexpected. Why should he love her? Yet he did.

If she accepted that, it was vital to come to a resolution. Love led to commitment. It was there that she found the wall solid, without footholds.

He lived on a remote island because he was basically a loner, because he preferred moving at his own pace, in his own time. She was a teacher who lived by a day-to-day schedule. Without the satisfaction of giving knowledge, she'd stagnate. In the structured routine of a college town, Ky would go mad.

Because she could find no compromise, Kate opted to do what she'd decided to do in the beginning. She'd ride with the current until the summer was over. Perhaps by then, an answer would come.

They spoke no more of percentages. Kate quietly dropped the notion of keeping her hotel room. These, she told herself, were small matters when so much more hung in the balance during her second summer with Ky.

The days went quickly with her and Ky working together with the prop-wash or by hand. Slowly, painstakingly, they uncovered more salvage. The candlesticks had turned out to be pewter, but the coin had been Spanish silver. Its date had been 1748.

In the next two-week period, they uncovered much more—a heavy intricately carved silver platter, more china and porcelain, and in another area dozens of nails and tools.

Kate documented each find on film, for practical and personal reasons. She needed the neat, orderly way of keeping track of the salvage. She wanted to be able to look back on those pictures and remember how she felt when Ky held up a crusted teacup or an oxidized tankard. She'd be able to look and remember how he'd played an outstaring game with a large lazy bluefish. And lost.

More than once Ky had suggested the use of a larger ship equipped for salvage. They discussed it, and its advantages, but they never acted on it. Somehow, they both felt they wanted to move slowly, working basically with their own hands until there came a time when they had to make a decision.

The cannons and the heavier pieces of ship's planking couldn't be brought up without help, so these they left to the sea for the time being. They continued to use tanks, rather than changing to a surface-supplied source of air, so they had to surface and change gear every hour or so. A diving rig would have saved time—but that wasn't their goal.

Their methods weren't efficient by professional salvor standards, but they had an unspoken agreement. Stretch time. Make it last.

The nights they spent together in the big four-poster, talking of the day's finds, or of tomorrow's, making love, marking time. They didn't speak of the future that loomed after the summer's end. They never talked of what they'd do the day after the treasure was found.

The treasure became their focus, something that kept them from reaching out when the other wasn't ready.

The day was fiercely hot as they prepared to dive. The sun was baking. It was mid-July. She'd been in Ocracoke for a month. For all her practicality, Kate told herself it was an omen. Today was the turning point of summer.

Even as she pulled the wet suit up to her waist, sweat beaded on her back. She could almost taste the cool freshness of the water. The sun glared on her tanks as she lifted them, bouncing off to spear her eyes.

"Here." Taking them from her, Ky strapped them onto her back, checking the gauges himself. "The water's going to feel like heaven."

"Yeah." Marsh tipped up a quart bottle of juice. "Think of me baking up here while you're having all the fun."

"Keep the throttle low, brother," Ky said with a grin as he climbed over the side. "We'll bring you a reward."

"Make it something round and shiny with a date stamped on it," Marsh called back, then winked at Kate as she started down the ladder. "Good luck."

She felt the excitement as the water lapped over her ankles. "Today, I don't think I need it."

The noise of the prop-wash disturbed the silence of

the water, but not the mystery. Even with technology and equipment, the water remained an enigma, part beauty, part danger. They went deeper and deeper until they reached the site with the scoops in the silt caused by their earlier explorations.

They'd already found what they thought had been the officers' and passengers' quarters, identifying it by the discovery of a snuff box, a silver bedside candleholder and Ky's personal favorite—a decorated sword. The few pieces of jewelry they'd found indicated a personal cache rather than cargo.

Though they fully intended to excavate in the area of the cache, it was the cargo they sought. Using the passengers' quarters and the galley as points of reference, they concentrated on what should have been the stern of the ship.

There were ballast rocks to deal with. This entailed a slow, menial process that required moving them by hand to an area they'd already excavated. It was time consuming, unrewarding and necessary. Still, Kate found something peaceful in the mindless work, and something fascinating about the ability to do it under fathoms of water with basically little effort. She could move a ballast pile as easily as Ky, whereas on land, she would have tired quickly.

Reaching down to clear another area, Ky's fingers brushed something small and hard. Curious, he fanned aside a thin layer of silt and picked up what at first looked like a tab on a can of beer. As he brought it closer, he saw it was much more refined, and though there were layers of crust on the knob of the circle, he felt his heart give a quick jerk.

He'd heard of diamonds in the rough, but he'd never thought to find one by simply reaching for it. He was no expert, but as he painstakingly cleaned what he could from the stone, he judged it to be at least two carats. With a tap on Kate's shoulder, he got her attention.

It gave him a great deal of pleasure to see her eyes widen and to hear the muffled sound of her surprise. Together, they turned it over and over again. It was dull and dirty, but the gem was there.

They were finding bits and pieces of civilization. Perhaps a woman had worn the ring while dining with the captain on her way to America. Perhaps some British officer had carried it in his vest pocket, waiting to give it to the woman he'd hoped to marry. It might have belonged to an elderly widow, or a young bride. The mystery of it, and its tangibility, were more precious than the stone itself. It was...lasting.

Ky held it out to her, offering. Their routine had fallen into a finders-keepers arrangement, in that whoever found a particular piece carried it in their own bag to the surface where everything was carefully cataloged on film and paper. Kate looked at the small, water-dulled piece of the past in Ky's fingers.

Was he offering her the ring because it was a woman's fancy, or was he offering her something else? Unsure, she shook her head, pointing to the bag on his belt. If he were asking her something, she needed it to be done with words.

Ky dropped the ring into his bag, secured it, then went back to work.

He thought he understood her, in some ways. In other ways, Ky found she was as much a mystery as the sea. What did she want from him? If it was love, he'd given her that. If it was time, they were both running out of it. He wanted to demand, was accustomed to demanding, yet she blocked his ability with a look.

She said she'd changed—that she was just beginning to feel in control of her life. He thought he understood that, as well as her fierce need for independence. And yet... He'd never known anything but independence. He, too, had changed. He needed her to give him the boundaries and the borders that came with dependence. His for her, and hers for him. Was the timing wrong again? Would it ever be right?

Damn it, he wanted her, he thought as he heaved another rock out of his way. Not just for today, but for tomorrow. Not tied against him, but bound to him. Why couldn't she understand that?

She loved him. It was something she murmured in the night when she was sleepy and caught close against him. She wasn't a woman to use words unless they had meaning. Yet with the love he offered and the love she returned, she'd begun to hold something back from him, as though he could have only a portion of her, but not all. Edged with frustration, he cleared more ballast. He needed, and would have, all.

Marriage? Was he thinking of marriage? Kate found herself flustered and uneasy. She'd never expected Ky to look for that kind of commitment, that kind of permanency. Perhaps she'd misread him. After all, it was difficult to be certain of someone's intention, yet she knew just how clearly Ky and she had been able to communicate underwater.

There was so much to consider, so many things to weigh. He wouldn't understand that, Kate mused. Ky was a man who made decisions in an instant and took the consequences. He wouldn't think about all the variables, all the what-ifs, all the maybes. She had to think about them all. She simply knew no other way.

Kate watched the silt and sand blowing away, causing a cuplike indentation to form on the ocean floor. Outside influences, she mused. They could eat away at the layers and uncover the core, but sometimes what was beneath couldn't stand up to the pressure.

Is that what would happen between her and Ky? How would their relationship hold up under the pressure of variant lifestyles—the demands of her profession and the free-wheeling tone of his? Would it stay intact, or would it begin to sift away, layer by layer? How much of herself would he ask her to give? And in loving, how much of herself would she lose?

It was a possibility she couldn't ignore, a threat she needed to build a solid defense against. Time. Perhaps time was the answer. But summer was waning.

The force of the wash made a small object spin up, out of the layer of silt and into the water. Kate grabbed at it and the sharp edge scraped her palm. Curious, she turned it over for examination. A buckle? she wondered. The shape seemed to indicate it, and she could just make out a fastening. Even as she started to hold it out for Ky another, then another was pushed off the ocean bed.

Shoe buckles, Kate realized, astonished. Dozens of them. No, she realized as more and more began to twist up in the water's spin and reel away. Hundreds. With a quick frenzy, she began to gather what she could. More than hundreds, she discovered as her heart thudded. There were thousands of them, literally thousands.

She held a buckle in her hand and looked at Ky in triumph. They'd found the cargo. There'd been shoe buckles on the manifest of the *Liberty*. Five thousand of them. Nothing but a merchantman carried something like that in bulk.

Proof. She waved the buckle, her arm sweeping out in slow motion to take in the swarm of them swirling away from the wash and dropping again. Proof, her mind shouted out. The cargo-hold was beneath them. And the treasure. They had only to reach it.

Ky took her hands and nodded, knowing what was in her mind. Beneath his fingers he could feel the race of her pulse. He wanted that for her, the excitement, the thrill that came from discovering something only half believed in. She brought the back of his hand to her cheek, her eyes laughing, buckles spinning around them. Kate wanted to laugh until she was too weak to stand. Five thousand shoe buckles would guide them to a chest of gold.

Kate saw the humor in his eyes and knew Ky's thoughts ran along the same path as hers. He pointed to himself, then thumbs up. With a minimum of signaling, he told Kate that he would surface to tell Marsh to shut off the engines. It was time to work by hand.

Excited, she nodded. She wanted only to begin. Resting near the bottom, Kate watched Ky go up and out of sight. Oddly, she found she needed time alone. She'd shared the heady instant of discovery with Ky, and now she needed to absorb it.

The *Liberty* was beneath her, the ship her father had searched for. The dream he'd kept close, carefully researching, meticulously calculating, but never finding.

Joy and sorrow mixed as she gathered a handful of the buckles and placed them carefully in her bag. For him. In that moment she felt she'd given him everything she'd always needed to.

Carefully, and this time for personal reasons rather than the catalog, she began to shoot pictures. Years from now, she thought. Years and years from now, she'd look at a snapshot of swirling silt and drifting pieces of metal, and she'd remember. Nothing could ever take that moment of quiet satisfaction from her.

She glanced up at the sudden silence. The wash had stilled. Ky had reached the surface. Silt and the pieces of crusted, decorated metal began to settle again without the agitation of the wash. The sea was a world without sound, without movement.

Kate looked down at the scoop in the ocean floor. They were nearly there. For a moment she was tempted to begin to fan and search by herself, but she'd wait for Ky. They began together, and they'd finish together. Content, she watched for his return.

When Kate saw the movement above her, she started

to signal. Her hand froze in place, then her arm, her shoulder and the rest of her body, degree by degree. It came smoothly through the water, sleek and silent. Deadly.

The noise of the prop-wash had kept the sea life away. Now the abrupt quiet brought out the curious. Among the schools of harmless fish glided the long bulletlike shape of a shark.

Kate was still, hardly daring to breathe as she feared even the trail of bubbles might attract him. He moved without haste, apparently not interested in her. Perhaps he'd already hunted successfully that day. But even with a full belly, a shark would attack what annoyed his uncertain temper.

She gauged him to be ten feet in length. Part of her mind registered that he was fairly small for what she recognized as a tiger shark. They could easily double that length. But she knew the jaws, those large sickle-shaped teeth, would be strong, merciless and fatal.

If she remained still, the chances were good that he would simply go in search of more interesting waters. Isn't that what she'd read sitting cozily under lamplight at her own desk? Isn't that what Ky had told her once when they'd shared a quiet lunch on his boat? All that seemed so remote, so unreal now, as she looked above and saw the predator between herself and the surface.

It was movement that attracted them, she reminded herself as she forced her mind to function. The movement a swimmer made with kicking feet and sweeping arms.

Don't panic. She forced herself to breathe slowly. No

sudden moves. She forced her nervous hands to form tight, still fists.

He was no more than ten feet away. Kate could see the small black eyes and the gentle movement of his gills. Breathing shallowly, she never took her eyes from his. She had only to be perfectly still and wait for him to swim on.

But Ky. Kate's mouth went dry as she looked toward the direction where Ky had disappeared moments before. He'd be coming back, any minute, unaware of what was lurking near the bottom. Waiting. Cruising.

The shark would sense the disturbance in the water with the uncanny ability the hunter had. The kick of Ky's feet, the swing of his arms would attract the shark long before Kate would have a chance to warn him of any danger.

He'd be unaware, helpless, and then... Her blood seemed to freeze. She'd heard of the sensation but now she experienced it. Cold seemed to envelop her. Terror made her head light. Kate bit down on her lip until pain cleared her thoughts. She wouldn't stand by idly while Ky came blindly into a death trap.

Glancing down, she saw the spear gun. It was over five feet away and unloaded for safety. Safety, she thought hysterically. She'd never loaded one, much less shot one. And first, she'd have to get to it. There'd only be one chance. Knowing she'd have no time to settle her nerves, Kate made her move.

She kept her eyes on the shark as she inched slowly toward the gun. At the moment, he seemed to be merely cruising, not particularly interested in anything. He never even glanced her way. Perhaps he would move on before Ky came back, but she needed the weapon. Fingers shaking, she gripped the butt of the gun. Time seemed to crawl. Her movements were so slow, so measured, she hardly seemed to move at all. But her mind whirled.

Even as she gripped the spear she saw the shape that glided down from the surface. The shark turned lazily to the left. To Ky.

No! her mind screamed as she rammed the spear into position. Her only thought that of protecting what she loved. Kate swam forward without hesitation, taking a path between Ky and the shark. She had to get close.

Her mind was cold now, with fear, with purpose. For the second time, she saw those small, deadly eyes. This time, they focused on her. If she'd never seen true evil before, Kate knew she faced it now. This was cruelty, and a death that wouldn't come easily.

The shark moved toward her with a speed that made her heart stop. His jaws opened. There was a black, black cave behind them.

Ky dove quickly, wanting to get back to Kate, wanting to search for what had brought them back together. If it was the treasure she needed to settle her mind, he'd find it. With it, they could open whatever doors they needed to open, lock whatever needed to be locked. Excitement drummed through him as he dove deeper.

When he spotted the shark, he pulled up short. He'd felt that deep primitive fear before, but never so sharply. Though it was less than useless against such a predator, he reached for his diver's knife. He'd left Kate alone. Cold-bloodedly, he set for the attack.

Like a rocket, Kate shot up between himself and the shark. Terror such as he'd never known washed over him. Was she mad? Was she simply unaware? Giving no time to thought, Ky barreled through the water toward her.

He was too far away. He knew it even as the panic hammered into him. The shark would be on her before he was close enough to sink the knife in.

When he saw what she held in her hand, and realized her purpose he somehow doubled his speed. Everything was in slow motion, and yet it seemed to happen in the blink of an eye. He saw the gaping hole in the shark's mouth as it closed in on Kate. For the first time in his life, prayers ran through him like water.

The spear shot out, sinking deep through the shark's flesh. Instinctively, Kate let herself drop as the shark came forward full of anger and pain. He would follow her now, she knew. If the spear didn't work, he would be on her in moments.

Ky saw blood gush from the wound. It wouldn't be enough. The shark jerked as if to reject the spear, and slowed his pace. Just enough. Teeth bared, Ky fell on its back, hacking with the knife as quickly as the water would allow. The shark turned, furious. Using all his strength, Ky turned with it, forcing the knife into the underbelly and ripping down. It ran through his mind that he was holding death, and it was as cold as the poets said.

From a few feet away, Kate watched the battle. She

was numb, body and mind. Blood spurted out to dissipate in the water. Letting the empty gun fall, she too reached for her knife and swam forward.

But it was over. One instant the fish and Ky were as one form, locked together. Then they were separate as the body of the shark sank lifelessly toward the bottom. She saw the eyes one last time.

Her arm was gripped painfully. Limp, Kate allowed herself to be dragged to the surface. Safe. It was the only clear thought her mind could form. He was safe.

Too breathless to speak, Ky pulled her toward the ladder, tanks and all. He saw her slip near the top and roll onto the deck. Even as he swung over himself, he saw two fins slice through the water and disappear below where the blood drew them.

"What the hell—" Jumping up from his seat, Marsh ran across the deck to where Kate still lay, gasping for air.

"Sharks." Ky cut off the word as he knelt beside her. "I had to bring her up fast. Kate." Ky reached a hand beneath her neck, lifting her up as he began to take off her tanks. "Are you dizzy? Do you have any pain—your knees, elbows?"

Though she was still gasping for air, she shook her head. "No, no, I'm all right." She knew he worried about decompression sickness and tried to steady herself to reassure him. "Ky, we weren't that deep after—when we came up."

He nodded, grimly acknowledging that she was winded, not incoherent. Standing, he pulled off his mask and heaved it across the deck. Temper helped alleviate the helpless shaking. Kate merely drew her knees up and rested her forehead on them.

"Somebody want to fill me in?" Marsh asked, glancing from one to the other. "I left off when Ky came up raving about shoe buckles."

"Cargo-hold," Kate murmured. "We found it."

"So Ky said." Marsh glanced at his brother whose knuckles were whitening against the rail as he looked out to sea. "Run into some company down there?"

"There was a shark. A tiger."

"She nearly got herself killed," Ky explained. Fury was a direct result of fear, and just as deadly. "She swam right in front of him." Before Marsh could make any comment, Ky turned on Kate. "Did you forget everything I taught you?" he demanded. "You manage to get a doctorate but you can't remember that you're supposed to minimize your movements when a shark's cruising? You know that arm and leg swings attract them, but you swim in front of him, flailing around as though you wanted to shake hands—holding a damn spear gun that's just as likely to annoy him as do any real damage. If I hadn't been coming down just then, he'd have torn you to pieces."

Kate lifted her head slowly. Whatever emotion she'd felt up to that moment was replaced by an anger so deep it overshadowed everything. Meticulously she removed her flippers, her mask and her weight belt before she rose. "If you hadn't been coming down just then," she said precisely, "there'd have been no reason for me to swim in front of him." Turning, she walked to the steps and down into the cabin.

For a full minute there was utter silence on deck. Above, a gull screeched, then swerved west. Knowing there'd be no more dives that day, Marsh went to the helm. As he glanced over he saw the deep stain of blood on the water's surface.

"It's customary," he began with his back to his brother, "to thank someone when they save your life." Without waiting for a comment, he switched on the engine.

Shaken, Ky ran a hand through his hair. Some of the shark's blood had stained his fingers. Standing still, he stared at it.

Not through carelessness, he thought with a jolt. It had been deliberate. Kate had deliberately put herself in the path of the shark. For him. She'd risked her life to save him. He ran both hands over his face before he started below deck.

He saw her sitting on a bunk with a glass in her hand. A bottle of brandy sat at her feet. When she lifted the glass to her lips her hand shook lightly. Beneath the tan the sun had given her, her face was drawn and pale. No one had ever put him first so completely, so unselfishly. It left him without any idea of what to say.

"Kate…"

"I'm not in the mood to be shouted at right now," she told him before she drank again. "If you need to vent your temper, you'll have to save it."

"I'm not going to shout." Because he felt every bit as unsteady as she did, he sat beside her and lifted the bottle, drinking straight from it. The brandy ran hot and strong through him. "You scared the hell out of me."

"I'm not going to apologize for what I did."

"I should thank you." He drank again and felt the nerves in his stomach ease. "The point is, you had no business doing what you did. Nothing but blind luck kept you from being torn up down there."

Turning her head, she stared at him. "I should've stayed safe and sound on the bottom while you dealt with the shark—with your diver's knife."

He met the look levelly. "Yes."

"And you'd have done that, if it'd been me?"

"That's different."

"Oh." Glass in hand, she rose. She took a moment to study him, that raw-boned, dark face, the dripping hair that needed a trim, the eyes that reflected the sea. "Would you care to explain that little piece of logic to me?"

"I don't have to explain it, it just is." He tipped the bottle back again. It helped to cloud his imagination which kept bringing images of what might have happened to her.

"No, it just isn't, and that's one of your major problems."

"Kate, have you any idea what could have happened if you hadn't lucked out and hit a vital spot with that spear?"

"Yes." She drained her glass and felt some of the edge dull. The fear might come back again unexpectedly, but she felt she was strong enough to deal with it. And the anger. No matter how it slashed at her, she would put herself between him and danger again. "I understand perfectly. Now, I'm going up with Marsh."

"Wait a minute." He stood to block her way. "Can't you see that I couldn't stand it if anything happened to you? I want to take care of you. I need to keep you safe."

"While you take all the risks?" she countered. "Is that supposed to be the balance of our relationship, Ky? You man, me woman? I bake bread, you hunt the meat?"

"Damn it, Kate, it's not as basic as that."

"It's just as basic as that," she tossed back. The color had come back to her face. Her legs were steady again. And she would be heard. "You want me to be quiet and content—and amenable to the way you choose to live. You want me to do as you say, bend to your will, and yet I know how you felt about my father."

It didn't seem she had the energy to be angry any longer. She was just weary, bone weary from slamming herself up against a wall that didn't seem ready to budge.

"I spent all my life doing what it pleased him to have me do," she continued in calmer tones. "No waves, no problems, no rebellion. He gave me a nod of approval, but no true respect and certainly no true affection. Now, you're asking me to do the same thing again with you." She felt no tears, only that weariness of spirit. "Why do you suppose the only two men I've ever loved should want me to be so utterly pliant to their will? Why do you suppose I lost both of them because I tried so hard to do just that?"

"No." He put his hands on her shoulders. "No, that's not true. It's not what I want from you or for you. I just want to take care of you."

She shook her head. "What's the difference, Ky?" she whispered. "What the hell's the difference?" Pushing past him, Kate went out on deck.

Chapter 12

Because in her quiet, immovable way Kate had demanded it, Ky left her alone. Perhaps it was for the best as it gave him time to think and to reassess what he wanted.

He realized that because of his fear for her, because of his need to care for her, he'd hurt her and damaged their already tenuous relationship.

On a certain level, she'd hit the mark in her accusations. He did want her to be safe and cared for while he sweated and took the risks. It was his nature to protect what he loved—in Kate's case, perhaps too much. It was also his nature to want other wills bent to his. He wanted Kate, and was honest enough to admit that he'd already outlined the terms in his own mind.

Her father's quiet manipulating had infuriated Ky and yet, he found himself doing the same thing. Not so quietly, he admitted, not nearly as subtly, but he was doing the same thing. Still, it wasn't for the same reasons. He wanted Kate to be with him, to align herself to him. It was as simple as that. He was certain, if she'd just let him, that he could make her happy.

But he never fully considered that she'd have demands or terms of her own. Until now, Ky hadn't thought how he'd adjust to them.

The light of dawn was quiet as Ky added the finishing touches to the lettering on his sailboat. For most of the night, he'd worked in the shed, giving Kate her time alone, and himself the time to think. Now that the night was over, only one thing remained clear. He loved her. But it had come home to him that it might not be enough. Though impatience continued to push at him, he reined it in. Perhaps he had to leave it to her to show him what would be.

For the next few days, they would concentrate on excavating the cargo that had sunk two centuries before. The longer they searched, the more the treasure became a symbol for him. If he could give it to her, it would be the end of the quest for both of them. Once it was over, they'd both have what they wanted. She, the fulfillment of her father's dream, and he, the satisfaction of seeing her freed from it.

Ky closed the shed doors behind him and headed back for the house. In a few days, he thought with a glance over his shoulder, he'd have something else to give her. Something else to ask her.

He was still some feet away from the house when he smelled the morning scents of bacon and coffee drifting through the kitchen windows. When he entered, Kate was standing at the stove, a long T-shirt over her tank suit, her feet bare, her hair loose. He could see the light dusting of freckles over the bridge of her nose, and the pale soft curve of her lips.

His need to gather her close rammed into him with such power, he had to stop and catch his breath. "Kate—"

"I thought since we'd be putting in a long day we should have a full breakfast." She'd heard him come in, sensed it. Because it made her knees weak, she spoke briskly. "I'd like to get an early start."

He watched her drop eggs into the skillet where the white began to sizzle and solidify around the edges. "Kate, I'd like to talk to you."

"I've been thinking we might consider renting a salvage ship after all," she interrupted, "and perhaps hiring another couple of divers. Excavating the cargo's going to be very slow work with just the two of us. It's certainly time we looked into lifting bags and lines."

Long days in the sun had lightened her hair. There were shades upon shades of variation so that as it flowed it reminded him of the smooth soft pelt of a deer. "I don't want to talk business now."

"It's not something we can put off too much longer." Efficiently, she scooped up the eggs and slid them onto plates. "I'm beginning to think we should expedite the excavation rather than dragging it out for what may very well be several more weeks. Then, of course, if we're talking about excavating the entire site, it would be months."

"Not now." Ky turned off the burner under the skillet. Taking both plates from Kate, he set them on the table. "Look, I have to do something, and I'm not sure I'll do it very well."

Turning, Kate took silverware from the drawer and went to the table. "What?"

"Apologize." When she looked back at him in her cool, quiet way, he swore. "No, I won't do it well."

"It isn't necessary."

"Yes, it's necessary. Sit down." He let out a long breath as she remained standing. "Please," he added, then took a chair himself. Without a word, Kate sat across from him. "You saved my life yesterday." Even saying it aloud, he felt uneasy about it. "It was no less than that. I never could have taken that shark with my diver's knife. The only reason I did was because you'd weakened and distracted him."

Kate lifted her coffee and drank as though they were discussing the weather. It was the only way she had of blocking out images of what might have been. "Yes."

With a frustrated laugh, Ky stabbed at his eggs. "Not going to make it easy on me, are you?"

"No, I don't think I am."

"I've never been that scared," he said quietly. "Not for myself, certainly not for anyone else. I thought he had you." He looked up and met her calm, patient eyes. "I was still too far away to do anything about it. If…"

"Sometimes it's best not to think about the ifs."

"All right." He nodded and reached for her hand. "Kate, realizing you put yourself in danger to protect me only made it worse somehow. The possibility of anything happening to you was bad enough, but the idea of it happening because of me was unbearable."

"You would've protected me."

"Yes, but—"

"There shouldn't be any buts, Ky."

"Maybe there shouldn't be," he agreed, "but I can't promise there won't be."

"I've changed." The fact filled her with an odd sense of power and unease. "For too many years I've channeled my own desires because I thought somehow that approval could be equated with love. I know better now."

"I'm not your father, Kate."

"No, but you also have a way of imposing your will on me. My fault to a point." Her voice was calm, level, as it was when she lectured her students. She hadn't slept while Ky had spent his hours in the shed. Like him, she'd spent her time in thought, in search for the right answers. "Four years ago, I had to give to one of you and deny the other. It broke my heart. Today, I know I have to answer to myself first." With her breakfast hardly touched, she took her plate to the sink. "I love you, Ky," she murmured. "But I have to answer to myself first."

Rising, he went to her and laid his hands on her shoulders. Somehow the strength that suddenly seemed so powerful in her both attracted him yet left him uneasy. "Okay." When she turned into his arms, he felt the world settle a bit. "Just let me know what the answer is."

"When I can." She closed her eyes and held tight. "When I can."

* * *

For three long days they dove, working away the silt to find new discoveries. With a small air lift and their own hands, they found the practical, the beautiful and the ordinary. They came upon more than eight thousand of the ten thousand decorated pipes on the *Liberty*'s manifest. At least half of them, to Kate's delight, had their bowls intact. They were clay, long-stemmed pipes with the bowls decorated with oak leaves or bunches of grapes and flowers. In a heady moment of pleasure, she snapped Ky's picture as he held one up to his lips.

She knew that at auction, they would more than pay for the investment she'd made. And, with them, the donation she'd make to a museum in her father's name was steadily growing. But more than this, the discovery of so many pipes on a wreck added force to their claim that the ship was English.

There were also snuff boxes, again thousands, leaving literally no doubt in her mind that they'd found the merchantman *Liberty*. They found tableware, some of it elegant, some basic utility-ware, but again in quantity. Their list of salvage grew beyond anything Kate had imagined, but they found no chest of gold.

They took turns hauling their finds to the surface, using an inverted plastic trash can filled with air to help them lift. Even with this, they stored the bulk of it on the sea floor. They were working alone again, without a need for Marsh to man the prop-wash. As it had been in the beginning, the project became a personal chore for only the two of them. What they found became a personal triumph. What they didn't find, a personal disappointment.

Kate delegated herself to deal with the snuff boxes, transporting them to the mesh baskets. Already, she was planning to clean several of them herself as part of the discovery. Beneath the layers of time there might be something elegant, ornate or ugly. She didn't believe it mattered what she found, as long as she found it.

Tea, sugar and other perishables the merchant ship had carried were long since gone without a trace. What she and Ky found now were the solid pieces of civilization that had survived centuries in the sea. A pipe meant for an eighteenth-century man had never reached the New World. It should have made her sad but, because it had survived, because she could hold it in her hand more than two hundred years later, Kate felt a quiet triumph. Some things last, whatever the odds.

Reaching down, she disturbed something that lay among the jumbled snuff boxes. Automatically, she jerked her hand back. Memories of the stingray and other dangers were still very fresh. When the small round object clinked against the side of a box and lay still, her heart began to pound. Almost afraid to touch, Kate reached for it. Between her fingers, she held a gold coin from another era.

Though she had read it was likely, she hadn't expected it to be as bright and shiny as the day it was minted. The pieces of silver they'd found had blackened, and other metal pieces had corroded, some of them crystalized almost beyond recognition. Yet, the gold, the small coin she'd plucked from the sea floor, winked back at her.

Its origin was English. The long-dead king stared out at her. The date was 1750.

Ky! Foolishly, she said his name. Though the sound was muffled and indistinguishable, he turned. Unable to wait, Kate swam toward him, clutching the coin. When she reached him, she took his hand and pressed the gold into his palm.

He knew at the moment of contact. He had only to look into her eyes. Taking her hand, he brought it to his lips. She'd found what she wanted. For no reason he could name, he felt empty. He pressed the coin back into her hand, closing her fingers over it tightly. The gold was hers.

Swimming beside her, Ky moved to the spot where Kate had found the coin. Together, they fanned, using all the patience each of them had stored. In the twenty minutes of bottom time they had left, they uncovered only five more coins. As if they were as fragile as glass, Kate placed them in her bag. Each took a mesh basket filled with salvage and surfaced.

"It's there, Ky." Kate let her mouthpiece drop as Ky hauled the first basket over the rail. "It's the *Liberty*, we've proven it."

"It's the *Liberty*," he agreed, taking the second basket from her. "You've finished what your father started."

"Yes." She unhooked her tanks, but it was more than their weight she felt lifted from her shoulders. "I've finished." Digging into her bag, she pulled out the six bright coins. "These were loose. We still haven't found the chest. If it still exists."

He'd already thought of that, but not how he'd tell her his own theory. "They might have taken the chest to another part of the boat when the storm hit." It was a possibility; it had given them hope that the chest was still there.

Kate looked down. The glittery metal seemed to mock her. "It's possible they put the gold in one of the lifeboats when they manned them. The survivor's story wasn't clear after the ship began to break up."

"A lot of things are possible." He touched her cheek briefly before he started to strip off his gear. "With a little luck and a little more time, we might find it all."

She smiled as she dropped the coins back into her bag. "Then you could buy your boat."

"And you could go to Greece." Stripped down to his bathing trunks, Ky went to the helm. "We need to give ourselves the full twelve hours before we dive again, Kate. We've been calling it close as it is."

"That's fine." She made a business of removing her own suit. She needed the twelve hours, she discovered, for more than the practical reason of residual nitrogen.

They spoke little on the trip back. They should've been ecstatic. Kate knew it, and though she tried, she couldn't recapture that quick boost she'd felt when she picked up the first coin.

She discovered that if she'd had a choice she would have gone back weeks, to the time when the gold was a distant goal and the search was everything.

It took the rest of the day to transport the salvage

from the *Vortex* to Ky's house, to separate and catalog it. She'd already decided to contact the Park Service. Their advice in placing many of the artifacts would be invaluable. After taxes, she'd give her father his memorial. And, she mused, she'd give Ky whatever he wanted out of the salvage.

Their original agreement no longer mattered to her. If he wanted half, she'd give it. All she wanted, Kate realized, was the first bowl she'd found, the blackened silver coin and the gold one that had led her to the five other coins.

"We might think about investing in a small electrolytic reduction bath," Ky murmured as he turned what he guessed was a silver snuff box in his palm. "We could treat a lot of this salvage ourselves." Coming to a decision, he set the box down. "We're going to have to think about a bigger ship and equipment. It might be best to stop diving for the next couple of days while we arrange for it. It's been six weeks, and we've barely scratched the surface of what's down there."

She nodded, not entirely sure why she wanted to weep. He was right. It was time to move on, to expand. How could she explain to him, when she couldn't explain to herself, that she wanted nothing else from the sea? While the sun set, she watched him meticulously list the salvage.

"Ky…" She broke off because she couldn't find the words to tell him what moved through her. Sadness, emptiness, needs.

"What's wrong?"

"Nothing." But she took his hands as she rose. "Come

upstairs now," she said quietly. "Make love with me before the sun goes down."

Questions ran through him, but he told himself they could wait. The need he felt from her touched off his own. He wanted to give her, and to take from her, what couldn't be found anywhere else.

When they entered the bedroom it was washed with the warm, lingering light of the sun. The sky was slowly turning red as he lay beside her. Her arms reached out to gather him close. Her lips parted. Refusing to rush, they undressed each other. No boundaries. Flesh against flesh they lay. Mouth against mouth they touched.

Kisses—long and deep—took them both beyond the ordinary world of place and time. Here, there were dozens of sensations to be felt, and no questions to be asked. Here, there was no past, no tomorrow, only the moment. Her body went limp under his, but her mouth hungered and sought.

No one else... No one else had ever taken her beyond herself so effortlessly. Never before had anyone made her so completely aware of her own body. A feathery touch along her skin drove pleasure through her with inescapable force.

The scent of sea still clung to both of them. As pleasure became liquid, they might have been fathoms under the ocean, moving freely without the strict rules of gravity. There were no rules here.

As his hands brought their emotions rising to the surface, so did hers for him. She explored the rippling muscles of his back, near the shoulders. Lingering there, she enjoyed just the feel of one of the subtle differences between them. His skin was smooth, but muscles bunched under it. His hands were gentle, but the palms were hard. He was lean, but there was no softness there.

Again and again she touched and tasted, needing to absorb him. Above all else, she needed to experience everything they'd ever had together this one time. They made love here, she remembered, that first time. The first time...and the last. Whenever she thought of him, she'd remember the quieting light of dusk and the distant sound of surf.

He didn't understand why he felt such restrained urgency from her, but he knew she needed everything he could give her. He loved her, perhaps not as gently as he could, but more thoroughly than ever before.

He touched. "Here," Ky murmured, using his fingertips to drive her up. As she gasped and arched, he watched her. "You're soft and hot."

He tasted. "And here..." With his tongue, he pushed her to the edge. As her hands gripped his, he groaned. Pleasure heaped upon pleasure. "You taste like temptation—sweet and forbidden. Tell me you want more."

"Yes." The word came out on a moan. "I want more."

So he gave her more.

Again and again, he took her up, watching the astonished pleasure on her face, feeling it in the arch of her body, hearing it in her quick breaths. She was helpless, mindless, his. He drove his tongue into her and felt her explode, wave after wave.

As she shuddered, he moved up her body, hands fast, mouth hot and open. Suddenly, on a surge of strength, she rolled on top of him. Within seconds, she'd dev-astated his claim to leadership. All fire, all speed, all woman, she took control.

Heedless, greedy, they moved over the bed. Mur-murs were incoherent, care was forgotten. They took with only one goal in mind. Pleasure—sweet, forbid-den pleasure.

Shaking, locked tight, they reached the goal together.

Dawn was breaking, clear and calm as Kate lay still, watching Ky sleep. She knew what she had to do for both of them, to both of them. Fate had brought them together a second time. It wouldn't bring them together again.

She'd bargained with Ky, offering him a share of gold for his skill. In the beginning, she'd believed that she wanted the treasure, needed it to give her all the options she'd never had before. That choice. Now, she knew she didn't want it at all. A hundred times more gold wouldn't change what was between her and Ky—what drew them to each other, and what kept them apart.

She loved him. She understood that, in his way, he loved her. Did that change the differences between them? Did that make her able and willing to give up her own life to suit his, or able and willing to demand that he do the same?

Their worlds were no closer together now than they'd been four years ago. Their desires no more in tune. With the gold she'd leave for him, he'd be able to do what he wanted with his life. She needed no treasure for that.

If she stayed... Unable to stop herself, Kate reached out to touch his cheek. If she stayed she'd bury herself for him. Eventually, she'd despise herself for it, and he'd resent her. Better that they take what they'd had for a few weeks than cover it with years of disappoinments.

The treasure was important to him. He'd taken risks for it, worked for it. She'd give her father his memorial. Ky would have the rest.

Quietly, still watching him sleep, she dressed.

It didn't take Kate long to gather what she'd come with. Taking her suitcase downstairs, she carefully packed what she'd take with her from the *Liberty*. In a box, she placed the pottery bowl wrapped in layers of newspaper. The coins, the blackened silver and the shiny gold, she zipped into a small pouch. With equal care, she packed the film she'd taken during their days under the ocean.

What she'd designated for the museum she'd already marked. Leaving the list on the table, she left the house.

She told herself it would be cleaner if she left no note, yet she found herself hesitating. How could she make him understand? After putting her suitcase in her car, she went back into the house. Quietly, she took the five gold coins upstairs and placed them on Ky's dresser. With a last look at him as he slept, she went back out again.

She'd have a final moment with the sea. In the quiet air of morning, Kate walked over the dunes.

She'd remember it this way—empty, endless and full of sound. Surf foamed against the sand, white on white.

What was beneath the surface would always call her—the memories of peace, of excitement, of sharing both with Ky. Only a summer, she thought. Life was made of four seasons, not one.

Day was strengthening, and her time was up. Turning, she scanned the island until she saw the tip of the lighthouse. Some things lasted, she thought with a smile. She'd learned a great deal in a few short weeks. She was her own woman at last. She could make her own way. As a teacher, she told herself that knowledge was precious. But it made her ache with loneliness. She left the empty sea behind her.

Though she wanted to, Kate deliberately kept herself from looking at the house as she walked back to her car. She didn't need to see it again to remember it. If things had been different… Kate reached for the door handle of her car. Her fingers were still inches from it when she was spun around.

"What the hell're you doing?"

Facing Ky, she felt her resolve crumble, then rebuild. He was barely awake, and barely dressed. His eyes were heavy with sleep, his hair disheveled from it. All he wore was a pair of ragged cut-offs. She folded her hands in front of her and hoped her voice would be strong and clear.

"I had hoped to be gone before you woke."

"Gone?" His eyes locked on hers. "Where?"

"I'm going back to Connecticut."

"Oh?" He swore he wouldn't lose his temper. Not this time. This time, it might be fatal for both of them. "Why?"

Her nerves skipped. The question had been quiet enough, but she knew that cold, flat expression in his eyes. The wrong move, and he'd leap. "You said it yourself yesterday, Ky, when we came up from the last dive. I've done what I came for."

He opened his hand. Five coins shone in the morning sun. "What about this?"

"I left them for you." She swallowed, no longer certain how long she could speak without showing she was breaking in two. "The treasure isn't important to me. It's yours."

"Damn generous of you." Turning over his hand, he dropped the coins into the sand. "That's how much the gold means to me, professor."

She stared at the gold on the ground in front of her. "I don't understand you."

"*You* wanted the treasure," he tossed at her. "It never mattered to me."

"But you said," she began, then shook her head. "When I first came to you, you took the job because of the treasure."

"I took the job because of you. You wanted the gold, Kate."

"It wasn't the money." Dragging a hand through her hair, she turned away. "It was never the money."

"Maybe not. It was your father."

She nodded because it was true, but it no longer hurt. "I finished what he started, and I gave myself something. I don't want any more coins, Ky."

"Why are you running away from me again?"

Slowly, she turned back. "We're four years older than we were before, but we're the same people."

"So?"

"Ky, when I went away before, it was partially because of my father, because I felt I owed him my loyalty. But if I'd thought you'd wanted me. *Me*," she repeated, placing her palm over her heart, "not what you wanted me to be. If I'd thought that, and if I'd thought you and I could make a future together, I wouldn't have gone. I wouldn't be leaving now."

"What the hell gives you the right to decide what I want, what I feel?" He whirled away from her, too furious to remain close. "Maybe I made mistakes, maybe I just assumed too much four years ago. Damn it, I paid for it, Kate, every day from the time you left until you came back. I've done everything I could to be careful this time around, not to push, not to assume. Then I wake up and find you leaving without a word."

"There aren't any words, Ky. I've always given you too many of them, and you've never given me enough."

"You're better with words than I am."

"All right, then I'll use them. I love you." She waited until he turned back to her. The restlessness was on him again. He was holding it off with sheer will. "I've always loved you, but I think I know my own limitations. Maybe I know yours too."

"No, you think too much about limitations, Kate, and not enough about possibilities. I let you walk away from me before. It's not going to be so easy this time."

"I have to be my own person, Ky. I won't live the rest of my life as I've lived it up to now."

"Who the hell wants you to?" he exploded. "Who the hell wants you to be anything but what you are? It's about time you stopped equating love with responsibility and started looking at the other side of it. It's sharing, giving and taking and laughing. If I ask you to give part of yourself to me, I'm going to give part of myself right back."

Unable to stop himself he took her arms in his hands, just holding, as if through the contact he could make his words sink in.

"I don't want your constant devotion. I don't want you to be obliged to me. I don't want to go through life thinking that whatever you do, you do because you want to please me. Damn it, I don't want that kind of responsibility."

Without words, she stared at him. He'd never said anything to her so simply, so free of half meanings. Hope rose in her. Yet still, he was telling her only what he didn't want. Once he gave her the flip side of that coin hope could vanish.

"Tell me what you do want."

He had only one answer. "Come with me a minute." Taking her hand, he drew her toward the shed. "When I started this, it was because I'd always promised myself I would. Before long, the reasons changed." Turning the latch, he pulled the shed doors open.

For a moment, she saw nothing. Gradually, her eyes adjusted to the dimness and she stepped inside. The boat was nearly finished. The hull was sanded and sealed and painted, waiting for Ky to take it outside and attach the mast. It was lovely, clean and simple.

Just looking at it, Kate could imagine the way it would flow with the wind. Free, light and clever.

"It's beautiful, Ky. I always wondered..." She broke off as she read the name printed boldly on the stern. *Second Chance.*

"That's all I want from you," Ky told her, pointing to the two words. "The boat's yours. When I started it, I thought I was building it for me. But I built it for you, because I knew it was one dream you'd share with me. I only want what's printed on it, Kate. For both of us." Speechless, she watched him lean over the starboard side and open a small compartment. He drew out a tiny box.

"I had this cleaned. You wouldn't take it from me before." Opening the lid, he revealed the diamond he'd found, sparkling now in a simple gold setting. "It didn't cost me anything and it wasn't made especially for you. It's just something I found among a bunch of rocks."

When she started to speak, he held up a hand. "Hold on. You wanted words, I haven't finished with them yet. I know you have to teach, I'm not asking you to give it up. I am asking that you give me one year here on the island. There's a school here, not Yale, but people still have to be taught. A year, Kate. If it isn't what you want after that, I'll go back with you."

Her brows drew together. "Back? To Connecticut? You'd live in Connecticut?"

"If that's what it takes."

A compromise...she thought, baffled. Was he offering to adjust his life for hers? "And if that isn't right for you?"

"Then we'll try someplace else, damn it. We'll find someplace in between. Maybe we'll move half a dozen times in the next few years. What does it matter?"

What did it matter? she wondered as she studied him. He was offering her what she'd waited for all of her life. Love without chains.

"I want you to marry me." He wondered if that simple statement shook her as much as it did him. "Tomorrow isn't soon enough, but if you'll give me the year, I can wait."

She nearly smiled. He'd never wait. Once he had her promise of the year, he'd subtly and not so subtly work on her until she found herself at the altar. It was nearly tempting to make him go through the effort.

Limitations? Had she spoken of limitations? Love had none.

"No," she decided aloud. "You only get the year if I get the ring. And what goes with it."

"Deal." He took her hand quickly as though she might change her mind. "Once it's on, you're stuck, professor." Pulling the ring from the box he slipped it onto her finger. Swearing lightly, he shook his head. "It's too big."

"It's all right. I'll keep my hand closed for the next fifty years or so." With a laugh, she went into his arms. All doubts vanished. They'd make it, she told herself. South, north or anywhere in between.

"We'll have it sized," he murmured, nuzzling into her neck.

"Only if they can do it while it's on my finger." Kate

closed her eyes. She'd just found everything. Did he know it? "Ky, about the *Liberty*, the rest of the treasure."

He tilted her face up to kiss her. "We've already found it."

* * * * *

Temptation

This book is dedicated with gratitude and affection to Nancy Jackson.

Chapter 1

"If there's one thing I hate," Eden mumbled, "it's six o'clock in the morning."

Sunlight poured through the thinly screened windows of the cabin and fell on the wooden floor, the metal bars of her bunk, and her face. The sound of the morning bell echoed dully in her head. Though she'd known that long, clanging ring for only three days, Eden already hated it.

For one fanciful moment, she buried her face under the pillow, imagining herself cuddled in her big four-poster. The Irish-linen sheets would smell ever-so-slightly of lemon. In her airy pastel bedroom, the curtains would be drawn against the morning, the scent of fresh flowers sweetening the air.

The pillowcase smelled of feathers and detergent.

With a grunt, Eden tossed the pillow to the floor, then struggled to sit up. Now that the morning bell had stopped, she could hear the cries of a couple of excited crows. From the cabin directly across the compound came a happy blast of rock music. With glazed eyes, she watched Candice Bartholomew bound out of the adjoining bunk. Her sharp-featured pixie's face was split by a grin.

"Morning." Candy's long, clever fingers ran through her thatch of red hair like scoops, causing it to bounce into further disarray. Candy was, Eden had always thought, all bounce. "It's a beautiful day," she announced, in a voice as cheerful as the rest of her. Watching her friend stretch in frilly baby-doll pajamas, Eden gave another noncommittal grunt. She swung her bare legs off the mattress and contemplated the accomplishment of putting her feet on the floor.

"I could grow to hate you." Eden's voice, still husky with sleep, carried the rounded tones of her finishing-school education. Eyes shut, she pushed her own tousled blond hair away from her face.

Grinning, Candy tossed open the cabin door so that she could breathe in the fresh morning air while she studied her friend. The strong summer sunlight shot through Eden's pale hair, making it look fragile where it lay against her forehead and cheeks. Her eyes remained shut. Her slender shoulders slumped, she let out an enormous yawn. Candy wisely said nothing, knowing Eden didn't share her enthusiasm for sunrise.

"It can't be morning," Eden grumbled. "I swear I only lay down five minutes ago." Resting her elbows on her knees, she dropped her face into her hands. Her complexion was creamy, with just a suggestion of rose on the crest of her cheekbones. Her nose was small, with a hint of an upward tilt at the tip. What might have been a coolly aristocratic face was gentled by a full, generous mouth.

Candy took in one last breath of air, then shut the door. "All you need is a shower and some coffee. The first week of camp's the toughest, remember?"

Eden opened wide, lake-blue eyes. "Easy for you to say. You're not the one who fell in the poison ivy."

"Still itching?"

"A little." Because her own foul mood was making her feel guilty, Eden managed a smile. Everything softened, eyes, mouth, voice. "In any case, this is the first time we're the campees instead of the campers." Letting out another fierce yawn, she rose and tugged on a robe. The air coming through the screens was fresh as a daisy, and chilly enough to make Eden's toes curl. She wished she could remember what she'd done with her slippers.

"Try under the bunk," Candy suggested.

Eden bent down and found them. They were embroidered pink silk, hardly practical, but it hadn't seemed worthwhile to invest in another pair. Putting them on gave her an excuse to sit down again. "Do you really think five consecutive summers at Camp Forden for Girls prepared us for this?"

Haunted by her own doubts, Candy clasped her hands together. "Eden, are you having second thoughts?"

Because she recognized distress in the bubbly voice, Eden buried her own doubts. She had both a financial and emotional interest in the newly formed Camp Liberty. Complaining wasn't going to put her on the road to success. With a shake of her head, she walked over to squeeze Candy's shoulder. "What I have is a terminal case of morning crankiness. Let me get that shower, then I'll be ready to face our twenty-seven tenants."

"Eden." Candy stopped her before she closed the bathroom door. "It's going to work, for both of us. I know it."

"I know it, too." Eden closed the bathroom door and leaned against it. She could admit it now, while she was alone. She was scared to death. Her last dime, and her last ray of hope, were tied up in the six cabins, the stables and the cafeteria that were Camp Liberty. What did Eden Carlbough, former Philadelphia socialite, know about managing a girls' summer camp? Just enough to terrify her.

If she failed now, with this, could she pick up the pieces and go on? Would there be any pieces left? Confidence was what was needed, she told herself as she turned the taps on. Once inside the narrow shower stall, she gave the tap optimistically marked HOT another twist. Water, lukewarm, dripped out halfheartedly. Confidence, Eden thought again as she shivered under the miserly spray. Plus some cold hard cash and a whole barrel of luck.

She found the soap and began to lather with the soft-scented French milled she still allowed herself to indulge in. A year ago she would never have considered something as lowly as soap an indulgence.

A year ago.

Eden turned so that the rapidly cooling water hit her

back. A year ago she would have risen at eight, had a leisurely, steaming shower, then breakfasted on toast and coffee, perhaps some shirred eggs. Sometime before ten, she would have driven to the library for her volunteer morning. There would have been lunch with Eric, perhaps at the Deux Cheminées before she gave her afternoon to the museum or one of Aunt Dottie's charities.

The biggest decision she might have made was whether to wear her rose silk suit or her ivory linen. Her evening might have been spent quietly at home, or at one of Philadelphia's elegant dinner parties.

No pressure. No problems. But then, Papa had been alive.

Eden sighed as she rinsed away the last of the lather. The light French scent clung to her even as she dried her skin with the serviceable camp-issue towel. When her father had been alive, she had thought that money was simply something to spend and that time was forever. She had been raised to plan a menu, but not to cook; to run a home, but not to clean it.

Throughout her childhood, she had been carelessly happy with her widowed father in the ageless elegance of their Philadelphia home. There had always been party dresses and cotillions, afternoon teas and riding lessons. The Carlbough name was an old and respected one. The Carlbough money had been a simple fact of life.

How quickly and finally things could change.

Now she was giving riding instructions and juggling

columns in a ledger with the vain hope that one and one didn't always make two.

Because the tiny mirror over the tiny sink was dripping with condensation, Eden rubbed it with the towel. She took a miserly dab of the half pot of imported face cream she had left. She was going to make it last through the summer. If *she* lasted through the summer herself, another pot would be her reward.

Eden found the cabin empty when she opened the bathroom door. If she knew Candy, and after twenty years she certainly did, the redhead would be down with the girls already. How easily she became acclimatized, Eden thought; then she reminded herself it was time she did the same. She took her jeans and her red T-shirt with CAMP LIBERTY emblazoned on the chest, and began to dress. Even as a teenager, Eden had rarely dressed so casually.

She had enjoyed her social life—the parties, the well-chaperoned ski trips to Vermont, the trips to New York for shopping or the theater, the vacations in Europe. The prospect of earning a living had never been considered, by her, or her father. Carlbough women didn't work, they chaired committees.

College years had been spent with the idea of rounding out her education rather than focusing on a career. At twenty-three, Eden was forced to admit she was qualified to do absolutely nothing.

She could have blamed her father. But how could she blame a man who had been so indulgent and loving? She had adored him. She could blame herself for being naive and shortsighted, but she could never blame her father. Even now, a year after his sudden death, she still felt pangs of grief.

She could deal with that. The one thing she had been taught to do, the one thing she felt herself fully qualified to accomplish, was to cover emotion with poise, with control, or with disdain. She could go day after day, week after week through the summer, surrounded by the girls at camp and the counselors Candy had hired, and none of them would know she still mourned her father. Or that her pride had been shattered by Eric Keeton.

Eric, the promising young banker with her father's firm. Eric, always so charming, so attentive, so suitable. It had been during her last year of college that she had accepted his ring and made her promises to him. And he had made promises to her.

When she discovered the hurt was still there, Eden coated it, layer by layer, with anger. Facing the mirror, she tugged her hair back in a short ponytail, a style her hairdresser would have shuddered at.

It was more practical, Eden told her reflection. She was a practical woman now, and hair waving softly to the shoulders would just have got in the way during the riding lessons she was to give that morning.

For a moment, she pressed her fingers against her eyes. Why were the mornings always the worst? She would wake, expecting to come out of some bad dream and find herself at home again. But it wasn't her home any longer. There were strangers living in it now. Brian Carlbough's death had not been a bad dream, but a horrible, horrible reality.

A sudden heart attack had taken him overnight, leaving Eden stunned with shock and grief. Even before the grief could fade, Eden had been struck with another shock.

There had been lawyers, black-vested lawyers with long, technical monologues. They had had offices that had smelled of old leather and fresh polish. With solemn faces and politely folded hands, they had shattered her world.

Poor investments, she had been told, bad market trends, mortgages, second mortgages, short-term loans. The simple fact had been, once the details had been sifted through, there had been no money.

Brian Carlbough had been a gambler. At the time of his death, his luck had turned, and he hadn't had time to recoup his losses. His daughter had been forced to liquidate his assets in order to pay off the debts. The house she had grown up in and loved was gone. She had still been numbed by grief when she had found herself without a home or an income. Crashing down on top of that had been Eric's betrayal.

Eden yanked open the cabin door and was met by the balmy morning air of the mountains. The breathtaking view of greening hills and blue sky didn't affect her. She was back in Philadelphia, hearing Eric's calm, reasonable voice.

The scandal, she remembered and began marching toward the big cabin where mess would be served. *His* reputation. *His* career. Everything she had loved had been taken away, but he had only been concerned with how he might be affected.

He had never loved her. Eden jammed her hands into her pockets and kept walking. She'd been a fool not to see it from the beginning. But she'd learned, Eden reminded herself. How she'd learned. It had simply been a merger to Eric, the Carlbough name, the Carlbough money and reputation. When they had been destroyed, he had cut his losses.

Eden slowed her quick pace, realizing she was out of breath, not from exertion but from temper. It would never do to walk into breakfast with her face flushed and her eyes gleaming. Giving herself a moment, she took a few deep breaths and looked around her.

The air was still cool, but by midmorning the sun would be warm and strong. Summer had barely begun.

And it was beautiful. Lining the compound were a half-dozen small cabins with their window flaps open to the morning. The sound of girlish laughter floated through the windows. Along the pathway between cabins four and five was a scattering of anemones. A dogwood, with a few stubborn blooms clinging to it, stood nearby. Above cabin two, a mockingbird chattered.

Beyond the main camp to the west were rolling hills, deeply green. Grazing horses and trees dotted them. There was an openness here, a sense of space which Eden found incredible. Her life had always been focused on the city. Streets, buildings, traffic, people, those had been the familiar. There were times when she felt a quick pang of need for what had been. It was still possible for her to have all that. Aunt Dottie had offered her home and her love. No one would ever know how long and hard Eden had wrestled with the temptation to accept the invitation and let her life drift.

Perhaps gambling was in Eden's blood, too. Why else would she have sunk what ready cash she had had left into a fledgling camp for girls in the hills?

Because she had had to try, Eden reminded herself. She had had to take the risk on her own. She could never go back into the shell of the fragile porcelain doll she had been. Here, centered in such open space, she would take the time to learn about herself. What was inside Eden Carlbough? Maybe, just maybe, by expanding her horizons, she would find her place.

Candy was right. Eden took a long last breath. It was going to work. They were going to make it work.

"Hungry?" Her hair damp from whatever shower she'd popped into, Candy cut across Eden's path.

"Starved." Content, Eden swung a friendly arm around Candy's shoulder. "Where did you run off to?"

"You know me, I can't let any part of this place run by itself." Like Eden, Candy swept her gaze over the camp. Her expression reflected everything inside her— the love, the fear, the fierce pride. "I was worried about you."

"Candy, I told you, I was just cranky this morning." Eden watched a group of girls rush out of a cabin and head for breakfast.

"Eden, we've been friends since we were six months old. No one knows better than I what you're going through."

No, no one did, and since Candy was the person she loved best, Eden determined to do a better job of concealing the wounds that were still open. "I've put it behind me, Candy."

"Maybe. But I know that the camp was initially my venture, and that I roped you in."

"You didn't rope me in. I wanted to invest. We both know it was a pitifully small amount."

"Not to me. The extra money made it possible for me to include the equestrian program. Then, when you agreed to come in and give riding lessons..."

"Just keeping a close eye on my investment," Eden said lightly. "Next year I won't be a part-time riding instructor and bookkeeper. I'll be a full-fledged counselor. No regrets, Candy." This time she meant it. "It's ours."

"And the bank's."

Eden shrugged that away. "We need this place. You, because it's what you've always wanted to do, always worked and studied toward. Me..." She hesitated, then sighed. "Let's face it, I haven't got anything else. The camp's putting a roof over my head, giving me three meals a day and a goal. I need to prove I can make it."

"People think we're crazy."

The pride came back, with a feeling of recklessness Eden was just learning to savor. "Let them."

With a laugh, Candy tugged at Eden's hair. "Let's eat."

Two hours later, Eden was winding up the day's first riding lesson. This was her specialty, her contribution to the partnership she and Candy had made. It had also been decided to trust Eden with the books, mainly because no one could have been more inept with figures than Candice Bartholomew.

Candy had interviewed and hired a staff of counselors, a nutritionist and a nurse. They hoped to have a pool and a swimming instructor one day, but for now there was supervised swimming and rowing on the lake, arts and crafts, hiking and archery. Candy had spent months refining a program for the summer, while Eden had juggled the profit-and-loss statements. She prayed the money would hold out while Candy ordered supplies.

Unlike Candy, Eden wasn't certain the first week of camp would be the toughest. Her partner had all the training, all the qualifications for running the camp, but Candy also had an optimist's flair for overlooking details like red ink on the books.

Pushing those thoughts aside, Eden signaled from the center of the corral. "That's all for today." She scanned the six young faces under their black riding hats. "You're doing very well."

"When can we gallop, Miss Carlbough?"

"After you learn to trot." She patted one of the horses' flanks. Wouldn't it be lovely, she thought, to gallop off into the hills, riding so fast even memories couldn't follow? Foolish, Eden told herself; she gave her attention back to the girls. "Dismount, then cool down your horses. Remember, they depend on you." The breeze tossed her bangs, and she brushed at them absently. "Remember to put all the tack in its proper place for the next class."

This caused the groans she expected. Riding and

playing with the horses was one thing, tidying up afterward was another. Eden considered exerting discipline without causing resentment another accomplishment. Over the past week, she'd learned to link the girls' faces and names. The eleven- and twelve-year-olds in her group had an enthusiasm that kept her on her toes. She'd already separated in her mind the two or three she instructed who had the kind of horse fever she recognized from her own adolescence. It was rewarding, after an hour on her feet in the sun, to answer the rapid-fire questions. Ultimately, one by one, she nudged them toward the stables.

"Eden!" Turning, she spotted Candy hustling toward her. Even from a distance, Eden recognized concern.

"What's happened?"

"We're missing three kids."

"What?" Panic came first, and quickly. Years of training had her pulling it back. "What do you mean, missing?"

"I mean they're nowhere in camp. Roberta Snow, Linda Hopkins and Marcie Jamison." Candy dragged a hand through her hair, a habitual gesture of tension. "Barbara was lining up her group for rowing, and they didn't show. We've looked everywhere."

"We can't panic," Eden said, as much to warn herself as Candy. "Roberta Snow? Isn't she the little brunette who stuck a lizard down one of the other girls' shirts? And the one who set off the morning bell at 3:00 a.m.?"

"Yes, that's her." Candy set her teeth. "The little darling. Judge Harper Snow's granddaughter. If she's skinned her knee, we'll probably face a lawsuit." With a shake of her head, Candy switched to an undertone. "The last anyone saw of her this morning, she was walking east." She pointed a finger, paint-spattered from her early art class. "No one noticed the other girls, but my bet is that they're with her. Darling Roberta is an inveterate leader."

"If she's walking that way, wouldn't she run into that apple orchard?"

"Yeah." Candy shut her eyes. "Oh, yeah. I'm going to have six girls up to their wrists in modeling clay in ten minutes, or I'd go off myself. Eden, I'm almost sure they headed for the orchard. One of the other girls admitted she heard Roberta planning to sneak over there for a few samples. We don't want any trouble with the owner. He's letting us use his lake only because I begged, shamelessly. He wasn't thrilled about having a girls' summer camp for a neighbor."

"Well, he has one," Eden pointed out. "So we'll all have to deal with it. I'm the one most easily spared around here, so I'll go after them."

"I was hoping you'd say that. Seriously, Eden, if they've snuck into that orchard, which I'd bet my last dime they have, we could be in for it. The man made no bones about how he feels about his land and his privacy."

"Three little girls are hardly going to do any damage to a bunch of apple trees." Eden began to walk, with Candy scurrying to keep pace.

"He's Chase Elliot. You know, Elliot Apples? Juice, cider, sauce, jelly, chocolate-covered apple seeds, whatever can be made from an apple, they do it. He made it abundantly clear that he didn't want to find any little girls climbing his trees."

"He won't find them, I will." Leaving Candy behind, Eden swung over a fence.

"Put Roberta on a leash when you catch up to her." Candy watched her disappear through the trees.

Eden followed the path from the camp, pleased when she found a crumpled candy wrapper. Roberta. With a grim smile, Eden picked it up and stuffed it in her pocket. Judge Snow's granddaughter had already earned a reputation for her stash of sweets.

It was warm now, but the path veered through a cool grove of aspens. Sunlight dappled the ground, making the walk, if not her errand, pleasant. Squirrels dashed here and there, confident enough in their own speed not to be alarmed at Eden's intrusion. Once a rabbit darted across her path, and disappeared into the brush with a frantic rustle. Overhead a woodpecker drummed, sending out an echo.

It occurred to Eden that she was more completely alone than she had ever been before. No civilization here. She bent down for another candy wrapper. Well, very little of it.

There were new scents here, earth, animal, vegetation, to be discovered. Wildflowers sprang up, tougher and more resilient than hothouse roses. It pleased her that she was even beginning to be able to recognize a few. They came back, year after year, without pampering, taking what came and thriving on it. They gave her hope. She could find a place here. Had found a place, she corrected herself. Her friends in Philadelphia might think her mad, but she was beginning to enjoy it.

The grove of aspens thinned abruptly, and the sunlight was strong again. She blinked against it, then shielded her eyes as she scanned the Elliot orchards.

Apple trees stretched ahead of her as far as she could see, to the north, south and east. Row after row after row of trees lined the slopes. Some of them were old and gnarled, some young and straight. Instantly she thought of early spring and the overwhelming scent of apple blossoms.

It would be magnificent, she thought as she stepped up to the fence that separated the properties. The fragrance, the pretty white-and-pink blossoms, the freshly green leaves, would be a marvelous sight. Now the leaves were dark and thick, and instead of blossoms, she could see fruit in the trees closest to her. Small, shiny, and green they hung, waiting for the sun to ripen them.

How many times had she eaten applesauce that had begun right here? The idea made her smile as she began to climb the fence. Her vision of an orchard had been a lazy little grove guarded by an old man in overalls. A quaint picture, but nothing as huge and impressive as the reality.

The sound of giggling took her by surprise. Shifting toward the direction of the sound, Eden watched an apple fall from a tree and roll toward her feet. Bending, she picked it up, tossing it away as she walked closer. When she looked up, she spotted three pairs of sneakers beneath the cover of leaves and branches.

"Ladies." Eden spoke coolly and was rewarded by

three startled gasps. "Apparently you took a wrong turn on your way to the lake."

Roberta's triangular, freckled face appeared through the leaves. "Hi, Miss Carlbough. Would you like an apple?"

The devil. But even as she thought it, Eden had to tighten her lips against a smile. "Down," she said simply, then stepped closer to the trunk to assist.

They didn't need her. Three agile little bodies scrambled down and dropped lightly onto the ground. In a gesture she knew could be intimidating, Eden lifted her left eyebrow.

"I'm sure you're aware that leaving camp property unsupervised and without permission is against the rules."

"Yes, Miss Carlbough." The response would have been humble if it hadn't been for the gleam in Roberta's eye.

"Since none of you seem interested in rowing today, Mrs. Petrie has a great deal of washing up to be done in the kitchen." Pleased by her own inspiration, Eden decided Candy would approve. "You're to report to Miss Bartholomew, then to Mrs. Petrie for kitchen detail."

Only two of the girls dropped their heads and looked down at the ground.

"Miss Carlbough, do you think it's fair to give us extra kitchen detail?" Roberta, one half-eaten apple still in hand, tilted her pointed chin. "After all, our parents are paying for the camp."

Eden felt her palms grow damp. Judge Snow was a wealthy and powerful man with a reputation for in-

dulging his granddaughter. If the little monster com-
plained... No. Eden took a deep breath and not by a
flicker showed her anxiety. She wouldn't be intimidated
or blackmailed by a pint-size con artist with apple juice
on her chin.

"Yes, your parents are paying for you to be entertained, instructed and disciplined. When they signed
you up for Camp Liberty, it was with the understanding that you would obey the rules. But if you prefer,
I'd be glad to call your parents and discuss this inci-
dent with them."

"No, ma'am." Knowing when to retreat, Roberta
smiled charmingly. "We'll be glad to help Mrs. Petrie,
and we're sorry for breaking the rules."

And I'm sure you have a bridge I could buy, Eden
thought, but she kept her face impassive. "Fine. It's
time to start back."

"My hat!" Roberta would have darted back up the
tree if Eden hadn't made a lucky grab for her. "I left
my hat up there. Please, Miss Carlbough, it's my Phillies cap, and it's autographed and everything."

"You start back. I'll get it. I don't want Miss Bartholomew to worry any longer than necessary."

"We'll apologize."

"See that you do." Eden watched them scramble over
the fence. "And no detours," she called out. "Or I keep
the cap." One look at Roberta assured her that that
bit of blackmail was all that was needed. "Monsters,"
she murmured as they jogged back into the grove, but
the smile finally escaped. Turning back, she studied
the tree.

All she had to do was climb up. It had looked simple enough when Roberta and her partners-in-crime had done it. Somehow, it didn't look as simple now. Squaring her shoulders, Eden stepped forward to grab a low-hanging branch. She'd done a little mountain-climbing in Switzerland; how much harder could this be? Pulling herself up, she hooked her foot in the first vee she found. The bark was rough against her palm. Concentrating on her goal, she ignored the scrapes. With both feet secured, she reached for the next branch and began to work her way up. Leaves brushed her cheeks.

She spotted the cap hanging on a short branch, two arms' lengths out of reach. When she made the mistake of looking down, her stomach clenched. So don't look, Eden ordered herself. What you can't see can't hurt you. She hoped.

Eden cautiously inched her way out to the cap. When her fingers made contact with it, she let out a low breath of relief. After setting it on her own head, she found herself looking out, beyond the tree, over the orchard.

Now it was the symmetry that caught her admiration. From her bird's height, she could see the order as well as the beauty. She could just barely glimpse a slice of the lake beyond the aspens. It winked blue in the distance. There were barnlike buildings, and what appeared to be a greenhouse, far off to the right. About a quarter of a mile away, there was a truck, apparently abandoned, on a wide dirt path. In the quiet, birds began to sing again. Turning her head, she saw the bright yellow flash of a butterfly.

The scent of leaves and fruit and earth was tangy,

basic. Unable to resist, Eden reached out and plucked a sun-warmed apple.

He'd never miss it, she decided as she bit into the skin. The tart flavor, not quite ripe, shot into her mouth. She shivered at the shock of it, the sensual appeal, then bit again. Delicious, she thought. Exciting. Forbidden fruit usually was, she remembered, but she grinned as she took a third bite.

"What in the devil are you doing?"

She started, almost unseating herself, as the voice boomed up from below. She swallowed the bite of apple quickly before peering down through the leaves.

He stood with his hands on his hips, narrow, lean, spare. A faded denim workshirt was rolled up past the elbows to show tan and muscle. Warily, Eden brought her eyes to his face. It was tanned like his arms, with the skin drawn tight over bone. His nose was long and not quite straight, his mouth full and firm and frowning. Jet-black and unruly, his hair fell over his brow and curled just beyond the collar of his shirt. Pale, almost translucent green eyes scowled up at her.

An apple, Eden, and now the serpent. The idea ran through her head before she drew herself back.

Wonderful, she thought. She'd been caught pinching apples by the foreman. Since disappearing wasn't an option, she opened her mouth to start a plausible explanation.

"Young lady, do you belong at the camp next door?"

The tone brought on a frown. She might be penniless, she might be scrambling to make a living, but she was still a Carlbough. And a Carlbough could certainly handle an apple foreman. "Yes, that's right. I'd like to—"

"Are you aware that this is private property, and that you're trespassing?"

The color of her eyes deepened, the only outward sign of her embarrassed fury. "Yes, but I—"

"These trees weren't planted for little girls to climb."

"I hardly think—"

"Come down." There was absolute command in his tone. "I'll have to take you back to the camp director."

The temper she had always gently controlled bubbled up until she gave serious consideration to throwing what was left of the apple down on his head. No one, absolutely no one, gave her orders. "That won't be necessary."

"I'll decide what's necessary. Come down here."

She'd come down all right, Eden thought. Then, with a few well-chosen words, he'd be put precisely in his place. Annoyance carried her from branch to branch, leaving no room for thoughts of height or inexperience. The two scrapes she picked up on the trip were hardly felt. Her back was to him as she lowered herself into a vee of the trunk. The pleasure of demolishing him with icy manners would be well worth the embarrassment of having been caught in the wrong place at the wrong time. She imagined him cringing and babbling an incoherent apology.

Then her foot slipped, and her frantic grab for a limb was an inch short of the mark. With a shriek that was equal parts surprise and dismay, she fell backward into space.

The breath whooshed back out of her as she connected with something solid. The tanned, muscled arms she'd seen from above wrapped around her. Momentum carried them both to the ground and, like the apple, they rolled. When the world stopped spinning, Eden found herself beneath a very firm, very long body.

Roberta's cap had flown off and Eden's face, no longer shadowed by the brim, was left unguarded in the sunlight. Chase stared down at her and felt soft breasts yield under him.

"You're not twelve years old," he murmured.

"Certainly not."

Amused now, he shifted his weight, but didn't remove it. "I didn't get a good look at you when you were in the tree." He had time to make up for that now, he decided, and he looked his fill. "You're quite a windfall." Carelessly, he brushed stray strands of hair away from her face. His fingertips were as rough against her skin as the bark had been to her palms. "What are you doing in a girls' summer camp?"

"Running it," she said coldly. It wasn't a complete lie. Because it would have bruised her dignity even more to squirm, she settled on sending him an icy look. "Would you mind?"

"Running it?" Since she had dropped out of one of his trees, he had no qualms about ignoring her request. "I met someone. Bartholomew—red hair, appealing face." He scanned Eden's classic features. "You're not her."

"Obviously not." Because his body was too warm, too male, and too close, she sacrificed some dignity by putting her hands to his shoulders. He didn't budge. "I'm her partner. Eden Carlbough."

"Ah, of the Philadelphia Carlboughs."

The humor in his voice was another blow to her pride. Eden combated it with a withering stare. "That's correct."

Intriguing little package, he thought. All manners and breeding. "A pleasure, Miss Carlbough. I'm Chase Elliot of the South Mountain Elliots."

Chapter 2

Perfect, just perfect, Eden thought as she stared up at him. Not the foreman, but the bloody owner. Caught stealing apples by, falling out of trees on and pinned to the ground under, the owner. She took a deep breath.

"How do you do, Mr. Elliot."

She might have been in the front parlor pouring tea, Chase thought; he had to admire her. Then he burst out laughing. "I do just fine, Miss Carlbough. And you?"

He was laughing at her. Even after the scandal and shame she had faced, no one had dared laugh at her. Not to her face. Her lips trembled once before she managed to control them. She wouldn't give the oaf the pleasure of knowing how much he infuriated her.

"I'm quite well, thank you, or will be when you let me up."

City manners, he thought. Socially correct and absolutely meaningless. His own were a bit cruder, but more honest. "In a minute. I'm finding this conversation fascinating."

"Then perhaps we could continue it standing up."

"I'm very comfortable." That wasn't precisely true. The soft, slender lines of her body were causing him some problems. Rather than alleviate them, Chase decided to enjoy them. And her. "So, how are you finding life in the rough?"

He was still laughing at her, without troubling to pretend otherwise. Eden tasted the fury bubbling up in her throat. She swallowed it. "Mr. Elliot—"

"Chase," he interrupted. "I think, under the circumstances, we should dispense with formalities."

Control teetered long enough for her to shove against his shoulders again. It was like pushing rock. "This is ridiculous. You *have* to let me up."

"I rarely have to do anything." His voice was a drawl now, and insolent, but no less imposing than the bellow that had first greeted her. "I've heard a lot about you, Eden Carlbough." And he'd seen the newspaper pictures that he now realized had been just shy of the mark. It was difficult to capture that cool sexuality in two dimensions. "I never expected a Carlbough of Philadelphia to fall out of one of my trees."

Her breathing became unsteady. All the training, the years she'd spent being taught how to coat every emotion with politeness, began to crack. "It was hardly my intention to fall out of one of your trees."

"Wouldn't have fallen out if you hadn't climbed up." He smiled, realizing how glad he was that he'd decided to check this section of the orchard himself.

This couldn't be happening. Eden closed her eyes a moment and waited for things to fall back into their proper places. She couldn't be lying flat on her back under a stranger. "Mr. Elliot." Her voice was calm and reasonable when she tried it again. "I'd be more than happy to give you a complete explanation if you'd let me up."

"Explanation first."

Her mouth quite simply fell open. "You are the most unbelievably rude and boorish man I have ever met."

"My property," he said simply. "My rules. Let's hear your explanation."

She almost shuddered with the effort to hold back the torrent of abuse that leaped to her tongue. Because of her position, she had to squint up at him. Already a headache was collecting behind her eyes. "Three of my girls wandered away from camp. Unfortunately, they climbed over the fence and onto your property. I found them, ordered them down and sent them back to the camp, where they are being properly disciplined."

"Tar and feathers?"

"I'm sure you'd prefer that, but we settled on extra kitchen detail."

"Seems fair. But that doesn't explain you falling out of my tree and into my arms. Though I've about decided not to complain about that. You smell like Paris." To Eden's amazement, he leaned down and buried his face in her hair. "Wicked nights in Paris."

"Stop it." Now her voice wasn't calm, wasn't disciplined.

Chase felt her heart begin to thud against his own. It

ran through his mind that he wanted to do more than sample her scent. But when he lifted his head, her eyes were wide. Along with the awareness in them was a trace of fear.

"Explanation," he said lightly. "That's all I intend to take at the moment."

She could hear her own pulse hammering in her throat. Of its own accord, her gaze fell upon his mouth. Was she mad, or could she almost taste the surge of masculine flavor that would certainly be on his lips? She felt her muscles softening, then instantly stiffened. She might very well be mad. If an explanation was what it took, she'd give it to him and get away. Far away.

"One of the girls…" Her mind veered vengefully to Roberta. "One of them left her cap in the tree."

"So you went up after it." He nodded, accepting her explanation. "That doesn't explain why you were helping yourself to one of my apples."

"It was mealy."

Grinning again, he ran a hand along her jawline. "I doubt that. I'd imagine it was hard and tart and delicious. I had my share of stomachaches from green apples years ago. The pleasure's usually worth the pain."

Something uncomfortably like need was spreading through her. The fear of it chilled both her eyes and voice. "You have your explanation, and your apology."

"I never heard an apology."

She'd be damned, she'd be twice damned if she'd give him one now. Glaring at him, she nearly managed to look regal. "I want you to let me up this instant. You're perfectly free to prosecute if you feel the need for compensation for a couple of worm-filled apples, but for now, I'm tired of your ridiculous backwoods arrogance."

His apples were the best in the state, the best in the country. But at the moment, he relished the idea of her sinking her pretty white teeth into a worm. "You haven't had a taste of backwoods arrogance yet. Maybe you should."

"You wouldn't dare," she began, only to have the last word muffled by his mouth.

The kiss caught her completely off guard. It was rough and demanding and as tart as the apple had been. Forbidden fruit. To a woman accustomed to coaxing, to requesting, the hard demand left her limp, unable to respond or protest. Then his hands were on her face, his thumbs tracing her jawline. Like the kiss, his palms were hard and thrilling.

He didn't regret it. Though he wasn't a man used to taking from a woman what wasn't offered, he didn't regret it. Not when the fruit was this sweet. Even though she lay very still, he could taste the panicked excitement on her lips. Yes, very sweet, he thought. Very innocent. Very dangerous. He lifted his head the moment she began to struggle.

"Easy," he murmured, still stroking her chin with his thumb. Her eyes were more frantic than furious. "It seems you're not the woman of the world you're reputed to be."

"Let me up." Her voice was shaking now, but she was beyond caring.

Getting to his feet, Chase brought her with him. "Want some help brushing off?"

"You are the most offensive man I've ever met."

"I can believe it. A pity you've been spoiled and pampered for so long." She started to turn away, but he caught her shoulders for one last look. "It should be interesting to see how long you last here without the basics—like hairdressers and butlers."

He's just like everyone else, she thought; she coated her hurt and doubt with disdain. "I'm very late for my next class, Mr. Elliot. If you'll excuse me?"

He lifted his hands from her shoulders, holding the palms out a moment before dropping them. "Try to keep the kids out of the trees," he warned. "A fall can be dangerous."

His smile had insults trembling on her lips. Clamping her tongue between her teeth, Eden scrambled over the fence.

He watched her, enjoying the view until she was swallowed up by the aspens. Glimpsing the cap at his feet, he bent down for it. As good as a calling card, he decided, tucking it into his back pocket.

Eden went through the rest of the day struggling not to think. About anything. She had deliberately avoided telling Candy about her meeting with Chase. In telling of it, she would have to think about it.

The humiliation of being caught up a tree was hard enough to swallow. Still, under other circumstances, she and Candy might have shared a laugh over it. Under any other circumstances.

But more than the humiliation, even more than the anger, were the sensations. She wasn't sure what they were, but each separate sensation she had experienced in the orchard remained fresh and vibrant throughout the day. She couldn't shake them off or cover them over, and she certainly couldn't ignore them. If she understood anything, she understood how important it was for her to close off her feelings before they could grow.

Ridiculous. Eden interrupted her own thoughts. She didn't know Chase Elliot. Moreover, she didn't want to know him. It was true that she couldn't block out what had happened, but she could certainly see that it never happened again.

Over the past year, she had taken control of the reins for the first time in her life. She knew what it was to fumble, what it was to fail, but she also knew she would never fully release those reins again. Disillusionment had toughened her. Perhaps that was the one snatch of silver lining in the cloud.

Because of it, she recognized Chase Elliot as a man who held his own reins, and tightly. She had found him rude and overbearing, but she had also seen his power and authority. She'd had her fill of dominating men. Rough-edged or polished, they were all the same underneath. Since her experience with Eric, Eden's opinion of men in general had reached a low ebb. Her encounter with Chase had done nothing to raise it.

It was annoying that she had to remind herself continually to forget about him.

Learning the camp's routine was enough to occupy her mind. Since she didn't have Candy's years of training and experience in counseling, her responsibilities were relatively few and often mundane, but at least she had the satisfaction of knowing she was more than a spectator. Ambition had become a new vice. If her role as apprentice meant she mucked out stalls and groomed horses, then Eden was determined to have the cleanest stables and the glossiest horses in Pennsylvania. She considered her first blister a badge of accomplishment.

The rush after the dinner bell still intimidated Eden. Twenty-seven girls aged ten to fourteen swarmed the cafeteria. It was one of Eden's new duties to help keep order. Voices were raised on topics that usually ranged from boys to rock stars, then back to boys. With a little luck, there was no jostling or shoving in line. But luck usually required an eagle eye.

Camp Liberty's glossy brochures had promised wholesome food. Tonight's menu included crispy chicken, whipped potatoes and steamed broccoli. Flatware rattled on trays as the girls shuffled, cafeteria-style, down the serving line.

"It's been a good day." Candy stood beside Eden, her eyes shifting back and forth as she managed to watch the entire room at once.

"And nearly over." Even as she said it, Eden realized her back didn't ache quite as much as it had the first couple of days. "I've got two girls in the morning riding session who show real promise. I was hoping I could give them a little extra time a couple of days a week."

"Great, we'll check the schedule." Candy watched one of the counselors convince a camper to put a stem of broccoli on her plate. "I wanted to tell you that you handled Roberta and company beautifully. Kitchen detail was an inspiration."

"Thanks." Eden realized how low her pride had fallen when such a small thing made her glow. "I did have a twinge of guilt about dumping them on Mrs. Petrie."

"The report is they behaved like troopers."

"Roberta?"

"I know." Candy's smile was wry. Both women turned to see the girl in question, already seated and eating daintily. "It's like waiting for the other shoe to drop. Eden, do you remember Marcia Delacroix from Camp Forden?"

"How could I forget?" With the bulk of the campers seated, Eden and Candy joined the line. "She was the one who put the garter snake in Miss Forden's lingerie drawer."

"Yeah." She turned to give Roberta another look. "Do you believe in reincarnation?"

With a laugh, Eden accepted a scoop of potatoes. "Let's just say I'll be checking my underwear." Hefting the tray, she started forward. "You know, Candy, I—" She saw it as if in slow motion. Roberta, the devil's own gleam in her eyes, held her fork vertically, a thick blob of potatoes clinging to the tines. Aim was taken as Roberta pulled back the business end of the fork with an expert flick. Even as Eden opened her mouth, Roberta sent the blob sailing into the hair of the girl across from her. Pandemonium.

Globs of potatoes flew. Girls screamed. More retaliated. In a matter of seconds, floors, tables, chairs and adolescents were coated in a messy layer of white. Like a general leading the way into battle, Candy stepped into the chaos and lifted her whistle. Before she had the chance to blow it, she was hit, right between the eyes.

A shocked silence fell.

With her tray still in her hands, Eden stood, afraid to breathe. One breath, one little breath, she thought, and she would dissolve into helpless laughter. She felt the pressure of a giggle in her lungs as Candy slowly wiped the dollop of potato from the bridge of her nose.

"Young ladies." The two words, delivered in Candy's most ferocious voice, had Eden's breath catching in her throat. "You will finish your meal in silence. Absolute silence. As you finish, you will line up against this wall. When the dinner hour is over, you will be issued rags, mops and buckets. The mess area will shine tonight."

"Yes, Miss Bartholomew." The acknowledgment came in murmured unison. Only Roberta, her hands folded neatly, her face a picture of innocence, responded in clear tones.

After a long ten seconds of silent staring, Candy walked back to Eden and picked up her tray. "If you laugh," she said in an undertone, "I'll tie your tongue into a square knot."

"Who's laughing?" Eden desperately cleared her throat. "I'm not laughing."

"Yes, you are." Candy sailed, like a steamship, to the head table. "You're just clever enough to do it discreetly."

Eden sat, then carefully smoothed her napkin on her lap. "You've got mashed potatoes in your eyebrows." Candy glared at her, and she lifted her coffee cup to hide a grin behind it. "Actually, it's very becoming. You may have found an alternative to hair gel."

Candy glanced down at the cooling potatoes on her own plate. "Would you like to try some?"

"Now, darling, you're the one who's always telling me we have to set an example." Eden took a satisfying bite of her chicken. "Mrs. Petrie's a gem, isn't she?"

It took the better part of two hours to clean the mess area and to mop up the puddles of water spilled by the inexperienced janitorial crew. By lights-out most of the girls were too tired to loiter. A pleasant late-evening hush covered the camp.

If the mornings were the worst for Eden, the evenings were invariably the best. A long day of physical activity left her comfortably tired and relaxed. The sounds of night birds and insects were becoming familiar. More and more, she looked forward to an hour of solitude with a sky full of stars. There was no theater to dress for, no party to attend. The longer she was away from her former life-style, the less she missed it.

She was growing up, she reflected, and she liked the idea. She supposed maturity meant recognizing what was really important. The camp was important, her friendship with Candy vital. The girls under their care for the summer, even the dastardly Roberta Snow, were what really mattered. She came to realize that even if everything she had once had was handed back to her, she would no longer be able to treat it in the same way.

She had changed. And even though she was certain there were still more changes to come, she liked the new Eden Carlbough. This Eden was independent, not financially, but internally. She'd never realized how dependent she had been on her father, her fiancé, the servants. The new Eden could cope with problems, large ones, small ones. Her hands were no longer elegantly manicured. The nails were neat, but short and rounded, unpainted. Practical, Eden thought as she held one up for inspection. Useful. She liked what she saw.

She continued her nightly ritual by walking to the stables. Inside it was cool and dark, smelling of leather, hay and horses. Just stepping inside helped to cement her confidence. This was her contribution. In most other areas, she still relied on pride and nerve, but here she had skill and knowledge.

She would check each of the six horses, then the tack, before she would consider her duties over for the day. Candy might be able to build a cathedral out of papier-mâché, but she knew nothing about strained tendons or split hooves.

Eden stopped at the first stall to stroke the roan gelding she called Courage. In her hand was a paper bag with six apple halves. It was a nightly ritual the horses had caught on to quickly. Courage leaned his head over the stall door and nuzzled her palm.

"Such a good boy," she murmured as she reached into the bag. "Some of the girls still don't know a bit from a stirrup, but we're going to change that." She held the apple in her palm and let him take it. While he chewed contentedly, Eden stepped into the stall to check him over. He'd been a bargain because of his age and his slight swayback. She hadn't been looking for thoroughbreds, but for dependability and gentleness. Satisfied that his grooming had been thorough, she latched the stall door behind her and went to the next.

Next summer they'd have at least three more mounts. Eden smiled as she worked her way from stall to stall. She wasn't going to question whether there would be a Camp Liberty next summer. There would be, and she'd be part of it. A real part.

She realized that she'd brought little with her other than money and a flair for horses. It was Candy who had the training, Candy who had had the three younger sisters and a family that had possessed more tradition than money. Unlike Eden, Candy had always known she would have to earn her own way and had prepared for it. But Eden was a quick learner. By Camp Liberty's second season, she would be a partner in more than name.

Her ambition was already spiraling upward. In a few years, Camp Liberty would be renowned for its equestrian program. The name Carlbough would be respected again. There might even come a time when her Philadelphia contemporaries would send their children to her. The irony of it pleased her.

After the fifth apple had been devoured, Eden moved to the last stall. Here was Patience, a sweet-tempered, aging mare who would tolerate any kind of ineptitude in a rider as long as she received affection. Sympathetic to old bones and muscles, Eden often spent an extra hour rubbing the mare down with liniment.

"Here you are, sweetheart." As the horse gnawed the apple, Eden lifted each hoof for inspection. "A pretty sketchy job," she mumbled before drawing a hoof pick out of her back pocket. "Let's see, wasn't it little Marcie who rode you last? I suppose this means we have to have a discussion on responsibility." With a sigh, Eden switched to another hoof. "I hate discussions on responsibility. Especially when I'm giving them." Patience snorted sympathetically. "Well, I can't leave all the dirty work to Candy, can I? In any case, I don't think Marcie meant to be inconsiderate. She's still a bit nervous around horses. We'll have to show her what a nice lady you are. There. Want a rubdown?" After sticking the pick back in her pocket, Eden rested her cheek against the mare's neck. "Oh, me too, Patience. A nice long massage with some scented oil. You can just lie there with your eyes closed while all the kinks are worked out, then your skin feels so soft, your muscles so supple." With a quick laugh, Eden drew away. "Well, since you can't oblige me, I'll oblige you. Just let me get the liniment."

Giving the mare a final pat, she turned. Her breath caught on a gasp.

Chase Elliot leaned against the open stall door. Shadows fell across his face, deepening its hollows. In the dim light, his eyes were like sea foam. She would have taken a step backward in retreat, but the mare blocked her way. He smiled at her predicament.

That triggered her pride. She could be grateful for that. It had thrown her that, in the shadowed light, he was even more attractive, more…compelling than he had been in the sun. Not handsome, she amended quickly. Certainly not in the smooth, conventional sense, the sense she had always gauged men's looks by before. Everything about him was fundamental. Not simple, she thought. No, not simple, but basic. Basic, like his kiss that morning. Warmth prickled along her skin.

"I'd be happy to help you with the massage." He smiled again. "Yours, or the mare's."

"No, thank you." She became aware that she was even more disheveled than she had been at their first meeting, and that she smelled, all too obviously, of horse. "Is there something I can do for you, Mr. Elliot?"

He liked her style, Chase decided. She might be standing in a stall that could use a bit of cleaning, but she was still the lady of the drawing room. "You've got a good stock here. A bit on the mature side, but solid."

Eden had to ward off a surge of pleasure. His opinion hardly mattered. "Thank you. I'm sure you didn't come to look over the horses."

"No." But he stepped inside the stall. The mare shifted to accommodate him. "Apparently you know your way around them." He lifted a hand to run it down the mare's neck. There was a simple gold ring on his right hand. Eden recognized its age and value, as well as the strength of the man who wore it.

"Apparently." There was no way past him, so she linked her fingers together and waited. "Mr. Elliot, you haven't told me what you're doing here."

Chase's lips twitched as he continued to stroke the mare. Miss Philadelphia was nervous, he thought. She covered it well enough with frigid manners, but her nerves were jumping. It pleased him to know that she hadn't been able to brush off that quick, impulsive kiss any more than he had. "No, I haven't." Before she could avoid it, he reached down for her hand. An opal gleamed dully in the shadowed light, nestled in a circle of diamond chips that promised to catch heat and fire.

"Wrong hand for an engagement ring." He discovered that the fact pleased him, perhaps more than it should have. "I'd heard you and Eric Keeton were to be married last spring. Apparently it didn't come off."

She would like to have sworn, shouted, yelled. That's what *he* wanted, Eden told herself, letting her hand lie passive in his. "No, it didn't. Mr. Elliot, for a, let's say, country squire, you have boundless curiosity about Philadelphia gossip. Don't your apples keep you busy enough?"

He had to admire anyone who could shoot straight and smile. "I manage to eke out a bit of free time. Actually, I was interested because Keeton's a family connection."

"He is not."

There, he'd ruffled her. For the first time since her initial surprise, she was really looking at him. Take a good look, Chase thought. You won't see any resemblance. "Distant, certainly." Capturing her other hand, he turned the palms up. "My grandmother was a Winthrop, and a cousin of his grandmother. Your Philadelphia hands have a couple of blisters. You should take care."

"A Winthrop?" Eden was surprised enough at the name to forget her hands.

"We've thinned the blood a bit in the last few generations." She should be wearing gloves, he thought, as he touched a blister with his thumb. "Still, I'd expected an invitation and was curious why you dumped him."

"I didn't dump him." The words came out like poisoned honey. "But to satisfy your curiosity, and to use your own crude phrase, he dumped me. Now if you'd give me back my hands, I could finish for the day."

Chase obliged, but continued to block her way out of the stall. "I'd never considered Eric bright, but I'd never thought him stupid."

"What a delightful compliment. Please excuse me, Mr. Elliot."

"Not a compliment." Chase brushed at the bangs over her forehead. "Just an observation."

"Stop touching me."

"Touching's a habit of mine. I like your hair, Eden. It's soft, but it goes its own way."

"A veritable bouquet of compliments." She managed one small step backward. He had her pulse thudding again. She didn't want to be touched, not physically, not emotionally, not by anyone. Instinct warned her how easily he could do both. "Mr. Elliot—"

"Chase."

"Chase." She acknowledged this with a regal nod. "The morning bell goes off at six. I still have several things to do tonight, so if there's a purpose in your being here, could we get to it?"

"I came to bring you back your hat." Reaching into his back pocket, he pulled out the Phillies cap.

"I see." One more black mark against Roberta. "It's

not mine, but I'd be happy to return it to its owner. Thank you for troubling."

"You were wearing it when you fell out of my tree." Chase ignored her outstretched hand and dropped the cap on her head. "Fits, too."

"As I've already explained—"

Eden's frigid retort was interrupted by the sound of running feet. "Miss Carlbough! Miss Carlbough!" Roberta, in an angelic pink nightgown and bare feet, skidded to a halt at the open stall. Beaming, she stared up at Chase. Her adolescent heart melted. "Hi."

"Hi."

"Roberta." Voice stern, teeth nearly clenched, Eden stepped forward. "It's almost an hour past lights-out."

"I know, Miss Carlbough. I'm sorry." When she smiled, Eden thought you could almost believe it. "I just couldn't get to sleep because I kept thinking about my cap. You promised I could have it back, but you never gave it to me. I helped Mrs. Petrie. Honest, you can ask. There were millions of pans, too. I even peeled potatoes, and—"

"Roberta!" The sharp tone was enough for the moment. "Mr. Elliot was kind enough to return your hat." Whipping it off her own head, Eden thrust it into the girl's hands. "I believe you should thank him, as well as apologize for trespassing."

"Gee, thanks." She treated him to a dazzling smile. "Are those your trees, really?"

"Yeah." With a fingertip, Chase adjusted the brim of her hat. He had a weakness for black sheep and recognized a kindred soul in Roberta.

"I think they're great. Your apples tasted a whole lot better than the ones we get at home."

"Roberta."

The quiet warning had the girl rolling her eyes, which only Chase could see. "I'm sorry I didn't show the proper respect for your property." Roberta turned her head to see whether Eden approved of the apology.

"Very nice, Roberta. Now straight back to bed."

"Yes, ma'am." She shot a last look at Chase. Her little heart fluttered. Crushing the cap down on her head, she raced to the door.

"Roberta." She whipped back around at the sound of Chase's voice. He grinned at her. "See you around."

"Yeah, see you." In love, Roberta floated off to her cabin. When the stable door slammed at her back, all Eden could manage was a sigh.

"It's no use," Chase commented.

"What isn't?"

"Pretending you don't get a kick out of her. A kid like that makes you feel good."

"You wouldn't be so sure of that if you'd seen what she can do with mashed potatoes." But Eden gave in enough to smile. "She's a monster, but an appealing one. Still, I have to admit, if we had twenty-seven Robertas in camp this summer, I'd end up in a padded room."

"Certain people just breed excitement."

Eden remembered the dinner hour. "Some call it chaos."

"Life flattens out quickly without a little chaos."

She looked at him, realizing she'd dropped her guard

enough to have an actual conversation. And realizing as well that they'd stopped talking about Roberta. The stables suddenly seemed very quiet. "Well, now that we've gotten that settled, I think—"

He took a step forward. She took a step back. A smile played around his lips again as he reached for her hand. Eden bumped solidly into the mare before she managed to raise her free hand to his chest.

"What do you want?" Why was she whispering, and why was the whisper so tremulous?

He wasn't sure what he wanted. Once, quickly, he scanned her face before bringing his gaze back to hers with a jolt. Or perhaps he was. "To walk with you in the moonlight, I think. To listen to the owls hoot and wait for the nightingale."

The shadows had merged. The mare stood quietly, breathing softly. His hand was in Eden's hair now, as if it belonged there. "I have to go in." But she didn't move.

"Eden and the apple," he murmured. "I can't tell you how tempting I've found that combination. Come with me. We'll walk."

"No." Something was building inside her, too quickly. She knew he was touching more than her hand, more than her hair. He was reaching for something he should not have known existed.

"Sooner or later." He'd always been a patient man. He could wait for her the way he waited for a new tree to bear fruit. His fingers slid down to her throat, stroking once. He felt her quick shudder, heard the unsteady indrawn breath. "I'll be back, Eden."

"It won't make any difference."

Smiling, he brought her hand to his lips, turning it palm up. "I'll still be back."

She listened to his footsteps, to the creak of the door as he opened it, then shut it again.

Chapter 3

The camp was developing its own routine. Eden adjusted hers to it. Early hours, long, physical days and basic food were both a solace and a challenge. The confidence she'd once had to work at became real.

There were nights during the first month of summer that she fell into her bunk certain she would never be able to get up in the morning. Her muscles ached from rowing, riding and endless hiking. Her head spun from weekly encounters with ledgers and account books. But in the morning the sun would rise, and so would she.

Every day it became easier. She was young and healthy. The daily regimented exercise hardened muscles only touched on by occasional games of tennis. The weight she had lost over the months since her father's death gradually came back, so that her look of fragility faded.

To her surprise, she developed a genuine affection for

the girls. They became individuals, not simply a group to be coped with or income on the books. It surprised her more to find that same affection returned.

Right from the start, Eden had been certain the girls would love Candy. Everyone did. She was warm, funny, talented. The most Eden had hoped for, for herself, was to be tolerated and respected. The day Marcie had brought her a clutch of wildflowers, Eden had been too stunned to do more than stammer a thank-you. Then there had been the afternoon she had given Linda Hopkins an extra half hour in the corral. After her first gallop, Linda had thrown herself into Eden's arms for a fierce and delightful hug.

So the camp had changed her life, in so many more ways than she'd expected.

The summer grew hot with July. Girls darted around the compound in shorts. Dips in the lake became a glorious luxury. Doors and windows stayed open at night to catch even the slightest breeze. Roberta found a garter snake and terrorized her cabin mates. Bees buzzed around the wildflowers and stings became common.

Days merged together, content, but never dull, so that it seemed possible that summer could last forever. As the time passed, Eden began to believe that Chase had forgotten his promise, or threat, to come back. She'd been careful to stay well within the borders of the camp herself. Though once or twice she'd been tempted to wander toward the orchards, she stayed away.

It didn't make sense for her to still be tense and uneasy. She could tell herself he'd only been a brief annoyance. Yet every time she went into the stables in the evening, she caught herself listening. And waiting.

Late in the evening, with the heat still shimmering, Eden stretched out on her bunk, fully dressed. Bribed by the promise of a bonfire the following night, the campers had quieted down early. Relaxed and pleasantly weary, Eden pictured it. Hot dogs flaming on sharpened sticks, marshmallows toasting, the blaze flickering heat over her face and sending smoke billowing skyward. Eden found herself looking forward to the evening every bit as much as the youngest camper. With her head pillowed on her folded arms, she stared up at the ceiling while Candy paced.

"I'm sure we could do it, Eden."

"Hmm?"

"The dance." Gesturing with the clipboard she was carrying, Candy stopped at the foot of the bunk. "The dance I've been talking about having for the girls. Remember?"

"Of course." Eden forced her mind back to business. "What about it?"

"I think we should go ahead with it. In fact, if it works out, I think it should be an annual event." Even after she plopped herself down on Eden's bed, her enthusiasm continued to bounce around the room. "The boys' camp is only twenty miles from here. I'm sure they'd go for it."

"Probably." A dance. That would mean refreshments for somewhere close to a hundred, not to mention music, decorations. She thought first of the red ink in the ledger, then about how much the girls would enjoy it. There had to be a way around the red ink. "I guess there'd be room in the mess area if we moved the tables."

"Exactly. And most of the girls have records with them. We could have the boys bring some, too." She began to scrawl on her clipboard. "We can make the decorations ourselves."

"We'd have to keep the refreshments simple," Eden put in before Candy's enthusiasm could run away with her. "Cookies, punch, that sort of thing."

"We can plan it for the last week of camp. Kind of a celebrational send-off."

The last week of camp. How strange, when the first week had been so wearing, that the thought of it ending brought on both panic and regret. No, summer wouldn't last forever. In September there would be the challenge of finding a new job, a new goal. She wouldn't be going back to a teaching job as Candy was, but to want ads and résumés.

"Eden? Eden, what do you think?"

"About what?"

"About planning the dance for the last week of camp?"

"I think we'd better clear it with the boys' camp first."

"Honey, are you okay?" Leaning forward, Candy took Eden's hand. "Are you worried about going back home in a few weeks?"

"No. Concerned." She gave Candy's hand a squeeze. "Just concerned."

"I meant it when I told you not to worry about a job right away. My salary takes care of the rent on the apartment, and I still have a little piece of the nest egg my grandmother left me."

"I love you, Candy. You're the best friend I've ever had."

"The reverse holds true, Eden."

"For that reason, there's no way I'm going to sit around while you work to pay the rent and put dinner on the table. It's enough that you've let me move in with you."

"Eden, you know I'm a lot happier sharing my apartment with you than I was living alone. If you look at it as a favor, you're going to feel pressured, and that's ridiculous. Besides, for the past few months, you were taking care of fixing all the meals."

"Only a small portion of which were edible."

"True." Candy grinned. "But I didn't have to cook. Listen, give yourself a little space. You'll need some time to find out what it is you want to do."

"What I want to do is work." With a laugh, Eden lay back on the bed again. "Surprise. I really want to work, to keep busy, to earn a living. The past few weeks have shown me how much I enjoy taking care of myself. I'm banking on getting a job at a riding stable. Maybe even the one I used to board my horse at. And if that doesn't pan out—" She shrugged her shoulders. "I'll find something else."

"You will." Candy set the clipboard aside. "And next year, we'll have more girls, a bigger staff and maybe even a profit."

"Next year, I'm going to know how to make a hurricane lamp out of a tuna can."

"And a pillow out of two washcloths."

"And pot holders."

Candy remembered Eden's one mangled attempt. "Well, maybe you should take it slow."

"There's going to be no stopping me. In the meantime, I'll contact the camp director over at—what's the name, Hawk's Nest?"

"Eagle Rock," Candy corrected her, laughing. "It'll be fun for us, too, Eden. They have counselors. *Male* counselors." Sighing, she stretched her arms to the ceiling. "Do you know how long it's been since I've spoken with a man?"

"You talked to the electrician just last week."

"He was a hundred and two. I'm talking about a man who still has all his hair and teeth." She touched her tongue to her upper lip. "Not all of us have passed the time holding hands with a man in the stables."

Eden plumped up her excuse for a pillow. "I wasn't holding hands. I explained to you."

"Roberta Snow, master spy, gave an entirely different story. With her, it appears to be love at first sight."

Eden examined the pad of callus on the ridge of her palm. "I'm sure she'll survive."

"Well, what about you?"

"I'll survive, too."

"No, I mean, aren't you interested?" After folding her legs under her, Candy leaned forward. "Remember, darling, I got a good look at the man when I was negotiating for the use of his lake. I don't think there's a woman alive who wouldn't sweat a bit after a look at those spooky green eyes."

"I never sweat."

Chuckling, Candy leaned back. "Eden, you're talking to the one who loves you best. The man was interested enough to track you down in the stables. Think of the possibilities."

"It's possible that he was returning Roberta's cap."

"And it's possible that pigs fly. Haven't you been tempted to wander over by the orchard, just once?"

"No." Only a hundred times. "Seen one apple tree, you've seen them all."

"The same doesn't hold true for an apple grower who's about six-two, with a hundred and ninety well-placed pounds and one of the most fascinating faces this side of the Mississippi." Concern edged into her voice. She had watched her friend suffer and had been helpless to do more than offer emotional support. "Have fun, Eden. You deserve it."

"I don't think Chase Elliot falls into the category of fun." Danger, she thought. Excitement, sexuality and, oh yes, temptation. Tossing her legs over the bunk, Eden walked to the window. Moths were flapping at the screen.

"You're gun-shy."

"Maybe."

"Honey, you can't use Eric as a yardstick."

"I'm not." With a sigh, she turned back. "I'm not pining or brooding over him, either."

The quick shrug was Candy's way of dismissing

someone she considered a weasel. "That's because you were never really in love with him."

"I was going to marry him."

"Because it seemed the proper thing to do. I know you, Eden, like no one else. Everything was very simple and easy with Eric. It all fit—click, click, click."

Amused, Eden shook her head. "Is something wrong with that?"

"Everything's wrong with that. Love makes you giddy and foolish and achy. You never felt any of that with Eric." She spoke from the experience of a woman who'd fallen in love, and out again, a dozen times before she'd hit twenty. "You would have married him, and maybe you would even have been content. His tastes were compatible with yours. His family mixed well with yours."

Amusement fled. "You make it sound so cold."

"It was. But you're not." Candy raised her hands, hoping she hadn't gone too far. "Eden, you were raised a certain way, to be a certain way; then the roof collapsed. I can only guess at how traumatic that was. You've picked yourself up, but still you've closed pieces of yourself off. Isn't it time you put the past behind you, really behind you?"

"I've been trying."

"I know, and you've made a good start, with the camp, with your outlook. Maybe it's time you started looking for a little more, just for yourself."

"A man?"

"Some companionship, some sharing, some affection. You're too smart to think that you need a man to make things work, but to cut them off because one acted like a weasel isn't the answer, either." She rubbed at a streak of red paint on her fingernail. "I guess I still believe that everyone needs someone."

"Maybe you're right. Right now I'm too busy pasting myself back together and enjoying the results. I'm not ready for complications. Especially when they're six foot two."

"You were always the romantic one, Eden. Remember the poetry you used to write?"

"We were children." Restless, Eden moved her shoulders. "I had to grow up."

"Growing up doesn't mean you have to stop dreaming." Candy rose. "We've started one dream here, together. I want to see you have other dreams."

"When the time's right." Touched, Eden kissed Candy's cheek. "We'll have your dance and charm your counselors."

"We could invite some neighbors, just to round things out."

"Don't press your luck." Laughing, Eden turned toward the door. "I'm going for a walk before I check on the horses. Leave the light on low, will you?"

The air was still, but not quiet. The first nights Eden had spent in the hills, the country quiet had disturbed her. Now, she could hear and appreciate the night music. The chorus of crickets in soprano, the tenor crying of an owl, the occasional bass lowing of the cows on a farm half a mile away all merged into a symphony accompanied by the rustling of small animals in the brush. The three-quarter moon and a galaxy of stars added soft light and dramatic shadows. The erratic yellow beams of an army of fireflies was a nightly light show.

As she strolled toward the lake, she heard the rushing song of peepers over the softer sound of lapping water. The air smelled as steamy as it felt, so she rounded the edge of the lake toward the cooler cover of trees.

With her mind on her conversation with Candy, Eden bent to pluck a black-eyed Susan. Twisting the stem between her fingers, she watched the petals revolve around the dark center.

Had she been a romantic? There had been poetry, dreamy, optimistic poetry, often revolving around love. Troubadour love, she thought now. The sort that meant long, wistful glances, sterling sacrifices and purity. Romantic, but unrealistic, Eden admitted. She hadn't written any poetry in a long time.

Not since she had met Eric, Eden realized. She had gone from dreamy young girl to proper young woman, exchanging verses for silver patterns. Now both the dreamy girl and the proper woman were gone.

That was for the best, Eden decided, and she tossed her flower onto the surface of the lake. She watched it float lazily.

Candy had been right. It had not been a matter of love with Eric, but of fulfilling expectations. When he had turned his back on her, he had broken not her heart, but her pride. She was still repairing it.

Eric had given her a suitable diamond, sent her roses at the proper times and had never been at a loss for a clever compliment. That wasn't romance, Eden mused, and it certainly wasn't love. Perhaps she'd never really understood either.

Was romance white knights and pure maidens? Was it Chopin and soft lights? Was it the top of the Ferris wheel? Maybe she'd prefer the last after all. With a quiet laugh, Eden wrapped her arms around herself and held her face up to the stars.

"You should do that more often."

She whirled, one hand pressing against her throat. Chase stood a few feet away at the edge of the trees, the edge of the shadows. It flashed through her mind that this was the third time she had seen him and the third time he had taken her by surprise. It was a habit she wanted to break.

"Do you practice startling people, or is it a natural gift?"

"I can't remember it happening much before you." The fact was, he hadn't come up on her, but she on him. He'd been walking since dusk, and had stopped on the banks of the lake to watch the water and to think of her. "You've been getting some sun." Her hair seemed lighter, more fragile against the honeyed tone of her skin. He wanted to touch it, to see if it was still as soft and fragrant.

"Most of the work is outdoors." It amazed her that she had to fight the urge to turn and run. There was something mystical, even fanciful, about meeting him here in the moonlight, by the water. Almost as if it had been fated.

"You should wear a hat." He said it absently, distracted by the pounding of his own heart. She might have been an illusion, long slender arms and legs gleaming in the moonlight, her hair loose and drenched with it. She wore white. Even the simple shorts and shirt seemed to glimmer. "I'd wondered if you walked here."

He stepped out of the shadows. The monotonous song of the crickets seemed to reach a crescendo. "I thought it might be cooler."

"Some." He moved closer. "I've always been fond of hot nights."

"The cabins tend to get stuffy." Uneasy, she glanced back and discovered she had walked farther than she'd intended. The camp, with its comforting lights and company, was very far away. "I didn't realize I'd crossed over onto your property."

"I'm only a tyrant about my trees." She was less of an illusion up close, more of a woman. "You were laughing before. What were you thinking of?"

Her mouth was dry. Even as she backed away, he seemed to be closer. "Ferris wheels."

"Ferris wheels? Do you like the drop?" Satisfying his own need, he reached for her hair. "Or the climb?"

At his touch, her stomach shot down to her knees. "I have to get back."

"Let's walk."

To walk with you in the moonlight. Eden thought of his words, and of fate. "No, I can't. It's late."

"Must be all of nine-thirty." Amused, he took her hand, then immediately turned it over. There was a hardening ridge of calluses on the pad beneath her fingers. "You've been working."

"Some people make a living that way."

"Don't get testy." He turned her hand back to run a thumb over her knuckles. Was it a talent of his, Eden wondered, to touch a woman in the most casual of ways and send her blood pounding? "You could wear gloves," Chase went on, "and keep your Philadelphia hands."

"I'm not in Philadelphia." She drew her hand away. Chase simply took her other one. "And since I'm pitching hay rather than serving tea, it hardly seems to matter."

"You'll be serving tea again." He could see her, seated in some fussy parlor, wearing pink silk and holding a china pot. But, for the moment, her hand was warm in his. "The moon's on the water. Look."

Compelled, she turned her head. There were such things as moonbeams. They gilded the dark water of the lake and silvered the trees. She remembered some old legend about three women, the moonspinners, who spun the moon on spindles. More romance. But even the new, practical Eden couldn't resist.

"It's lovely. The moon seems so close."

"Some things aren't as close as they seem; others aren't so far away."

He began to walk. Because he still had her hand, and because he intrigued her, Eden walked with him. "I suppose you've always lived here." Just small talk, she told herself. She didn't really care.

"For the most part. This has always been headquarters for the business." He turned to look down at her. "The house is over a hundred years old. You might find it interesting."

She thought of her home and of the generations of

Carlboughs who had lived there. And of the strangers who lived there now. "I like old houses."

"Are things going well at camp?"

She wouldn't think of the books. "The girls keep us busy." Her laugh came again, low and easy. "That's an understatement. We'll just say their energy level is amazing."

"How's Roberta?"

"Incorrigible."

"I'm glad to hear it."

"Last night she painted one of the girls while the girl was asleep."

"Painted?"

Eden's laugh came again, low and easy. "The little darling must have copped a couple of pots of paint from the art area. When Marcie woke up, she looked like an Indian preparing to attack a wagon train."

"Our Roberta's inventive."

"To say the least. She told me she thought it might be interesting to be the first woman chief justice."

He smiled at that. Imagination and ambition were the qualities he most admired. "She'll probably do it."

"I know. It's terrifying."

"Let's sit. You can see the stars better."

Stars? She'd nearly forgotten who she was with and why she had wanted to avoid being with him. "I don't think I—" Before she'd gotten the sentence out, he'd tugged her down on a soft, grassy rise. "One wonders why you bother to ask."

"Manners," he said easily as he slipped an arm around her shoulders. Even as she stiffened, he relaxed. "Look at the sky. How often do you notice it in the city?"

Unable to resist, she tilted her face up. The sky was an inky black backdrop for countless pinpoints of lights. They spread, winking, shivering, overhead with a glory that made Eden's throat ache just in the looking. "It isn't the same sky that's over the city."

"Same sky, Eden. It's people who change." He stretched out on his back, crossing his legs. "There's Cassiopeia."

"Where?" Curious, Eden searched, but saw only stars without pattern.

"You can see her better from here." He pulled her closer to him, and before she could protest, he was pointing. "There she is. Looks like a W this time of year."

"Yes!" Delighted, she reached for his wrist and outlined the constellation herself. "I've never been able to find anything in the sky."

"You have to look first. There's Pegasus." Chase shifted his arm. "He has a hundred and sixty-six stars you can view with the naked eye. See? He's flying straight up."

Eyes narrowed, she concentrated on finding the pattern. Moonlight splashed on her face. "Oh yes, I see." She shifted a bit closer to guide his hand again. "I named my first pony Pegasus. Sometimes I'd imagine he sprouted wings and flew. Show me another."

He was looking at her, at the way the stars reflected in her eyes, at the way her mouth softened so generously with a smile. "Orion," he murmured.

"Where?"

"He stands with his sword behind him and his shield lifted in front. And a red star, thousands of times brighter than the sun, is the shoulder of his sword arm."

"Where is he? I—" Eden turned her head and looked directly into Chase's eyes. She forgot the stars and the moonlight and the soft, sweet grass beneath her. The hand on his wrist tightened until the rhythm of his pulse was the rhythm of hers.

Her muscles contracted and held as she braced for the kiss. But his lips merely brushed against her temple. Warmth spread through her as softly as the scent of honeysuckle spread through the air. She heard an owl call out to the night, to the stars, or to a lover.

"What are we doing here?" she managed.

"Enjoying each other." Without rushing, his lips moved over her face.

Enjoying? That was much too mild a word for what was burning through her. No one had ever made her feel like this, so weak and hot, so strong and desperate. His lips were soft, the hand that rested on the side of her face was hard. Beneath his, her heart began to gallop uncontrolled. Eden's fingers slipped off the reins.

She turned her head with a moan and found his mouth with hers. Her arms went around him, holding him close as her lips parted in demand. In all her life she had never known true hunger, not until now. This was breathless, painful, glorious.

He'd never expected such unchecked passion. He'd been prepared to go slowly, gently, as the innocence he'd felt in her required. Now she was moving under him, her fingers pressing and kneading the muscles of his back, her mouth hot and willing on his. The patience that was so much a part of him drowned in need.

Such new, such exciting sensations. Her body gave as his pressed hard against it. Gods and goddesses of the sky guarded them. He smelled of the grass and the earth, and he tasted of fire. Night sounds roared in her head, and her own sigh was only a dim echo when his lips slid down to her throat.

Murmuring his name, Eden combed her fingers through his hair. He wanted to touch her, all of her. He wanted to take her now. When her hand came to rest on his face, he covered it with his own and felt the smooth stone of her ring.

There was so much more he needed to know. So little he was sure of. Desire, for the moment, couldn't be enough. Who was she? He lifted his head to look down at her. Who the hell was she, and why was she driving him mad?

Pulling himself back, he tried to find solid ground. "You're full of surprises, Eden Carlbough of the Philadelphia Carlboughs."

For a moment, she could only stare. She'd had her ride on the Ferris wheel, a wild, dizzying ride. Somewhere along the line, she'd been tossed off to spiral madly in the air. Now she'd hit the ground, hard. "Let me up."

"I can't figure you, Eden."

"You aren't required to." She wanted to weep, to curl up into a ball and weep, but she couldn't focus on the reason. Anger was clearer. "I asked you to let me up."

He rose, holding out a hand to help her. Ignoring it, Eden got to her feet. "I've always felt it was more constructive to shout when you're angry."

She shot him one glittering look. Humiliation. It was something she'd sworn she would never feel again. "I'm sure you do. If you'll excuse me."

"Damn it." He caught her arm and swung her back to face him. "Something was happening here tonight. I'm not fool enough to deny that, but I want to know what I'm getting into."

"We were enjoying each other. Wasn't that your term?" Nothing more, Eden repeated over and over in her head. Nothing more than a moment's enjoyment. "We've finished now, so good night."

"We're far from finished. That's what worries me."

"I'd say that's your problem, Chase." But a ripple of fear—of anticipation—raced through her, because she knew he was right.

"Yeah, it's my problem." My God, how had he passed so quickly from curiosity to attraction to blazing need? "And because it is, I've got a question. I want to know why Eden Carlbough is playing at camp for the summer rather than cruising the Greek Isles. I want to know why she's cleaning out stables instead of matching silver patterns and planning dinner parties as Mrs. Eric Keeton."

"My business." Her voice rose. The new Eden wasn't as good as the old one at controlling emotion. "But if you're so curious, why don't you call one of your family connections? I'm sure any of them would be delighted to give you all the details."

"I'm asking you."

"I don't owe you any explanations." She jerked her arm away and stood trembling with rage. "I don't owe you a damn thing."

"Maybe not." His temper had cooled his passion and cleared his head. "But I want to know who I'm making love with."

"That won't be an issue, I promise you."

"We're going to finish what we started here, Eden." Without stepping closer, he had her arm again. The touch was far from gentle, far from patient. "That I promise you."

"Consider it finished."

To her surprise and fury, he only smiled. His hand eased on her arm to one lingering caress. Helpless against her response, she shivered. "We both know better than that." He touched a finger to her lips, as if reminding her what tastes he'd left there. "Think of me."

He slipped back into the shadows.

Chapter 4

It was a perfect night for a bonfire. Only a few wispy clouds dragged across the moon, shadowing it, then freeing it. The heat of the day eased with sunset, and the air was balmy, freshened by a calm, steady breeze.

The pile of twigs and sticks that had been gathered throughout the day had been stacked, tepeelike, in a field to the east of the main compound. In the clearing, it rose from a wide base to the height of a man. Every one of the girls had contributed to the making of it, just as every one of them circled around the bonfire now, waiting for the fire to catch and blaze. An army of hot dogs and marshmallows was laid out on a picnic table. Stacked like swords were dozens of cleaned and sharpened sticks. Nearby was the garden hose with a tub full of water, for safety's sake.

Candy held up a long kitchen match, drawing out the drama as the girls began to cheer. "The first annual bonfire at Camp Liberty is about to begin. Secure your hot dogs to your sticks, ladies, and prepare to roast."

Amid the giggles and gasps, Candy struck the match, then held it to the dry kindling at the base. Wood crackled. Flames licked, searched for more fuel, and spread around and around, following the circle of starter fluid. As they watched, fire began its journey up and up. Eden applauded with the rest.

"Fabulous!" Even as she watched, smoke began to billow. Its scent was the scent of autumn, and that was still a summer away. "I was terrified we wouldn't get it started."

"You're looking at an expert." Catching her tongue between her teeth, Candy speared a hot dog with a sharpened stick. Behind her, the bonfire glowed red at the center. "The only thing I was worried about was rain. But just look at those stars. It's perfect."

Eden tilted her head back. Without effort, without thought, she found Pegasus. He was riding the night sky just as he'd been riding it twenty-four hours before. One day, one night. How could so much have happened? Standing with her face lifted to the breeze and her hands growing warm from the fire, she wondered if she had really experienced that wild, turbulent moment with Chase.

She had. The memories were too ripe, too real for dreams. The moment had happened, and all the feelings and sensations that had grown from it. Deliberately she turned her gaze to a riot of patternless stars.

It didn't change what she remembered, or what she still felt. The moment had happened, she thought again, and it had passed. Yet, somehow, she wasn't certain it was over.

"Why does everything seem different here, Candy?"

"Everything *is* different here." Candy took a deep breath, drawing in the scents of smoke, drying grass and roasting meat. "Isn't it marvelous? No stuffy parlors, no boring dinner parties, no endless piano recitals. Want a hot dog?"

Because her mouth was watering, Eden accepted the partially blackened wiener. "You simplify things, Candy." Eden ran a thin line of ketchup along the meat and stuck it in a bun. "I wish I could."

"You will once you stop thinking you're letting down the Carlbough name by enjoying a hot dog by a bonfire." When Eden's mouth dropped open, Candy gave her a friendly pat. "You ought to try the marshmallows," she advised before she wandered off to find another stick.

Is that what she was doing? Eden wondered, chewing automatically. Maybe, in a way that wasn't quite as basic as Candy had said, it was. After all, she had been the one who had sold the house that had been in the family for four generations. In the end, it had been she who had inventoried the silver and china, the paintings and the jewelry for auction. So, in the end, it had been she who had liquidated the Carlbough tradition to pay off debts and to start a new life.

Necessary. No matter how the practical Eden accepted the necessity, the grieving Eden still felt the loss, and the guilt.

With a sigh, Eden stepped back. The scene that

played out in front of her was like a memory from her own childhood. She could see the column of gray smoke rising toward the sky, twirling and curling. At the core of the tower of wood, the fire was fiercely gold and greedy. The smell of outdoor cooking was strong and summery, as it had been during her own weeks at Camp Forden for Girls. For a moment, there was regret that she couldn't step back into those memories of a time when life was simple and problems were things for parents to fix.

"Miss Carlbough."

Brought out of a half-formed dream, Eden glanced down at Roberta. "Hello, Roberta. Are you having fun?"

"It's super!" Roberta's enthusiasm was evident from the smear of ketchup on her chin. "Don't you like bonfires?"

"Yes, I do." Smiling, she looked back at the crackling wood, one hand dropping automatically to Roberta's shoulder. "I like them a lot."

"I thought you looked sort of sad, so I made you a marshmallow."

The offering dripped, black and shriveled, from the end of a stick. Eden felt her throat close up the same way it had when another girl had offered her a clutch of wildflowers. "Thanks, Roberta. I wasn't sad really, I was just remembering." Gingerly, Eden pulled the melted, mangled marshmallow from the stick. Half of it plopped to the ground on the way to her mouth.

"They're tricky," Roberta observed. "I'll make you another one."

Left with the charred outer hull, Eden swallowed valiantly. "You don't have to bother, Roberta."

"Oh, I don't mind." She looked up at Eden with a glowing, generous grin. Somehow, all her past crimes didn't seem so important. "I like to do it. I thought camp was going to be boring, but it's not. Especially the horses. Miss Carlbough..." Roberta looked down at the ground and seemed to draw her courage out of her toes. "I guess I'm not as good as Linda with the horses, but I wondered if maybe you could—well, if I could spend some more time at the stables."

"Of course you can, Roberta." Eden rubbed her thumb and forefinger together, trying fruitlessly to rid herself of the goo. "And you don't even have to bribe me with marshmallows."

"Really?"

"Yes, really." Attracted despite herself, Eden ruffled Roberta's hair. "Miss Bartholomew and I will work it into your schedule."

"Gee, thanks, Miss Carlbough."

"But you'll have to work on your posting."

Roberta's nose wrinkled only a little. "Okay. But I wish we could do stuff like barrel racing. I've seen it on TV."

"Well, I don't know about that, but you might progress to small jumps before the end of camp."

Eden had the pleasure of seeing Roberta's eyes saucer with pleasure. "No fooling?"

"No fooling. As long as you work on your posting."

"I will. And I'll be better than Linda, too. Wow,

jumps." She spun in an awkward pirouette. "Thanks a lot, Miss Carlbough. Thanks a lot."

She was off in a streak, undoubtedly to spread the word. If Eden knew Roberta, and she was beginning to, she was certain the girl would soon have talked herself into a gold medal for equestrian prowess at the next Olympic Games.

But, as she watched Roberta spin from group to group, Eden realized she wasn't thinking of the past any longer; nor was she regretting. She was smiling. As one of the counselors began to strum a guitar, Eden licked marshmallow goop from her fingers.

"Need some help with that?"

With her fingers still in her mouth, Eden turned. She should have known he'd come. Perhaps, in her secret thoughts, she had hoped he would. Now she found herself thrusting her still-sticky fingers behind her back.

He wondered if she knew how lovely she looked, with the fire at her back and her hair loose on her shoulders. There was a frown on her face now, but he hadn't missed that one quick flash of pleasure. If he kissed her now, would he taste that sweet, sugary flavor she had been licking from her fingers? Through it would he find that simmering, waiting heat he'd tasted once before? The muscles in his stomach tightened, even as he dipped his thumbs into his pockets and looked away from her toward the fire.

"Nice night for a bonfire."

"Candy claims she arranged it that way." Confident there was enough distance between them, and that there were enough people around them, Eden allowed herself to relax. "We weren't expecting any company."

"I spotted your smoke."

That made her glance up and realize how far the smoke might travel. "I hope it didn't worry you. We notified the fire department." Three girls streaked by behind them. Chase glanced their way and had them lapsing into giggles. Eden caught her tongue in her cheek. "How long did it take you to perfect it?"

With a half smile, Chase turned back to her. "What?"

"The deadly charm that has females crumpling at your feet?"

"Oh, that." He grinned at her. "I was born with it."

The laugh came out before she could stop it. To cover her lapse, Eden crossed her arms and took a step backward. "It's getting warm."

"We used to have a bonfire on the farm every Halloween. My father would carve the biggest pumpkin in the patch and stuff some overalls and a flannel shirt with straw. One year he dressed himself up as the Headless Horseman and gave every kid in the neighborhood a thrill." Watching the fire, he remembered and wondered why until tonight he hadn't thought of continuing the tradition. "My mother would give each of the kids a caramel apple, then we'd sit around the fire and tell ghost stories until we'd scared ourselves silly. Looking back, I think my father got a bigger kick out of it than any of us kids."

She could see it, just as he described, and had to smile again. For her, Halloween had been tidy costume parties where she'd dressed as a princess or ballerina.

Though the memories were still lovely, she couldn't help wishing she'd seen one of the bonfires and the Headless Horseman.

"When we were planning tonight, I was as excited as any of the girls. I guess that sounds foolish."

"No, it sounds promising." He put a hand to her cheek, turning her slightly toward him. Though she stiffened, her skin was warm and soft. "Did you think of me?"

There it was again—that feeling of drowning, of floating, of going under for the third time. "I've been busy." She told herself to move away, but her legs didn't respond. The sound of singing and strumming seemed to be coming from off in the distance, with melody and lyrics she couldn't quite remember. The only thing that was close and real was his hand on her cheek.

"I-it was nice of you to drop by," she began, struggling to find solid ground again.

"Am I being dismissed?" He moved his hand casually from her cheek to her hair.

"I'm sure you have better things to do." His fingertip skimmed the back of her neck and set every nerve end trembling. "Stop."

The smoke billowed up over her head. Light and shadow created by the fire danced over her face and in her eyes. He'd thought of her, Chase reminded himself. Too much. Now he could only think what it would be like to make love with her near the heat of the fire, with the scent of smoke, and night closing in.

"You haven't walked by the lake."

"I told you, I've been busy." Why couldn't she make

her voice firm and cool? "I have a responsibility to the girls, and the camp, and—"

"Yourself?" How badly he wanted to walk with her again, to study the stars and talk. How badly he wanted to taste that passion and that innocence again. "I'm a very patient man, Eden. You can only avoid me for so long."

"Longer than you think," she murmured, letting out a sigh of relief as she spotted Roberta making a beeline for them.

"Hi!" Delighted with the quick fluttering of her heart, Roberta beamed up at Chase.

"Hi, Roberta," he said. She was thrilled that he'd remembered her name. He gave her a smile, and his attention, without releasing Eden's hair. "You're taking better care of your cap, I see."

She laughed and pushed up the brim. "Miss Carlbough said if I wandered into your orchard again, she'd hold my cap for ransom. But if you invited us to come on a tour, that would be educational, wouldn't it?"

"Roberta." Why was it the child was always one step ahead of everyone else? Eden lifted her brow in a quelling look.

"Well, Miss Bartholomew said we should think of interesting things." Roberta put her most innocent look to good use. "And I think the apple trees are interesting."

"Thanks." Chase thought he heard Eden's teeth clench. "We'll give it some thought."

"Okay." Satisfied, Roberta stuck out a wrinkled black tube. "I made you a hot dog. You have to have a hot dog at a bonfire."

"Looks terrific." Accepting it, he pleased Roberta by taking a generous bite. "Thanks." Only Chase and his stomach knew that the meat was still cold on the inside.

"I got some marshmallows and sticks, too." She handed them over. "It's more fun to do it yourself, I guess." Because she was on the border between childhood and womanhood, Roberta picked up easily on the vibrations around her. "If you two want to be alone, you know, to kiss and stuff, no one's in the stables."

"Roberta!" Eden pulled out her best camp director's voice. "That will do."

"Well, my parents like to be alone sometimes." Undaunted, she grinned at Chase. "Maybe I'll see you around."

"You can count on it, kid." As Roberta danced off toward a group of girls, Chase turned back. The moment he took a step toward her, Eden extended her skewered marshmallow toward the fire. "Want to go kiss and stuff?"

It was the heat of the fire that stung her cheeks with color, Eden assured herself. "I suppose you think it would be terribly amusing for Roberta to go home and report that one of the camp directors spent her time in the stables with a man. That would do a lot for Camp Liberty's reputation."

"You're right. You should come to my place."

"Go away, Chase."

"I haven't finished my hot dog. Have dinner with me."

"I've had a hot dog already, thank you."

"I'll make sure hot dogs aren't on the menu. We can talk about it tomorrow."

"We will not talk about it tomorrow." It was anger that made her breathless, just as it was anger that made her unwise enough to turn toward him. "We will not talk about anything tomorrow."

"Okay. We won't talk." To show how reasonable he was, he bent down and closed the conversation, his mouth covering hers. He wasn't holding her, but it took her brain several long, lazy seconds before it accepted the order to back away.

"Don't you have any sense of propriety?" she managed in a strangled voice.

"Not much." He made up his mind, looking down at her eyes, dazed and as blue as his lake, that he wasn't going to take no for an answer—to any question. "We'll make it about nine tomorrow morning at the entrance to the orchard."

"Make what?"

"The tour." He grinned and handed her his stick. "It'll be educational."

Though she was in an open field, Eden felt her back press into a corner. "We have no intention of disrupting your routine."

"No problem. I'll pass it on to your co-director before I go back. That way, you'll be sure to be coordinated."

Eden took a long breath. "You think you're very clever, don't you?"

"Thorough, just thorough, Eden. By the way, your marshmallow's on fire."

With his hands in his pockets, he strolled off while she blew furiously on the flaming ball.

She'd hoped for rain but was disappointed. The morning dawned warm and sunny. She'd hoped for support but was faced with Candy's enthusiasm for a field trip through one of the most prestigious apple orchards in the country. The girls were naturally delighted with any shift in schedule, so as they walked as a group the short distance to the Elliot farm, Eden found herself separated from the excitement.

"You could try not to look as though you're walking to the guillotine." Candy plucked a scrawny blue flower from the side of the road and stuck it in her hair. "This is a wonderful opportunity—for the girls," she added quickly.

"You managed to convince me of that, or else I wouldn't be here."

"Grumpy."

"I'm not grumpy," Eden countered. "I'm annoyed at being manipulated."

"Just a small piece of advice." Picking another flower, Candy twirled it. "If I'd been manipulated by a man, I'd make certain he believed it was my idea in the first place. Don't you think it would throw him off if you walked up to the gates with a cheery smile and boundless enthusiasm?"

"Maybe." Eden mulled the idea over until her lips began to curve. "Yes, maybe."

"There now. With a little practice, you'll find out that deviousness is much better in some cases than dignity."

"I wouldn't have needed either if you'd let me stay behind."

"Darling, unless I miss my guess, a certain apple baron would have plucked you up from whatever corner you'd chosen to hide in, tossed you over his wonderfully broad shoulder and dragged you along on our little tour, like it or not." Pausing, Candy let a sigh escape. "Now that I think about it, that would have been more exciting."

Because she was well able to picture it herself, Eden's mood hardened again. "At least I thought I could count on support from my best friend."

"And you can. Absolutely." With easy affection, Candy draped an arm over Eden's shoulder. "Though why you think you need my support when you have a gorgeous man giving you smoldering kisses, I can't imagine."

"That's just it!" Because several young heads turned when she raised her voice, Eden fought for calm again. "He had no business pulling something like that in front of everyone."

"I suppose it is more fun in private."

"Keep this up, and you may find that garter snake in your underwear yet."

"Just ask him if he's got a brother, or a cousin. Even an uncle. Ah, here we are," she continued before Eden could reply. "Now smile and be charming, just like you were taught."

"You're going to pay for this," Eden promised her in an undertone. "I don't know how, I don't know when, but you'll pay."

They brought the group to a halt when the road forked. On the left were stone pillars topped with an arching wrought-iron sign that read ELLIOT. Sloping away from the pillars was a wall a foot thick and high as a man. It was old and sturdy, proving to Eden that the penchant for privacy hadn't begun with Chase.

The entrance road, smooth and well-maintained, ribboned back over the crest of a hill before it disappeared. Along the road were trees, not apple but oak, older and sturdier than the wall.

It was the continuity that drew her, the same symmetry she had seen and admired in the groves. The stone, the trees, even the road, had been there for generations. Looking, Eden understood his pride in them. She, too, had once had a legacy.

Then he strode from behind the wall and she fought back even that small sense of a common ground.

In a T-shirt and jeans, he looked lean and capable. There was a faint sheen of sweat on his arms that made her realize he'd already been working that morning. Drawn against her will, she dropped her gaze to his hands, hands that were hard and competent and unbearably gentle on a woman's skin.

"Morning, ladies." He swung the gates open for them.

"Oh Lord, he's something," Eden heard one of the counselors mumble. Remembering Candy's advice, she straightened her shoulders and fixed on her most cheerful smile.

"This is Mr. Elliot, girls. He owns the orchards we'll tour today. Thank you for inviting us, Mr. Elliot."

"My pleasure—Miss Carlbough."

The girlish murmurs of agreement became babbles of excitement as a dog sauntered to Chase's side. His fur was the color of apricots and glistened as though it had been polished in the sunlight. The big, sad eyes studied the group of girls before the dog pressed against Chase's leg. Eden had time to think that a smaller man might have been toppled. The dog was no less than three feet high at the shoulder. More of a young lion than a house pet, she thought. When he settled to sit at Chase's feet, Chase didn't have to bend to lay a hand on the dog's head.

"This is Squat. Believe it or not, he was the runt of his litter. He's a little shy."

Candy gave a sigh of relief when she saw the enormous tail thump the ground. "But friendly, right?"

"Squat's a pushover for females." His gaze circled the group. "Especially so many pretty ones. He was hoping he could join the tour."

"He's neat." Roberta made up her mind instantly. Walking forward, she gave the dog's head a casual pat. "I'll walk with you, Squat."

Agreeable, the dog rose to lead the way.

There was more to the business of apples than Eden had imagined. It wasn't all trees and plump fruit to be plucked and piled into baskets for market. Harvesting wasn't limited to autumn with the variety of types that were planted. The season, Chase explained, had been extended into months, from early summer to late fall.

They weren't just used for eating and baking. Even

cores and peelings were put to use for cider, or dried and shipped to Europe for certain champagnes. As they walked, the scent of ripening fruit filled the air, making more than one mouth water.

The Tree of Life, Eden thought as the scent tempted her. Forbidden fruit. She kept herself surrounded by girls and tried to remember that the tour was educational.

He explained that the quick-maturing trees were planted in the forty-foot spaces between the slow growers, then cut out when the space was needed. A practical business, she remembered, organized, with a high level of utility and little waste. Still, it had the romance of apple blossoms in spring.

Masses of laborers harvested the summer fruit. While they watched the men and machines at work, Chase answered questions.

"They don't look ripe," Roberta commented.

"They're full-size." Chase rested a hand on her shoulder as he chose an apple. "The changes that take place after the fruit's reached maturity are mainly chemical. It goes on without the tree. The fruit's hard, but the seeds are brown. Look." Using a pocketknife with casual skill, he cut the fruit in half. "The apples we harvest now are superior to the ones that hang longer." Reading Roberta's expression correctly, Chase tossed her half the fruit. The other half Squat took in one yawning bite.

"Maybe you'd like to pick some yourself." The reaction was positive, and Chase reached up to demonstrate. "Twist the fruit off the stem. You don't want to break the twig and lose bearing wood."

Before Eden could react, the girls had scattered to nearby trees. She was facing Chase. Perhaps it was the way his lips curved. Perhaps it was the way his eyes seemed so content to rest on hers, but her mind went instantly and completely blank.

"You have a fascinating business." She could have kicked herself for the inanity of it.

"I like it."

"I, ah…" There must be a question, an intelligent question, she could ask. "I suppose you ship the fruit quickly to avoid spoilage."

He doubted that either of them gave two hoots about apples at the moment, but he was willing to play the game. "It's stored right after picking at thirty-two degrees Fahrenheit. I like your hair pulled back like that. It makes me want to tug on the string and watch it fall all over your shoulders."

Her pulse began to sing, but she pretended she hadn't heard. "I'm sure you have various tests to determine quality."

"We look for richness." Slowly, he turned the fruit over in his hand, but his gaze roamed to her mouth. "Flavor." He watched her lips part as if to taste. "Firmness," he murmured, as he circled her throat with his free hand. "Tenderness."

Her breath seemed to concentrate, to sweeten into the sound of a sigh. It was almost too late when she bit it off. "It would be best if we stuck to the subject at hand."

"Which subject?" His thumb traced along her jawline.

"Apples."

"I'd like to make love with you in the orchards, Eden, with the sun warm on your face and the grass soft at your back."

It terrified her that she could almost taste what it would be like, to be with him, alone. "If you'll excuse me."

"Eden." He took her hand, knowing he was pushing too hard, too fast, but unable to stop himself. "I want you. Maybe too much."

Though his voice was low, hardly more than a whisper, she felt her nerves jangling. "You should know you can't say those things to me here, now. If the children—"

"Have dinner with me."

"No." On this, she told herself she would stand firm. She would not be manipulated. She would not be maneuvered. "I have a job, Chase, one that runs virtually twenty-four hours a day for the next few weeks. Even if I wanted to have dinner with you, which I don't, it would be impossible."

He considered all this reasonable. But then, a great many smoke screens were. "Are you afraid to be alone with me? Really alone."

The truth was plain and simple. She ignored it. "You flatter yourself."

"I doubt a couple hours out of an evening would disrupt the camp's routine, or yours."

"You don't know anything about the camp's routine."

"I know that between your partner and the counselors, the girls are more than adequately supervised. And I know that your last riding lesson is at four o'clock."

"How did you—"

"I asked Roberta," he said easily. "She told me you have supper at six, then a planned activity or free time from seven to nine. Lights-out is at ten. You usually spend your time after supper with the horses. And sometimes you ride out at night when you think everyone's asleep."

She opened her mouth, then shut it again, having no idea what to say. She had thought those rides exclusively hers, exclusively private.

"Why do you ride out alone at night, Eden?"

"Because I enjoy it."

"Then tonight you can enjoy having dinner with me."

She tried to remember there were girls beneath the trees around them. She tried to remember that a display of temper was most embarrassing for the person who lost control. "Perhaps you have some difficulty understanding a polite refusal. Why don't we try this? The last place I want to be tonight, or at any other time, is with you."

He moved his shoulders before he took a step closer. "I guess we can just settle all this now. Here."

"You wouldn't..." She didn't bother to finish the thought. By now she knew very well what he would dare. One quick look around showed her that Roberta and Marcie were leaning against the trunk of a tree, happily munching apples and enjoying the show. "All right, stop it." So much for not being manipulated. "I have no idea why you insist on having dinner with someone who finds you so annoying."

"Me, either. We'll discuss it tonight. Seven-thirty." Tossing Eden the apple, he strolled over toward Roberta.

Eden hefted the fruit. She even went so far as to draw a mental bull's-eye on the back of his head. With a sound of disgust, she took a hefty bite instead.

Chapter 5

Vengefully, Eden dragged a brush through her hair. Despite the harsh treatment, it sprang back softly to wisp around her face and wave to her shoulders. She wouldn't go to any trouble as she had for other dates and dinners, but leave it loose and unstyled. Though he was undoubtedly too hardheaded to notice that sort of female subtlety.

She didn't bother with jewelry, except for the simple pearl studs she often wore around camp. In an effort to look cool, even prim, she wore a high-necked white blouse, regretting only the lace at the cuffs. Matching it with a white skirt, she tried for an icy look. The result was an innocent fragility she couldn't detect in the one small mirror on the wall.

Intending on making it plain that she had gone to no trouble for Chase's benefit, she almost ignored makeup. Grumbling to herself, Eden picked up her blusher.

Basic feminine vanity, she admitted; then she added a touch of clear gloss to her lips. There was, after all, a giant step between not fussing and looking like a hag. She was reaching for her bottle of perfume before she stopped herself. No, that was definitely fussing. He would get soap, and soap only. She turned away from the mirror just as Candy swung through the cabin door.

"Wow." Stopping in the doorway, Candy took a long, critical look. "You look terrific."

"I do?" Brow creased, Eden turned back to the mirror. "Terrific wasn't exactly what I was shooting for. I wanted something along the lines of prim."

"You couldn't look prim if you wore sackcloth and ashes, any more than I could look delicate even with lace at my wrists."

With a sound of disgust, Eden tugged at the offending lace. "I knew it. I just knew it was a mistake. Maybe I can rip it off."

"Don't you dare." Laughing, Candy bounded into the room to stop Eden from destroying her blouse. "Besides, it isn't the clothes that are important. It's the attitude, right?"

Eden gave the lace a last tug. "Right. Candy, are you sure everything's going to be under control here? I could still make excuses."

"Everything's already under control." Candy flopped down on her bunk, then began to peel the banana she held. "In fact, things are great. I've just taken a five-minute break to see you off and stuff my face." She took a big bite to prove her point. "Then," she continued over a mouthful of banana, "we're getting together in the mess area to take an inventory of our record collection for the dance. The girls want some practice time before the big night."

"You could probably use extra supervision."

Candy waved her half-eaten banana. "Everyone's going to be in the same four walls for the next couple of hours. You go enjoy your dinner and stop worrying. Where are you going?"

"I don't know." She stuffed some tissue in her bag. "And I really don't care."

"Come on, after nearly six weeks of wholesome but god-awful boring food, aren't you just a little excited about the prospect of oysters Rockefeller or escargots?"

"No." She began to clasp and unclasp her bag. "I'm only going because it was simpler than creating a scene."

Candy broke off a last bite of banana. "Certainly knows how to get his own way, doesn't he?"

"That's about to end." Eden closed her purse with a snap. "Tonight."

At the sound of an approaching car, Candy propped herself up on an elbow. She noticed Eden nervously biting her lower lip, but she only gestured toward the door with her banana peel. "Well, good luck."

Eden caught the grin and paused, her hand on the screen door. "Whose side are you on, anyway?"

"Yours, Eden." Candy stretched, and prepared to go rock and roll. "Always."

"I'll be back early."

Candy grinned, wisely saying nothing as the screen door slammed shut.

However hard Eden might have tried to look remote, icy, disinterested, the breath clogged up in Chase's lungs the moment she stepped outside. They were still an hour from twilight, and the sun's last rays shot through her hair. Her skirt swirled around bare legs honey-toned after long days outdoors. Her chin was lifted, perhaps in anger, perhaps in defiance. He could only see the elegant line of her throat.

The same slowly drumming need rose up inside him the moment she stepped onto the grass.

She'd expected him to look less…dangerous in more formal attire. Eden discovered she had underestimated him again. The muscles in his arms and shoulders weren't so much restricted as enhanced by the sports jacket. The shirt, either by design or good fortune, matched his eyes and was left open at the throat. Slowly and easily he smiled at her, and her lips curved in automatic response.

"I imagined you looking like this." In truth, he hadn't been sure she would come, or what he might have done if she had locked herself away in one of the cabins and refused to see him. "I'm glad you didn't disappoint me."

Feeling her resolve weaken, Eden made an effort to draw back. "I made a bargain," she began, only to fall silent when he handed her a bunch of anemones freshly picked from the side of the road. He wasn't supposed to be sweet, she reminded herself. She wasn't supposed to be vulnerable to sweetness. Still, unable to resist, she buried her face in the flowers.

That was a picture he would carry with him forever, Chase realized. Eden, with wildflowers clutched in both hands; her eyes, touched with both pleasure and confusion, watching him over the petals.

"Thank you."

"You're welcome." Taking one of her hands, he brought it to his lips. She should have pulled away. She knew she should. Yet there was something so simple, so right in the moment—as if she recognized it from some long-ago dream. Bemused, Eden took a step closer, but the sound of giggling brought her out of the spell.

Immediately she tried to pull her hand away. "The girls." She glanced around quickly enough to catch the fielder's cap as it disappeared around the corner of the building.

"Well, then, we wouldn't want to disappoint them?" Turning her hand over, Chase pressed a kiss to her palm. Eden felt the heat spread.

"You're being deliberately difficult." But she closed her hand as if to capture the sensation and hold it.

"Yes." He smiled, but resisted the impulse to draw her into his arms and enjoy the promise he'd seen so briefly in her eyes.

"If you'd let me go, I'd like to put the flowers in water."

"I'll do it." Candy left her post by the door and came outside. Even Eden's glare didn't wipe the smile from her face. "They're lovely, aren't they? Have a good time."

"We'll do that." Chase linked his fingers with Eden's and drew her toward his car. She told herself the sun had been in her eyes. Why else would she have missed the low-slung white Lamborghini parked beside the cabin. She settled herself in the passenger's seat with a warning to herself not to relax.

The moment the engine sprang to life, there was a chorus of goodbyes. Every girl and counselor had lined up to wave them off. Eden disguised a chuckle with a cough.

"It seems this is one of the camp's highlights this summer."

Chase lifted a hand out of the open window to wave back. "Let's see if we can make it one of ours."

Something in his tone made her glance over just long enough to catch that devil of a smile. Eden made up her mind then and there. No, she wouldn't relax, but she'd be damned if she'd be intimidated either. "All right." She leaned back in her seat, prepared to make the best of a bad deal. "I haven't had a meal that wasn't served on a tray in weeks."

"I'll cancel the trays."

"I'd appreciate it." She laughed, then assured herself that laughing wasn't really relaxing. "Stop me if I start stacking the silverware." The breeze blowing in the open window was warm and as fresh as the flowers Chase had brought her. Eden allowed herself the pleasure of lifting her face to it. "This is nice, especially when I was expecting a pickup truck."

"Even country bumpkins can appreciate a well-made machine."

"That's not what I meant." Ready with an apology, she turned, but saw he was smiling. "I suppose you wouldn't care if it was."

"I know what I am, what I want and what I can do."

As he took a curve he slowed. His eyes met hers briefly. "But the opinions of certain people always matter. In any case, I prefer the mountains to traffic jams. What do you prefer, Eden?"

"I haven't decided." That was true, she realized with a jolt. In a matter of weeks her priorities, and her hopes, had changed direction. Musing on that, she almost missed the arching ELLIOT sign when Chase turned between the columns. "Where are we going?"

"To dinner."

"In the orchard?"

"In my house." With that he changed gears and had the car cruising up the gravel drive.

Eden tried to ignore the little twist of apprehension she felt. True, this wasn't the crowded, and safe, restaurant she had imagined. She'd shared private dinners before, hadn't she? She'd been raised from the cradle to know how to handle any social situation. But the apprehension remained. Dinner alone with Chase wouldn't be, couldn't possibly be, like any other experience.

Even as she was working out a polite protest, the car crested the hill. The house rose into view.

It was stone. She couldn't know it was local stone, quarried from the mountains. She saw only that it was old, beautifully weathered. At first glance, it gave the appearance of being gray, but on a closer look colors glimmered through. Amber, russet, tints of green and umber. The sun was still high enough to make the chips of mica and quartz glisten. There were three stories, with the second overhanging the first by a skirting balcony. Eden could see flashes of red and buttercup yellow from the pots of geraniums and marigolds. She caught the scent of lavender even before she saw the rock garden.

A wide, sweeping stone stairway, worn slightly in the center, led to double glass doors of diamond panes. A redwood barrel was filled with pansies that nodded in the early evening breeze.

It was nothing like what she had expected, and yet... the house, and everything about it, was instantly recognizable.

His own nervousness caught Chase off guard. Eden said nothing when he stopped the car, still nothing when he got out to round the hood and open her door. It mattered, more than he had ever imagined it could, what she thought, what she said, what she felt about his home.

She held her hand out for his in a gesture he knew was automatic. Then she stood beside him, looking at what was his, what had been his even before his birth. Tension lodged in the back of his neck.

"Oh, Chase, it's beautiful." She lifted her free hand to shield her eyes from the sun behind the house. "No wonder you love it."

"My great-grandfather built it." The tension had dissolved without his being aware of it. "He even helped quarry the stone. He wanted something that would last and that would carry a piece of him as long as it did."

She thought of the home that had been her family's for generations, feeling the too-familiar burning behind her eyes. She'd lost that. Sold it. The need to tell him was almost stronger than pride, because in that moment she thought he might understand.

He felt her change in mood even before he glanced down and saw the glint of tears in her eyes. "What is it, Eden?"

"Nothing." No, she couldn't tell him. Some wounds were best left hidden. Private. "I was just thinking how important some traditions are."

"You still miss your father."

"Yes." Her eyes were dry now, the moment past. "I'd love to see inside."

He hesitated a moment, knowing there had been more and that she'd been close to sharing it with him. He could wait, Chase told himself, though his patience was beginning to fray. He would have to wait until she took that step toward him rather than away from him.

With her hand still in his, he climbed the steps to the door. On the other side lay a mountain of apricot fur known as Squat. Even after Chase opened the door, the mound continued to snore.

"Are you sure you should have such a vicious watchdog unchained?"

"My theory is most burglars wouldn't have the nerve to step over him." Catching Eden around the waist, Chase lifted her up and over.

The stone insulated well against the heat, so the hall was cool and comfortable. High, beamed ceilings gave the illusion of unlimited space. A Monet landscape caught her eye, but before she could comment on it, Chase was leading her through a set of mahogany doors.

The room was cozily square, with window seats recessed into the east and west walls. Instantly Eden could imagine the charm of watching the sun rise or set. Comfort was the theme of the room, with its range of blues from the palest aqua to the deepest indigo. Hand-hooked rugs set off the American antiques. There were fresh flowers here, too, spilling out of a Revere Ware bowl. It was a touch she hadn't expected from a bachelor, particularly one who worked with his hands.

Thoughtful, she crossed the room to the west window. The slanting sun cast long shadows over the buildings he had taken them through that morning. She remembered the conveyor belts, the busy sorters and packers, the noise. Behind her was a small, elegant room with pewter bowls and wild roses.

Peace and challenge, she realized, and she sighed without knowing why. "I imagine it's lovely when the sun starts to drop."

"It's my favorite view." His voice came from directly behind her, but for once she didn't stiffen when he rested his hands on her shoulders. He tried to tell himself it was just coincidence that she had chosen to look out that window, but he could almost believe that his own need for her to see and understand had guided her there. It wouldn't be wise to forget who she was and how she chose to live. "There's no Symphony Hall or Rodin Museum."

His fingers gently massaged the curve of her shoulders. But his voice wasn't as patient. Curious, she turned. His hands shifted to let her slide through, then settled on her shoulders again. "I don't imagine they're missed. If they were, you could visit, then come back to this." Without thinking, she lifted her hand to brush the hair from his forehead. Even as she caught herself, his hand closed around her wrist. "Chase, I—"

"Too late," he murmured; then he kissed each of her fingers, one by one. "Too late for you. Too late for me."

She couldn't allow herself to believe that. She couldn't accept the softening and opening of her emotions. How badly she wanted to let him in, to trust again, to need again. How terrifying it was to be vulnerable. "Please don't do this. It's a mistake for both of us."

"You're probably right." He was almost sure of it himself. But he brushed his lips over the pulse that hammered in her wrist. He didn't give a damn. "Everyone's entitled to one enormous mistake."

"Don't kiss me now." She lifted a hand but only curled her fingers into his shirt. "I can't think."

"One has nothing to do with the other."

When his mouth touched hers, it was soft, seeking. *Too late*. The words echoed in her head even as she lifted her hands to his face and let herself go. This is what she had wanted, no matter how many arguments she had posed, no matter how many defenses she had built. She wanted to be held against him, to sink into a dream that had no end.

He felt her fingers stream through his hair and had to force himself not to rush her. Desire, tensed and hungry, had to be held back until it was tempered with acceptance and trust. In his heart he had already acknowledged that she was more than the challenge he had first considered her. She was more than the summer fling he might have preferred. But as her slim, soft body pressed against his, as her warm, willing mouth opened for him, he could only think of how he wanted her, now, when the sun was beginning to sink toward the distant peaks to the west.

"Chase." It was the wild, drumming beat of her heart that frightened her most. She was trembling. Eden could feel it start somewhere deep inside and spread out until it became a stunning combination of panic and excitement. How could she fight the first and give in to the second? "Chase, please."

He had to draw himself back, inch by painful inch. He hadn't meant to take either of them so far, so fast. Yet perhaps he had, he thought as he ran a hand down her hair. Perhaps he had wanted to push them both toward an answer that still seemed just out of reach.

"The sun's going down." His hands weren't quite steady when he turned her toward the window again. "Before long, the light will change."

She could only be grateful that he was giving her time to regain her composure. Later she would realize how much it probably had cost him.

They stood a moment in silence, watching the first tints of rose spread above the mountains. A loud, rasping cough had her already-tense nerves jolting.

"S'cuze me."

The man in the doorway had a grizzled beard that trailed down to the first button of his red checked shirt. Though he was hardly taller than Eden, his bulk gave the impression of power. The folds and lines in his face all but obscured his dark eyes. Then he grinned, and she caught the glint of a gold tooth.

So this was the little lady who had the boss running around in circles. Deciding she was prettier than a barrelful of prime apples, he nodded to her by way of greeting. "Supper's ready. Unless you want to eat it cold, you best be moving along."

"Eden Carlbough, Delaney." Chase only lifted a brow, knowing Delaney had already sized up the situation. "He cooks and I don't, which is why I haven't fired him yet."

This brought on a cackle. "He hasn't fired me because I wiped his nose and tied his shoes."

"We could add that that was close to thirty years ago."

She recognized both affection and exasperation. It pleased her to know someone could exasperate Chase Elliot. "It's nice to meet you, Mr. Delaney."

"Delaney, ma'am. Just Delaney." Still grinning, he pulled on his beard. "Mighty pretty," he said to Chase. "It's smarter to think of settling down with someone who isn't an eyesore at breakfast. Supper's going to get cold," he added. Then he was gone.

Though Eden had remained politely silent during Delaney's statement, it took only one look at Chase's face to engender a stream of laughter. The sound made Chase think more seriously about gagging Delaney with his own beard.

"I'm glad you're amused."

"Delighted. It's the first time I've ever seen you speechless. And I can't help being pleased not to be considered an eyesore." Then she disarmed him by offering him her hand. "Supper's going to get cold."

Instead of the dining room, Chase led her out to a jalousied porch. Two paddle fans circled overhead, making the most of the breeze that crept in the slanted windows. A wind chime jingled cheerfully between baskets of fuchsia.

"Your home is one surprise after another," Eden commented as she studied the plump love seats and the glass-and-wicker table. "Every room seems fashioned for relaxation and stunning views."

The table was set with colorful stoneware. Though the sun had yet to drop behind the peaks, two tapers were already burning. There was a single wild rose beside her plate.

Romance, she thought. This was the romance she had once dreamed of. This was the romance she must now be very wary of. But, wary or not, she picked up the flower and smiled at him. "Thank you."

"Did you want one, too?" As she laughed, Chase drew back her chair.

"Sit down. Sit down. Eat while it's hot." Despite his bulk, Delaney bustled into the room. In his large hands was an enormous tray. Because she realized how easily she could be mowed down, Eden obeyed. "Hope you got an appetite. You could use a little plumping up, missy. Then, I've always preferred a bit of healthy meat on female bones."

As he spoke, he began to serve an exquisite seafood salad. "Made my special, Chicken Delaney. It'll keep under the covers if you two don't dawdle over the salad. Apple pic's on the hot plate, biscuits in the warmer." He stuck a bottle of wine unceremoniously in an ice bucket. "That's the fancy wine you wanted." Standing back, he took a narrowed-eyed glance around before snorting with satisfaction. "I'm going home. Don't let my chicken get cold." Wiping his hands on his jeans, he marched to the door and let it swing shut behind him.

"Delaney has amazing style, doesn't he?" Chase took the wine from the bucket to pour two glasses.

"Amazing," Eden agreed, finding it amazing enough that those gnarled hands had created anything as lovely as the salad in front of her.

"He makes the best biscuits in Pennsylvania." Chase lifted his glass and toasted her. "And I'd put his Beef Wellington up against anyone's."

"Beef Wellington?" With a shake of her head, Eden sipped her wine. It was cool, just a shade tart. "I hope you'll take it the right way when I say he looks more like the type who could charcoal a steak over a backyard grill." She dipped her fork in the salad and sampled it. "But..."

"Appearances can be deceiving," Chase finished for her, pleased with the way her eyes half shut as she tasted. "Delaney's been cooking here as long as I can remember. He lives in a little cottage my grandfather helped him build about forty years ago. Nose-wiping and shoe-tying aside, he's part of the family."

She only nodded, looking down at her plate for a moment as she remembered how difficult it had been to tell her longtime servants she was selling out. Perhaps they had never been as familiar or as informal as Chase's Delaney, but they, too, had been part of the family.

It was there again, that dim candle glow of grief he'd seen in her eyes before. Wanting only to help, he reached over to touch her hand. "Eden?"

Quickly, almost too quickly, she moved her hand and began to eat again. "This is wonderful. I have an aunt back home who would shanghai your Delaney after the first forkful."

Home, he thought, backing off automatically. Philadelphia was still home.

The Chicken Delaney lived up to its name. As the sun set, the meal passed easily, even though they disagreed on almost every subject.

She read Keats and he read Christie. She preferred Bach and he Haggard, but it didn't seem to matter as the glass walls filtered the rosy light of approaching twilight. The candles burned lower. The wine shimmered in crystal, inviting one more sip. Close and clear and quick came the two-tone call of a quail.

"That's a lovely sound." Her sigh was easy and content. "If things are quiet at camp, we can hear the birds in the evening. There's a whippoorwill who's taken to singing right outside the cabin window. You can almost set your watch by her."

"Most of us are creatures of habit," he murmured. He wondered about her, what habits she had, what habits she had changed. Taking her hand, he turned it up. The ridge of callus had hardened. "You didn't take my advice."

"About what?"

"Wearing gloves."

"It didn't seem worth it. Besides..." Letting the words trail off, she lifted her wine.

"Besides?"

"Having calluses means I did something to earn them." She blurted it out, then sat swearing at herself and waiting for him to laugh.

He didn't. Instead he sat silently, passing his thumb over the toughened skin and watching her. "Will you go back?"

"Go back?"

"To Philadelphia."

It was foolish to tell him how hard she'd tried not to think about that. Instead, she answered as the practical Eden was supposed to. "The camp closes down the last week in August. Where else would I go?"

"Where else?" he agreed, but when he released her hand she felt a sense of loss rather than relief. "Maybe there comes a time in everyone's life when they have to take a hard look at the options." He rose, and her hands balled into fists. He took a step toward her, and her heart rose up to her throat. "I'll be back."

Alone, she let out a long, shaky breath. What had she been expecting? she asked herself. What had she been hoping for? Her legs weren't quite steady when she rose, but it could have been the wine. But wine would have made her warm, and she felt a chill. To ward it off, she rubbed her arms with her hands. The sky was a quiet, deepening blue but for a halo of scarlet along the horizon. She concentrated on that, trying not to imagine how it would look when the stars came out.

Maybe they would look at the stars together again.

They could look, picking out the patterns, and she would again feel that click that meant her needs and dreams were meshing. With his.

Pressing a hand to her lips, she struggled to block off that train of thought. It was only that the evening had been lovelier than she had imagined. It was only that they had more in common than she had believed possible. It was only that he had a gentleness inside him that softened parts of her when she least expected it. And when he kissed her, she felt as though she had the world pulsing in the palm of her hand.

No. Uneasy, she wrapped her hands around her forearms and squeezed. She was romanticizing again, spinning daydreams when she had no business dreaming at all. She was just beginning to sort out her life, to make her own place. It wasn't possible that she was looking to him to be any part of it.

She heard the music then, something low and unfamiliar that nonetheless had tiny shivers working their way up her spine. She had to leave, she thought quickly. And right away. She had let the atmosphere get to her. The house, the sunset, the wine. Him. Hearing his footsteps, she turned. She would tell him she had to get back. She would thank him for the evening, and...escape.

When he came back into the room, she was standing beside the table so that the candlelight flickered over her skin. Dusk swirled behind her with its smoky magic. The scent of wild roses from the bush outside the window seemed to sigh into the room. He wondered, if he touched her now, if she would simply dissolve in his hands.

"Chase, I think I'd better—"

"Shh." She wouldn't dissolve, he told himself as he went to her. She was real, and so was he. One hand captured hers, the other slipping around her waist. After one moment of resistance, she began to move with him. "One of the pleasures of country music is dancing to it."

"I, ah, I don't know the song." But it felt so good, so very good, to sway with him while darkness fell.

"It's about a man, a woman and passion. The best songs are."

She shut her eyes. She could feel the brush of his jacket against her cheek, the firm press of his hand at her waist. He smelled of soap, but nothing a woman would use. This had a tang that was essentially masculine. Wanting to taste, she moved her head so that her lips rested against his neck.

His pulse beat there, quick, surprising her. Forgetting caution, she nestled closer and felt its sudden rise in speed. As her own raced to match it, she gave a murmur of pleasure and traced it with the tip of her tongue.

He started to draw her away. He meant to. When he'd left her, he'd promised himself that he would slow the pace to one they could both handle. But now she was cuddled against him, her body swaying, her fingers straying to his neck, and her mouth... With an oath, Chase dragged her closer and gave in to hunger.

The kiss was instantly torrid, instantly urgent. And somehow, though she had never experienced anything like it, instantly familiar. Her head tilted back in surrender. Her lips parted. Here and now, she wanted the fire and passion that had only been hinted at.

Perhaps he lowered her to the love seat, perhaps she drew him to it, but they were wrapped together, pressed against the cushions. An owl hooted once, then twice, then gave them silence.

He'd wanted to believe she could be this generous. He'd wanted to believe his lips would touch hers and find unrestricted sweetness. Now his mind spun with it. Whatever he had wanted, whatever he had dreamed of, was less, so much less than what he now held in his arms.

He stroked a hand down her body and met trembling response. With a moan, she arched against him. Through the sheer fabric of her blouse, he could feel the heat rising to her skin, enticing him to touch again and yet again.

He released the first button of her blouse, then the second, following the course with his lips. She shivered with anticipation. Her lace cuffs brushed against his cheeks as she lifted her hands to his hair. It seemed her body was filling, flooding with sensations she'd once only imagined. Now they were so real and so clear that she could feel each one as it layered over the next.

The pillows at her back were soft. His body was hard and hot. The breeze that jingled the wind chime overhead was freshened with flowers. Behind her closed eyes came the flicker and glow of candlelight. In teams of thousands, the cicadas began to sing. But more thrilling, more intense, was the sound of her name whispering from him as he pressed his lips against her skin.

Suddenly, searing, his mouth took hers again. In the kiss she could taste everything, his need, his desire, the passion that teetered on the edge of sanity. As her own madness hovered, she felt her senses swimming with him. And she moaned with the ecstasy of falling in love.

For one brief moment, she rose on it, thrilled with the knowledge that she had found him. The dream and the reality were both here. She had only to close them both in her arms and watch them become one.

Then the terror of it fell on her. She couldn't let it be real. How could she risk it? Once she had given her trust and her promise, if not her heart. And she had been betrayed. If it happened again, she would never recover. If it happened with Chase, she wouldn't want to.

"Chase, no more." She turned her face away and tried to clear her head. "Please, this has to stop."

Her taste was still exploding in his mouth. Beneath his, her body was trembling with a need he knew matched his own. "Eden, for God's sake." With an effort that all but drained him, he lifted his head to look down at her. She was afraid. He recognized her fear immediately and struggled to hold back his own needs. "I won't hurt you."

That almost undid her. He meant it, she was sure, but that didn't mean it wouldn't happen. "Chase, this isn't right for me. For either of us."

"Isn't it?" Tension knotted in his stomach as he drew her toward him. "Can you tell me you didn't feel how right it was a minute ago?"

"No." It was both confusion and fear that had her

dragging her hands through her hair. "But this isn't what I want. I need you to understand that this can't be what I want. Not now."

"You're asking a hell of a lot."

"Maybe. But there isn't any choice."

That infuriated him. She was the one who had taken his choice away, simply by existing. He hadn't asked her to fall into his life. He hadn't asked her to become the focus of it before he had a chance for a second breath. She'd given in to him to the point where he was half-mad for her. Now she was drawing away. And asking him to understand.

"We'll play it your way." His tone chilled as he drew away from her.

She shuddered, recognizing instantly that his anger could be lethal. "It's not a game."

"No? Well, in any case, you play it well."

She pressed her lips together, understanding that she deserved at least a part of the lash. "Please, don't spoil what happened."

He walked to the table and, lifting his glass, studied the wine. "What did happen?"

I fell in love with you. Rather than answer him, she began to button her blouse with nerveless fingers.

"I'll tell you." He tossed back the remaining wine, but it didn't soothe him. "Not for the first time in our fascinating relationship, you blew hot and cold without any apparent reason. It makes me wonder if Eric backed out of the marriage out of self-defense."

He saw her fingers freeze on the top button of her blouse. Even in the dim light, he could watch the color wash out of her face. Very carefully, he set his glass down again. "I'm sorry, Eden. That was uncalled-for."

The fight for control and composure was a hard war, but she won. She made her fingers move until the button was in place, then, slowly, she rose. "Since you're so interested, I'll tell you that Eric jilted me for more practical reasons. I appreciate the meal, Chase. It was lovely. Please thank Delaney for me."

"Damn it, Eden."

When he started forward, her body tightened like a bow. "If you could do one thing for me, it would be to take me back now and say nothing. Absolutely nothing."

Turning, she walked away from the candlelight.

Chapter 6

During the first weeks of August, the camp was plagued with one calamity after another. The first was an epidemic of poison ivy. Within twenty-four hours, ten of the girls and three of the counselors were coated with calamine lotion. The sticky heat did nothing to make the itching more bearable.

Just as the rashes started to fade came three solid days of rain. As the camp was transformed into a muddy mire, outdoor activities were canceled. Tempers soared. Eden broke up two hair-pulling battles in one day. Then, as luck would have it, lightning hit one of the trees and distracted the girls from their boredom.

By the time the sun came out, they had enough pot holders, key chains, wallets and pillows to open their own craft shop.

Men with Jeeps and chain saws came to clear away

the debris from the tree. Eden wrote out a check and
prayed the last crisis was over.

It was doubtful the check had even been cashed when
the secondhand restaurant stove she and Candy had
bought stopped working. In the three days the parts
were on order, cooking was done in true camp style—
around an open fire.

The gelding, Courage, developed an infection that
settled in his lungs. Everyone in camp worried about
him and fussed over him and pampered him. The vet
dosed him with penicillin. Eden spent three sleepless
nights in the stables, nursing him and waiting for the
crisis to pass.

Eventually the horse's appetite improved, the mud in
the compound dried and the stove was back in working
order. Eden told herself that the worst had to be over
as the camp's routine picked up again.

Yet oddly, the lull brought out a restlessness she'd
been able to ignore while the worst was happening.
At dusk, she wandered to the stables with her sackful
of apples. It wasn't hard to give a little extra attention
to Courage. He'd gotten used to being pampered during his illness. Eden slipped him a carrot to go with
the apple.

Still, as she worked her way down the stalls, she
found the old routine didn't keep her mind occupied.
The emergencies over the past couple of weeks had
kept her too busy to take a second breath, much less
think. Now, with calm settling again, thinking was un-
avoidable.

She could remember her evening with Chase as if it

had been the night before. Every word spoken, every touch, every gesture, was locked in her mind as it had been when it had been happening. The rushing, tumbling sensation of falling in love was just as vital now, and just as frightening.

She hadn't been prepared for it. Her life had always been a series of preparations and resulting actions. Even her engagement had been a quiet step along a well-paved road. Since then, she'd learned to handle the detours and the roadblocks. But Chase was a sudden one-way street that hadn't been on any map.

It didn't matter, she told herself as she finished Patience's rubdown. She would navigate this and swing herself back in the proper direction. Having her choices taken away at this point in her life wasn't something she would tolerate. Not even when the lack of choice seemed so alluring and so right.

"I thought I'd find you here." Candy leaned against the stall door to give the mare a pat. "How was Courage tonight?"

"Good." Eden walked to the little sink in the corner to wash liniment from her hands. "I don't think we have to worry about him anymore."

"I'm glad to know that you'll be using your bunk instead of a pile of hay."

Eden pressed both hands to the small of her back and stretched. No demanding set of tennis had ever brought on this kind of ache. Strangely enough, she liked it. "I never thought I'd actually look forward to sleeping in that bunk."

"Well, now that you're not worried about the gelding, I can tell you I'm worried about you."

"Me?" Eden looked for a towel and, not finding one, dried her hands on her jeans. "Why?"

"You're pushing yourself too hard."

"Don't be silly. I'm barely pulling my weight."

"That stopped being even close to the truth the second week of camp." Now that she'd decided to speak up, Candy took a deep breath. "Damn it, Eden, you're exhausted."

"Tired," Eden corrected her. "Which is nothing a few hours on that miserable bunk won't cure."

"Look, it's okay if you want to avoid the issue with everyone else, even with yourself. But don't do it with me."

It wasn't often Candy's voice took on that firm, no-nonsense tone. Eden lifted a brow and nodded. "All right, what is the issue?"

"Chase Elliot," Candy stated, and she saw Eden freeze up. "I didn't hound you with questions the night you came back from dinner."

"And I appreciate that."

"Well, don't, because I'm asking now."

"We had dinner, talked a bit about books and music, then he brought me back."

Candy closed the stall door with a creak. "I thought I was your friend."

"Oh, Candy, you know you are." With a sigh, Eden closed her eyes a moment. "All right, we did exactly what I said we did, but somewhere between the talk and the ride home, things got a little out of hand."

"What sort of things?"

Eden found she didn't even have the energy to laugh. "I've never known you to pry."

"I've never known you to settle comfortably into depression."

"Am I?" Eden blew her bangs out of her eyes. "God, maybe I am."

"Let's just say that you've jumped from one problem to the next in order to avoid fixing one of your own." Taking a step closer, Candy drew Eden down on a small bench. "So let's talk."

"I'm not sure I can." Linking her hands, Eden looked down at them. The opal ring that had once been her mother's winked back at her. "I promised myself after Papa died and everything was in such a mess that I would handle things and find the best way to solve the problems. I've needed to solve them myself."

"That doesn't mean you can't lean on a friend."

"I've leaned on you so much I'm surprised you can walk upright."

"I'll let you know when I start limping. Eden, unless my memory's faulty, we've taken turns leaning on each other since before either of us could walk. Tell me about Chase."

"He scares me." With a long breath, Eden leaned back against the wall. "Everything's happening so fast, and everything I feel seems so intense." Dropping the last of her guard, she turned her face to Candy's. "If things had worked out differently, I'd be married to another man right now. How can I even think I might be in love with someone else so soon?"

"You're not going to tell me you think you're fickle." The last thing Eden had expected was Candy's bright, bubbling laughter, but that was what echoed off the stable walls. "Eden, I'm the fickle one, remember? You've always been loyal to a fault. Wait, I can see you're getting annoyed, so let's take this logically." Candy crossed her ankles and began to count off on her fingers.

"First, you were engaged to Eric—the slime—because of all the reasons we've discussed before. It seemed the proper thing to do. Were you in love with him?"

"No, but I thought—"

"Irrelevant. No is the answer. Second, he showed his true colors, the engagement's been off for months, and you've met a fascinating, attractive man. Now, let's even take it a step further." Warming up to the subject, Candy shifted on the bench. "Suppose—God forbid—that you had actually been madly in love with Eric. After he had shown himself to be a snake, your heart would have been broken. With time and effort, you would have pulled yourself back together. Right?"

"I certainly like to think so."

"So we agree."

"Marginally."

That was enough for Candy. "Then, heart restored, if you'd met a fascinating and attractive man, you would have been equally free to fall for him. Either way, you're in the clear." Satisfied, Candy rose and dusted her palms on her jeans. "So what's the problem?"

Not certain she could explain, or even make sense of it herself, Eden looked down at her hands. "Because

I've learned something. Love is a commitment, it's total involvement, promises, compromises. I'm not sure I can give those things to anyone yet. And if I were, I don't know if Chase feels at all the same way."

"Eden, your instincts must tell you he does."

With a shake of her head, she rose. She did feel better having said it all out loud, but that didn't change the bottom line. "I've learned not to trust my instincts, but to be realistic. Which is why I'm going to go hit the account books."

"Oh, Eden, give it a break."

"Unfortunately, I had to give it a break during the poison ivy, the lightning, the stove breakdown and the vet visits." Hooking her arm through Candy's, she started to walk toward the door. "You were right, and talking it out helped, but practicality is still the order of the day."

"Meaning checks and balances."

"Right. I'd really like to get to it. The advantage is I can frazzle my brain until the bunk really does feel like a feather bed."

Candy pushed open the door, then squared her shoulders. "I'll help."

"Thanks, but I'd like to finish them before Christmas."

"Oh, low blow, Eden."

"But true." She latched the door behind them. "Don't worry about me, Candy. Talking about it cleared my head a bit."

"Doing something about it would be better, but it's a start. Don't work too late."

"A couple of hours," Eden promised.

The office, as Eden arrogantly called it, was a small side room off the kitchen. After switching on the gooseneck lamp on the metal army-surplus desk, she adjusted the screen, flap up. As an afterthought, she switched the transistor radio on the corner of the desk to a classical station. The quiet, familiar melodies would go a long way toward calming her.

Still, as always, she drew in a deep breath as she took her seat behind the desk. Here, she knew too well, things were black-and-white. There were no multiple choices, no softening the rules as there could be in other areas of the camp. Figures were figures and facts were facts. It was up to her to tally them.

Opening the drawers, she pulled out invoices, the business checkbook and the ledger. She began systematically sorting and entering as the tape spilled out of the adding machine at her elbow.

Within twenty minutes, she knew the worst. The additional expenses of the past two weeks had stretched their capital to the limit. No matter how many ways Eden worked the numbers, the answer was the same. They weren't dead broke, but painfully close to it. Wearily, she rubbed the bridge of her nose between her thumb and forefinger.

They could still make it, she told herself. She pressed her hand down on the pile of papers, letting her palm cover the checks and balances. By the skin of their teeth, she thought, but they could still make it. If there were no more unexpected expenses. And if, she continued, the pile seeming to grow under her hand, she and Candy lived frugally over the winter. She imagined the pile growing another six inches under her restraining hand. If they got the necessary enrollments for the next season, everything would turn around.

Curling her fingers around the papers, she let out a long breath. If one of those *if*s fell through, she still had some jewelry that could be sold.

The lamplight fell across her opal-and-diamond ring, but she looked away, feeling guilty at even considering selling it. But she would. If her other choices were taken away, she would. What she wouldn't do was give up.

The tears began so unexpectedly that they fell onto the blotter before she knew she had shed them. Even as she wiped them away, new ones formed. There was no one to see, no one to hear. Giving in, Eden laid her head on the piles of bills and let the tears come.

They wouldn't change anything. With tears would come no fresh ideas or brilliant answers, but she let them come anyway. Quite simply, her strength had run out.

He found her like that, weeping almost soundlessly over the neat stacks of paper. At first Chase only stood there, with the door not quite shut at his back. She looked so helpless, so utterly spent. He wanted to go to her, but held himself back. He understood that the tears would be private. She wouldn't want to share them, particularly not with him. And yet, even as he told himself to step back, he moved toward her.

"Eden."

Her head shot up at the sound of her name. Her eyes were drenched, but he saw both shock and humiliation in them before she began to dry her cheeks with the backs of her hands.

"What are you doing here?"

"I wanted to see you." It sounded simple enough, but didn't come close to what was moving inside him. He wanted to go to her, to gather her close and fix whatever was wrong. He stuck his hands in his pockets and remained standing just inside the door. "I just heard about the gelding this morning. Is he worse?"

She shook her head, then struggled to keep her voice calm. "No, he's better. It wasn't as serious as we thought it might be."

"That's good." Frustrated by his inability to think of something less inane, he began to pace. How could he offer comfort when she wouldn't share the problem? Her eyes were dry now, but he knew it was pride, and pride alone, that held her together. The hell with her pride, he thought. He needed to help.

When he turned back, he saw she had risen from the desk. "Why don't you tell me about it?"

The need to confide in him was so painfully strong that she automatically threw up the customary shield. "There's nothing to tell. It's been a rough couple of weeks. I suppose I'm overtired."

It was more than that, he thought, though she did look exhausted. "The girls getting to you?"

"No, really, the girls are fine."

Frustrated, he looked for another answer. The radio was playing something slow and romantic. Glancing toward it, Chase noticed the open ledger. The tail of adding-machine tape was spilling onto the floor. "Is it money? I could help."

Eden closed the book with a snap. Humiliation was a bitter taste at the back of her throat. At least it dried the last of her tears. "We're fine," she told him in a voice that was even and cool. "If you'd excuse me, I still have some work to do."

Rejection was something Chase had never fully understood until he'd met her. He didn't care for it. Nodding slowly, he searched for patience. "It was meant as an offer, not an insult." He would have turned and left her then, but the marks of weeping and sleeplessness gave her a pale, wounded look. "I'm sorry about the trouble you've been having the past year, Eden. I knew you'd lost your father, but I didn't know about the estate."

She wanted, oh so badly, to reach out, to let him gather her close and give her all the comfort she needed. She wanted to ask him what she should do, and have him give her the answers. But wouldn't that mean that all the months of struggling for self-sufficiency had been for nothing? She straightened her shoulders. "It isn't necessary to be sorry."

"If you had told me yourself, it would have been simpler."

"It didn't concern you."

He didn't so much ignore the stab of hurt as turn it into annoyance. "Didn't it? I felt differently—feel differently. Are you going to stand there and tell me there's nothing between us, Eden?"

She couldn't deny it, but she was far too confused,

far too afraid, to try to define the truth. "I don't know how I feel about you, except that I don't want to feel anything. Most of all, I don't want your pity."

The hands in his pockets curled into fists. He didn't know how to handle his own feelings, his own needs. Now she was treating them as though they didn't matter. He could leave, or he could beg. At the moment, Chase saw no choice between the two. "Understanding and pity are different things, Eden. If you don't know that, there's nothing else to say."

Turning, he left her. The screen door swished quietly behind him.

For the next two days, Eden functioned. She gave riding instructions, supervised meals and hiked the hills with groups of girls. She talked and laughed and listened, but the hollowness that had spread inside her when the door had closed at Chase's back remained.

Guilt and regret. Those were the feelings she couldn't shake, no matter how enthusiastically she threw herself into her routine. She'd been wrong. She'd known it even as it was happening, but pride had boxed her in. He had offered to help. He had offered to care, and she'd refused him. If there was a worse kind of selfishness, she couldn't name it.

She'd started to phone him, but hadn't been able to dial the number. It hadn't been pride that had held her back this time. Every apology that formed in her mind was neat and tidy and meaningless. She couldn't bear to give him a stilted apology, nor could she bear the possibility that he wouldn't care.

Whatever had started to grow between them, she had squashed. Whatever might have been, she had cut off before it had begun to flower. How could she explain to Chase that she'd been afraid of being hurt again? How could she tell him that when he'd offered help and understanding she'd been afraid to accept it because it was so easy to be dependent?

She began to ride out alone at night again. Solitude didn't soothe her as it once had; it only reminded her that she had taken steps to insure that she would remain alone. The nights were warm, with the lingering scent of honeysuckle bringing back memories of a night where there had been pictures in the sky. She couldn't look at the stars without thinking of him.

Perhaps that was why she rode to the lake, where the grass was soft and thick. Here she could smell the water and wild blossoms. The horse's hooves were muffled, and she could just hear the rustle of wings in flight— some unseen bird in search of prey or a mate.

Then she saw him.

The moon was on the wane, so he was only a shadow, but she knew he was watching her. Just as she had known, somehow, that she would find him there tonight. Reining in, she let the magic take her. For the moment, even if it were only a moment, she would forget everything but that she loved him. Tomorrow would take care of itself.

She slid from the horse and went to him.

He said nothing. Until she touched him, he wasn't sure she wasn't a dream. In silence, she framed his face

in her hands and pressed her lips to his. No dream had
ever tasted so warm. No illusion had ever felt so soft.

"Eden—"

With a shake of her head, she cut off his words. There
were weeks of emptiness to fill, and no questions that
needed answering. Rising on her toes, she kissed him
again. The only sound was her sigh as his arms finally
came around her. She discovered a bottomless well of
giving inside her. Something beyond passion, something beyond desire. Here was comfort, strength and
the understanding she had been afraid to accept.

His fingers trailed up to her hair, as if each touch reassured him she was indeed real. When he opened his
eyes again, his arms wouldn't be empty, but filled with
her. Her cheek rubbed his, smooth skin against a day's
growth of beard. With her head nestled in a curve of
his shoulder, she watched the wink and blink of fireflies and thought of stars.

They stood in silence while an owl hooted and the
horse whinnied in response.

"Why did you come?" He needed an answer, one he
could take back with him when she had left him again.

"To see you." She drew away, wanting to see his face.
"To be with you."

"Why?"

The magic shimmered and began to dim. With a
sigh, she drew back. Dreams were for sleeping, Eden
reminded herself. And questions had to be answered.
"I wanted to apologize for the way I behaved before.
You were being kind." Searching for words, she turned
to pluck a leaf from the tree that shadowed them. "I

know how I must have seemed, how I sounded, and I am sorry. It's difficult, still difficult for me to..." Restless, she moved her shoulders. "We were able to muffle most of the publicity after my father died, but there was a great deal of gossip, of speculation and not-so-quiet murmurs."

When he said nothing, she shifted again, uncomfortable. "I suppose I resented all of that more than anything else. It became very important to me to prove myself, that I could manage, even succeed. I realize that I've become sensitive about handling things myself and that when you offered to help, I reacted badly. I apologize for that."

Silence hung another moment before he took a step toward her. Eden thought he moved the way the shadows did. Silently. "That's a nice apology, Eden. Before I accept it, I'd like to ask if the kiss was part of it."

So he wasn't going to make it easy for her. Her chin lifted. She didn't need an easy road any longer. "No."

Then he smiled and circled her throat with his hand. "What was it for then?"

The smile disturbed her more than the touch, though it was the touch she backed away from. Strange how you could take one step and find yourself sunk to the hips. "Does there have to be a reason?" When she walked toward the edge of the lake, she saw an owl swoop low over the water. That was the way she felt, she realized. As if she were skimming along the surface of something that could take her in over her head. "I wanted to kiss you, so I did."

The tension he'd lived with for weeks had vanished,

leaving him almost light-headed. He had to resist the urge to scoop her up and carry her home, where he'd begun to understand she belonged. "Do you always do what you want?"

She turned back with a toss of her head. She'd apologized, but the pride remained. "Always."

He grinned, nudging a smile from her. "So do I."

"Then we should understand each other."

He trailed a finger down her cheek. "Remember that."

"I will." Steady again, she moved past him to the gelding. "We're having a dance a week from Saturday. Would you like to come?"

His hand closed over hers on the reins. "Are you asking me for a date?"

Amused, she swung her hair back before settling a foot in the stirrup. "Certainly not. We're short of chaperons."

She bent her leg to give herself a boost into the saddle, but found herself caught at the waist. She dangled in midair for a moment before Chase set her on the ground again, turning her to face him. "Will you dance with me?"

She remembered the last time they had danced and saw from the look in his eyes that he did as well. Her heart fluttered in the back of her dry throat, but she lifted a brow and smiled. "Maybe."

His lips curved, then descended slowly to brush against hers. She felt the world tilt, then steady at an angle only lovers understand. "A week from Saturday," he murmured, then lifted her easily into the saddle. His hand remained over hers another moment. "Miss me."

He stayed by the water until she was gone and the night was silent again.

Chapter 7

The last weeks of summer were hot and long. At night, there was invariably heat lightning and rumbling thunder, but little rain. Eden pushed herself through the days, blocking out the uncertainty of life after September.

She wasn't escaping, she told herself. She was coping with one day at a time. If she had learned one important lesson over the summer, it was that she could indeed make changes, in herself and in her life.

The frightened and defeated woman who had come to Camp Liberty almost as if it were a sanctuary would leave a confident, successful woman who could face the world on her own terms.

Standing in the center of the compound, she ran her hands down her narrow hips before dipping them into the pockets of her shorts. Next summer would be even better, now that they'd faced the pitfalls and learned how to maneuver around them. She knew she was skipping over months of her life, but found she didn't want to dwell on the winter. She didn't want to think of Philadelphia and snowy sidewalks, but of the mountains and what she had made of her life there.

If it had been possible, she would have found a way to stay behind during the off-season. Eden had begun to understand that only necessity and the need for employment were taking her back east. It wasn't her home any longer.

With a shake of her head, Eden pushed away thoughts of December. The sun was hot and bright. She could watch it shimmer on the surface of Chase's lake and think of him.

She wondered what would have happened if she had met him two years earlier when her life had been so ordered and set and mapped-out. Would she have fallen in love with him then? Perhaps it was all a matter of timing; perhaps she would have given him a polite howdo-you-do and forgotten him.

No. Closing her eyes, she could recall vividly every sensation, every emotion he'd brought into her life. Timing had nothing to do with something so overwhelming. No matter when, no matter where, she would have fallen in love with him. Hadn't she fought it all along, only to find her feelings deepening?

But she'd thought herself in love with Eric, too.

She shivered in the bright sun and watched a jay race overhead. Was she so shallow, so cold, that her feelings could shift and change in the blink of an eye? That was what held her back and warned her to be cautious.

If Eric hadn't turned his back on her, she would have married him. His ring would be on her finger even now. Eden glanced down at her bare left hand.

But that hadn't been love, she reassured herself. Now she knew what love felt like, what it did to heart and mind and body. And yet... How did he feel? He cared, and he wanted, but she knew enough of love now to understand that wasn't enough. She, too, had once cared and wanted. If Chase was in love with her, there wouldn't be any *before*. Time would begin now.

Don't be a fool, she told herself with a flash of annoyance. That kind of thinking would only make her drift back to dependence. There was a before for both of them, and a future. There was no way of being sure that the future would merge with what she felt today.

But she wanted to be a fool, she realized with a quick, delicious shudder. Even if only for a few weeks, she wanted to absorb and concentrate all those mad feelings. She'd be sensible again. Sensible was for January, when the wind was sharp and the rent had to be paid. In a few days she would dance with him, smile up at him. She would have that one night of the summer to be a fool.

Kicking off her shoes, Eden plucked them up in one hand and ran the rest of the way to the dock. Girls, already separated into groups, were waiting for the signal to row out into the lake.

"Miss Carlbough!" In her camp uniform and her familiar cap, Roberta hopped up and down on the grass near the rowboats. "Watch this." With a quick flurry of motion, she bent over, kicked up her feet and stood on her head. "What do you think?" she demanded through teeth clenched with effort. Her triangular face reddened.

"Incredible."

"I've been practicing." With a grunt, Roberta tumbled onto the grass. "Now, when my mom asks what I did at camp, I can stand on my head and show her."

Eden lifted a brow, hoping Mrs. Snow got a few more details. "I'm sure she'll be impressed."

Still sprawled on the grass, arms splayed out to the sides, Roberta stared up at Eden. She was just old enough to wish that her hair was blond and wavy. "You look real pretty today, Miss Carlbough."

Touched, and more than a little surprised, Eden held out a hand to help Roberta up. "Why, thank you, Roberta. So do you."

"Oh, I'm not pretty, but I'm going to be once I can wear makeup and cover my freckles."

Eden rubbed a thumb over Roberta's cheek. "Lots of boys fall for freckles."

"Maybe." Roberta tucked that away to consider later. "I guess you're soft on Mr. Elliot."

Eden dropped her hand back in her pocket. "Soft on?"

"You know." To demonstrate, Roberta sighed and fluttered her eyes. Eden wasn't sure whether to laugh or give the little monster a shove into the lake.

"That's ridiculous."

"Are you getting married?"

"I haven't the vaguest idea where you come up with such nonsense. Now into the boat. Everyone's ready to go."

"My mom told me people sometimes get married when they're soft on each other."

"I'm sure your mother's quite right." Hoping to close the subject, Eden helped Roberta into their assigned rowboat, where Marcie and Linda were already waiting. "However, in this case, Mr. Elliot and I barely know each other. Everyone hook their life jackets, please."

"Mom said she and Daddy fell in love at first sight." Roberta hooked on the preserver, though she thought it was a pain when she swam so well. "They kiss all the time."

"I'm sure that's nice. Now—"

"I used to think it was kind of gross, but I guess it's okay." Roberta settled into her seat and smiled. "Well, if you decide not to marry Mr. Elliot, maybe I will."

Eden was busy locking in the oars, but she glanced up. "Oh?"

"Yeah. He's got a neat dog and all those apple trees." Roberta adjusted the brim of her cap over her eyes. "And he's kind of pretty." The two girls beside her giggled in agreement.

"That's certainly something to think about." Eden began to row. "Maybe you can discuss the idea with your mother when you get home."

"'Kay. Can I row first?"

Eden could only be grateful that the girl's interest span was as fast-moving as the rest of her. "Fine. You and I will row out. Marcie and Linda can row back."

After a bit of drag and a few grunts, Roberta matched her rhythm to Eden's. As the boat began to glide, it occurred to Eden that she was rowing with the same three girls who had started the adventure in the apple orchard. With a silent chuckle, she settled into sync with Roberta and let her mind drift.

What if she had never gone up in that tree? Absently, she touched her lower lip with her tongue, recalling the taste and feel of Chase. If she had it to do over, would she run in the opposite direction?

Smiling, Eden closed her eyes a moment, so that the sun glowed red under her lids. No, she wouldn't run. Being able to admit it, being able to be sure of it, strengthened her confidence. She wouldn't run from Chase, or from anything else in life.

Perhaps she was soft on him, as Roberta had termed it. Perhaps she could hug that secret to herself for a little while. It would be wonderful if things could be as simple and uncomplicated as Roberta made them. Love equaled marriage, marriage equaled happiness. Sighing, Eden opened her eyes and watched the surface of the lake. For a little while she could believe in poetry and dreams.

Daydreams… They were softer and even more mystical than dreams by night. It had been a long time since Eden had indulged in them. Now the girls were chattering and calling to their friends in the other boats. Someone was singing, deliberately off-key. Eden's arms moved in a steady rhythm as the oars cut smoothly into the water and up into the air again.

So she was floating…dreaming with her eyes open… silk and ivory and lace. The glitter of the sun on water was like candlelight. The call of crows was music to dance by.

She was riding on Pegasus. High in a night sky, his white wings effortlessly cut through the air. She could taste the cool, thin wind that took them through clouds. Her hair was free, flying behind her, twined with flowers. More clouds, castle-like, rose up in the distance, filmy and gray and secret. Their secrets were nothing to her. She had freedom for the first time, full, unlimited freedom.

And he was with her, riding the sky through snatches of light and dark. Higher, still higher they rose, until the earth was only mist beneath them. And the stars were flowers, the white petals of anemones that she could reach out and pick as the whim struck her.

When she turned in his arms, she was his without boundaries. All restrictions, all doubts, had been left behind in the climb.

"Hey, look. It's Squat!"

Eden blinked. The daydream disintegrated. She was in a rowboat, with muscles that were just beginning to ache from exertion. There were no flowers, no stars, only water and sky.

They'd rowed nearly the width of the lake. A portion of Chase's orchard spread back from the shore, and visible was one of the greenhouses he had taken the camp through on the day of the tour. Delighted with the company, Squat dashed back and forth in the shallow water near the lake's edge. His massive paws scattered a flurry of water that coated him until he was a sopping, shaggy mess.

Smiling as the girls called out greetings to the dog, Eden wondered if Chase was home. What did he do with his Sundays? she thought. Did he laze around the house with the paper and cups of coffee? Did he switch on the ball game, or go out for long, solitary drives? Just then, as if to answer her questions, he and Delaney joined the dog on the shore. Across the water, Eden felt the jolt as their eyes met.

Would it always be like that? Always stunning, always fresh? Always immediate? Inhaling slowly, she coaxed her pulse back to a normal rate.

"Hey, Mr. Elliot!" Without a thought for the consequences, Roberta dropped her oar and jumped up. Excitement had her bouncing up and down as the boat teetered.

"Roberta." Acting by instinct, Eden locked her oars. "Sit down, you'll turn us over." Eden started to grab for her hand as the other girls took Roberta's lead and jumped to their feet.

"Hi, Mr. Elliot!"

The greeting rang out in unison, just before the boat tipped over.

Eden hit the water headfirst. After the heat of the sun it seemed shockingly cold, and she surfaced sputtering with fury. With one hand, she dragged the hair out of her eyes and focused on the three bobbing heads. The girls, buoyed by their life jackets, waved unrepentantly at the trio on shore.

Eden grabbed the edge of the upended boat. "Roberta!"

"Look, Miss Carlbough." Apparently the tone, said through gritted teeth, passed over the girl's head. "Squat's coming out."

"Terrific." Treading water, Eden plucked Roberta by the arm and tried to drag her back to the capsized boat. "Remember the rules of boating safety. Stay here." Eden went for the next girl, but twisted her head to see the dog paddling toward them. Uneasy with his progress, she looked back toward shore.

Her request that Chase call back his dog caught in her throat as she spotted his grin. Though she couldn't hear the words, she saw Delaney turn to him with some remark. It was enough to see Chase throw back his head and laugh. That sound carried.

"Want some help?" he called out.

Eden pulled at the next giggling girl. "Don't put yourself out," she began, then shrieked when Squat laid a wet, friendly nose on her shoulder. Her reaction seemed to amuse everyone, dog included. Squat began to bark enthusiastically in her ear.

Fresh pandemonium broke out as the girls began to splash water at each other and the dog. Eden found herself caught in the crossfire. In the other boats, campers and counselors looked on, grinning or calling out encouraging words. Squat paddled circles around her as she struggled to restore some kind of order.

"All right, ladies. Enough." That earned her a mouthful of lake. "It's time to right the boat."

"Can Squat take a ride with us?" Roberta giggled as he licked water from her face.

"No."

"That hardly seems fair."

Eden nearly submerged before Chase gripped her arm. She'd been too busy trying to restore order and her own dignity to notice that he'd swum the few yards from shore. "He came out to help."

His hair was barely damp, while hers was plastered to her head. Chase hooked an arm around her waist to ease her effort to tread water.

"You'd better right the boat," he said to the girls, who immediately fell to doing so with a vengeance. "Apparently you do better with horses." His voice was soft and amused in Eden's ear.

She started to draw away, but her legs tangled with his. "If you and that monster hadn't been on shore—"

"Delaney?"

"No, not Delaney." Frustrated, Eden pushed at her hair.

"You're beautiful when you're wet. Makes me wonder why I haven't thought of swimming with you before."

"We're not supposed to be swimming, we're supposed to be boating."

"Either way, you're beautiful."

She wouldn't be moved. Even though the girls had already righted the boat, Eden knew she was in over her head. "It's that dog," she began. Even as she said it, the girls were climbing back into the boat and urging Squat to join them.

"Roberta, I said—" Chase gently dunked her. Surfacing, she heard him striking the bargain.

"We'll swim back. You bring Squat. He likes boats."

"I said—" Again, she found herself under water. This time when she came up for air, she gave Chase her full attention. The swing she took at him was slow and sluggish because of the need to tread water.

He caught her fist and kissed it. "Beat you back."

Narrowing her eyes, Eden gave him a shove before striking out after the boat. The water around her ears muffled the sound of Squat's deep barking and the girls' excited cheering. With strong, even strokes, she kept a foot behind the boat and made certain the girls behaved.

Less than twenty feet from shore, Chase caught her by the ankle. Laughing and kicking, Eden found herself tangled in his arms.

"You cheat." As he rose, he swept her off her feet so that her accusation ended in another laugh. His bare chest was cool and wet under her palms. His hair was dripping so that the sunlight was caught in each separate drop of water. "I won."

"Wrong." She should have seen it coming. Without effort, he pitched her back in the lake. Eden landed bottom first. "I won."

Eden stood to shake herself off. Managing to suppress a smile, she nodded toward the whooping girls. "And that, ladies, is a classic example of poor sportsmanship." She reached up to squeeze the water out of her hair, unaware that her shirt clung to every curve. Chase felt his heart stop. She waded toward shore, with the clear lake water clinging to her tanned legs. "Good afternoon, Delaney."

"Ma'am." He gave her a gold, flashing grin. "Nice day for a swim."

"Apparently."

"I was about to pick me some blackberries for jam." He cast his gaze over the three dripping girls. "If I had some help, could be I'd have a jar or so extra for some neighbors."

Before Eden could consent or refuse, all the girls and Squat were jumping circles around her. She had to admit that a ten- or fifteen-minute break would make the row back to camp a little more appealing. "Ten minutes," she told them before turning back to signal to the other boats.

Delaney toddled off, sandwiched between girls who were already barraging him with questions. As they disappeared into a cluster of trees, a startled flock of birds whizzed out. She laughed, turning back to see Chase staring at her.

"You're a strong swimmer."

She had to clear her throat. "I think I've just become more competitive. Maybe I should keep an eye on the girls so—"

"Delaney can handle them." He reached out to brush a bead of water from her jawline. Beneath his gentle touch, she shivered. "Cold?"

More than the sun had taken the lake's chill from her skin. Eden managed to shake her head. "No." But when his hands came to her shoulders, she stepped back.

He wore only cutoffs, faded soft from wear. The shirt he had peeled off before diving into the lake had been tossed carelessly to the ground. "You don't feel cold," he murmured as he stroked his hands down her arms.

"I'm not." She heard the laughter beyond the trees. "I really can't let them stay long. They'll have to change."

Patient, Chase took her hand. "Eden, you're going to end up in the lake again if you keep backing up."

He was frightening her. Frustrated, he struggled not to push. It seemed that every time he thought he'd gained her trust, he saw that quick flash of anxiety in her eyes again. He smiled, hoping the need that was roiling inside him didn't show. "Where are your shoes?"

Off-balance, she looked down and stared at her own bare feet. Slowly, her muscles began to relax again. "At the bottom of your lake." Laughing, she shook her wet hair back, nearly destroying him. "Roberta always manages to keep things exciting. Why don't we give them a hand with the berry-picking."

His arm came across her body to take her shoulder before she could move past him. "You're still backing away, Eden." Lifting a hand, he combed his fingers through her sleek, wet hair until they rested at the base of her neck. "It's hard to resist you this way, with your face glowing and your eyes aware and just a bit frightened."

"Chase, don't." She put her hand to his.

"I want to touch you." He shifted so that the full length of her body was against his. "I need to touch you." Through the wet cotton, she could feel the texture of his skin on hers. "Look at me, Eden." The slightest pressure of his fingers brought her face up to his. "How close are you going to let me get?"

She could only shake her head. There weren't any words to describe what she was feeling, what she wanted, what she was still too afraid to need. "Chase, don't do this. Not here, not now." Then she could only moan, as his mouth traveled with a light, lazy touch over her face.

"When?" He had to fight the desire to demand rather than to ask, to take rather than to wait. "Where?" This time the kiss wasn't lazy, but hard, bruising. Eden felt rational thought spiral away even as she groped for an answer. "Don't you think I know what happens to you when we're like this?" His voice thickened as his patience stretched thinner and thinner. "Good God, Eden, I need you. Come with me tonight. Stay with me."

Yes, yes. Oh, yes. How easy it would be to say it, to give in, to give everything without a thought for tomorrow. She clung to him a moment, wanting to believe dreams were possible. He was so solid, so real. But so were her responsibilities.

"Chase, you know I can't." Fighting for rationality, she drew away. "I have to stay at camp."

Before she could move away again, he caught her face in his hands. She thought his eyes had darkened, a stormier green now, with splashes of gold from the sun. "And when summer's over, Eden? What then?"

What then? How could she have the answer, when the answer was so cold, so final? It wasn't what she wanted, but what had to be. If she was to keep her promise to herself, to make her life work, there was only one answer. "Then I'll go back, back to Philadelphia, until next summer."

Only summers? Was that all she was willing to give? It was the panic that surprised him and kept the fury at bay. When she left, his life would be empty. He took her shoulders again, fighting back the panic.

"You'll come to me before you go." It wasn't a question. It wasn't a demand. It was a simple statement. The demand she could have rebelled against; the question she could have refused.

"Chase, what good would it do either of us?"

"You'll come to me before you go," he repeated. Because if she didn't, he'd follow her. There would be no choice.

Chapter 8

Red and white crepe paper streamed from corner to corner, twined together in elongated snakes of color. Balloons, bulging with air from energetic young lungs, were crowded into every available space. Stacked in three uneven towers were all the records deemed fit to play.

Dance night was only a matter of hours away.

Under Candy's eagle eye, tables were carried outside, while others were grouped strategically around the mess area. This simple chore took twice as long as it should have, as girls had to stop every few feet to discuss the most important aspect of the evening: boys.

Although her skills with paint and glue were slim at best, Eden had volunteered for the decorating committee — on the understanding that her duties were limited to hanging and tacking what was already made. In addition to the crepe paper and balloons, there were banners and paper flowers that the more talented members of campers and staff had put together by hand. The best of these was a ten-foot banner dyed Camp Liberty red and splashed with bold letters that spelled out WELCOME TO CAMP LIBERTY'S ANNUAL SUMMER DANCE.

Candy had already taken it for granted that it would be the first of many. In her better moods, Eden hoped she was right. In her crankier ones, she wondered if they could swing a deal with the boys' camp to split the cost of refreshments. For the moment, she pushed both ideas aside, determined to make this dance the best-decorated one in Pennsylvania.

Eden let an argument over which records had priority run its course below her as she climbed a stepladder to secure more streamers. Already, the record player at the far end of the room was blaring music.

It was silly. She told herself that yet again as she realized she was as excited about the evening as any of the girls. She was an adult, here only to plan, supervise and chaperon. Even as she reminded herself of this, her thoughts ran forward to the evening, when the mess area would be filled with people and noise and laughter. Like the girls below her, her thoughts kept circling back to vital matters—like what she should wear.

It was fascinating to realize that this simple end-of-the-summer dance in the mountains was more exciting for her than her own debutante ball. That she had taken lightly, as the next step along the path that had been cleared for her before she was born. This was new, untried and full of possibilities.

It all centered on Chase. Eden was nearly ready to accept that as a new song blared into life. Since it was one she'd heard dozens of times before, she began to hum along with it. Her ponytail swayed with the movement as she attached another streamer.

"We'll ask Miss Carlbough." Eden heard the voices below, but paid little attention, as she had a tack in her mouth and five feet of crepe paper held together by her thumb. "She always knows, and if she doesn't, she finds out."

She had started to secure the tack, but as the statement drifted up to her, she stopped pushing. Was that really the way the girls saw her? Dependable? With a half laugh, she sent the tack home. To her, the statement was the highest of compliments, a sign of faith.

She'd done what she had set out to do. In three short months, she had accomplished something she had never done in all her years of living. She had made something of herself, by herself. And, perhaps more importantly, for herself.

It wasn't going to stop here. Eden dropped the rest of the tacks into her pocket. The summer might be nearly over, but the challenge wasn't. Whether she was in South Mountain or Philadelphia, she wasn't going to forget what it meant to grow. Twisting on the ladder, she started down to find out what it was the girls had wanted to ask her. On the second rung, she stopped, staring.

The tall, striking woman strode into the mess. The tail of her Hermès scarf crossed the neck of a cerise suit and trailed on behind. Her bone-white hair was perfect, as was the double strand of pearls that lay on her bosom. Tucked in the crook of one arm was a small piece of white fluff known as BooBoo.

"Aunt Dottie!" Delighted, Eden scrambled down from the ladder. In seconds she was enveloped by Dottie's personal scent, an elusive combination of Paris and success. "Oh, it's wonderful to see you." Drawing back from the hug, Eden studied the lovely, strong-boned face. Even now, she could see shadows of her father in the eyes and around the mouth. "You're the last person I expected to see here."

"Darling, have you grown thorns in the country?"

"Thorns? I—oh." Laughing, Eden reached in her pocket. "Thumbtacks. Sorry."

"The hug was worth a few holes." Taking Eden's hand, she stepped back to make her own study. Though her face remained passive, she let out a quiet sigh of relief. No one knew how many restless nights she'd spent worrying over her brother's only child. "You look beautiful. A little thin, but with marvelous color." With Eden's hand still in hers, she glanced around the room. "But darling, what an odd place you've chosen to spend the summer."

"Aunt Dottie." Eden just shook her head. Throughout the weeks and months after her father's death, Dottie had stubbornly refused to accept Eden's decision not to use Dottie's money as a buffer, her home as a refuge. "If I have marvelous color, credit the country air."

"Hmm." Far from convinced, Dottie continued to look around as a new record plopped down to continue the unbroken cycle of music. "I've always considered the south of France country enough."

"Aunt Dottie, tell me what you're doing here. I'm amazed you could even find the place."

"It wasn't difficult. The chauffeur reads a map very well." Dottie gave the fluff in her arms a light pat. "BooBoo and I felt an urge for a drive to the country."

"I see." And she did. Like everyone else she had left behind, Eden knew that her aunt considered her camp venture an impulse. It would take more than one summer to convince Dottie, or anyone else, that she was serious. After all, it had taken her most of the summer to convince herself.

"Yes, and since I was in the neighborhood…" Dottie let that trail off. "What a chic outfit," she commented, taking in Eden's paint-spattered smock and tattered sneakers. "Then, perhaps bohemian's coming back. What do you have there?"

"Crepe paper. It goes with the thumbtacks." Eden extended her hand. BooBoo regally allowed her head to be patted.

"Well, give them both to one of these charming young ladies and come see what I've brought you."

"Brought me?" Obeying automatically, Eden handed over the streamers. "Start these around the tables, will you, Lisa?"

"Do you know," Dottie began as she linked her arm through Eden's, "the nearest town is at least twenty miles from here? That is if one could stretch credibility and call what we passed through a town. There, there, BooBoo, I won't set you down on the nasty ground."

She cuddled the dog as they stepped outside. "BooBoo's a bit skittish out of the city, you understand."

"Perfectly."

"Where was I? Oh yes, the town. It had one traffic light and a place called Earl's Lunch. I was almost curious enough to stop and see what one did at Earl's Lunch."

Eden laughed, and leaned over to kiss Dottie's cheek. "One eats a small variety of sandwiches and stale potato chips and coffee while exchanging town gossip."

"Marvelous. Do you go often?"

"Unfortunately, my social life's been a bit limited."

"Well, your surprise might just change all that." Turning, Dottie gestured toward the canary-yellow Rolls parked in the main compound. Eden felt every muscle, every emotion freeze as the man straightened from his easy slouch against the hood.

"Eric."

He smiled, and in a familiar gesture, ran one hand lightly over his hair. Around him, a group of girls had gathered to admire the classic lines of the Rolls and the classic looks of Eric Keeton.

His smile was perfectly angled as he walked toward her. His walk was confident, just a shade too conservative for a swagger. As she watched him, Eden saw him in the clear light of disinterest. His hair, several shades darker than her own, was perfectly styled for the boardroom or the country club. Casual attire, which included pleated slacks and a polo shirt, fit neatly over his rather narrow frame. Hazel eyes, which had a tendency to look bored easily, smiled and warmed now. Though she hadn't offered them, he took both her hands.

"Eden, how marvelous you look."

His hands were soft. Strange, she had forgotten that. Though she didn't bother to remove hers, her voice was cool. "Hello, Eric."

"Lovelier than ever, isn't she, Dottie?" Her stiff greeting didn't seem to disturb him. He gave her hands an intimate little squeeze. "Your aunt was worried about you. She expected you to be thin and wan."

"Fortunately, I'm neither." Now, carefully, deliberately, Eden removed her hands. She would have been greatly pleased, though she had no way of knowing it, that her eyes were as cold as her voice. It was so easy to turn away from him. "Whatever possessed you to drive all this way, Aunt Dottie? You weren't really worried?"

"A tad." Concerned with the ice in her niece's voice, Dottie touched Eden's cheek. "And I did want to see the—the place where you spent the summer."

"I'll give you a tour."

A thin left brow arched in a manner identical to Eden's. "How charming."

"Aunt Dottie!" Red curls bouncing, Candy raced around the side of the building. "I knew it had to be you." Out of breath and grinning broadly, Candy accepted Dottie's embrace. "The girls were talking about a yellow Rolls in the compound. Who else could it have been?"

"As enthusiastic as ever." Dottie's smile was all affection. She might not have always understood Candice

Bartholomew, but she had always been fond of her. "I hope you don't mind a surprise visit."

"I love it." Candy bent down to the puff of fur. "Hi, BooBoo." Straightening, she let her gaze drift over Eric. "Hello, Eric." Her voice dropped an easy twenty-five degrees. "Long way from home."

"Candy." Unlike Dottie, he had no fondness for Eden's closest friend. "You seem to have paint all over your hands."

"It's dry," she said, carelessly, and somewhat regretfully. If the paint had been wet, she would have greeted him more personally.

"Eden's offered to take us on a tour." Dottie was well aware of the hostility. She'd driven hundreds of miles from Philadelphia for one purpose. To help her niece find happiness. If it meant she had to manipulate…so much the better. "I know Eric's dying to look around, but if I could impose on you—" She laid her hand on Candy's. "I'd really love to sit down with a nice cup of tea. BooBoo, too. The drive was a bit tiring."

"Of course." Manners were their own kind of trap. Candy sent Eden a look meant to fortify her. "We'll use the kitchen, if you don't mind the confusion."

"My dear, I thrive on it." With that she turned to smile at Eden and was surprised by the hard, knowing look in Eden's eyes.

"Go right ahead, Aunt Dottie. I'll show Eric what the camp has to offer."

"Eden, I—"

"Go have your tea, darling." She kissed Dottie's cheek. "We'll talk later." She turned, leaving Eric to follow or not. When he fell into step beside her, she began. "We've six sleeping cabins this season, with plans to add two more for next summer. Each cabin has an Indian name to keep it distinct."

As they passed the cabins, she saw that the anemones were still stubbornly blooming. They gave her strength. "Each week, we have a contest for the neatest cabin. The reward is extra riding time, or swimming time, or whatever the girls prefer. Candy and I have a small shower in our cabin. The girls share facilities at the west end of the compound."

"Eden." Eric cupped her elbow in his palm in the same manner he had used when strolling down Broad Street. She gritted her teeth, but didn't protest.

"Yes?" The cool, impersonal look threw him off. It took him only a moment to decide it meant she was hiding a broken heart.

"What have you been doing with yourself?" He waved his hand in a gesture that took in the compound and the surrounding hills. "Here?"

Holding on to her temper, Eden decided to take the question literally. "We've tried to keep the camp regimented, while still allowing for creativity and fun. Over the past few weeks, we've found that we can adhere fairly tightly to the schedule as long as we make room for fresh ideas and individual needs." Pleased with herself, she dipped her hands into the pockets of her smock. "We're up at six-thirty. Breakfast is at seven sharp. Daily inspection begins at seven-thirty and activities at eight. For the most part, I deal with the horses and stables, but when necessary, I can pitch in and help in other areas."

"Eden." Eric stopped her by gently tightening his fingers on her elbow. Turning to him, she watched the faint breeze ruffle his smooth, fair hair. She thought of the dark confusion of Chase's hair. "It's difficult to believe you've spent your summer camping out in a cabin and overseeing a parade of girls on horseback."

"Is it?" She merely smiled. Of course it was difficult for him. He owned a stable, but he'd never lifted a pitchfork. Rather than resentment, Eden felt a stirring of pity. "Well, there's that, among a few other things such as hiking, smoothing over cases of homesickness and poison ivy, rowing, giving advice on teenage romance and fashion, identifying fifteen different varieties of local wildflowers and seeing that a group of girls has fun. Would you like to see the stables?" She headed off without waiting for his answer.

"Eden." He caught her elbow again. It took all her willpower not to jab it back into his soft stomach. "You're angry. Of course you are, but I—"

"You've always had a fondness for good horseflesh." She swung the stable door open so that he had to back off or get a faceful of wood. "We've two mares and four geldings. One of the mares is past her prime, but I'm thinking of breeding the other. The foals would interest the girls and eventually become part of the riding stock. This is Courage."

"Eden, please. We have to talk."

She stiffened when his hands touched her shoulders.

But she was calm, very calm, when she turned and removed them. "I thought we were talking."

He'd heard the ice in her voice before, and he understood it. She was a proud, logical woman. He'd approach her on that level. "We have to talk about us, darling."

"In what context?"

He reached for her hand, giving a small shrug when she drew it away. If she had accepted him without a murmur, he would have been a great deal more surprised. For days now, he'd been planning exactly the proper way to smooth things over. He'd decided on regretful, with a hint of humble thrown in.

"You've every right to be furious with me, every right to want me to suffer."

His tone, soft, quiet, understanding, had her swallowing a ball of heat. Indifference, she reminded herself, disinterest, was the greatest insult she could hand him. "It doesn't really concern me if you suffer or not." That wasn't quite true, she admitted. She wouldn't be averse to seeing him writhe a bit. That was because he had come, she realized. Because he had had the gall to come and assume she'd be waiting.

"Eden, you have to know that I have suffered, suffered a great deal. I would have come before, but I wasn't sure you'd see me."

This was the man she had planned to spend her life with. This was the man she had hoped to have children with. She stared at him now, unsure whether she was in the midst of a comedy or a tragedy. "I'm sorry to hear that, Eric. I don't see any reason why you should have suffered. You were only being practical, after all."

Soothed by her placid attitude, he stepped toward her. "I admit that, rightly or wrongly, I was practical." His hands slid up her arms in an old gesture that made her jaw clench. "These past few months have shown me that there are times when practical matters have to take second place."

"Is that so?" She smiled at him, surprised that he couldn't feel the heat. "What would go first?"

"Personal..." He stroked a finger over her cheek. "Much more personal matters."

"Such as?"

His lips were curved as his mouth lowered. She felt the heat of anger freeze into icy disdain. Did he think her a fool? Could he believe himself so irresistible? Then she nearly did laugh, as she realized the answer to both questions was yes.

She let him kiss her. The touch of his lips left her totally unmoved. It fascinated her that, only a few short months before, his kisses had warmed her. It had been nothing like the volcanic heat she experienced with Chase, but there had been a comfort and an easy pleasure. That was all she had thought there was meant to be.

Now there was nothing. The absence of feeling in itself dulled the edge of her fury. She was in control. Here, as in other areas of her life, she was in control. Though his lips coaxed, she simply stood, waiting for him to finish.

When he lifted his head, Eden put her hands on his

arms to draw herself away. It was then she saw Chase just inside the open stable door.

The sun was at his back, silhouetting him, blinding her to the expression on his face. Even so, her mouth was dry as she stared, trying to see through shadow and sun. When he stepped forward, his eyes were on hers.

Explanations sprang to her tongue, but she could only shake her head as his gaze slid over her and onto Eric.

"Keeton." Chase nodded, but didn't extend his hand. He knew if he had the other man's fingers in his he would take pleasure in breaking them, one by one.

"Elliot." Eric returned the nod. "I'd forgotten. You have land around here, don't you?"

"A bit." Chase wanted to murder him, right there in the stables, while Eden watched. Then he would find it just as satisfying to murder her.

"You must know Eden, then." Eric placed a hand on her shoulder in a casually possessive movement. Chase followed the gesture before looking at her again. Her instinctive move to shrug away Eric's hand was stopped by the look. Was it anger she saw there, or was it disgust?

"Yes. Eden and I have run into each other a few times." He dipped his hands into his pockets as they balled into fists.

"Chase was generous enough to allow us to use his lake." Her right hand groped for her left until they were clasped together. "We had a tour of his orchards." Though pride suffered, her eyes pleaded with him.

"Your land must be very near here." Eric hadn't

missed the exchange of looks. His hand leaned more heavily on Eden's shoulder.

"Near enough."

Then they were looking at each other, not at her. Somehow that, more than anything, made her feel as though she'd been shifted to the middle. If there was tension and she was the cause of it, she wanted to be able to speak on her own behalf. But the expression in Chase's eyes only brought confusion. The weight of Eric's hand only brought annoyance. Moving away from Eric, she stepped toward Chase.

"Did you want to see me?"

"Yes." But he'd wanted more than that, a great deal more. Seeing her in Eric's arms had left him feeling both murderous and empty. He wasn't ready to deal with either yet. "It wasn't important."

"Chase—"

"Oh, hello." The warmth in Candy's voice came almost as a shock. She stepped through the doorway with Dottie at her side. "Aunt Dottie, I want you to meet our neighbor, Chase Elliot."

Even as Dottie extended her hand, her eyes were narrowed speculatively. "Elliot? I'm sure I know that name. Yes, yes, didn't we meet several years ago? You're Jessie Winthrop's grandson."

Eden watched his lips curve, his eyes warm, but he wasn't looking at her. "Yes, I am, and I remember you very well, Mrs. Norfolk. You haven't changed."

Dottie's laugh was low and quick. "It's been fifteen years if it's been a day. I'd say there's been a change or two. You were about a foot shorter at the time." She sized him up approvingly in a matter of ten seconds. "It's apples, isn't it? Yes, of course, it is. Elliot's."

And, oh my God, she realized almost as quickly, I've brought Eric along and jammed up the works. A person would have to have a three-inch layer of steel coating not to feel the shock waves bouncing around the stables.

What could be done, she told herself, could be undone. Smiling, she looked at her niece. "Candy's been telling me about the social event of the season. Are we all invited?"

"Invited?" Eden struggled to gather her scattered wits. "You mean the dance?" She had to laugh. Her aunt was standing in the stables in Italian shoes and a suit that had cost more than any one of the horses. "Aunt Dottie, you don't intend to stay here?"

"Stay here?" The white brows shot up. "I should say not." She twisted the pearls at her neck as she began to calculate. She didn't intend to bunk down in a cabin, but neither was she about to miss the impending fireworks. "Eric and I are staying at a hotel some miles away, but I'd be heartbroken if you didn't ask us to the party tonight." She put a friendly hand on Chase's arm. "You're coming, aren't you?"

He knew a manipulator when he saw one. "Wouldn't miss it."

"Wonderful." Dottie slid Candy's hand back into the crook of her arm, then patted it. "We're all invited then."

Fumbling, Candy looked from Eric to Eden. "Well, yes, of course, but—"

"Isn't this sweet?" Dottie patted her hand again. "We'll have a delightful time. Don't you think so, Eden?"

"Delightful," Eden agreed, wondering if she could hitch a ride out of town.

Chapter 9

Eden had problems—big problems. But not the least of them were the sixty adolescents in the mess hall. However she handled Eric, however she managed to explain herself to Chase, sixty young bodies couldn't be put on hold.

The boys arrived in vans at eight o'clock. Unless Eden missed her guess, they were every bit as nervous as the girls. Eden remembered her own cotillion days, the uncertainty and the damp palms. The blaring music helped cover some of the awkwardness as the boys' counselors trooped them in.

The refreshment table was loaded. There was enough punch stored in the kitchen to bathe in. Candy gave a brief welcoming speech to set the tone, the banners and the paper flowers waving at her back. A fresh record was set spinning on the turntable. Girls stood on one side of the room, boys on the other.

The biggest problem, naturally, was that no one wanted to go first. Eden had worked that out by making up two bowls of corresponding numbers. Boys picked from one, girls from another. You matched, you danced. It wasn't imaginative, but it was expedient.

When the first dance was half over, she slipped into the kitchen to check on backup refreshments, leaving Candy to supervise and to mingle with the male counselors.

When she returned, the dance floor wasn't as crowded, but this time the partners had chosen for themselves.

"Miss Carlbough?"

Eden turned her head as she bent to place a bowl of chips in an empty space on the long crowded table. Roberta's face was spotless. Her thatch of wild hair had been tamed into a bushy ponytail and tied with a ribbon. She had little turquoise stars in her ears to match a ruffled and not-too-badly-wrinkled blouse. The dusting of freckles over her face had been partially hidden by a layer of powder. Eden imagined she had conned it out of one of the older girls, but let it pass.

"Hi, Roberta." Plucking two pretzels from a bowl, she handed one over. "Aren't you going to dance?"

"Sure." She glanced over her shoulder, confident and patient. "I wanted to talk to you first."

"Oh?" It didn't appear that she needed a pep talk. Eden had already seen the skinny, dark-haired boy Roberta had set her sights on. If Eden was any judge, he didn't stand a chance. "What about?"

"I saw that guy in the Rolls."

Eden's automatic warning not to speak with her mouth full was postponed. "You mean Mr. Keeton?"

"Some of the girls think he's cute."

"Hmm." Eden nibbled on her own pretzel.

"A couple of them said you were soft on him. They think you had a lovers' quarrel, you know, like Romeo and Juliet or something. Now he's come to beg you to forgive him, and you're going to realize that you can't live without him and go off and get married."

The pretzel hung between two fingers as Eden listened. After a moment, she managed to clear her throat. "Well, that's quite a scenario."

"I said it was baloney."

Trying not to laugh, she bit into the pretzel. "Did you?"

"You're smart, all the girls say so." Reaching behind Eden, she took a handful of chips. "I said you were too smart to be soft on the guy in the Rolls, because he's not nearly as neat as Mr. Elliot." Roberta glanced over her shoulder as if in confirmation. "He's shorter, too."

"Yes." Eden had to bite her lip. "Yes, he is."

"He doesn't look like he'd jump in the lake to fool around."

The last statement had Eden trying to imagine Eric diving into the cool waters of the lake half-dressed. Or bringing her a clutch of wildflowers. Or finding pictures in the sky. Her lips curved dreamily. "No, Eric would never do that."

"That's why I knew it was all baloney." Roberta devoured the chips. "When Mr. Elliot comes, I'm going to dance with him, but now I'm going to dance with

Bobby." Shooting Eden a smile, she walked across the room and grabbed the hand of the lanky, dark-haired boy. As Eden had thought, he didn't have a chance.

She watched the dancing, but thought of Chase. It came to her all at once that he was the only man she knew whom she hadn't measured against her father. Comparisons had never occurred to her. She hadn't measured Chase against anyone but had fallen in love with him for himself. Now all she needed was the courage to tell him.

"So this is how young people entertain themselves these days."

Eden turned to find Dottie beside her. For Camp Liberty's summer dance, she had chosen mauve lace. The pearls had been exchanged for a single, sensational ruby. BooBoo had a clip of rhinestones—Eden sincerely hoped they were only rhinestones—secured on top of her head. Feeling a wave of affection, Eden kissed her aunt. "Are you settled into your hotel?"

"So to speak." Accepting a potato chip, Dottie took her own survey. The powder-blue voile was the essence of simplicity with its cap sleeves and high neck, but Dottie approved the way it depended on the wearer for its style. "Thank God you haven't lost your taste."

Laughing, Eden kissed her again. "I've missed you. I'm so glad you came."

"Are you?" Always discreet, Dottie led her toward the screen door. "I was afraid you weren't exactly thrilled to see me here." She let the screen whoosh shut as they stepped onto the porch. "Particularly with the surprise I brought you."

"I was glad to see you, Aunt Dottie."

"But not Eric."

Eden leaned back on the rail. "Did you think I would be?"

"Yes." She sighed, and brushed at the bodice of her lace. "I suppose I did. It only took five minutes to realize what a mistake I'd made. Darling, I hope you understand I was trying to help."

"Of course I do, and I love you for it."

"I thought that whatever had gone wrong between you would have had time to heal over." Forgetting herself, Dottie offered BooBoo the rest of the chip. "To be honest, the way he's been talking to me, I was sure by bringing him to you I'd be doing the next-best thing to saving your life."

"I can imagine," Eden murmured.

"So much for grand gestures." Dottie moved her shoulders so that the ruby winked. "Eden, you never told me why you two called off the wedding. It was so sudden."

Eden opened her mouth, then closed it again. There was no reason to hurt and infuriate her aunt after all these months. If she told her now, it would be for spite or, worse, for sympathy. Eric was worth neither. "We just realized we weren't suited."

"I always thought differently." There was a loud blast of music and a chorus of laughter. Dottie cast a glance over her shoulder. "Eric seems to think differently, too. He's been to see me several times in recent weeks."

Pushing the heavy fall of hair from her shoulders, Eden walked to the edge of the porch. Perhaps Eric had

discovered that the Carlbough name wasn't so badly
tarnished after all. It gave her no pleasure to be cynical, but it was the only answer that seemed right. It
wouldn't have taken him long to realize that eventually she would come into money again, through inher-
itances. She swallowed her bitterness as she turned
back to her aunt.

"He's mistaken, Aunt Dottie. Believe me when I say
he doesn't have any genuine feelings for me. Perhaps
he thinks he does," she added, when she saw the frown
centered between Dottie's brows. "I'd say it's a matter
of habit. I didn't love Eric." Her hands outstretched, she
went to take her aunt's. "I never did. It's taken me some
time to understand that I was going to marry him for all
the wrong reasons—because it was expected, because
it was easy. And…" She drew in her breath. "Because
I mistakenly thought he was like Papa."

"Oh, darling."

"It was my mistake, so most of it was my fault." Now
that it was said, and said aloud, she could accept it. "I
always compared the men I dated with Papa. He was
the kindest, most caring man I've ever known, but even
though I loved and admired him, it was wrong of me
to judge other men by him."

"We all loved him, Eden." Dottie drew Eden into
her arms. "He was a good man, a loving man. A gambler, but—"

"I don't mind that he was a gambler." Now, when
she drew back, Eden could smile. "I know if he hadn't
died so suddenly, he'd have come out on top again. But
it doesn't matter, Aunt Dottie, because I'm a gambler,

too." She turned so that her gesture took in the camp. "I've learned how to make my own stake."

"How like him you are." Dottie was forced to draw a tissue out of her bag. "When you insisted on doing this, even when I first came here today, I could only think my poor little Eden's gone mad. Then I looked, really looked, at your camp, at the girls, at you, and I could see you'd made it work." After one inelegant sniff, she stuffed the tissue back in her bag. "I'm proud of you, Eden. Your father would have been proud of you."

Now it was Eden's eyes that dampened. "Aunt Dottie, I can't tell you how much that means to me. After he died and I had to sell everything, I felt I'd betrayed him, you, everyone."

"No." Dottie cupped Eden's chin in her hand. "What you did took tremendous courage, more than I had. You know how badly I wanted to spare you all of that."

"I know, and I appreciate it, but it had to be this way."

"I think I understand that now. I want you to know that I hurt for you, Eden, but I was never ashamed. Even now, knowing you don't need it, I'll tell you that my house is yours whenever you like."

"Knowing that is enough."

"And I expect this to be the finest camp in the east within five years."

Eden laughed again, and all the weight she'd carried with her since her father's death slipped off her shoulders. "It will be."

With a nod, Dottie took a step along the rail and looked out at the compound. "I do believe you should have a pool. Girls should have regulated, regimented swimming lessons. Splashing in the lake doesn't meet those standards. I'm going to donate one."

Eden's back went up immediately. "Aunt Dottie—"

"In your father's name." Dottie paused and cocked a brow. "Yes, I can see you won't argue with that. If I can donate a wing to a hospital, I can certainly donate a swimming pool in my brother's name to my favorite niece's camp. In fact, my accountant's going to be thrilled. Now, would you like Eric and me to go?"

Barely recovered from being so neatly maneuvered, Eden only sighed. "Having Eric here means nothing now. I want you to stay as long as you like."

"Good. BooBoo and I are enjoying ourselves." Dottie bent down to nuzzle in the dog's fur. "The delightful thing about BooBoo is that she's so much more tractable than any of my children were. Eden, one more thing before I go inside and absorb culture. I would swear that I felt, well, how to put it? One might almost say earth tremors when I walked into the stables this afternoon. Are you in love with someone else?"

"Aunt Dottie—"

"Answer enough. I'll just add my complete approval, not that it matters. BooBoo was quite charmed."

"Are you trying to be eccentric?"

With a smile, Dottie shifted the bundle in her arms. "When you can't rely on beauty any longer, you have to fall back on something. Ah, look here." She stepped aside as the Lamborghini cruised up. Lips pursed, Dottie watched Chase climb out. "Hello again," she called. "I admire your taste." She gave Eden a quick pat. "Yes,

I do. I think I'll just pop inside and try some punch. It isn't too dreadful, is it?"

"I made it myself."

"Oh." Dottie rolled her eyes. "Well, I've some gambler in me as well."

Bracing herself, Eden turned toward Chase. "Hello. I'm glad you could—"

His mouth covered hers so quickly, so completely, that there wasn't even time for surprise. She might think of the hard possessiveness of the kiss later, but for now she just slid her hands up his back so that she could grip his shoulders. Instantly intense, instantly real, instantly right.

She hadn't felt this with Eric. That was what Chase told himself as she melted against him. She'd never felt this with anyone else. And he was going to be damn sure she didn't. Torn between anger and need, he drew her away.

"What—" She had to stop and try again. "What was that for?"

He gathered her hair in his hand to bring her close again. His lips tarried a breath from hers. "As someone once said to me, I wanted to kiss you. Any objections?"

He was daring her. Her chin angled in acceptance. "I can't think of any."

"Mull it over. Get back to me." With that, he propelled her toward the lights and music.

She didn't like to admit that cowardice might be part of the reason she carefully divided her time between the girls and the visiting counselors. Eden told herself it was a matter of courtesy and responsibility. But she knew she needed to have her thoughts well in hand before she spoke privately with Chase again.

She watched him dance with Roberta and wanted to throw herself into his arms and tell him how much she loved him. How big a fool would that make her? He hadn't asked about Eric, so how could she explain? It hummed through her mind that if he hadn't asked, it didn't matter to him. If it didn't matter, he wasn't nearly as involved as she was. Still, she told herself that before the evening was over she would find the time to talk it through with him, whether he wanted to hear it or not. She just wanted to wait until she was sure she could do a good job of it.

There was no such confusion about the evening in general. The summer dance was a hit. Plans between the camp coordinators were already under way to make it an annual event. Already Candy was bubbling with ideas for more joint ventures.

As always, Eden would let Candy plan and organize; then she would tidy up the details.

By keeping constantly on the move, Eden avoided any direct confrontation with Eric or Chase. Of course they spoke, even danced, but all in the sanctuary of the crowded mess hall. Eric's conversation had been as mild as hers, but there had been something dangerous in Chase's eyes. It was that, and the memory of that rocketing kiss, that had her postponing the inevitable.

"I guess you like her a lot," Roberta ventured as she saw Chase's gaze wander toward Eden yet again.

"What?" Distracted, Chase looked back at his dance partner.

"Miss Carlbough. You're soft on her. She's so pretty," Roberta added with only the slightest touch of envy. "We voted her the prettiest counselor, even though Miss Allison has more—" She caught herself, realizing suddenly that you didn't discuss certain parts of a woman's anatomy with a man, even with Mr. Elliot. "More, ah…"

"I get the picture." Charmed, as always, Chase swung her in a quick circle.

"Some of the other girls think Mr. Keeton's a honey."

"Oh?" Chase's smile turned into a sneer as he glanced at the man in question.

"I think his nose is skinny."

"It was almost broken," Chase muttered.

"And his eyes are too close together," Roberta added for good measure. "I like you a lot better."

Touched, and remembering his first crush, Chase tugged on her ponytail to tilt her face to his. "I'm pretty soft on you, too."

From her corner, Eden watched the exchange. She saw Chase bend down and saw Roberta's face explode into smiles. A sigh nearly escaped her before she realized she was allowing herself to be envious of a twelve-year-old. With a shake of her head, she told herself that it was the strain of keeping herself unavailable that was beginning to wear on her. The music never played below loud. Uncountable trips to the kitchen kept the refreshment table full. Boys and girls shouted over the music to make themselves heard.

Five minutes, she told herself. She would steal just five quiet, wonderful minutes by herself.

This time, when she slipped back into the kitchen, she kept going. The moist summer air soothed her the moment she stepped outside. It smelled of grass and honeysuckle. Grateful for the fresh air after the cloying scent of fruit punch, Eden breathed deeply.

Tonight, the moon was only a sliver in the sky. She realized she had seen it change, had watched its waning and waxing more in the past three months than she had in all of her life. This was true of more than the moon. She would never look at anything else exactly the same way again.

She stood for a moment, finding the pictures in the sky that Chase had shown her. With the air warm on her face, she wondered if there would ever be a time when he would show her more.

As she crossed the grass, the light was silvery. From behind her came the steady murmur of music and voices. She found an old hickory tree and leaned against it, enjoying the solitude and the distance.

This was what warm summer nights were for, she thought. For dreams and wishes. No matter how cold it got during the winter, no matter how far away summer seemed, she would be able to take this night out of her memory and live it again.

The creak and swish of the back door cut through her concentration.

"Eric." She straightened, not bothering to disguise the irritation in her voice.

He came to her until he, too, stood under the hickory. Starlight filtered through the leaves to mix with the shadows. "I've never known you to leave a party."

"I've changed."

"Yes." Her eyes were calm and direct. He shifted uncomfortably. "I've noticed." When he reached out to touch her, she didn't step back. She didn't even feel his touch. "We never finished talking."

"Yes, we did. A long time ago."

"Eden." Moving cautiously, he lifted a finger to trace her jawline. "I've come a long way to see you, to make things right between us."

Eden merely tilted her head to the side. "I'm sorry you were inconvenienced, but there's nothing to make right." Oddly, the anger, even the bitterness, had become diluted. It had started weakening, she knew, when he had kissed her that afternoon. Looking at him now, she felt detached, as if he were someone she'd known only vaguely. "Eric, it's foolish for either of us to drag this out. Let's just leave things alone."

"I admit I was a fool." He blocked her exit, as if by simply continuing in the same vein he could put things back in the order he wanted. "Eden, I hurt you, and I'm sorry, but I was thinking of you as well as myself."

She wanted to laugh, but found she didn't even have the energy to give him that much. "Of me, Eric? All right, have it your way. Thank you and goodbye."

"Don't be difficult," he said, displaying a first trace of impatience. "You know how difficult it would have been for you to go through with the wedding while the scandal was still fresh in everyone's mind."

That stopped her, more than his hand had. She leaned

back against the tree and waited. Yes, there was still a trace of anger, she discovered. It was mild, and buried quite deep, but it was still there. Perhaps it would be best to purge everything from her system. "Scandal. By that I assume you mean my father's poor investments."

"Eden." He moved closer again to put a comforting hand on her arm. "Your position changed so dramatically, so abruptly, when your father died and left you..."

"To earn my own way," she finished for him. "Yes, we can agree on that. My position changed. Over the past few months I've become grateful for that." There was annoyance now, but only as if he were a pesky fly she had to swat away. "I've learned to expect things from myself and to realize money had very little to do with the way I was living."

She saw by his frown that he didn't understand, would never understand the person who had grown up from the ashes of that old life. "You might find this amazing, Eric, but I don't care what anyone thinks about my altered circumstances. For the first time in my life, I have what I want, and I earned it myself."

"You can't expect me to believe that this little camp is what you want. I know you, Eden." He twined a lock of hair around his finger. "The woman I know would never choose something like this over the life we could have together in Philadelphia."

"You might be right again." Slowly, she reached up to untangle his hand from her hair. "But I'm no longer the woman you knew."

"Don't be ridiculous." For the first time he felt a twinge of panic. The one thing he had never considered was driving hundreds of miles to be humiliated. "Come back to the hotel with me tonight. Tomorrow we can go back to Philadelphia and be married, just as we always planned."

She studied him for a moment, trying to see if there was some lingering affection for her there, some true emotion. No, she decided almost at once. She wished it had been true, for then she could have had some kind of respect for him.

"Why are you doing this? You don't love me. You never did, or you couldn't have turned your back on me when I needed you."

"Eden—"

"No, let me finish. Let's finish this once and for all." She pushed him back a foot with an impatient movement of her hands. "I'm not interested in your apologies or your excuses, Eric. The simple truth is you don't matter to me."

It was said so calmly, so bluntly, that he very nearly believed it. "You know you don't mean that, Eden. We were going to be married."

"Because it was convenient for both of us. For that much, Eric, I'll share the blame with you."

"Let's forget blame, Eden. Let me show you what we can have."

She held him off with a look. "I'm not angry anymore, and I'm not hurt. The simple fact is, Eric, I don't love you, and I don't want you."

For a moment, he was completely silent. When he did speak, Eden was surprised to hear genuine emotion in his voice. "Find someone to replace me so soon, Eden?"

Temptation

She could almost laugh. He had jilted her almost two steps from the altar, but now he could act out the role of betrayed lover. "This grows more and more absurd, but no, Eric, it wasn't a matter of replacing you, it was a matter of seeing you for what you are. Don't make me explain to you what that is."

"Just how much does Chase Elliot have to do with all of this?"

"How dare you question me?" She started past him, but this time he grabbed her arm, and his grip wasn't gentle. Surprised by his refusal to release her, she stepped back and looked at him again. He was a child, she thought, who had thrown away a toy and was ready to stamp his feet now that he wanted it back and couldn't have it. Because her temper was rising, she fell back on her attitude of icy detachment. "Whatever is or isn't between Chase and me is none of your concern."

This cool, haughty woman was one he recognized. His tone softened. "Everything about you concerns me."

Weary, she could only sigh. "Eric, you're embarrassing yourself."

Before she could rid herself of him again, the screen door opened for a second time.

"Apparently I'm interrupting again." Hands in pockets, Chase stepped down from the porch.

"You seem to be making a habit of it." Eric released Eden, only to step between her and Chase. "You should be able to see that Eden and I are having a private conversation. They do teach manners, even here in the hills, don't they?"

Chase wondered if Eric would appreciate his style of manners. No, he doubted the tidy Philadelphian would appreciate a bloody nose. But then, he didn't give a damn what Eric appreciated. He'd taken two steps forward before Eden realized his intent.

"The conversation's over," she said quickly, stepping between them. She might as well have been invisible. As she had felt herself being shifted to the middle that afternoon, now she felt herself being nudged aside.

"Seems you've had considerable time to say what's on your mind." Chase rocked back on his heels, keeping his eyes on Eric.

"I don't see what business it is of yours how long I speak with my fiancée."

"Fiancée!" Eden's outraged exclamation was also ignored.

"You've let some months slip past you, Keeton." Chase's voice remained mild. His hands remained in his pockets. "Some changes have been made."

"Changes?" This time Eden turned to Chase, with no better results. "What are you talking about?"

Calmly, without giving her a glance, he took her hand. "You promised me a dance."

Instantly, Eric had her other arm. "We haven't finished."

Chase turned back, and for the first time the danger in his eyes was as clear as glass. "Yes, you have. The lady's with me."

Infuriated, Eden yanked herself free of both of them. "Stop it!" She'd had enough of being pulled in two directions without being asked if she wanted to move in either. For the first time in her life, she forgot manners, courtesy and control and did what Chase had once advised. When you're mad, he'd said, yell.

"You are both so *stupid*!" A toss of her head had the hair flying into her eyes to be dragged back impatiently. "How dare you stand here like two half-witted dogs snarling over the same bone? Don't either of you think I'm capable of speaking my own mind, making my own decisions? Well, I've got news for both of you. I can speak my own mind just fine. You." She turned to face Eric. "I meant every word I said to you. Understand? *Every single word.* I tried to phrase things as politely as possible, but if you push, let me warn you, you won't receive the same courtesy again."

"Eden, darling—"

"No, no, no!" She slapped away the hand he held out to her. "You dumped me the moment things got rough. If you think I'll take you back now, after you've shown yourself to be a weak, callous, insensitive—" oh, what was Candy's word? "—weasel," she remembered with relish, "you're crazy. And if you dare, if you *dare* touch me again, I'll knock your caps loose."

God, what a woman, Chase thought. He wondered how soon he could take her into his arms and show her how much he loved her. He'd always thought her beautiful, almost ethereal; now she was a Viking. More than he'd wanted anything in his life, he wanted to hold that passion in his arms and devour it. He was smiling at her when she whirled on him.

"And you." Taking a step closer to Chase, she began to stab him in the chest with her finger. "You go find someone else to start a common brawl over. I'm not flattered by your Neanderthal attempts at playing at the white knight."

It wasn't quite what he'd had in mind. "For God's sake, Eden, I was—"

"Shut up." She gave him another quick jab. "I can take care of myself, Mr. Macho. And if you think I appreciate your interference in my affairs, you're mistaken. If I wanted some—some muscle-flexing he-man to clean up after me, I'd rent one."

Sucking in a deep breath, she turned to face both of them. "The two of you have behaved with less common sense than those children in there. Just for future reference, I don't find it amusing that two grown men should feel it necessary for their egos to use me as a Ping-Pong ball. I make my own choices, and I've got one for you, so listen carefully. I don't want either one of you."

Turning on her heel, she left them standing under the hickory, staring after her.

Chapter 10

The last day of the session was pandemonium. There was packing and tears and missing shoes. Each cabin gave birth to its own personal crisis. Gear had to be stored until the following summer, and an inventory had to be made of kitchen supplies.

Beds were stripped. Linen was laundered and folded. Eden caught herself sniffling over a pillowcase. Somehow, during the first inventory, they came up short by two blankets and counted five towels more than they'd started with.

Eden decided to leave her personal packing until after the confusion had died down. It even crossed her mind to spend one last night in camp and leave fresh the following morning. She told herself it was more practical, even more responsible, for one of them to stay behind so that a last check could be made of the empty cabins. In truth, she just couldn't let go.

She wasn't ready to admit that. Leaving the laundry area for the stables, she began counting bridles. The only reason she was considering staying behind, she lectured herself, was to make certain all the loose ends were tied up. As she marked numbers on her clipboard, she struggled to block out thoughts of Chase. He certainly had nothing to do with her decision to remain behind. She counted snaffle bits twice, got two different totals, then counted again.

Impossible man. She slashed the pencil over the paper, marking and totaling until she was satisfied. Without pausing, she started a critical study of reins, checking for wear. A good rubbing with saddle soap was in order, she decided. That was one more reason to stay over one more night. But, as it often had during the past week, her confrontation with Chase and Eric ran through her mind.

She had meant everything she'd said. Just reaffirming that satisfied her. Every single word, even though she had shouted it, had come straight from the heart. Even after seven days her indignation, and her resolve, were as fresh as ever.

She had simply been a prize to be fought over, she remembered, as indignation began to simmer toward rage. Is that all a woman was to a man, something to yank against his side and stretch his ego on? Well, that wasn't something she would accept. She had only truly forged her own identity in recent months. That wasn't something she was going to give up, or even dilute, for anyone, for any man.

Fury bubbling, Eden crossed over to inspect the saddles. Eric had never loved her. Now, more than ever, that was crystal clear. Even without love, without caring, he'd wanted to lay some sort of claim. My woman. My property. My *fiancée*! She made a sound, somewhere between disgust and derision, that had one of the horses blowing in response.

If her aunt hadn't taken him away, Eden wasn't sure what she might have done. And, at this point, she was equally unsure she wouldn't have enjoyed it immensely.

But worse, a hundred times worse, was Chase. As she stared into space, her pencil drummed a rapid rat-a-tat-tat on the clipboard. He'd never once spoken of love or affection. There had been no promises asked or given, and yet he'd behaved just as abominably as Eric.

That was where the comparison ended, she admitted, as she pressed the heel of her hand to her brows. She was in love with Chase. Desperately in love. If he'd said a word, if he'd given her a chance to speak, how different things might have been. But now she was discovering that leaving him was infinitely more difficult than it had been to leave Philadelphia.

He hadn't spoken; he hadn't asked. The compromises she might have made for him, and only him, would never be needed now. Whatever might have been was over, she told herself, straightening her shoulders. It was time for new adjustments, new plans and, again, a new life. She had done it once, and she could do it again.

"Plans," she muttered to herself as she studied the clipboard again. There were so many plans to make for the following season. It would be summer again before she knew it.

Her fingers clutched the pencil convulsively. Was that how she would live her life, from summer to summer? Would there only be emptiness in between, emptiness and waiting? How many times would she come back and walk along the lake hoping to see him?

No. This was the mourning period. Eden closed her eyes for a moment and waited for the strength to return. You couldn't adjust and go on unless you'd grieved first. That was something else she had learned. So she would grieve for Chase. Then she would build her life.

"Eden. Eden, are you in there?"

"Right here." Eden turned as Candy rushed into the tack room.

"Oh, thank God."

"What now?"

Candy pressed a hand to her heart as if to push her breath back. "Roberta."

"Roberta?" Her stomach muscles balled like a fist. "Is she hurt?"

"She's gone."

"What do you mean, gone? Did her parents come early?"

"I mean gone." Pacing, Candy began to tug on her hair. "Her bags are all packed and stacked in her cabin. She's nowhere in camp."

"Not again." More annoyed than worried now, Eden tossed the clipboard aside. "Hasn't that child learned anything this summer? Every time I turn around she's off on a little field trip of her own."

"Marcie and Linda claim that she said she had something important to take care of before she left." Candy lifted her hands, then let them fall. "She didn't tell them what she was up to, that I'm sure of. You and I both know that she might only have gone to pick some flowers for her mother, but—"

"We can't take any chances," Eden finished.

"I've got three of the counselors out looking, but I thought you might have some idea where she could have gone before we call out the marines." She paused to catch her breath. "What a way to round out the summer."

Eden closed her eyes a minute to concentrate. Conversations with Roberta scattered through her memory until she focused on one in particular. "Oh, no." Her eyes shot open. "I think I know where she's gone." She was already rushing out of the tack room as Candy loped to keep up.

"Where?"

"I'll need to take the car. It'll be quicker." Thinking fast, Eden dashed to the rear of their cabin, where the secondhand compact was parked under a gnarled pear tree. "I'd swear she's gone to say goodbye to Chase, but make sure the orchard gets checked."

"Already done, but—"

"I'll be back in twenty minutes."

"Eden—"

The gunning of the motor drowned out Candy's words. "Don't worry, I'll bring the little darling back." She set her teeth. "If I have to drag her by her hair."

"Okay, but—" Candy stepped back as the compact shot forward. "Gas," she said with a sigh as Eden drove away. "I don't think there's much gas in the tank."

Eden noticed that the sky was darkening and decided to blame Roberta for that as well. She would have sworn an oath that Roberta had gone to see Chase one last time. A three-mile hike would never have deterred a girl of Roberta's determination.

Eden drove under the arching sign, thinking grimly of what she would say to Roberta once she had her. The pleasure she got from that slid away as the car bucked and sputtered. Eden looked down helplessly as it jolted again, then stopped dead. The needle of the gas gauge registered a flat *E*.

"Damn!" She slapped a hand on the steering wheel, then let out a yelp. Padded steering wheels weren't part of the amenities on cars as old as this one. Nursing her aching wrist, she stepped out of the car just as the first blast of thunder shook the air. As if on cue, a torrent of rain poured down.

For a moment, Eden merely stood beside the stalled car, her throbbing hand at her mouth, while water streamed over her. Her clothes were soaked through in seconds. "Perfect," she mumbled; then, on the heels of that: "Roberta." Casting one furious look skyward, she set off at a jogging run.

Lightning cracked across the sky like a whip. Thunder bellowed in response. Each time, Eden's heart leaped toward her throat. As each step brought her closer to Chase's home, her fear mounted.

What if she'd been wrong? What if Roberta wasn't there, but was caught somewhere in the storm, wet and frightened? What if shc was lost or hurt? Her breath began to hitch as anxiety ballooned inside her.

She reached Chase's door, soaked to the skin and terrified.

Her pounding at the door sounded weak against the cannoning thunder. Looking back over her shoulder, Eden could see nothing but a solid wall of rain. If Roberta was out there, somewhere... Whirling back, she pounded with both fists, shouting for good measure.

When Chase opened the door, she nearly tumbled over his feet. He took one look at her soaked, bedraggled figure and knew he'd never seen anything more beautiful in his life. "Well, this is a surprise. Get you a towel?"

Eden grabbed his shirt with both hands. "Roberta," she managed, trying to convey everything with one word.

"She's in the front room." Gently, he pushed the hair out of her eyes. "Relax, Eden, she's fine."

"Oh, thank God." Near tears, Eden pressed her fingers to her eyes. But when she lowered them, her eyes were dry and furious. "I'll murder her. Right here, right now. Quickly."

Before she could carry through with her threat, Chase stepped in front of her. Now that he'd had a good taste of her temper, he no longer underestimated it. "I think I have an idea how you feel, but don't be too rough on her. She came by to propose."

"Just move aside, or I'll take you down with her." She shoved him aside and strode past him. The moment she stood in the doorway, Eden drew a breath. "Roberta." Each syllable was bitten off. The girl on the floor stopped playing with the dog and looked up.

"Oh, hi, Miss Carlbough." She grinned, apparently pleased with the company. After a moment her teeth dropped down to her lower lip. Though perhaps an optimist, Roberta was no fool. "You're all wet, Miss Carlbough."

The low sound deep in Eden's throat had Squat's ears pricking. "Roberta," she said again as she started forward. Squat moved simultaneously. Drawing up short, Eden gave the dog a wary glance. He sat now, his tail thumping, directly between Eden and Roberta. "Call off your dog," she ordered without bothering to look at Chase.

"Oh, Squat wouldn't hurt you." Roberta scurried across the floor to leap lovingly on his neck. Squat's tail thumped even harder. Eden thought for a moment that he was smiling. She was certain she'd gotten a good view of his large white teeth. "He's real friendly," Roberta assured her. "Just hold your hand out and he'll sniff it."

And take it off at the wrist—which was giving her enough trouble as it was. "Roberta," Eden began again, staying where she was. "After all these weeks, aren't you aware of the rules about leaving camp?"

"Yes, ma'am." Roberta hooked an arm around Squat's neck. "But it was important."

"That isn't the point." Eden folded her hands. She was aware of how she looked, how she sounded, and she knew that if she turned her head she would see Chase grinning at her. "Rules have a purpose, Roberta. They aren't made up just to spoil your fun, but to see to order and safety. You've broken one of the most important ones today, and not for the first time. Miss Bartholomew and I are responsible for you. Your parents expect, and rightfully so, that we'll..."

Eden trailed off as Roberta listened, solemn-eyed. She opened her mouth again, prepared to complete the lecture, but only a shuddering breath came out. "Roberta, you scared me to death."

"Gee, I'm sorry, Miss Carlbough." To Eden's surprise, Roberta jumped up and dashed across the room to throw her arms around Eden's waist. "I didn't mean to, really. I guess I didn't think anyone would miss me before I got back."

"Not miss you?" A laugh, a little shaky, whispered out as Eden pressed a kiss to the top of Roberta's head. "You monster, don't you know I've developed radar where you're concerned?"

"Yeah?" Roberta squeezed hard.

"Yeah."

"I am sorry, Miss Carlbough, really I am." She drew back so that her freckled, triangular face was tilted to Eden's. "I just had to see Chase for a minute." She sent Eden an intimate, feminine glance that had Eden looking quickly over at Chase.

"Chase?" Eden repeated, knowing her emphasis on Roberta's use of the first name would get her nowhere.

"We had a personal matter to discuss." Chase dropped down onto the arm of a chair. He wondered if Eden had any idea how protectively she was holding Roberta.

Though it was difficult, Eden managed to display some dignity in her dripping clothes. "I realize it's too much to expect a twelve-year-old to show a consistent sense of responsibility, but I would have expected more from you."

"I called the camp," he said, taking the wind out of her sails. "Apparently I just missed catching you. They know Roberta's safe." Rising, he walked over and grabbed the tail of her T-shirt. A flick of the wrist had water dripping out. "Did you walk over?"

"No." Annoyed that he had done exactly what he should have done, Eden smacked his hand away. "The car..." She hesitated, then decided to lie. "Broke down." She turned to frown at Roberta again. "Right before the storm."

"I'm sorry you got wet," Roberta said again.

"And so you should be."

"Didn't you put gas in the car? It was out, you know."

Before Eden could decide to murder her after all, they were interrupted by the blast of a horn.

"That'll be Delaney." Chase walked to the window to confirm it. "He's going to run Roberta back to camp."

"That's very kind of him." Eden held her hand out for Roberta's. "I appreciate all the trouble."

"Just Roberta." Chase caught Eden's hand before she could get away from him again. Ready and willing, or kicking and screaming, he was holding on to what he needed. "You'd better get out of those wet clothes before you come down with something."

"As soon as I get back to camp."

"My mother says you catch a chill if your feet stay wet." Roberta gave Squat a parting hug. "See you next year," she said to Chase, and for the first time Eden saw a hint of shyness. "You really will write?"

"Yeah." Chase bent down, tilted her head and kissed both cheeks. "I really will write."

Her freckles all but vanished under her blush. Turning, she threw herself into Eden's arms again. "I'll miss you, Miss Carlbough."

"Oh, Roberta, I'll miss you, too."

"I'm coming back next year and bringing my cousin. Everyone says we're so much alike we should be sisters."

"Oh," Eden managed weakly. "Wonderful." She hoped one winter was enough time to recharge.

"This was the best summer ever." Roberta gave one last squeeze as tears began to cloud Eden's eyes. "Bye!"

The front door was slamming behind her before Eden had taken the first step. "Roberta——"

"It was my best summer ever, too." Chase took her free hand before she could try for the door.

"Chase, let me go. I have to get back."

"Dry clothes. Though, as I may have mentioned before, you look wonderful wet and dripping."

"I'm not staying," she said, even as he tugged her toward the stairs.

"Since I just heard Delaney pull off, and your car's out of gas, I'd say you are." Because she was shivering now, he hurried her up. "And you're leaving puddles on the floor."

"Sorry." He propelled her through his bedroom. Eden had a fleeting impression of quiet colors and a brass bed before she was nudged into the adjoining bath.

"Chase, this is very nice of you, but if you could just drive me back—"

"After you've had a hot shower and changed."

A hot shower. He could have offered her sable and emeralds and not tempted her half so much. Eden hadn't had a hot shower since the first week of June. "No, I really think I should get back."

But the door was already closing behind him.

Eden stared at it; then, her lower lip caught between her teeth, she looked back at the tub. Nothing she'd ever seen in her life had seemed so beautiful, so desirable. It took her less than ten seconds to give in.

"Since I'm here anyway..." she mumbled, and began to peel out of her clothes.

The first sizzle of hot spray stole her breath. Then, with a sigh of pure greed, she luxuriated in it. It was sinful, she thought as the water sluiced over her head. It was heaven.

Fifteen minutes later, she turned the taps off, but not without regret. On the rack beside the tub was a thick, thirsty bath towel. She wrapped herself in it and decided it was nearly as good as the shower. Then she noticed her clothes were gone.

For a moment, she only frowned at the empty rail where she'd hung them. Then she gripped the towel tighter. He must have come in and taken them while she was in the shower. Lips pursed, Eden studied the frosted glass doors and wondered how opaque they really were.

Be practical, she told herself. Chase had come in and taken her clothes because they needed to be dried. He was simply being a considerate host. Still, her nerves drummed a bit as she lifted the navy-blue robe from the hook on the back of the door.

It was his, of course. His scent clung to the material so that she felt he was all but in the room with her as she drew it on. It was warm and thick, but she shivered once as she secured the belt.

It was practical, she reminded herself. The robe was nothing more than an adequate covering until her clothes were dry again. But she tilted her head so that her chin rubbed along the collar.

Fighting off the mood, she took the towel and rubbed the mist away from the mirror. What she saw was enough to erase any romantic fantasies from her mind. True, the hot water from the shower had brought some color to her cheeks, but she hadn't even a trace of mascara left to darken her lashes. With the color of the robe to enhance them, her eyes dominated her face. She looked as though she'd been saved just before going under for the third time. Her hair was wet, curling in little tendrils around her face. Eden dragged a hand through it a few times, but couldn't bring it to order without a brush.

Charming, she thought before she pulled the door open. In Chase's bedroom she paused, wanting to look, wanting even more to touch something that belonged to him. With a shake of her head, she hurried through the bedroom and down the stairs. It was only when she stopped in the doorway of the front room and saw him that her nerves returned in full force.

He looked so right, so at ease in his workshirt and

jeans as he stood in front of a nineteenth-century cabinet pouring brandy from a crystal decanter. She'd come to realize that it was his contradictions, as much as anything else, that appealed to her. At the moment, reasons didn't matter. She loved him. Now she had to get through this last encounter before burying herself in the winter months.

He turned and saw her. He'd known she was there, had felt her there, but had needed a moment. When he'd come into the bath to take her wet clothes, she'd been humming. He'd only seen a shadow of her behind the glass but had wanted, more than he could remember wanting anything, to push the barrier aside and take her. To hold her with her skin wet and warm, her eyes huge and aware.

He wanted her as much, as sharply, now as she stood in the doorway dwarfed by his robe.

So he'd taken a moment, for the simple reason that he had to be sure he could speak.

"Better?"

"Yes, thanks." Her hand reached automatically for the lapels of the robe and fidgeted there. He crossed the room to offer her a snifter.

"Drink. This should ward off the danger of wet feet."

As she took the glass, Chase closed the doors at her back. Eden found herself gripping the snifter with both hands. She lifted it slowly, hoping the brandy would clear her head.

"I'm sorry about all this." She made certain her tone was as polite and as distant as she could manage. She kept her back to the doors.

"No trouble." He wanted to shake her. "Why don't you sit down?"

"No, I'm fine." But when he continued to stand in front of her, she felt it necessary to move. She walked to the window, where the rain was still pouring from the sky. "I don't suppose this can keep up for long."

"No, it can't." The amusement he was beginning to feel came out in his voice. Wary, Eden turned back to him. "In fact, I'm amazed it's gone on this long." Setting his brandy aside, he went to her. "It's time we stopped it, Eden. Time you stopped backing away."

She gave a quick shake of her head and skirted around him. "I don't know what you mean."

"The hell you don't." He was behind her quickly, and there was nowhere to run. He took the snifter from her nerveless fingers before turning her to face him again. Slowly, deliberately, he gathered her hair in his hands, drawing it back until her face was unframed. There was a flash of fear in her eyes, but beneath it, waiting, was the need he'd wanted to see.

"We stood here once before, and I told you then it was too late."

The sun had been streaming through the glass then. Now the rain was lashing against it. As she stood there, Eden felt past and present overlap. "We stood here once before, and you kissed me."

His mouth found hers. Like the storm, the kiss was fierce and urgent. He'd expected hesitation and found demand. He'd expected fear and found passion. Drawing her closer, he found hunger and need and shimmering desire. What he had yet to find, what he discovered he needed most, was acceptance.

Trust me. He wanted to shout it at her, but her hands were in his hair, entangling him and pulling him to her.

The rain beat against the windowpanes. Thunder walked across the sky. Eden was whirling in her own private storm. She wanted him, wanted to feel him peeling the robe from her shoulders and touching her. She wanted that first delirious sensation of skin meeting skin. She wanted to give her love to him where it could be alive and free, but knew she had to keep it locked inside, secret, lonely.

"Chase. We can't go on like this." She turned her head away. "I can't go on like this. I have to leave. People are waiting for me."

"You're not going anywhere. Not this time." He slid a hand up her throat. His patience was at an end.

She sensed it and backed away. "Candy will be wondering where I am. I'd like to have my clothes now."

"No."

"No?"

"No," he said again as he lifted his brandy. "Candy won't be wondering where you are, because I phoned her and told her you weren't coming back. She said you weren't to worry, that things were under control. And no—" he sipped his brandy "—you can't have your clothes. Can I get you something else?"

"You phoned her?" All the fear, all the anxiety, drained away to make room for temper. Her eyes darkened, losing their fragility. Chase almost smiled. He loved the cool woman, the nervous one, the determined one, but he adored the Viking.

"Yeah. Got a problem with that?"

"Where did you possibly get the idea that you had a right to make my decisions for me?" She pushed a hand, covered by the cuff of his robe, against his chest. "You had no business calling Candy, or anyone else. More, you had no business assuming that I'd stay here with you."

"I'm not assuming anything. You are staying here. With me."

"Guess again." This time, when she shoved, there was enough power behind it to take him back a step. He knew that if he hadn't already been mad about her, he would have fallen in love at that moment. "God, but I'm sick to death of dealing with overbearing, dictatorial men who think all they have to do is want something to have it."

"You're not dealing with Eric now, Eden." His voice was soft, perhaps a shade too soft. "You're not dealing with other men, but with me. Only me."

"Wrong again, because I'm through dealing with you. Give me my clothes."

He set the snifter down very carefully. "No."

Her mouth would have fallen open if her jaw hadn't been clenched so tightly. "All right, I'll walk back in this." Ready to carry out her threat, she marched to the door and yanked it open. Squat lay across the threshold. As they spotted each other, he rose on his haunches with what Eden was certain was a leer. She took one more step, then, cursing herself for a coward, turned back.

"Are you going to call off that beast?"

Chase looked down at Squat, knowing the dog would do nothing more dangerous than slobber on her bare feet. Hooking his thumb in his pocket, he smiled. "He's had his shots."

"Terrific." With her mind set on one purpose, she strode to the window. "I'll go out this way then." Kneeling on the window seat, she began to struggle with the sash. When Chase caught her around the waist, she turned on him.

"Take your hands off me. I said I was leaving, and I meant it." She took a swing, surprising them both when it landed hard in his gut. "Here, you want your robe back. I don't need it. I'll walk the three miles naked." To prove her point, she began fighting the knot at the belt.

"I wouldn't do that." As much for his sake as hers, he caught her hands. "If you do, we won't spend much time talking this through."

"I'm not spending any time at all." She squirmed until they both went down on the cushions of the window seat. "I don't have anything else to say to you." She managed to kick until the robe was hitched up to her thighs. "Except that you have the manners of a pig, and I can't wait until I'm hundreds of miles away from you. I decided the other night, when I was given the choice between a boring fool and a hardheaded clod, that I'd rather join a convent. Now take your hands off me, or I swear, I'll hurt you. No one, but no one, pushes me around."

With that, she put all her energy into one last shove. It sent them both tumbling off the cushions and onto the floor. As he had done once before, Chase rolled with her until he had her pinned beneath him. He stared at her now as he had then, while she fought to get her breath back.

"Oh God, Eden, I love you." Laughing at them both, he crushed his lips to hers.

She didn't fight the kiss. She didn't even move, though her fingers stiffened under his. Each breath took such an effort that she thought her heart had slowed down to nothing. When she could speak again, she did so carefully.

"I'd appreciate it if you'd say that again."

"I love you." He watched her eyes close and felt that quick twinge of panic. "Listen to me, Eden. I know you've been hurt, but you have to trust me. I've watched you take charge of your life this summer. It hasn't been the easiest thing I've ever done to stand back and give you the space you needed to do that."

She opened her eyes again. Her heart wasn't beating at a slow rhythm now, but seemed capable of bursting out of her chest. "Was that what you were doing?"

"I understood that you needed to prove something to yourself. And I think I knew that until you had, you wouldn't be ready to share whatever that was with me."

"Chase—"

"Don't say anything yet." He brought her hand to his lips. "Eden, I know you're used to certain things, a certain way of life. If that's what you need, I'll find a way to give it to you. But if you give me a chance, I can make you happy here."

She swallowed, afraid of misunderstanding. "Chase, are you saying you'd move back to Philadelphia if I asked you to?"

"I'm saying I'd move anywhere if it was important to you, but I'm not letting you go back alone, Eden. Summers aren't enough."

Her breath came out quietly. "What do you want from me?"

"Everything." He pressed his lips to her hand again, but his eyes were no longer calm. "A lifetime, starting now. Love, arguments, children. Marry me, Eden. Give me six months to make you happy here. If I can't, we'll go anywhere you like. Just don't back away."

"I'm not backing away." Her fingers entwined with his. "And I don't want to be anyplace but here."

She saw the change in his eyes even as his fingers tightened on hers. "If I touch you now, there's no going back."

"You've already told me it was too late." She drew him down to her. Passion and promises merged as they strained closer. She felt again that she had the world in the palm of her hand and held it tightly. "Don't ever let me go. Oh, Chase, I could feel my heart breaking when I thought of leaving here today, leaving you when I loved you so much."

"You wouldn't have gotten far."

Her lips curved at that. Perhaps, in some areas, she could accept a trace of arrogance. "You'd have come after me?"

"I'd have come after you so fast I'd have been there before you."

She felt pleasure grow, and glow. "And begged?"

His brow lifted at the glint in her eyes. "Let's just say I'd have left little doubt as to how much I wanted you."

"And crawled," she said, twining her arms around his neck. "I'm almost sorry I missed that. Maybe you could do it now."

He took a quick nip at her ear. "Don't press your luck."

Laughing, she held on. "One day this will be gray," she murmured as she trailed her fingers through his hair. "And I still won't be able to keep my hands out of it." She drew his head back to look at him, and this time there was no laughter, only love. "I've waited for you all my life."

He buried his face in her throat, fighting back the need to make her his, then and there. With Eden it would be perfect, it would be everything dreams were made of. He drew away to trace the line of her cheekbone. "You know, I wanted to murder Eric when I saw him with his hands on you."

"I didn't know how to explain when I saw you there. Then, later..." Her brow arched. "Well, you behaved very badly."

"You were magnificent. You scared Eric to death."

"And you?"

"You only made me want you more." He tasted her again, feeling the wild, sweet thrill only she had ever brought to him. "I had plans to kidnap you from camp. Bless Roberta for making it easy."

"I hope she's not upset you're going to marry me instead. You have a neat dog, and you're kind of cute." She pressed her lips to the sensitive area just below his ear.

"She understood perfectly. In fact, she approves."

Eden stopped her lazy exploration of his throat. "Approves? You mean you told her you were going to marry me?"

"Sure I did."

"Before you asked me?"

Grinning, Chase leaned down to nip at her bottom lip. "I figured Squat and I could convince you."

"And if I'd said no?"

"You didn't."

"There's still time to change my mind." He touched his lips to hers again, letting them linger and warm. "Well," she said with a sigh, "maybe just this once I'll let you get away with it."

* * * * *

MILLS & BOON®

Why shop at millsandboon.co.uk?

Each year, thousands of romance readers find their perfect read at millsandboon.co.uk. That's because we're passionate about bringing you the very best romantic fiction. Here are some of the advantages of shopping at www.millsandboon.co.uk:

* **Get new books first**—you'll be able to buy your favourite books one month before they hit the shops

* **Get exclusive discounts**—you'll also be able to buy our specially created monthly collections, with up to 50% off the RRP

* **Find your favourite authors**—latest news, interviews and new releases for all your favourite authors and series on our website, plus ideas for what to try next

* **Join in**—once you've bought your favourite books, don't forget to register with us to rate, review and join in the discussions

Visit **www.millsandboon.co.uk**
for all this and more today!